THE WRITE KNIGHT

L. B. Martin

Copyright © 2023 L. B. Martin

All rights reserved

Brantley Greenwald is affiliated with L. B. Martin.
Edited by Chasity Mahala

The characters and events portrayed in this book are fictitious. Any similarity to real persons, living or dead, is coincidental and not intended by the author.

No part of this book may be reproduced, or stored in a retrieval system, or transmitted in any form or by any means, electronic, mechanical, photocopying, recording, or otherwise, without express written permission of the publisher.

ISBN: 9798387192210

Cover design by: Samuel Greenwald
Library of Congress Control Number: 2018675309
Printed in the United States of America

Acknowledgement

This book is dedicated to two particularly important people in my life. To my husband, Sam, thank you for always encouraging me to keep going and always believing in me even when I didn't. You have always been my rock. And to my best friend, Dakota, thank you for inspiring me to be okay with my true self and not the one everyone wanted me to be. Your crazy matches mine. Also, thanks for reading every chapter after I edited them a million times and always being on call when I need synonyms and input on the spicy scenes. You are the true MVP!

P.S. Dad, I would have been a terrible doctor. People are safer this way.

P.S.S., I think Taylor Swift said it best. Haters gonna hate, hate, hate, hate, hate.

"Out of suffering have emerged the strongest souls; the most massive characters are seared with scars."

KHALIL GIBRAN

CONTENTS

Title Page
Copyright
Dedication
Epigraph
Playlist
Prologue — 1
Chapter 1 — 6
Chapter 2 — 13
Chapter 3 — 26
Chapter 4 — 35
Chapter 5 — 49
Chapter 6 — 57
Chapter 7 — 64
Chapter 8 — 73
Chapter 9 — 80
Chapter 10 — 88
Chapter 11 — 99
Chapter 12 — 110
Chapter 13 — 114
Chapter 14 — 119
Chapter 15 — 126

Chapter 16	132
Chapter 17	140
Chapter 18	146
Chapter 19	152
Chapter 20	158
Chapter 21	171
Chapter 22	180
Chapter 23	191
Chapter 24	198
Chapter 25	209
Chapter 26	217
Chapter 27	226
Chapter 28	236
Chapter 29	247
Chapter 30	260
Chapter 31	269
Chapter 32	278
Chapter 33	286
Chapter 34	290
Chapter 35	296
Chapter 36	304
Chapter 37	308
Epilogue	318
About The Author	323
Praise For Author	325
Books In This Series	327

PLAYLIST

Darkside – Neoni
Daydream – Lily Meola
Control – Zoe Wees
Where Have You Been – Rihanna
Yellow – Coldplay
Don't Let Me Down – The Chainsmokers
Never Let Me Go – Florence + The Machine
Ungodly Hour – The Fray
Heal – Tom Odell
Walls We're All Against – Ross Copperman
Say Anything – Tristian Prettyman
Say You Won't Let Go – James Arthur
Keep on Loving You – Cigarettes After Sex
Recovery – James Arthur
Take on the World - You Me At Six
Twin Flame – Machine Gun Kelly
Trophy – TAELA
Unstoppable – Sia
Dirty Thoughts – Chloe Adams
Inside Her Head – Bryce Savage
Anti-Hero – Taylor Swift
Iris – Goo Goo Dolls
All of Me – Jasmine Thompson

Get You the Moon (feat. SnØw) – Kina
Lonely – Machine Gun Kelly
Play This When I'm Gone – Machine Gun Kelly

PROLOGUE

Elizabeth
Fourteen years ago...

Darkness.

It surrounds me. Threatening to pull me into its shadowy depths. I don't know which way to go, but I know I need to run. Run to escape it. Run from the hold it seems to have on my body, my mind. Tingles prickle the back of my neck, and I know I'm soon to be in its sinewy grasp. My throat clogs in fear and my lungs ache as the emotion consumes me. I feel the shift in the air and know I've lost the battle. It has me in its hold, and I'm being pulled under to where darkness knows no bounds.

I awaken with a jolt of electricity thrumming through my body. I gasp for air that seems thick in my lungs. My pajamas cling to my body from the sweat coating my skin. My heart is pounding in my chest, demanding to be set free of its confines. I gasp as I open my eyes and realize I am safe in bed. I scrunch my eyes closed trying to recall any details from the nightmare, but the more I try and concentrate, the more it evaporates from my mind, like rain on asphalt on a hot summer day. I sigh as I drop back to the bed and shield my eyes from the sun streaming right through the windows. Taking deep breaths to calm my nerves, the minutes pass and the dream fades further and further away. I can never remember them, but I know they are dark. Always dark and consuming. I've had night terrors since I was little, most of the time brought by the onset of an illness, but sometimes I feel as if they are a foreboding of what's to come. A shiver runs down my spine as fear ricochets through my chest like a pin ball machine, and then takes hold in my stomach as a wave of nausea passes over me. I wrap my arms around myself, willing the fear to leave my body. It was just a dream. Just a dream. I'm safe. There is nothing wrong. *It's just in your head, Elizabeth.* These dreams only come occasionally, but every time I have the same reactions... drenched with sweat, heart pounding, and the feeling of being suffocated to death. The feeling of losing all control.

Focus. Deep breaths. Breathe in through your nose and out through your mouth. Repeat. In. Out. In. Out. I continue until my heart begins to slow.

When I regain my composure, I realize I'm not in my room, and remember coming to spend the weekend at my aunt and uncle's house. I get up from the bed and look over to see if my cousin is still asleep. Cathy is a bit older than me, but we have always gotten along. Everyone says I am mature for my age, and I suppose I agree. I don't really get along with my classmates at school except for my best friend, Sarah. She and I seem to have been destined to be friends.

I remember the first day that I met Sarah in elementary school. She was a new student and didn't know a soul. I, myself, didn't have many friends, either. About a week passed before we spoke to one another. She sat directly behind me in class, and one day she came in and tapped me on the shoulder. When I looked back at her, she smiled and said, "I love your new haircut!" I smiled back as my heart fluttered because someone noticed me.

"I'm Sarah," she continued anxiously as she wrung her hands together under her desk.

I knew it took a lot of courage to be the first one to speak to a total stranger. I understood that probably as much as she did. Her smile faltered a bit before I could reply. "Thank you. I didn't think anyone would notice. I'm Elizabeth," I said as I watched her relax back into her seat. It didn't take long before we became inseparable. Instant friends just from one comment. On the weekends, I was either at her house or she was at mine. We had so much in common that we referred to each other as sisters. And she was, even if not by blood.

When I see that Cathy isn't in the room, I climb out of the bed and change into a new set of clothes I packed for the weekend. I bundle the sweat-soaked ones up beside my bag before I leave the room and head toward the bathroom. The hardwood floor creaks as I walk along the hallway. This house is old, but it isn't without southern charm. I could see it being built back in colonial times. Who knows? Maybe it was. It's a beautiful two-story brick home with wooden trim around the perimeter. There are large white columns on the front of the house that remind me of the homes in *The Patriot* movie with Mel Gibson. Although the outside of the house has a classical style, the interior has mostly been renovated to incorporate modern design. Except the floors. They creak so badly that I find myself tiptoeing to avoid the sound.

Once in the bathroom, I look at my appearance in the mirror. Cringing at what I see before me; I get to work on making myself somewhat presentable. My hair is still damp from sweat and going all different directions, the epitome of "bed head." My face is a bit rosy, and my eyes have a weariness to them. I turn on the sink and splash water on my face several times to wash away the memories of this morning. Taking a towel that's hanging nearby, I wipe my face. I look back at myself, and at least, I look more awake and less like a zombie. I run my hands through my long black hair to try and rid it of the obvious tangles. I give up, reach for a rubber band and put my hair in a messy bun. After brushing my teeth, I turn the light off, and walk toward the stairs that lead downstairs. Again, I tiptoe because I hate the loud creaking that comes from this old staircase; I'm not trying to sneak up on anyone. Then I hear hushed voices in the kitchen as I reach the bottom of the stairs. I hold back behind the door and don't immediately walk in. I don't want to interrupt if there is a family discussion going on. I'm about to turn away when I hear my mother and father's names fall from my aunt's lips. I pause, not knowing what to do. I hear a faint whimper, and then someone blowing their nose. My heart begins to race for the second time today. Fear washes over me as I think back to the nightmare. That feeling of dread seems lodged back in my throat. I know something is wrong.

Unable to stay hidden any longer, I will my legs to carry me to the kitchen to see what has happened. As soon as I step in, I see my aunt, uncle, and cousin talking at the table. I'm seen the instant I round the corner to the kitchen, and my aunt jumps up from her chair to come over to me. Panic sweeps through me as I see her puffy eyes staring down at me. Before I can get anything out, she asks, "Did you sleep well, honey? I made some biscuits and gravy. Go on and take a seat, and I'll get you some." She points me in the direction of the table, and I take a moment to look at the expressions on everyone's faces. They appear to have wiped away any remnant of the conversation they were having by plastering on fake smiles. Cathy pats the seat next to her playfully, but her eyes tell a different story. One that I'm not familiar with. Sadness? Worry? Surely if something had happened, they would tell me or whisk me off to my parents, right? *Definitely*.

My aunt puts the plate down in front of me and begins moving about the kitchen as if nothing is wrong. My uncle clears his throat and begins perusing through the newspaper that was lying in front of him. Cathy gets up and helps her mother clean the breakfast dishes. Everyone seemed fine, as if I was hearing things before I came in. I'm not sure what I walked in on, but I obviously heard incorrectly. My anxiety seems to melt away, and I look around again before digging into my delicious, homestyle breakfast.

After breakfast has been cleared away, I go to the living room to watch some television. Before I plop down on the couch, my aunt comes in looking for me.

"We are going to drop you off at home in a little bit. We have plans that we forgot about," she says looking at me with a new softness to her eyes.

"Oh, okay," I respond. Again, I have this feeling that they are hiding something from me. I am about to ask if there is something going on when she scurries out of the room and up the stairs. I'm disappointed to be leaving because I was planning on staying the whole weekend, but I understand that things can come up. I'll call Sarah when I get home and maybe she can come over. There are only two weeks left of school, and I will officially be a high schooler. That thought lifts my spirits as I head back upstairs to pack my things.

Nothing can prepare me for what awaits me at home. I'm clueless as to what I'm walking into, but from this day forward, I will never be the same. The day that began with darkness, will end with much more than I could have ever imagined.

CHAPTER 1

Elizabeth

"Lizzie, you are coming with me tonight. No excuses this time!" Sarah yells from the kitchen. "You know all the A-list people will be there. Plus, this is *the* club to be at tonight!"

Here we go again. I love Sarah to death, but she can be a bit much at times. We have been best friends since third grade and roommates since our freshmen year in college. She majored in Public Relations and is a rockstar at it. I majored in English Literature with a minor in British Lit. I have always been a literary enthusiast at heart, so there was no doubt in my mind about what I would be studying. Although it wasn't what my parents expected of me, I did what I always do and marched to the beat of my own drum. I've always been the black sheep of the family, even counting my cousins. My father wanted me to continue in his footsteps and become a successful lawyer, then take over his practice one day. In my opinion, I can't think of anything that I would less like to do. And so, with my decision to become a writer, my relationship with my father became strained, to say the least. Well, that is, if it could possibly become more strained than it already was. My mother just wanted me to do something I was passionate about and would make me financially stable. Apparently, they didn't have faith that I had what it takes to be a successful writer. I still hear it in her voice when we speak on the phone as she mentions, ever so casually, that it's not too late to take classes to become an English teacher. At least then, I would be using some of my degree, she always says.

My mother and I have been close since my father filed for a divorce from her after twenty-eight years of marriage. I was twelve at the time and the news came as a shock to everyone, me more than most. I never even saw my parents fight. Not very much anyway. Not enough to throw away all those years together at the drop of a hat. I was spending the weekend with my cousin the night it happened, and when I got home the next day, my father had moved out. He was just up and gone in the night. *How did he pack so quickly? Was he already prepared? Was he waiting on me to leave for the weekend?* Those questions used to plague my thoughts constantly after that day. My whole life was turned upside down, or the life that I knew.

I had always been a "daddy's girl" from the time I could walk. We bonded over his teaching me how to play sports, namely softball. He even eventually became my head coach. I played from age five to eighteen, except for the year that my parents got divorced. I didn't have the energy or will to play that year. I couldn't bear to even look at the ballfield, much less step foot on it. I didn't want to see all my friends' parents in the stands cheering them on. When the next season came, I played with my fellow teammates, but it was never the same again. At that point, I refused to play for my father. He walked out on us, so I was not going to let him share in our love of softball. Petty, I know, but I was a teenager.

After the divorce was finalized, my father quickly moved on and married another woman. I am pretty sure they were already together, but I don't have proof, and frankly I don't need any. I know he was unfaithful to my mother, and that's something I can never look past, no matter how many years it has been. My parents went from loving spouses to not being able to be in the same room with one another. It was so intense that from then on, every holiday had to be celebrated twice. That might seem like a dream for some, but to me it sucked. Who wants to have two birthday parties? I didn't. I wanted one where my whole family and my friends could attend. A party that wouldn't be so intense or have unnecessary comments and expressions of pity. My friends would have to pick which party to attend, either my mother's or father's. It was hell to say the least. And don't get me started on how they would fight over who got to be with me on the actual day of my birthday. It's safe to say that birthdays were effectively ruined for me. I began to despise celebrating them, so eventually I stopped. That divorce triggered something deep inside of me that didn't surface until I started to date. I guess it ruined me for thinking "happily-ever-afters" were obtainable.

Sarah knows all about the struggles with my family. She was there through the best and worst of times. She's my shoulder to cry on and my light in the darkness. I consider her family more than my own most days, and she treats me the same. I let out a deep sigh. I haven't thought of that shit show in a while. I don't know what made it bubble up in my mind, but I don't want it to stay there. I cast it aside and respond to Sarah before she thinks I am ignoring her.

"I have to work at the restaurant until ten, so I won't have time to get back here and change to go out tonight. Sorry girl, next time, I promise," I shout from the bathroom in an effort to mollify her enough, so that I can stay in tonight. The door bursts open, and Sarah is wearing that expression I know all too well. The one that says I won't be getting out of this little excursion tonight.

"Elizabeth Brighton, you haven't been out since you found Jacob and his dirty little secretary in his office. It is time to move on! Here's what's going to happen. You are going to come home and get that gross restaurant smell off you, and then I will give you a makeover. Plus, you know that no one shows up to these things right when they open. Besides, I did some major PR for this club, and I'm going to celebrate my success with my best friend. It's going to be the greatest night, and who knows, maybe you will meet some hunky guy to get you over your ex!" Sarah exclaims as she puts her hands on her hips, looking fabulous as always.

She has beautiful, pale skin, and her hair is cut into a straight blonde bob that suits her personality perfectly. She stands a few inches shorter than me, so I glance downward to see her green eyes staring at me waiting for an answer.

"Fine, but only because you full named me, and I know how hard you worked on this project."

Sarah landed this huge PR job with a new club that is opening, and she's been working her ass off to give it the attention it needs; and tonight, is the big opening. On top of her bonus, she was given two VIP tickets to tonight's unveiling. Apparently, this club is super exclusive and only for the rich and famous.

I do need to get out. It's been six months since Jacob and I broke up, so I know she is right about that. Since I started dating in high school, I only seem to attract the lying, cheating, asshole type of men. It's sad how many "relationships" I have been in that ended because the guy cheated on me.

My first boyfriend, Michael, was a real charmer, and we were together for two years, until that fateful day when I caught him and a server that he worked with in a storage room. Then there was James. I should have seen the red flags from the beginning. He was secretive, would flirt with other girls when we were together, and ogled them when he thought I wasn't looking. He was so gross and so obvious, but I was clueless until it was brought to my attention. Next, there was Kevin; he was in the Marines, and we got along so well at first. Then one day, I surprised him at his apartment, and he was in bed with a so-called "friend" of mine. He even had the audacity to run after me and tell me he still loved me.

All these men told me they loved me, and I foolishly believed them. I don't know if I really loved any of them. Sure, my first boyfriend could probably be described as puppy love, and I was young. Turns out, they are all just like dear ol' dad. Should have stuck with that warning from the beginning and saved myself the time and energy. How hard is it to just tell me you aren't interested anymore or want to see other people? That's so much better than finding out the hard way, which inevitably causes more heartache and embarrassment for both parties involved.

I could probably write the ultimate breakup song, like Taylor Swift, with all the heartaches I've had to endure. Maybe I should just go into songwriting? I mean, I definitely have enough material to last a while. I suppose the lyrics wouldn't be as powerful unless they were coming from my lips, and that is certainly not happening. My extent of singing consists of in the shower or when I'm drunk and at a karaoke bar. Both sound like someone is being murdered or a bag of cats being thrown about.

Anyways, after Jacob, I decided that enough was enough and I was not going to date anymore for the foreseeable future. The truth is, I don't trust men. I've seen the same thing happen time and time again, and now I am putting my foot down. I don't have faith in men, plain and simple. At least not the ones that I encounter. I seem to be a magnet for the asshole, douchebag types, and I don't have time for that. I don't really believe in that kind of love anymore. Life isn't a fairytale, and I will not get swept up in another affair that will break my heart. I have carefully constructed walls around my heart, and they won't crumble. I know I sound like a cynical ice queen, maybe Elsa had the right idea. I've not had the privilege of coming across a man who wasn't an egotistical asshat, except for my brother. He didn't take after my father, and I love him all the more because of it.

It's Friday night, and I just want to come home and lay on the couch with some wine and binge watch a new show on Netflix, and maybe even work on my book that I have been trying to write for over a year. Jacob hated that I wanted to spend my free time drafting my book. He said that it would never amount to anything, and I should look for a "real" career. That sounds familiar, right? I almost did just that until I caught him that night with *her*. It was a blessing in disguise, really. Now, more than ever, I am determined to finish this book and get it published. I will do whatever it takes. I've decided not to let anything get in my way. I just need to get over this writer's block that seems to have plagued my mind.

"Just so you know, I am totally over that jerk! Just because I haven't been out in a while does not mean that I am still stuck on him!" I continue. Looking back, I don't think I ever loved Jacob. Maybe I loved the idea of having someone, but in my soul, I know that we weren't a good match. He was overly possessive and had a very bad temper.

"Anyways, I am not looking for a man right now. I don't need any distractions from finishing my book. We are just going to get some drinks and dance the night away," I add. My voice is a little louder now, but I am not intending to be rude. I just want her to know that she can stop hassling me about Jacob or any other man for that matter. Jacob is history, just like my dating life. End of discussion.

Sarah begins jumping up and down, clapping her hands, and squealing at my declaration to join her tonight. Plus, I know she loves to give me makeovers whenever I'll let her.

"We are going to have so much fun! Single ladies on the town tonight! Whoop! I've got to pick out some clothes and shoes! Oh, I can't wait until you get back. I am so excited.

Thank you. Thank you. Thank you!" she exclaims, while she squeezes me tight, does a little dance, then runs to her closet and begins pulling out dresses that I am sure will be part of my "makeover." I can't help but chuckle at her enthusiasm.

"I'm not wearing those dreaded heels that almost killed me the night we went to that Broadway show! I'm lucky I can even walk at all now!"

She peaks her head out of her room, giving me a stern look. "Nothing was wrong with those shoes, Liz. It was you that couldn't handle them. But don't worry, I will have something fabulous ready for you when you get back here. I can already envision it!" She disappears back into her room with the sound of hangers being thrown all around. She isn't the most organized person on the planet, and I can already sense the disaster that is going to be her room. Tonight is going to be interesting, that's for sure.

I check my watch and realize I am running late if I want to stop at my favorite little coffee shop on the way to work. I finish putting on a few strokes of mascara and some lipstick. I don't have time to put in more effort on the makeup front. My hair is cascading down my back in soft black waves. I run my fingers through it to get out any lingering tangles. I glance at the mirror and take in my appearance. That will have to do. I run to my closet and slip into an emerald green, wrap-around dress and my favorite black knee-high boots. I add a black belt to the dress and grab a jacket from the closet by the front door of our apartment. I take a quick glance at the floor length mirror in the hall, then grab my bag and hurry to the door, picking up my keys and phone as I shout, "I'm leaving! My coffee is calling me! I will see you tonight!" The door slams shut behind me, but not before I hear her laughing at me. She knows how real my coffee obsession is.

CHAPTER 2

Miles

I wake up before my alarm goes off this morning. A tiny sliver of light streams through my window where my curtains weren't completely closed last night. I rest my arm over my eyes trying to go back to sleep. I can feel the exhaustion deep inside my bones. I need a vacation, but I know I won't be getting one of those in the near future. I stayed up late going over all the details of an upcoming novel release. The board thinks this will be an immediate bestseller, but I am not entirely convinced. I know the book will do well, but I want something that knocks my socks off. I want to read something fresh and new. I want our readers to be completely smitten with the books that we publish. Lately, the only manuscripts that fall on my desk are mediocre at best. I'm looking for that spark that my father had a knack for finding. A needle in a haystack if you will. I know I will find it eventually. I *must* find it. I want to prove to the company and to myself that I can do this job just as well as my father. I'm just hoping this obscure gem appears sooner rather than later. When I find that diamond, I will do everything in my power to grab ahold of it and make it the largest bestseller of our time. The board at least knows that I am determined and a hard worker. I won't take no for an answer when I find that special author.

    I sigh and toss the covers off me, knowing that more sleep will not come. I get up from the comfort of my king-sized bed and make my way to my attached ensuite. I turn on the light, and the brightness of the white walls along with the reflection of the white marble flooring make my eyes squint for a moment until they adjust to the change. I splash some cold water on my face and brush my teeth. I lean against the countertop as I take a look in the mirror and see the weariness in my once bright blue eyes. I've been working myself to death, but I can't bring myself to slow down.

With a groan, I stand back up, run my hands through my dark hair, and walk back out to my room. I take in the sight of the manuscripts sprawled across my bed along with my laptop. I fell asleep working, like I do most nights. I scrub my hand over my face and walk into my closet to put on some workout shorts and walk to the downstairs gym in my penthouse. I need to sweat out this frustration and anxiety that I feel building inside of me. Having my own gym has made a huge impact on my stress level, meaning it has decreased immensely. Well, at least while I am pushing my body, I don't think of the mounds of work and responsibility that await me. Going to the public gym was a nightmare because everywhere I go, I am almost instantly recognized. Then, I constantly get interrupted by women and sometimes even men, and I could never get a good workout in. I got tired of being gawked at and constantly disturbed when I was trying to exercise; so, when I bought my new place, I knew it had to come with a private gym. Don't get me wrong; I'm not saying that I didn't use to love all the attention because it made the women come to me easy and willing, but it got old quickly.

I get to my private elevator and punch the button for the second floor where my gym is located. As the elevator opens, I take in the room. This is one of my special places to come when I need a distraction. There is a wall full of floor-to-ceiling windows that are tinted. It allows me to see out but not the other way around. I didn't just want a gym with four walls. The thought of that made me claustrophobic. No, I needed a space that would double as a gym and a secret haven to observe the environment outside without fear of onlookers. My stationary bike, treadmill, and elliptical sit facing the windows, and my weights are off to the side of the room along with a full bathroom.

I put in my ear pods and hop on the treadmill, losing myself in the rhythmic steps as the anxiety begins to melt away. After thirty minutes, I move to my weights. This is the least favorite part of my workout, but I got used to it when I was playing basketball in high school and college. Even after I graduated, I continued working out because it was always a good stress reliever for me and allows me to clear my mind before a busy day of work. After two hours of sweating my ass off, I grab a towel and head back upstairs to my shower. I rarely use the one in the gym, but it's there if I need it or when my brother comes to workout with me.

By 7:00 am, I am showered, dressed, and in my kitchen making my morning protein shake before I leave for work. I'm pretty much a creature of habit. I need a schedule and want to live by it. That's how to truly utilize all the hours of the day. It helps my day go smoothly, so this is my usual morning routine. If I stay on task, then I will grow to be the best, and that's what I want to be.

When my father passed away unexpectedly, he bequeathed to me his publishing company. He built the company from the ground up with his bare hands and always wanted it to stay within the family. Since I was a young boy, he'd groomed me to take over the business. I would go to work with him and see how he interacted with authors, investors, and employees. He was always kind but led with a firm hand. I always looked up to him and never questioned whether I wanted the company or not. This company is part of my blood, so I stepped into the position immediately, without hesitation.

My father passed away from a massive heart attack a year ago, and I am still trying to make my way in the company and fill his large shoes. It's intimidating to have that kind of pressure thrust onto you. I have had to fight hard, work hard, and drive a hard ship around the office to prove that I am worthy to be the CEO of Knight Publishing Company, the largest publishing company in the United States. As soon as I was appointed, the press had a field day with me and everything surrounding my personal life. They dug up old stories of my playboy years and the board of directors questioned my ability to run this enterprise. Yes, I admit that I have always liked to have fun, and I never cared much about what it looked like to others. Being a trust-fund baby and the son of Benjamin Miles Knight Sr., I have always been in the limelight. My brother and mine's every move is written about and spewed across tabloids for everyone to read. However, after stepping into this position, I have tried to be on my best behavior per our PR's orders. I want our investors to believe they can trust this company, and by extension, me.

But, if I am being honest, my party days were already nearing the end. It just didn't have the same effect on me that it used to. I don't want the trouble of picking up total strangers, and then taking them to a nice hotel. Yes, always a hotel. I never brought a woman to my penthouse. This is my private sanctuary, and I didn't want to sully it with a rotation of women. That part of my life is in the past. As I near my thirties, I am ready to find the one woman I am meant to settle down with, I just don't think I have the time or energy to find her. I want someone that will be there when I get home every day. Someone happy to see me. Someone to share life experiences with and to start a family. That's what I genuinely want, but I fear that's in the very distant future, if ever. I want what my parents had. They were high school sweethearts and got married young, but they remained in love until my father passed away. My brother and I grew up in a happy home that was filled with love and respect, and we learned about that special love from our parents. We were fortunate to have them in our lives. Of course, my parents had their share of fights and problems, but they worked through them and came out stronger on the other side.

My father sat me down, a few years before he died, to have a chat about soulmates. He said, *"Son, I knew the moment I saw your mother that she was meant to be mine. I can't explain how I knew, other than this intense feeling in my chest, unlike anything I had ever felt. When I saw her in the school hallway that day, I knew, without a doubt, she was the one. When her sparkling green eyes met mine, I fell in love. I walked straight to her, introducing myself, and well, the rest is history, son. She later told me that she felt the same way."* He hesitated for a moment and took a sip of his bourbon. *We were sitting in his study at my childhood home. I came for dinner, and then we retired to his study to have a nightcap. I've heard how my parents met many times before but not in this depth. I'm not sure why he is picking now to tell me this, though. He looks intently at the amber liquid as he spins it around in his glass. He looks back up at me with more emotion in his eyes.* "I want you to find that, Miles. You need to stop with the frivolous women and find your forever; trust me, you will know when you do. She is out there somewhere." *I take a deep breath and bring my glass to my lips, feeling the burn as the liquid runs down the back of my throat. I do want to settle down some day, but I think my parents just got lucky in love. He always told us to believe in love at first sight and soulmates. Both of my parents were adamant that love would find you when you least expected it.* "I hope that I am as lucky as you one day." *I reply back to him. He put his hand over mine and patted it. His eyes intent on mine he stated,* "You will, my boy, but in the meantime, how about not go through all the women in New York, huh? Don't look at me like that. I know you and your brother's reputation." *I nod as I take another sip of bourbon and lean my head back against the chair to think about everything he just told me.*

I do wish that I could find that special someone, but it seems like more of a pipe dream now, more than ever. I'm just so concentrated on work right now, and if that woman is out there, then I know she will stumble into my path. However, finding this woman will be easier said than done. The only women that I attract are always solely interested in my status and wealth. I can tell instantly when a woman approaches me that she is after my name, not me. I admit that it seems impossible to find that special someone when I am looked at like an elite social status and ATM.

I shake the thoughts from my mind as my phone buzzes in my pocket alerting me that my driver is here. I chug my shake, grab my wallet and keys, and head down the elevator, then through the lobby. I like to drive, but traffic in this city it is a nightmare. My gun metal gray, 5.2 Liter, V12 Aston Martin DB11 is my baby. She was the gift from my parents when I graduated from Princeton University. I wish that I had more time to take her out for a spin. I would drive her every day if it wouldn't take me an hour to get somewhere.

My chauffeur is waiting right outside the doors.

"Morning, Mr. Knight," Thomas says as he opens the door for me to get in.

"Good morning, Thomas. How is Marie doing?"

As he slides into the driver's seat, he answers, "Oh, doing much better. Thank you for the dinner you sent us last night. It was a wonderful treat."

Thomas has been my driver for a few years now, and I know his wife is going through tough times with her chemotherapy treatment. She has been in and out of hospitals for months now. I know that must take a toll on them, so I try to help out whenever I can. I was able to pull some strings and get her into the best medical facility in New York. They have a new treatment available, that otherwise wouldn't have been a possibility financially for Thomas and his wife, so I paid for everything. My parents instilled this behavior in my brother,

Sebastian, and me since we were little. My mother always says that "Actions speak louder than words." So, I wanted to let Thomas know, he is an integral part of this company.

"It was no trouble at all. I'm happy you could have a relaxing night together. Thomas, I need to grab a coffee before heading into the office today," I reply, as I get out my phone and begin scrolling through the piles of emails that have accumulated overnight.

Damnit, it's only been eight hours since I last checked my emails, and they are already sky high. As I finish replying to an investor that wants to meet next week, the car comes to a stop in front of the little coffee shop that I frequent since it is right around the corner from my office.

Thomas speaks up getting my attention, "We have arrived, sir. I'll wait here for you unless you would like me to fetch your order for you this morning?"

"Thank you for the offer, Thomas, but I think I would like to get some fresh air for a bit. Would you care for anything?"

"No, thank you. Marie packed me a thermos today. She's such a good woman."

As I get out of the car, I remark, "You are a lucky man to have found the one." With a smile he nods, and I head toward the shop. Walking through the throngs of people on the sidewalk, I replay the words my father once told me, and smile. Thomas found his one, too. Maybe there is hope for me after all.

As I step through the doors, I am hit with the wonderful aroma of coffee. I don't see how anyone can get anything done without coffee. I drink at least three cups a day. I know, I know, it's not healthy, but it's essential when you work the hours that I do. Usually, I have my assistant bring them to me, but I thought I would grab one on the way this morning. The shop is a bit crowded today, but I am almost certain it's because it's Black Friday. Everyone and their mother are out and about shopping and obviously getting their caffeine fill in the process. When I finally approach the counter, I put in my usual order and under the name "Austen", which I always use to have a sense of anonymity.

I have been using this name at coffee shops and such since I was in college. My friends used to think it was hilarious that I couldn't go anywhere without a crowd gathering around, like some kind of royalty. I hated it and they knew it; but they liked giving me shit about it. I didn't want that experience in college. I wanted to just feel normal for once, and so that's when I began giving a fake name at coffee shops. Obviously, it didn't shield me from everyone like Clark Kent's glasses, but it helped. Over time it became a habit, one that I still use today.

Since I am named after my father, Benjamin Miles Knight Sr., I go by Miles instead of Benjamin, unlike him. Miles is a common enough name, but I still use aliases to get by as unnoticed as possible. Since being in the headlines lately for an incident involving the company, I would rather not cause a spectacle. Even a short trip to a coffee shop can cause an uproar in the tabloids. I honestly don't understand the appeal for people to read about this type of thing, but it still happens.

I keep my head down and move to the waiting area, pull out my phone again, and see that my brother has texted me. Sebastian is three years younger than I, and he is the CFO of Knight Publishing Company. He may be my little brother, but he is also my best friend.

Seb: We have plans tonight. I hope you are ready.

Miles: I thought the Calloway investors were rescheduled?

Seb: They did. I'm not talking about that. That new club VIBE has its opening tonight, and we are on the VIP list. You're going. No excuses!

I sigh, looking down at the message. It's been a long week. I haven't left the office before 9:00 p.m. one night this entire week, and then I have more work waiting for me when I get home. Maybe I need to hire another assistant. I was looking forward to enjoying a drink on my balcony overlooking New York City and maybe get a few manuscripts read before Monday.

Seb: I know you read the message. You need to get out, and tonight is the night.

Miles: You are just wanting a wingman. Why not ask Samuel?

Samuel is our first cousin and just got back from a tour in Afghanistan. He was honorably discharged from the Army after he received a Purple Heart medal for sustaining injuries from an IED—improvised explosive device—during combat.

Seb: I do not need a wingman. The ladies just come to me. You know this! I just want to spend some time with my bro outside of the office and have a bit of fun. What's the harm in that? Besides, Samuel is still healing. I texted him to see if he would like to join us.

Miles: There better not be news outlets there. And you better not make another scene. I don't think we pay Marcie enough to cover up your shenanigans as it is.

Seb: This is a private club. We aren't going to have to worry about fan girls tonight. And for your peace of mind, I will be on my absolute best behavior, big brother. ;)

I roll my eyes at that last text. Sebastian doesn't know how to be on his best behavior. At least I will be there with him tonight, so I can keep an eye on him. Marcie, our public relations representative, has her hands full with my brother, and some with myself on occasion, but she does an excellent job of keeping us out of the press and mostly out of trouble.

Miles: Fine, I'll go. I'll be in the office in fifteen. Just grabbing a coffee.

"Austen, your coffee is ready," the barista behind the counter yells. As I make my way through the throng of people to the counter, a woman comes out of nowhere and grabs the coffee at the same time I do. Our hands graze and a bolt of electricity shoots up my arm and through my body. The sensation is one that I haven't felt before. I am momentarily annoyed that someone would have the audacity to steal another's coffee. Who would do that? I look down at the culprit standing next to me that has her hand on my coffee and am temporarily speechless.

The crowd around us seems to fade into the background as I gaze at this magnificent creature. This woman is stunning. She has olive skin, and her rich black hair falls down her back in these beautiful, soft waves. When she looks up at me, I am taken aback at the glow of her lustrous brown eyes. They are large and exquisite with gold flakes sprinkled in them, and her long black eyelashes seem to flutter up and down in slow motion as she stares up at me. The smell of her vanilla perfume assaults my senses in the best possible way, and it's hard for me to stop staring at her. Her green dress hugs her delicious curves, and the black belt and boots accentuate the color of her hair. She obviously knows her style. This woman is utterly breathtaking. I realize that she is still staring at me, and I manage to ask with a bit more accusation than I intended, "Is your name Austen?"

She looks nervous and starts to fidget as she drops her hold onto the cup and looks back to me. "No, well, yes in this case. I oftentimes use different authors' names when I place a coffee order."

A smile quirks on my face. "That's a very intriguing idea. So, today I assume you are Jane Austen?" A blush creeps on her face as she looks up into my eyes. I feel like they are looking into my very soul. I can see that her eyes are surprised but smiling that I recognize the author's name. It's mesmerizing looking into those expressive chocolate pools, and I don't see a hint of recognition of who I am, which is very unexpected. I don't remember the last time someone was this close to me and didn't instantly recognize me from the tabloids or media in general. Women fall all over me, mainly because of my billionaire/CEO title. It makes it difficult to find a genuine person in this huge city. This makes her even more intriguing.

"Yes, well, she was on my mind this morning, and it seemed fitting to use."

She smiles. Her perfect white teeth light up her face. My breath catches in my throat at the sight. I suddenly want to reach out and gently stroke my knuckles over her cheek to feel the softness there. My eyes roam over her face and land on her plump lips. The bottom is slightly larger than the top, and in that moment, I want to know how they would feel against my own. *Calm down, Miles, it's just a woman in a coffee shop. Is this what my father was talking about?* I can still feel her touch on my skin, even though she moved her hand away. I clear my throat to get my mind back to the present. I open my mouth to speak but am interrupted.

"Austen, your coffee is ready," the barista shouts over the customers. The beautiful woman beside of me begins to chuckle as I grasp the newest cup that has been placed on the counter. I can't help but smile, hearing her sweet laugh. It's like a refreshing melody.

"I suppose this one is mine then. I have to say that I have never had this happen before," I say. I raise my cup to her and say, "Cheers. To hoping we got our correct orders." We tap the cups, and she laughs. I can't help it, but I want to keep making her laugh. I try to think of something else to say, but my thoughts elude me. This kind of thing doesn't happen to me. I am a successful businessman, and I pride myself on my ability to have a quick tongue, especially in stressful business meetings.

She continues to look up at me, and then says, "It was good to meet you, Austen. Next time I will have to use a different name so there is no confusion." She chuckles as she smiles and turns to walk toward the exit.

I don't want to correct her of my real name because I am enjoying this too much, but I call out to her, "Maybe I will run into you again, Jane." She turns enough for me to see that beautiful smile and then walks out the door. I want to call out and ask her for her real name and phone number, and to see if we can meet again sometime, but I just watch in awe as the beauty steps out into the traffic of people rushing about. As I stand there in the middle of the crowded shop, a huge smile forms on my face. That was the most authentic interaction I have had in a long time, and I crave to have it again. I take my coffee, nodding to the barista as I stuff some bills in the tip jar and head toward the exit.

Thomas is on the sidewalk waiting. I look around the busy street, but I don't see her anywhere. When he sees me, he opens the door of the Bentley. As I get in, all I can think about is a gorgeous black-haired goddess with intense brown eyes. *What am I even doing?* I don't think I have ever wanted to see a woman again so badly. I don't even know anything about her. Well, that's not true. She is obviously a literature enthusiast. I am suddenly appreciating my mother's insistence that I take literature courses in college. That may come in handy when I see her again. Yes, I will be seeing her again. I just know it.

Thomas pulls up to the front of Knight Publishing Company. "Thank you, Thomas. I won't be needing you for lunch today. I will have my assistant pick something up."

"Very good, sir. I will see you this afternoon."

I walk into my office which is on the eightieth floor. I have the best view of the city from up here. I like to sit and watch the hustle and bustle from the people below. I set my cup of coffee on my desk and smile as I stare at it. I take a seat, and the only thing I can think about is the interaction I just had at the coffee shop. Her smile keeps replaying in my mind. *I wonder who her favorite author is? Does she read contemporary literature? Has she read something that we have published?* I've got to get her out of my head, or I won't be able to get any work done today, and I can't be here all night since my brother made plans for us. With one last thought of her magnetic eyes, I open my laptop and get to work, taking a sip of the overly sweet coffee that definitely isn't mine.

CHAPTER 3

Elizabeth

I make it to my favorite little coffee shop, Raven's Brew, just in time to get a cup and head to work, only I didn't consider that it's Black Friday! I'm screwed. I open the door and instantly see the lengthy line of customers waiting to order and the ones waiting for their orders. I heave a heavy sigh and get in line. I don't want to be late for work, but I also can't survive the day without coffee. And coffee will always win out in my opinion. So, in the line, I wait. I've never seen so many people here. That's why this is where I come. It's normally quiet and peaceful, and they have the best coffee in the city, if you ask me. Hopefully, they have a full staff today because I need to get on my way as soon as possible. I stand in the corner after I order, willing the baristas to work quickly and trying not to get in the way of all the people bustling about.

    I really need to get to the bookstore before Edith comes in. I've been working at Much Ado About Books for two years now, and I still enjoy it, for the most part. It's a secondhand bookstore, and I love to see the inventory that comes in. You never know what book will come through the door. It's thrilling. I once found a rare first addition *Sense and Sensibility*, and Edith was kind enough to sell it to me at a reasonable price; otherwise, there is no way that I would ever own such an incredible book. It's one of my most prized possessions. I keep in on my nightstand in a glass case.

    Over the crowd, I barely hear the barista yell, "Austen,

your coffee is ready." I rush up to the counter to grab my coffee just as someone else places his hand on the cup as well. A charge runs through my body at the touch. I almost jerk my hand back at the feeling. I look up at the man, and it's like looking at a Greek god. An aggravated god, by the looks of it. Still, I have never seen a more beautiful human than the one in front of me. Is there some sort of GQ photoshoot going on around here that I'm unaware of? Because he is definitely cover page material. He is every page material, to be honest, and I would buy that shit in a heartbeat. I feel like I'm drooling. *Am I drooling? Geez, get a grip Lizzie. This is just some man. We just talked about this; men are unwelcome news. Especially ones that look like this.* Definitely ones that look like this! Still, I can't help but want to touch his masculine jaw and trace it with my fingers. *Lizzie, snap out of it!*

He is the epitome of tall, dark, and handsome. *How cliche, Lizzie.* But it's the truth. I have to look up to see him because he's so much taller than I am, well over the six-foot range. His eyes are blue like the most stunning sapphires I have ever seen. Albeit, at the moment, they look like a tumultuous sea, ready to wreak havoc on any ship that dares to sail its waters. His dark hair is wavy and longer on top, and it looks like he's been running his hands through it, as if he has already worked a full day. His sharp cheek bones and sculpted jaw could rival Michelangelo's David. His attire says businessman, but his body is built like a professional athlete with broad shoulders and what seems like a very toned body. His gray suit looks like it was made just for him, which I'm sure it was. I bet this man intimidates everyone around him. But right now, without coffee pumping through my brain to make me more amicable or even sane, for that matter, I'm taking his expression as a threat to my coffee. And that's just not something someone wants to do to me. Just ask Sarah.

I can't take my eyes off him. It's like a magnet drawing me in. I realize that we are still just staring at each other, and my hand is still holding onto the coffee cup. I quickly drop my hand and clench it at my side. *Am I even going to be able to speak?* No words are coming out of my mouth because I feel the anger begin to boil over. I don't have time for this. I should already be at work. *Say something, Lizzie. Anything. Literally, anything at all.*

Finally, he speaks up and asks, "Is your name Austen?" With a questionable look, like I am a coffee thief.

I'm the one that should be getting upset; he grabbed my drink. "No, well, yes in this case. I oftentimes use different authors' names when I place a coffee order," I say matter-of-factly, like it's the most normal thing in the world. I know I'm quirky, get over it.

Why am I nervous? Other than the fact that this is the most handsome man I have ever seen in my life, and he is looking at me with such intensity that I can't seem to look away. But didn't I just tell Sarah I wasn't looking for a man. It's ironic that after that confession, I happen to run into a perfect one. At least on the outside. *He could be your Mr. Darcy! Stop it, Lizzie, you must get to work. Plus, he is totally out of my league. I mean, this guy probably dates super models.*

Interrupting my thoughts, he says, "That's a very curious idea. So, today I assume you are Jane Austen?" I can feel the blush creeping up my face. When was the last time I blushed like this? I can't deny that I am pleased that he knows who Jane Austen is. Although everyone knows who she is, right? Maybe Sarah was right; I really need to get out more. My heart begins to beat rapidly in my chest. My body should not be reacting like this. Yes, he's handsome, but so are a lot of men. *This is not a hero in your book, Lizzie. He actually looks like he could play the villain. Snap out of it.* "Yes, well, she was on my mind this morning, and it seemed fitting to use," I manage to say. He studies me for a moment, and I almost see a twinkle in his eyes as he looks me up and down. I should probably be either offended or embarrassed, but I feel good today and confident, and even more so since the stunning man in front of me checked me out, however briefly. Just then, the barista calls out another coffee for, "Austen."

This arrogant but stunning stranger turns to grab it and quips, "I suppose this one is mine then." He holds the first cup out for me to grab and our fingers meet for a second time. A small smile spreads over his face and I see his perfect teeth. I think my ovaries just exploded. Damn, this guy looks like a prototype of the perfect man. *Someone come clone this man for the sake of all womankind.* I have never had this instant attraction to someone in my life. I feel like I have this electric current running through my veins that is way more potent than any coffee could ever be. It's very disconcerting.

He suddenly raises his cup to mine, bumping the rims together. "Cheers. To hoping we got our correct orders."

I chuckle because I really do hope that I got my right order, but also this is such a bizarre situation. The irritation that he showed earlier seems to have dissipated. He appears to be gazing at me just as intently as I have been at him. It feels like there is electricity crackling around us. Surely, it's just because of the coffee confusion, but he almost looks interested in me. It's like we are the only people in this shop. He is staring at me like I am the only one he sees. Obviously, I am daydreaming, hallucinating, gone too long without coffee? That's what it is. It's intoxicating, though. Jacob certainly never looked at me like that. *Ugh, stop thinking of that scumbag.* I break eye contact and glance at my watch, then look back to him, "It was good to meet you, Austen. Next time I will use a different name."

I turn and head toward the exit when I hear him say, "Maybe I will run into you again, Jane."

Okay, swoon. I glance back and give him a big smile,

then hurry out of the shop. I need to get out of here before I start to drool for real and make a fool of myself. Besides, he looks like a lady's man for sure. That's a heartbreak waiting to happen. I wouldn't be opposed to seeing him again, although the chances of that are slim. I mean this is New York City with a population of eight million people. I must focus on my novel. Nothing good can come from dating. I know this all too well. But, wow, I can't get his eyes out of my head. They were the bluest of blues. I facepalm myself to get my focus back on reality.

As I walk the two blocks to the bookstore, I watch all the people out and about, hurrying from store to store. This is a special time of year in New York. Feeling as though my coffee has cooled off a bit, I take a large gulp and almost choke. A few people give me worried expressions as they pass by me. I swallow the coffee and curse the coffee gods for mixing up my drink order. It. Is. Black. Coffee. That's it! No sugar or cream or delicious caramel. Literally, the bare minimum coffee beverage one could ask for. Damn, he's even more intense than I thought. I rushed out of my apartment for this, waited in a ridiculous line, and had the most bizarre encounter with Loki, the God of Mischief. What a disaster. I sigh as I chuck the coffee in the closest trash bin. I will definitely be dragging now without my caffeine fix.

I make it to work with two minutes to spare and still the bitter taste occupies my mouth. Bleh. Relief washes over me when I realize that I got here before Edith. She always says that I am late if I arrive after she does, even if I am technically on time. It's frustrating, but I enjoy it here; so, I make it a point to leave my apartment with plenty of time to spare. As I enter the shop, I let out a deep breath that I didn't realize I was holding. I hang my jacket on the hooks by the door and put my purse under the register. This is a small shop that's sandwiched between two larger clothing boutiques. There is a cute little spot in the back of the shop where you can sit and read in a little nook. I love sitting there when I get the chance. The atmosphere here is so comforting, like being wrapped in your favorite blanket.

I love the smell of old books. The first thing I do when I get a book is smell the inside. It's such an intimate experience. These books have been all over; they could have changed people's lives, and they somehow made their way to this little secondhand bookstore. I also love to look on the inside of the covers to see if someone has written a personal note as a gift to the receiver of the book. I love books, which is obvious. I think I became obsessed in high school when I had an English teacher that had so much love and joy for them. You could see her fascination pouring out of her with every line she read. She became the reason that I studied literature in college. I would sit in my dorm room and drink in the words of the most celebrated British authors. Those have always been my favorite. Their stories took root in my brain and have been there since. It's calming to sit down with a classic and let the world around you fall away as you emerge as a character on the pages. This escapism I know all too well.

I start going through the new inventory and put the books in the computer. This keeps me busy for most of my shift, probably because I kept stopping and thinking about the Austen guy from the coffee shop. He didn't look like an Austen. I'm not even sure what name would fit him. Something strong and manly. I grin when I think of his beautiful smile, with his dimples shining through. Breaking my daydream, Edith calls, "You need to shelve those new books before you leave." I groan and with that I am back to work.

As I walk out of the bookstore, I head to a little café to have something to eat before my shift at the restaurant. The only thing that keeps me going is knowing that when I publish my book, I hopefully won't have to work two jobs. That is, if I ever finish it, which is harder than it seems because I am always working. It's a vicious cycle.

After I finish my sandwich, I jog to the restaurant because now I am in danger of being late again. I go in through the back doors and head to the lockers so I can change into my uniform and add a bit more makeup. This is an upscale Italian restaurant called the Ziti Dish, and my manager is always fussing about the wait staff looking perfect. I pull my hair up in a ponytail and walk to the bar to see what section I will be working in tonight. Hopefully, it will be one that will allow me to get out of here at a reasonable time so I can make it back to my apartment for my "makeover". I still can't believe that I agreed to that. I laugh thinking what Sarah must be doing right now to get everything ready. Oddly enough, I am looking forward to tonight. I'm a tad nervous too, but I don't know why.

The shift goes by quickly because it's so busy. Everyone has been out shopping today, and now they are wanting to eat out before going home to unload their gifts. The night goes by in a blur of serving food and drinks over and over again. By the time I am off, my feet are killing me, but at least I am off tomorrow, and I made some good tip money that will buy us some delicious drinks tonight. The rest will go to rent. I go back to the lockers and change back into my clothes from earlier today. I put my apron and ticket book in my locker and grab my purse before locking it up. Then I pull out my phone and see several messages from Sarah telling me to hurry up. I tell her I'm on the way and put my phone back in my purse.

I leave the restaurant and quickly walk the few blocks to my apartment. When I get up the stairs, I hear music coming from our apartment. I walk in and Sarah shoves a glass of champaign in my hand, takes my purse from me, and puts it by the door.

"Welcome home. This is to get our celebration started. Cheers to best friends, a night on the town, and VIP tickets to the hottest club in the city!" Sarah clinks my glass.

I take a sip and enjoy the bubbles as they go down my throat. Yum, I love champaign. Sarah is really excited and it's kind of rubbing off on me now. I'm looking forward to seeing what this club VIBE has to offer. Apparently, it's exclusive so only the wealthiest in the city get in. Other than us, of course. Thinking about who I could see or meet tonight, I remember the man from the coffee shop.

"So, I sort of met this guy today at the coffee shop down the street. We both had Austen on our cups, and we grabbed one of the cups at the same time…" I pause and smile thinking of him, "…and he looked like a Greek god. Seriously, I couldn't stop staring at him."

Sarah rushes over, "Did he ask you out? Did he get your number? How long did you talk for? What does he look like? I need all the details, NOW!"

I can't stop laughing at her excitement. "I hate to break it to you, but he didn't ask me out or get my number. I will probably never see him again. But man, he was so handsome. He was a tall, dark, and gorgeous drink of water." I down the rest of my champaign and get up to refill my glass.

"Well, that's a shame. I was hoping for something juicy," she says.

"Sorry to disappoint. However, I believe we have a club to get to, and I think I was promised a makeover, so you better get to it because you have your work cut out for you."

Sarah puts her hands on her hips and rolling her eyes at me says, "You don't even need a makeover; you're already gorgeous. I am just going to accentuate those curves and beautiful brown eyes. Now come on."

I step out of the shower, and Sarah is waiting for me with a pile of dresses for me to go through. I end up picking a short red dress that has an overlay of lace. It fits perfectly, hugging all the right places. The dress falls just above my knees. It's the perfect amount of revealing but not too much. The perfect little holiday dress. Sarah goes with a smoky look on my eyes and chooses red lipstick for my mouth. I slide into some tall heels and gaze into my floor length mirror. I feel like I don't even know who is looking back at me. It has been so long since I made such an effort in my appearance. My hair is curled and hanging down my back with it pinned up on one side. I feel so sexy and confident in my appearance. I'm so thankful for Sarah. She knows exactly how to work her magic on me.

Sarah comes out of her room in a black dress that's tight at the top then flows out. Her makeup is perfect, as usual. She comes over and links her arm through mine, and we look in the mirror together.

"We are some hotties tonight! Are you ready to go?" she asks.

"Yes, let me grab my purse and phone."

We lock up the apartment and get down to the street to hail a cab. "Tonight is going to be one for the books. I can just feel it."

Sarah smiles at me. We slide into the cab and the driver asks us where to. "Club VIBE," Sarah answers. Just like that, we are on the way. I've got butterflies in my belly for some reason, but I am looking forward to this night. Tonight, seems like anything could happen. I guess that's my literary romantic side coming out, but the thought is still there. I've never been this optimistic about a night out. I wonder if it has anything to do with Austen. It doesn't matter. I have sworn off men and I'm not about to change my mind. I am going out with Sarah to dance and have a good time. That's all.

CHAPTER 4

Miles

Our driver lets us out at the curb of the club. Instantly, I can hear the bass of the music coming from inside. The outside of the club seems ordinary enough, except for a red carpet that paves the way to the entrance. And of course, I spot cameras flashing. Sebastian gives me an "I'm sorry" look as we head to the entrance. I keep my head down as I walk, trying to draw less attention.

Reporters start shouting when they see us approaching.

"Miles Knight!"

"Sebastian Knight!"

"Can we get a picture?"

"How are you doing with the stresses of running the largest publishing company in the country? Any comments?"

Cameras are flashing all over and microphones are held out as far as they can reach over the railing. Ah, hell. And so, it begins. Well, we are already here now. Best make the most of it. This isn't the first time we have been bombarded, and it sure as hell won't be the last. Sebastian and I pause quickly for a few photos, and then I wave my hand to the rest of them. "No comments at this time. Have a good night." We stride quickly to the entrance of the club just in time for us to be ushered inside, without having to deal with more press. Seb and I will be all over the internet by the end of the night, and I'm sure some will use this opportunity to throw shade our way.

We walk into the elegantly decorated lobby of the club. The lights are dim, and it takes a moment for my eyes to adjust from the flashes that were just going off outside. Immediately, we are greeted by a waiter holding a silver platter full of champaign flutes. I wave him off because I didn't come here to drink champaign; I'm heading for the good stuff. We walk toward the set of double glass doors that are simultaneously opened for us to walk through. I notice there is already a fairly large crowd of people here. We go straight to the bar and order two shots of Patron and two whiskeys. The bartender slides the shots over to us, and Sebastian raises his to gesture a toast. I hold mine up as he says, "To brothers and new adventures." We clink our shots and down them. Feeling the burn, I'm grateful that my whiskey is here, so I can get the tequila taste out of my mouth. We take our drinks and walk over to a high-top table at the far end of the club.

"This is an impressive turn out for a new club. The PR must have been phenomenal. We need to look into who represented them," I say to Sebastian.

"I agree. It's impressive, but no more shop talk tonight. I want to actually have a good time and that doesn't involve talking about the company," he says coolly.

"You're right. We need a break." I respond.

A few gentlemen that we've done business with in the past, come up to our table and start up a conversation about work, then switch to basketball. These men played basketball in college and that's what we bonded over when we did business a few months ago. I engage in the conversation, offering who I believe will make it to the playoffs. We all chat for a while. As the topic changes to something that doesn't interest me, I begin looking around the club. The décor is trendy but sophisticated. Throughout the space, there are different areas that seem to have different themes, but it still matches as a whole. The walls are painted in a dark gray that offsets the white-framed, abstract paintings hanging throughout with spotlights that illuminate each of them, no doubt commissioned by a noted artist. Without the bar and all the tables, this club could be conceived as an art gallery. The high-top tables are silver metal with white and black marble tops. Long loungers line the walls in the back of the club for a more comfortable sitting area. This place is decorated nicely, and it feels more upscale than the usual clubs.

Just as I glance toward the bar, I see her. The woman from the coffee shop is here. What are the chances of this happening, especially twice in one day? I stare for a moment making sure that it's really her and not my imagination. As I watch, I know for sure that it's the Jane Austen woman. I knew in my heart that I would be seeing her again, but in this moment, I'm paralyzed looking at her. My heart begins to race, and I feel anxious. This is a reaction that I have never had toward a woman. I'm taking this as a sign that I need to get to know her. I sit at my table and watch. She is wearing a stunning red dress that hugs her curves perfectly. Her long black hair covers her back, making her look like a goddess. She seems so charismatic. I see her laugh and can't help but smile. I remember that laugh. It has been playing in my head on repeat all day. I've got to go and talk to her. It's like there is a magnet pulling me toward her. I hear my father's words in my head again, and I smile. This woman is mine; she just doesn't know it yet. I can feel it in my soul. She's the one.

"Excuse me, gentlemen, I will be back," I advise, looking at the men at our table and my brother. He looks at me quizzically but doesn't say anything, just nods. I get up and head toward the bar where she is standing. The closer I get, the more radiant she becomes. Suddenly, I can't think of what to say. I don't have trouble talking to any females, but everything about her seems different than any other woman I've ever encountered. I need something special to break the ice. A sudden thought comes to mind that just might work.

I slide in beside her at the bar, but she has her back to me because she's still talking with her friend. I stand and listen to her voice and the enthusiasm as she is speaking. There is a pause in the conversation, and I know this is my chance to speak up. I lean into her space, so she can hear me as I say, "I certainly have not the talent, which some people possess, of conversing easily with those I have never seen before." She turns her head quickly to look at me with surprise in her eyes as I continue, "I cannot catch their tone of conversation, or appear interested in their concerns, as often I see done." I smile at her. "Fancy seeing you here." I smirk while leaning into her. I am instantly hit by the intoxicating smell of vanilla on her skin.

"Austen," she says breathlessly. I smile at that because I know she feels the same connection that I do. I chuckle and respond, "Actually, my name is Miles."

She looks up at me with a playful expression in her eyes, "Do you go around to every woman and recite *Pride and Prejudice* to them?" she asks.

"This is a first for me, truly," I sigh, and then continue, "I knew you liked Jane Austen from our meeting this morning. I saw you from across the club, and I knew I had to come speak to you."

She smiles a bright, beautiful smile that reaches her eyes. She holds out her hand for me to shake and says, "My name is Elizabeth, but since the first time I read *Pride and Prejudice,* I insist that people call me Lizzie."

As our hands slide together, that same jolt of electricity runs up my arm. She seems to notice as well and looks up at me with her lips slightly parted. "It's nice to officially meet you,

Lizzie," I muse, still holding her hand and not wanting to let go. I hold it for a few seconds longer than appropriate but drop it before she thinks I'm some creep. I instantly miss her warmth. Her friend has now come up beside her. She is also beautiful but not in the way Elizabeth is. She has on a black dress that is very flattering to her figure. She looks at me up and down with a large grin on her face, and I'm almost certain that she recognizes me.

I am about to speak up when Elizabeth says, "This is my best friend, Sarah." Elizabeth motions to the woman next to her. I take her hand as I say, "Nice to meet you. I'm Miles."

She shakes my hand and replies, "Nice to meet you." She drops her hand and leans in to whisper something in Elizabeth's ear, and she heads toward the dance floor with a drink in hand. As I turn to look back at Elizabeth, I am again struck by her beauty. Pulling me out of my gaze, she asks, "So, where did you study literature, or are you just a Jane Austen enthusiast?"

"I actually went to Princeton and studied marketing. However, during my undergraduate I took many literature courses, one of them being British lit. That is when I began to fully appreciate Austen's work, along with many others." She studies me for a minute but seems impressed with my answer. I mentally give myself a pat on the back. And so, I ask, "Did you study literature?"

Her smile grows as she replies, "Yes, actually, in great detail. I majored in literature, and I had a minor in British lit. It is a passion of mine. I became obsessed with it in high school, and I knew that's what I wanted to study when I went to college…" she pauses with a slight frown, then continues, "…although, it wasn't what my father wanted. I'm sorry. I don't usually talk about him. I'm not sure why that slipped out." She blushes and looks a bit uneasy.

"And what is it that your father wanted you to study?" I ask.

She takes a deep breath and says, "He wanted me to study law and take over his practice one day." She sounds a little bitter.

I don't want to push further into that subject because I sense there is something deeper there, and I don't want to try my luck. So instead, I change the subject. "So, I have now met you twice today. I believe the universe is trying to tell us something," I say, smiling widely.

She laughs loudly and looks back at me. "Do you truly believe in the universe aligning moments like this?" she asks quizzically but with a sparkle in her eyes.

"No, I confess I normally do not. I believe in making my own dreams come true with hard work, but this seems like more than a coincidence, and I think we would be fools to ignore it," I reply. She studies me for a moment. I'm not sure if she is going to laugh in my face or accept that this chance meeting must mean something.

She seems to be considering my response when she suddenly says, "Would you like to dance?" She gestures toward the dance floor. I cringe inwardly because I am not the best dancer, but I am pleased that she doesn't want to get rid of me just yet.

"Absolutely," I say. "Lead the way."

I hold my hand out for her to take and feel the warmth immediately return when she places her hand in mine. I look down at our entwined fingers and get a sense of rightness. It is something I wouldn't be able to explain in a million years other than fate, like two puzzle pieces coming together. I have never had that kind of thought in my life, but here I am thinking about Elizabeth. I hardly know her, but I feel as though I've known her for years. It's contradictory to everything I have come to know. She is so easy to talk to. Also, she doesn't know who I really am, so I know that she is being genuine. We make our way through the crowd to the dance floor. The music playing is loud, and the lighting is dimmer, making a sensual energy beat throughout. As I look around, every couple seems to be in their own world. I look down at Elizabeth and confess, "I have to admit I am not very good at this."

She looks up at me with those big brown eyes that seem to pierce my soul. She leans in closer, and I can smell her vanilla perfume again. With her eyes still on me, she says, "Put your hands on my hips and let the music move you."

I do as she says and, feeling her waist, I pull her closer to me, holding her tightly. Elizabeth is pressed up against me and is swaying her hips to the music. This feels so unbelievably right. Her body molds to mine perfectly, and I can't help but feel like this is exactly where I belong. Thank the stars for bringing us together again. The warmth of her body against mine feels like something I have been missing my whole life. She has her hands on my shoulders and lightly runs her hands through the back of my hair. It's the best sensation I've ever felt. I want her hands to stay there. I gently rub my hands up and down her hips, and they are delicious. I get lost in her warmth and touch. I lean down and whisper in her ear breathlessly, "You're good at this." Goosebumps break out over her skin as she looks up at me. Those intoxicating eyes penetrate my soul, and again, I am mesmerized at this stunning woman that I'm holding.

I'm not sure how long we stay like this, but then she asks, "Do you want to go get a drink, and then find somewhere to sit?" I nod and she leads me from the dance floor to the bar area. I instantly miss the warmth of her body pressed against mine, but I hold onto her hand tightly. I'm not letting her go. Not now or ever. When we come to the bar, I see Sebastian is standing there with a tall blonde. That's his usual type. We walk up to where they are, and I give him a pat on the back. "Lizzie, this is my brother, Sebastian," I say to introduce the two of them. I see the smile in his eyes as he looks her over, and a sense of possessiveness comes over me. I don't want anyone to look at her like that. *Why am I acting like a caveman? It's not like she is mine. Yet. Well in my mind she is, I'll just have to get her on board as soon as possible.* Sebastian reaches out to take her hand, and then leans in to put a chaste kiss on her cheek. I slide my hand around Elizabeth's waist and pull her closer to me. I know it's barbaric, but my need to claim her is strong. Sebastian gestures toward the woman he was speaking with and says, "This is Tiffany. Tiffany, this is my brother Miles."

Her eyes light up in recognition, and I immediately regret approaching my brother. Before she can say anything, I reply, "Nice to meet you. We were just going to grab a drink. I will see you later, Seb." As we walk off, he gives me a smirk and a wink. I roll my eyes and lead Elizabeth to the other side of the bar where there is an opening. "What would you like?" I ask Elizabeth.

"Vodka cranberry martini, please," she replies. I order our drinks, and then I look back at Elizabeth to see that she had been watching me. I try to hide my grin, but I'm sure she can see. The drinks come quickly; I thank the bartender and put down more than enough money for the two drinks. We take our glasses and I lead Elizabeth to an empty booth in the back. As we walk, I place my hand on the small of her back, and the heat of her body travels up my arm and straight to my heart. We get to the table and take our seats. Silence falls over us as we both take a sip of our drinks.

"So, what do you do, Miles?" she asks.

I knew this question was coming, and I should have prepared for it. I don't want to lie to her. I want her to be able to trust me because I really think we have a connection. This is a bond that I have never felt before and because of that, I'm scared to tell her who I really am. I know that I will tell her eventually, but I don't want it to be tonight. I just want to be Miles tonight, not Benjamin Miles Knight Jr. I think for a minute and say, "I'm in marketing. I got my doctorate from Princeton, so I enjoy all aspects of business." That's not a lie. I did get my doctorate at Princeton, and I am involved in marketing at KPC. I just didn't tell her that I also happen to be the CEO. "What about you?" I ask her before she can ask any questions.

"Currently, I work at a secondhand bookstore, Much Ado About Books, and I am also a waiter at the Ziti Dish. But that is all temporary until I can get my book published. It has been difficult to write the past few months." She looks a little embarrassed of her job positions, but that's not what caught me off guard. *She is a writer? How can she, of all people, not know who I am? Is she pretending, so she can get close to me?* My body instantly begins to tense at the thought. No, she isn't like that. She can't be. She didn't seem to know who I was at the coffee shop. I would have been able to see it in her eyes if she knew who I was. Also, she probably would have shoved her manuscript in my face and begged me to read it. I get that all the time. No, Elizabeth is different. I can feel it. She's real and down to earth and the most alluring woman I have ever seen.

"So, you are a writer? Have you ever been published?" I ask her.

She shakes her head and says, "No, this will be my first book. It has been in the works for over a year, and I am really trying to finish it. I went through a tough time, and I didn't have the motivation I needed to get the writing done. But now I am determined to finish it. I need to see if I have what it takes to be like one of the greats."

I know I am phishing for answers, but I ask, "Do you have a publisher in mind?"

She shakes her head again. "I don't know. I haven't thought that far ahead yet. I need to get the manuscript completed, and then I guess I will do some research and send it to several publishing companies. My friend that you met, Sarah, is in Public Relations, and I think she worked for a publisher a few years back. But other than that, I haven't given it much thought. I just need to get the words down on paper first."

Relief spreads through my body, and I let out a breath that I didn't know I was holding in. She doesn't know who I am, or she would have just said so. Thank God. "Wow, which will be such a huge accomplishment when you complete it, Lizzie. What type of book are you writing?" I question.

She immediately replies, "It's a romantic comedy. I know it's a bit cliché with all the authors out there that are writing the same thing, but I feel like I can bring a new and unique story to the table. Well, at least that's how I feel. I haven't let anyone else read it, so I may just be biased," she comments with a huge smile on her face. She continues to tell me the synopsis of the story, and I am very intrigued. I love how animated she is when she talks about something that she's passionate about. I can't help but get a flurry of butterflies in the pit of my stomach at the sight of her in her element. *Do, men get butterflies? Sebastian is going to give me so much shit about this when he finds out.* She is unlike anyone I have ever met, and I couldn't be happier about it. She is right. She is unique, a one-of-a-kind woman that will be mine. I can't deny this chemistry that we have, and I know without a doubt that she is exactly who my father was talking about. I smile at the thought. I know he is smiling down at me, and I think for a moment that he sent her to me. He knew I needed a push.

Then I get another idea. Could this woman be the author I have been looking for? Is she the spark that I've been searching for? These meetings haven't been by chance. Fate brought us together, and I will make sure she realizes that. I smile and reply, "Your face lights up when you talk about your writing. I can see how passionate you are about it. You're uniquely beautiful."

She blushes at my words and mutters a thank you as she takes another sip of her drink. "I'm in love with books," she says. "Not just contemporary but the classics as well. You already know my love for Jane Austen. But it's more than love. I get enveloped in the words and am transported to the time of the story. In the secondhand bookstore I work for, we get in many books that are incredibly old, and each day I hope that I will come across a first edition of some kind. But those are hard to come by, obviously." She pauses for a moment and then continues, " Sorry for rambling, I suppose literature gets me excited, and you are very easy to talk to." She looks surprised at her admission, and I can see a bit of tension in her face.

"You don't ever have to apologize to me. I like hearing you talk about things you enjoy and are passionate about." She simply nods her head at my statement. I'm not sure how the energy between us has shifted, but she seems to be putting up walls; I won't have that. Elizabeth is going to be mine. I'm not sure it was love at first sight, but it was something. Something I won't let slip through my fingers. "You know, I didn't want to come tonight. My brother forced me here, but I'm glad that he did. I wanted to see you again after our meeting this morning," I say in hopes of making her relax or at least make her more comfortable. I'm not sure what's going on in that head of hers, but I don't want her to shut me out. I can't let that happen. I know what this is between us, and if she needs reassurance or time, I will be there to give her just that. But I'm not letting her go.

She seems surprised and says, "That's what happened to me, as well. Sarah had to beg me to come out. She had these VIP tickets, and she pretty much made me come." She chuckles.

The sound hits me in the heart like an arrow, and I can't help but smile.

"It's curious that we both had to be talked in to coming here, and now look at us, meeting for the second time today. I believe I reiterated my earlier comment that this is more than a coincidence," I say. Her eyes are stuck on mine, she seems to be considering this. "I promise I'm not some sappy romantic that believes in all that, but I also can't deny this connection I feel toward you. I felt it this morning as well. And I don't ever feel like that toward anyone, Lizzie."

I'm about to continue when she says, "I don't really believe in fairytale happy endings and such. I know I write about them, but they are just fiction. I've never had luck in the love department, so it's hard for me to believe this is more than a chance meeting. I'm not trying to discredit your beliefs; I am just going on experience."

Ah, so she's been hurt before, and that's why she has her guard up. I understand that. I will just work that much harder to show her I'm trustworthy, and I am the man for her. "I'm sorry that you have had relationships that have caused you to guard yourself, but I intend on showing you my worthiness. Elizabeth, these kinds of feelings I'm having don't ever happen to me. I want you to know that I'm not just trying to get you in bed," I respond.

Elizabeth opens her mouth to respond when Sarah stumbles to our table. She has obviously had too much to drink. Startled by the appearance of Sarah, Elizabeth says "Sarah, are you okay? How much have you had to drink? Do I need to take you home?" Sarah just starts laughing and stumbling around as she tries to dance to the music. Elizabeth gets up to steady her friend. She looks at me apologetically and says, "I'm so sorry. I really think I need to get her home and into bed before she passes out on me."

I stand up as well and offer a hand to Sarah. "I'll help you get her outside through this crowd."

She smiles and says, "Thank you so much; I appreciate that." I go around to the other side of Sarah, and we make our way to the exit, stopping to get their coats, and I help them both into them. As we leave the club, the fresh, cool air hits my face. It's a chilly and mild November night.

"I need to order an uber to…"

Before she can finish, I offer, "No need, I will have my driver take you both home. It's not a problem." She looks at me for a minute as shock crosses into her features, and I'm unsure of what she's thinking. So, I repeat, "It really is no trouble. Please, let me assist you."

She looks at Sarah who looks like she is about to pass out, then looks back at me and says, "Thank you. I really am grateful for that."

I really need to get her friend home as soon as possible. "Great," I reply, as I pull out my phone and send a message to Thomas. "He will be here in three minutes." She looks stunned. We stand in silence for a few moments as we both hold on to Sarah, and then Thomas pulls up to the curb. He gets out and opens the door as we lead her friend to the car. We slide Sarah inside while Elizabeth and I stand next to the door. "Thank you, Thomas. Will you see that these women get home safely?"

Elizabeth replies, "You aren't riding with us?"

"No, unfortunately, I have to go back into the club and make sure my brother makes it home as well," I say.

She nods her head, then smiles. "This is very generous of you. How can I repay you?"

I'm surprised. No one has ever asked to give me something in return for favors; but thinking quickly, I say with a quirk, "How about your number?" She laughs and stares into my eyes. Man, I love her smile. It's infectious. I just want to keep it on her face.

I can see her trying to decide in her mind, when she finally says, "Are you sure that's what you want? Your offer is way more generous."

Without hesitation, I reply, "I actually believe I am getting the better arrangement here." She blushes and nods her head in agreement.

"Deal." She gives me her number and goes to slide into the car, but before she can, I kiss her cheek. Her face reddens instantly, and she smiles. She gets in and says, "I'm glad I met you, Miles. Twice."

I wink at her and say, "We'll talk soon." She nods, and I close the door. I watch as they drive away until I can no longer see the brake lights. I turn around and head back into the club to get my brother, but all I can think about is Elizabeth. I knew I would see her again, but never did I think it would be the same day. I chuckle because I know that this is the beginning of something great. I can feel it.

CHAPTER 5

Elizabeth

I give the driver our apartment's address, and then turn to make sure Sarah is all right, lying on the seat next to me. Leaning over, I brush the hair out of her face and pull her coat up over her more to keep her warm. When I sit back up, I take in the fancy interior of this car. What type of marketing does Miles do for a living to be able to afford the luxury of a chauffeur? I knew the club was exclusive, but I guess I hadn't thought that Miles was one of those people. I figured he scored tickets like we had. But as I look around, I'm pretty sure Miles is one of the high-end customers the club was targeting. I wish Sarah was awake to see where we are right now. She would flip out.

I lean my head back as my mind begins to replay the events of the evening. Never in a million years did I think I would run into the man from the coffee shop. *I knew his name wasn't Austen*, I think to myself. The brief interaction in the coffee shop did not do his looks justice; he is simply gorgeous... like Superman status. I could look into his beautiful blue eyes for hours while drooling all over myself. His long black eyelashes accentuate his eyes perfectly. His rugged black hair, that he runs his hand through when he is thinking about something, is so sexy. I chuckle to myself. He is so far out of my league; we aren't even in the same universe. Not that he was interested in me. He was just being polite, I'm sure. Especially with him insisting that we use his car to take us home. He was just being chivalrous. Obviously, chivalry isn't dead, as I previously thought. Or maybe Miles is just the exception to the rule. At first, I bet he thought we were invited for our social status as well, which can't be further from the truth. I might as well be Cinderella to his Prince Charming self. I sigh as I run my hands over my face. Why am I even entertaining these thoughts? I don't want a man. I'm not looking for anyone. I'm on a break from men, at the moment. It's my newest mantra and I will stick to it.

I roll my head to the side and look through the window at the sights passing. Miles has great hair. I want to run my hands through it again, like when we were dancing. While we were on the dance floor, I could feel his body's warmth against me, and I wanted to get closer to bask in it. He smelled like sandalwood and spice and whiskey. A dangerous combination in my book. Those smells hit me to my very core. I couldn't help but to be entranced by him. The way he came over and introduced himself tonight, using a quote from Jane Austen, it's like something out of a romance novel. I still can't believe I was the one on the receiving end of that line. I mean, obviously, it was a pickup line. Right? I feel chill bumps creep over my skin when I remember turning around and seeing him standing there beside me. Something came over me; it was like we were the only people in the room tonight, that is, until Sarah stumbled our way.

I look over at her in the car, and she is resting against the opposite window. As the limo comes to a stop, the driver lets us know that we have arrived. I shake the thoughts from my head and focus on how the hell I'm supposed to get Sarah up to our apartment. Thomas comes around to open the door for us, and he insists on helping me get Sarah to our apartment, which is a miracle because I don't think I would have been able to do it alone. We probably wouldn't have made it past the first set of stairs.

"Thank you so much for the ride home and helping me get her inside. You have been a life saver, Thomas." I wish there was something I could do for him in return. Should I tip him? I don't even know what to do in this situation. Is it like a bellhop helping me bring up my luggage? I mean, Sarah was like a dead weight, so she kind of was my luggage. I smile, thinking of the look on her face if she knew I was thinking of her as a piece of luggage to be toted around.

"Not a problem, ma'am. I'm happy I could help. You have a good night, dear," he replies.

As he turns to go back to the car, I ask, "How long have you worked for Miles?"

He turns back around and says, "I've worked for him for three years, but I have been with their family for twenty years." He must sense that I want to know more, so he adds, "He is a great person, and he has a heart of gold." With that, he turns on his heels and heads toward the car.

I turn back to Sarah on the couch and help get her to bed. After getting her tucked in, I put a glass of water and Tylenol on her nightstand and a trashcan close to her bed. Hopefully, she won't get sick, but I would rather be safe than have to help in that cleanup. I cringe at the thought. I quietly slip out of her room and go to my own. As I pull on my pajamas, I sit on my bed finally alone with my thoughts.

Although Miles is handsome and charming, I need to stand by my previous promise to stay away from men. I don't have time for that type of distraction in my life right now; I also don't have the time to nurse a new broken heart, which would only be inevitable. If my parents' divorce taught me anything, it's that even after twenty-eight years together, you can still end up with a broken heart.

Even with that resolve in my mind, it doesn't stop me from recounting tonight. Miles seemed so different from other men. He looked at me like I was the only one he was seeing in the whole club. It doesn't make sense. He is obviously wealthy, and I told him that I work two jobs. Someone like him would never have something to do with someone like me. Unbelievingly, he still seemed interested in me after that confession. However, obviously, we are from different classes. I mean he has his own driver, for Pete's sake! But I still can't help but to fantasize what it would be like to be with a man like that. Not the wealth part, which doesn't interest me. It's his confidence and intelligence that call to me, not to mention his dangerously handsome looks. He was so attentive, but is that because he only had one thing on his mind, which would be closing the deal at the end of the night? He said himself that's not what he was after, but don't all men say something like that to get the girl?

Even asking myself that question, I have the urge to put that thought away, because he didn't seem at all displeased that I had to cut the night short when I told him that I needed to get Sarah home. Although, he didn't leave when we did, so maybe he went back into the club and found another woman that he could take home for the night. Still, I can't help but smile that he offered us his personal car and driver to get us home. Who does that? It was a very kind and thoughtful gesture, and he seemed sincere about it. Maybe I am thinking about this too much. It's not like he'll be calling me. I did give him my number, but I'm not expecting anything. I hope he doesn't call because I'm not looking for a man. *Keep telling yourself that, Lizzie.* Even if he happens to look like a Greek god, he did seem genuinely interested in me and thought that it was fate that we ended up at the same place twice in one day. I do agree that it's strange how that happened, but I don't believe in that type of thing, do I? I mean, that's fairytale talk, and it can't be real. There is no such thing as love at first sight and soulmates. *Right?* But I still feel this connection with him that I can't deny. *Why can't I deny it? I NEED to deny it.* But even though I don't know tons about him, there was like a tiny thread drawing me to him, pulling us closer together. I have never felt like that in my life. When he whispered in my ear, my whole body reacted with goosebumps. I shiver just thinking about his warm breath on my neck. *Okay, calm down, Lizzie. Nothing is going to come of this. It was just a cool night to tell Sarah about later.* I must protect myself. I have a feeling that his fire will burn me, and I won't go hopping down that rabbit hole. I take a few deep breaths to try and put the thoughts of all things Miles out of my head.

I stand up and walk to the kitchen to get a glass of water and return to my bed. I get under the covers and turn on my side, placing a pillow under my arm to snuggle with. The last thing I see as I drift off to sleep is my first edition of *Sense and Sensibility* that sits on my nightstand. I smile to myself, and within minutes, I'm fast asleep.

***

Bang. Bang. Bang. What is that sound? Bang. Bang. Bang. I hear knocking. Is that on our door? Am I still dreaming? Ugh, what time is it? I peek open my eyes and see the sunlight streaming through my golden black-out curtains that I forgot to close last night before I fell asleep. I roll over to grab my phone and see that it's eight in the morning. Who would be here this early?

"Sarah, did you order something?" I call out. No answer comes. I'm sure she's still passed out from last night. I shuffle out of bed and pull on my robe and slippers and head to the door. I check the peephole and see... Miles' driver? Thomas, I think? What is going on? I open the door and he's got a huge grin on his face. Just then, I notice the flowers in his hand. It's the largest bouquet I've ever seen. Beautiful white lilies are perfectly placed in this intricate crystal vase.

"Good morning, Miss Elizabeth. These are for you," he

says, offering me the flowers.

I take the vase in my hands, looking down at them in disbelief. "Oh, um… are you sure these are for me?" I ask, confused, with a blush that I know he can see. He just chuckles and motions to the card inside the bouquet. I look down and see my name handwritten on the paper. When I look back up, I see Thomas has already started to walk toward the stairs. "Thank you," I manage to croak out because I'm too stunned to say anything else.

I walk back into the apartment, closing the door behind me. I place the flowers on the kitchen counter and stare at them for a moment. I'm a bit speechless and still half asleep to really register what is going on right now. I don't even know if someone has ever sent me flowers, except when I was in the hospital when I was younger. And that was from family members. These are from Miles? Maybe his driver drove another woman home, and these were meant for her? Or a girlfriend and he got confused? But then I remember the card that has my name on it, and I snatch it up right away because I need to know what is going on. The front of the card has, 'Lizzie' scrolled on the envelope in a man's perfect handwriting. I can feel my cheeks flush, and my body starts coursing with nerves. Geez, this man can do this to me just by seeing my handwritten name! I've got a genuine problem. I can't believe this is real. I open the envelope and turn the card over.

Lizzie,

Thank you for your company last night.

"To be fond of dancing was a

certain step toward falling in love."

-J. Austen

Have dinner with me. Pick you up at eight.

Miles

I read and reread the card over and over with a smile plastered on my face. Wow, this man has some serious charming skills. This is the second time he's recited Jane Austen to me. It is like he knows what my soul yearns to hear and is speaking straight to it. Am I living in a Hallmark movie right now? I mean, this can't be my life. No man has ever taken the time to use one of my passions to flirt with me or ask me out. I stare at the lilies; they are so beautiful and unique. He didn't send roses, almost like he knew that I didn't like them, which is silly. We barely know anything about each other. But there is still this weird feeling like I already know him. Is he really unlike any of the other men I have dated? He seems different. Is this crazy? Yes, it's crazy. I have only known this man for a day. That is all. And here I am holding a card from him staring at beautiful flowers. Am I going to go on this date? I don't have his number; he only has mine. There is no way for me to decline his offer. Did he know I wouldn't be able to say no? I chuckle to myself. "Oh, Miles, what am I going to do with you?" I whisper. *Maybe it's not a date and just two people having dinner like friends*, but as soon as I utter the words to myself, I know it might not to be true. This is indeed a date. My heart begins to race in my chest, and my palms become sweaty because this scares me. It scares me because he has already gotten under my skin in a way that no man has before. I can't get hurt again; I won't survive it. I must keep my heart guarded at all costs, but I can't help admitting that he may have chinked a small piece of my armor off in the past twenty-four hours. I take a deep breath and read the card again. He will be here at eight tonight, and I will have to be ready. I never thought I would say this again, especially this soon, but I'm going on a date tonight. The thought both terrifies and excites me.

As I place the card on the counter, I get a great idea for my book in progress. I run to my room, grabbing my laptop and flopping on my bed. I spend the rest of the day with words flowing out of my mind and through my fingers. The motivation is back. My fingers momentarily pause above the keyboard. Is this because of Miles, I wonder? Whatever the reason, I am going to take advantage of it. So, I dive back into my writing as the day drifts away.

CHAPTER 6

Miles

It's early Saturday morning, and I have already worked out and showered. I usually try and sleep in a bit on the weekends, but it eluded me last night. I called Thomas to take me to the florist down the street, so I could pick something out for Elizabeth. I didn't want to call and just have something put together. I wanted to do it myself, and I also wanted the card handwritten. I had an idea while I was in the shower for the perfect thing to write on the card. Another Jane Austen quote came to mind, and I couldn't help but smile. This woman is something special, and I want to treat her as such. I've never done anything like this before. I haven't ever wanted to be romantic and thoughtful, but it almost seems natural to do it for her. I have never put this much effort into charming a woman, but I find myself wanting to go the extra mile for her. I want to see her smile and make her happy. I want to spend more time with her. Elizabeth did tell me she hasn't had the best relationships in the past, and it makes me angry that someone could do whatever they did to her. I already feel protective over her. I don't even want to think of those past assholes; they had their chance. I'm damn excited that they screwed up, just not at the cost of her feelings. But I will get her to trust me and see I'm nothing like anyone she has ever been with.

Thomas drops me back at my place, and then goes to deliver the flowers to her. He knows where she lives because he took her home last night, which worked to my benefit. As I am sipping my second cup of coffee on my balcony, my phone vibrates in my pocket. I take it out and read the text from Thomas that says one word. **Delivered**. Perfect, now it's time to plan the perfect date. I make a few calls and set everything up. I hope that I'm not going overboard with these details. I barely know Lizzie, but I also feel like my soul already knows her. I have never put this much energy into organizing a date. *She's different*, I keep saying to myself. I cannot wait to see her face when she sees where I'm taking her. The excitement I feel in my chest is spilling over into my entire body, and I have this energy that has me unable to sit still. I have hours before I need to get ready, so I must find something to keep my mind occupied until then. I walk toward my office and sit at my desk. Opening the laptop, I see there are dozens of emails that need my attention. So, for the remainder of the afternoon, I work which always keeps my focus.

***

Elizabeth

My hands begin to cramp from typing, and I look out of my bedroom window, realizing the sun is setting. I have been writing for hours. I haven't gotten this much done, in well, ever. Wow, that spark came out of nowhere. I smile when I look back at my laptop and see how much I've accomplished today. The book is still far from being completed, but I finally feel like this is exactly where I need to be and what I need to be doing. I save the file, put my laptop on my nightstand, and scoot down from my vintage cream bedspread. I found this gem when I was thrift shopping, and I had to have it. My whole room has a 19th century feel to it. I love that era. I often think I should have been born in that time period. *Would I have become an influential writer if I was from that time? Would I have been like Jane Austen?* The thought makes me smile. Maybe this book will be a success, and people will know my name. Maybe, someday, I will have some of the impact that Jane Austen did in her day and is still having.

I hear Sarah squeal from the kitchen, and I run out of my room to see what the problem is. However, when I get to the kitchen, she is smiling and jumping up and down. What on Earth? "What are you so giddy about?" I ask, shaking my head.

"Um, hello? Where did these flowers come from?" She looks at me with a wide grin. "Oh, is it the guy from last night? From the club? I told you that you would find a new guy! Tell me everything," she squeaks.

"Well, if you hadn't passed out on me last night, then you would know. But since you did, and you have been asleep all day, I haven't had the chance to fill you in on my... interesting night," I reply, smiling.

"Do you remember the coffee shop guy I mentioned yesterday?" She nods, looking puzzled. "Well, it turns out we ended up having another surprise meeting... at the club last night. That's who came up to us at the bar before you went to go dance," I say matter-of-factly.

"WHAT??" she shrieks. "That was the tall, dark, and handsome man that grabbed your coffee? And he just so happened to be at the same club opening as you? This is fate. FATE! I'm telling you. What is he like?" she asks eagerly for more details. I pause and think over yesterday, what is he like?

"He's sweet and intelligent. He knows Jane Austen enough to whisper a line in my ear last night. Hang on. Why do you think it's fate? That's the same thing he said. There is no such thing," I object.

She gives me a look that says I'm about to get a lesson. I can't help but chuckle. "Fate is real, my friend. And the fact that he mentioned it means he believes that, too. He sounds romantic, and it doesn't hurt that he's sexy as hell!" As she takes a large gulp of coffee she persists, "So, tell me more!"

"We danced, and then we got a table and talked a little about my book. He also mentioned it was not a coincidence that we met twice in one day. I told him I didn't really believe that because of my failed relationships. Then you stumbled over to our table, and I had to get you out of there. He helped me get you out of the club and offered us his chauffeur to drive us home. Then he gave me a kiss on the cheek, and I woke up to this delivery this morning," I say, trying to think if I left anything out. "So, he wants to take me out tonight, but I don't know. I'm nervous, but I have no way to contact him and tell him no. What do I do?" I ask. She looks at me like I have asked the silliest thing in the world.

"What you are going to do is get in the shower now, and I will go find you a dress and shoes! Makeup and hair next! Don't look at me like that! You *are* going on this date! No man has ever gone to this much trouble for a date with either of us. In my opinion, he sounds like Prince Charming. And I don't want to hear that you've sworn off men because this is a whole new situation entirely. He is definitely not in the same league as the rest of those dirtbags you've dated in the past. Now, go get in that shower, girl! I'm so excited for you!" she exclaims.

I sigh and smile at the same time. I already knew I was going on this date, but I needed some reassurance from my best friend. She knows me so well and understands my hesitation. However, she is right; I feel like he is different somehow.

"I'm going to take a bath and try to get my nerves under control," I reply as I head to the bathroom. I love our tub. It's white porcelain with claw feet. It is one of the features that sold me on this apartment. I start the water and sprinkle in some lavender bath salts. The steam begins to fill the room, and I step out of my robe, then lower myself into the tub. Man, this feels good. I can feel the tension just melting right away. I need to make more time for baths. I think I tell myself that every time I get in here, but I rarely do. I'm always on such a tight schedule that I normally just hop in the shower as quickly as possible. I have some instrumental piano music playing from my phone, and I lay my head back against the tub, then close my eyes.

I must drift off because Sarah comes barging in, startling me. The water is now tepid, and I realize that I did doze off for a bit, but I was so relaxed it was hard not to.

"You have to get out of there if you want to be ready when he gets here!" she says as she throws me a towel. I get out, drain the tub, and follow her to her bedroom to see what she has picked out for me. When I step in, I see the most beautiful cream-colored dress. It has a form-fitting bodice with lace and sporadic little rhinestones. From the bodice, the dress flows out from the waist with a sheer overlay. It has a baby doll neckline with a matching sheer material that drapes over one shoulder. I walk up to the dress and feel the material in my hands.

"Is this new? I have never seen this before," I whisper, maybe a little in shock of its beauty.

She beams and says, "I got it on clearance the other day when you were at work. I was walking by a shop and saw it in the window. I had to go in and have a closer look and instantly had to have it!"

"You don't mind if I wear it? This seems like a special occasion dress," I reply. She takes my shoulders in her hands and looks me in the eyes. "This IS a special occasion. You are putting yourself out there again, and I couldn't be prouder of you. You need to wear this dress as your suit of armor. The better you feel about yourself, the better you feel about this big jump you're making," she says reassuringly. She always knows just what to say. She's right. Special occasions call for special outfits. And this date is a new milestone in my life. I can feel it. I slip into the dress and the matching five-inch cream heels with matching rhinestones that she picked out. She works on my hair and makeup, and I'm dressed and ready with five minutes to spare. I get out my wristlet and slide my phone and keys into it. I walk over to the floor length mirror to look at myself. I feel beautiful and confident and not at all nervous. Okay, so that last part isn't entirely true. I'm super nervous, but I can do this. I take several deep breaths and give myself a mental pep talk.

Then, there's a knock on the door. I look at Sarah, and she gives me two thumbs up. I walk to the door and peer out of the peephole to make sure it's him, and it is. I unlock the door and open it. My breath catches in my throat when I see him standing there in my doorway. He is wearing a grey suit that fits him perfectly. I can see the outline of his perfect muscles. He has on a light blue collared shirt without a tie. He looks like he just walked off the runway, again. I become aware that no one has spoken as Sarah comes to the door and holds her hand out.

"Hi. I'm Sarah, Lizzie's roommate. I know we met last night, but I don't recall all the details of that, unfortunately. Thank you for getting us home safely." They both chuckle and shake hands.

"It was no problem at all. Anytime," he says., He turns his gaze toward me and remarks, "You look stunning!"

I can feel the blush sneaking up into my cheeks; I smile and say, "Thank you. You don't look too bad yourself."

He chuckles and holds his arm out for me to take. "Are you ready to get this date started?"

I nod, grabbing my bag. "Let me get my coat." I retrieve it

from the closet by the door and kiss Sarah on the cheek. "I will be back later. Love you," I say to her as I put my hand on Miles' forearm. I hear the door close behind us as we walk toward the stairs. I look up at him, and he is already staring back at me. I smile, too, and turn my gaze back to the stairs so I don't fall. That would just be my luck. He is even more handsome than I remember. *How is that even possible?* He places his hand on the small of my back and bolts of electricity shoot through my body. *Oh boy, here we go.*

CHAPTER 7

Miles

When Lizzie opens the door to her apartment, I feel momentarily paralyzed. It's as if all the breath in my lungs has been sucked out of me. She's even more stunning than I remember. My eyes sweep over her body of their own accord. The cream dress compliments her gorgeous olive complexion. Her silky black hair, curled loosely, runs over her shoulders and down her back. She has one side pulled up with a silver flower pinning it in place. We stare into each other's eyes for a moment without either one of us speaking. I only break my gaze when her roommate comes over to reintroduce herself. I offer my arm to Elizabeth, and she takes it after she gets her coat. She closes the door, and I walk her toward the stairs. I can't keep my gaze from looking her over. She is the most intoxicating woman I have ever laid eyes on. I move my hand down the backless part of her dress to the small of her back and feel the goosebumps erupt over her skin as it did last night when I touched her. I sense she feels this connection like I do, even if she is scared to jump in this with me. I don't even take in my surroundings until I realize that we have reached my car. I open the passenger door for her, and she smiles, sliding in and giving me a small thank you. I make sure she's settled before I close the door, and then jog to my side of the car.

 I thought tonight would be a good chance to take my own car. I wanted her alone and not uncomfortable, having Thomas drive us around. Once inside, I look back over to her.

She is studying my car, her eyes wide. "So, where are you taking me tonight?" she asks as she glances at me.

"It's a surprise," I say with a grin and a wink. She blushes. Damn, I don't know the last time I made a woman blush like this, but I love it. I love that I have that effect on her. I crank the engine and pull out into the traffic.

"Oh," she says. "I didn't thank you for the flowers and the card. Thank you, Miles. Actually, my favorite flower is the lily, and the card made my day. Are you a huge Jane Austen fan or is it because you know that I am?" she asks.

"Well, I mentioned before that I took literature classes in college, but Jane Austen has always stood out to me. I've read many of her novels, several times each. I appreciate her work," I reply, looking over at her as she takes in that information. I can tell that I win some points with that answer. She gives me a bright smile.

"I love snuggling up on the couch and reading something written by Jane Austen. I feel like I travel through the words, and the world around me melts away," Lizzie states.

"I know that exact feeling. I, too, have had the pleasure of diving into a book that completely consumes me." I glance over to Lizzie and smile at how deep and thoughtful she can be. She doesn't seem superficial but completely down to Earth. I want to know everything there is to know about her. I want to know her hopes and her fears, what her family is like, where she grew up, her happy place. Everything.

We strike up a casual conversation as I drive toward our destination. When I pull up to the New York Public Library, she gives me a quizzical look, and I just smile at her. I get out, open her door, and offer her my hand. When she slides hers into mine, I feel electricity run up my arm again. I won't ever tire of that feeling. I walk her to the entrance, hand in hand.

"Good evening, Mr. Knight. Everything is all set and ready to go," says the director of the library.

I wince as he says my last name, and I hope that Lizzie wasn't paying attention to that. She's too in awe of our location, which is the exact reaction I was hoping for. The director opens the door for us, and I lead her inside. "Thank you, Travis," I tell him.

She looks up at me once the door closes. "What is this? Where is everyone?" she questions.

"I called in a few favors and was able to get the library closed down for just the two of us tonight."

Her eyes widen as big as saucers, and she puts her hand over her mouth as she gasps. "Really?

"Yes, it's just us tonight. Well, us and the servers," I add as one is walking toward us with champagne on a silver tray. I take one of the bubbling, crystal flutes from him and hand it to Lizzie, then I take my own. She looks at me with amazement in her eyes. "To new adventures. 'It isn't what we say or think that defines us, but what we do.' Cheers," I say as we clink our glasses together. I give her a wink and take a sip of the champaign.

"Another Austen quote? Do you have some written on your hand or have a notecard full of them?" she asks me teasingly. I can see the playfulness in her eyes.

"Yes, another quote, but no, I don't have any notes with me," I pause and take a sip of my champaign, enjoying the taste swishing through my mouth. "I can't seem to help it when I'm around you. You know my mother always told me that 'actions speak louder than words,' so I suppose I get that from her. She is another literature enthusiast. She would adore you," I declare because I know that I will be introducing them soon.

"She sounds like an amazing woman, and she raised you

well." She gestures to the empty library in front of us. "I'm sure I would like her, also."

I can't help but watch her as she takes in everything. I feel like I'm seeing it all for the first time even though I have been here hundreds of times. "This has always been my favorite place in New York. I come here when I need to think or when I just want to get away from the world. It's my solace. Although, I admit, I have never rented the whole library out," I tell her.

"This is absolutely perfect, Miles. I love it. Thank you for doing this for me. I have never experienced something like this in my life. It's surreal. We are in the same building with the most precious authors gathered around us. Thank you. This means more than you know," she as she stares straight in my eyes.

I want to kiss her right this moment. I can feel the magnet that's pulling us toward each other, and I don't want to resist it any longer. I lean down, cupping the side of her face and look into her eyes. "Can I kiss you, Lizzie?" She just nods, and I lean in closer to where our noses are almost touching. Our eyes are still locked on one another. I graze my lips over hers, and she shivers. I smile and deepen the kiss. Her lips are perfect and soft and warm. She lets out a small moan, and I take the invitation to further explore her mouth. My tongue sweeps in, and she tastes like the sweet champaign along with something else that is entirely Lizzie. My hand slides into her hair, and I want my fingers to get tangled in the luscious waves. I pull her closer with my forearm and silently curse that we are still holding our glasses. I want both of my hands on her. She is so responsive to my touches. I break the kiss, so we can both catch our breath. She looks up at me with a blush on her cheeks and a smile across her now swollen lips. "How about we take a tour?" I whisper as I kiss her forehead. I take her hand and she intertwines her fingers through mine, then we set off. After an hour of perusing the shelves, stacked with the classics and many other brilliantly acclaimed writers, I lead her to where the next surprise awaits us.

"Where are we going now?" she questions.

"You'll see," is all I offer with a smirk.

We walk into a room with a Jane Austen exhibit, and in the middle, sits a small round table covered with a white linen tablecloth with tapered candles lit in the middle. I lead her to the table and pull the chair out for her. She takes a seat, and I gently steal a kiss to her cheek as I take mine.

"I don't even have the words to say or express… which is highly unusual, because I always have plenty of words," she says. "You did all this just for me?" She looks at me in disbelief.

"I did. I have never done anything like this before, but I wanted to do it for you. I knew you would love this library as I do, and I also knew they had a Jane Austen exhibit going on. I wanted to do something special for you," I reply honestly.

"Why did you want to do something so special? You hardly know me," she says breathlessly as she studies my face.

"I suppose that's true, but I feel like I know you. This probably sounds bizarre, but I feel like I was meant to meet you. Even after our brief meeting at the coffee shop, I wanted to see you again. Then we end up at the same club, and I can't help thinking there is a reason for that. I've never had this instant connection with someone before. It's an insane feeling, but I want to get to know you more. I want to spend more time with you," I reply, as our waiter comes to the table and sets our dishes down before us. He also refills our flutes, then disappears out of the room.

She doesn't take her eyes off me the entire time the waiter is at our table. She isn't giving away what she's thinking, and for a moment, I feel like I may have taken this too far, too quickly. I take a moment and gaze at her from across the table, the candlelight flickering on her face. Every time I look at her, she takes my breath away.

"You know," she begins, "I mentioned last night that I haven't had the best luck with dating. Although, that's putting it lightly. I have to say that honesty seems to have been the problem in my past relationships. As in, they were never honest with me." She pauses for a moment, and my hands are balled into fists, just hearing about those men who have hurt her before. She sighs and continues, "I guess what I am trying to say is you seem different somehow. I'm not even sure how I have that feeling since I haven't known you long. I do feel a connection toward you, as well. It's kind of terrifying, given my history."

Before she can finish, I reach over the table and grasp her hand. My thumb begins running circles over her wrist, and she looks back up at me when I say, "I'm not like them. I would never lie to you. I want to explore what's between us. Will you take a chance with me?" I ask. She seems to ponder the question for a minute, which gets my heart racing even more. *Have I overstepped? Did I rush into this? Am I going to scare her off?* I've never asked anyone to take a chance with me. Honestly, all my past relationships and conquests have gravitated toward me, without my having to make much of an effort. Her eyes meet mine, and I see the twinkle in them, which gives me a little relief that she may feel the same way. I know she's scared. Hell, I'm scared, too. This is all unfamiliar territory for me, but I want to jump in headfirst. Lizzie squeezes my hand, which brings me back to the conversation.

"Yes, I will, Miles." Those four words shoot straight through my heart, and I know that I will do anything to prove to her that we are meant to be together. Forever. I can't help but smile so large I'm sure I look ridiculous. I get up from my chair and hold out a hand to her, saying "Good, dance with me,

Lizzie."

I pull her up from her chair and put my hands around her waist, then pull her close. She drapes her arms over my shoulders as we sway to the piano ballad that is playing for us. I look down at her, and my heart swells with the happiness she has just brought me. I lean down to kiss her forehead, but she looks up at the same time and our lips meet. It's a soft, but intimate kiss. It seems like a promise. The words that we haven't said are in this kiss, and it's more than I could have hoped for. The music stops and we continue to sway for a bit longer. I then lead her back to her chair, and instantly miss the warmth of her body pressed up against me.

We eat our dinner that was prepared by a friend of mine who just so happens to be a chef. We talk about lighter topics over dinner, and after the plates are cleared away, I take her hands in mine. This is it. I must tell her who I am and hope that she isn't upset that I haven't told her sooner.

"I need to tell you something," I huskily whisper. She swallows the champaign that she just drank and looks at me fearfully, which instantly guts me. I need her to trust me like I need my next breath. "I wanted to tell you my whole name. It's Miles Knight Jr."

A flicker of recognition crosses her face as I continue. "I am the CEO of Knight Publishing Company. I know when you asked me what I did for a living, my answer was a bit vague. But I really do marketing at the company. I do a bit of everything. I guess I didn't mention it before because I could tell that you didn't recognize me, which is so rare nowadays. It was like a breath of fresh air. The only women I normally attract are after me for my name or wealth. I apologize for keeping you in the dark, but I want this to work, and I want to be honest with you." I blow out a breath and wait for her to say something to me.

"Wow, I definitely didn't recognize you, although I don't really read the papers much, so it's not a surprise that I didn't. Thank you for telling me, and I understand why you kept it quiet. I can't imagine what you must go through daily. Although I am curious. What made you think you could trust me? How do you know that I'm not like those other women?" she asks quietly.

I know my answer right away, without even thinking, "I can tell you are an exception to those other women because there is something about you that feels genuine. I saw how you cared for Sarah last night, and how you didn't want to use my driver until I persuaded you. You are compassionate and caring and intelligent. Then you asked how you could repay me. I have never had anyone ask that. I was stunned when I heard the words. You are exactly what I have been looking for, Lizzie."

She lets out a deep breath and says, "Wow, thank you for saying those things about me. No one has ever called me all those kind words before. I feel a little self-conscious because I work two jobs. I'm not ashamed of that, but I feel like I'm probably not in the same social circle that you are. Well, I know I'm not. But you were right, I am not one of those women. I'm only interested in you as a person, Miles. I was interested at the coffee shop when I thought your name was Austen." She takes a minute and quietly chuckles. "Thank you for trusting me with this information and also for being honest with me, especially after what I told you about my past."

A frown briefly crosses her face and I know there's more she isn't telling me about her past, but I will let her tell me when she's ready. "I don't want you to feel self-conscious, I was given this position. I am still trying to earn it and navigate my way through it. And I like you for who you are, not what you do for a living. I'm not so shallow to believe two people can't be together because of their differences in social prestige." I squeeze her hands gently. She gives me a nod and a smile that meets her sparkling brown eyes. "Let's get out of here," I happily blurt as I take her hand and pull her up against me. I lean down and kiss the top of her head. The scent of lavender wafts through my senses. I hold her hand as I lead her to the exit.

CHAPTER 8

Elizabeth

As we are walking to Miles' car, I am filled with so many emotions: happiness, fearfulness, excitement, and maybe just a little smitten. I mean, I just went on the most romantic date of my life with the most handsome man that I have ever laid my eyes on. Oh, speaking of eyes, I could get lost in his forever. The deep blue reminds me of the ocean, and they feel like they pierce my heart. We approach his car hand in hand, and he opens the door for me; but before I can get in, he catches me in his arms and bends toward me until our lips meet. It's sweet and tender; I can still taste the champaign on his lips. He breaks off from the kiss and gives me a quick peck on the cheek.

"This has been the most romantic night of my life. Thank you, Miles, for taking the time to put in so much effort for me," I say as I slide into his car. He makes sure I'm settled in before he leans in and buckles my seat belt for me. Can I just take a moment to catch my breath because this man is blowing my mind? He runs his thumb over my cheek before he stands back up and closes the door.

After he gets behind the wheel, he looks over at me and just gazes into my eyes for a moment, then replies, "The pleasure has been all mine. The company was the best I've ever had!" He winks at me with a smile, and then starts the engine. I can't stop smiling. I know he can probably see the blush that I have on my face, but I can't hide it. And I guess I don't care that he sees. I'm sure he's seen me blushing throughout the night. That's just what he does to me. This date really has made me happy. It's surprising that I enjoyed it so much. Well, only surprising by how spectacular it was. Most of my previous dates have been dinner and a movie, maybe some walking around; but never have I experienced anything quite like this. Well, I've never experienced anything like Miles Knight. Yes, I'm still floored by that information. I didn't want him to see the shock in my eyes because I really didn't recognize him, but I have heard of him. I mean every author who hopes to make it big has heard of his company.

We ride in comfortable silence as we head toward my apartment. Miles reaches over and grabs my hand to hold. I glance over at him; he looks so relaxed and not at all nervous, the way I feel. Is he like this with all his dates? Does he go this extravagant for the other women that he goes out with? I can't help but feel a little jealous. *Stop thinking that, Lizzie. He said he hasn't done this before. He hasn't given you any reason to doubt him, well, except not telling you his real name. But that's understandable. If the roles were reversed, I don't think I would have told him my name either.*

As we arrive back at my apartment, he pulls into a spot and cuts the engine. He turns to look at me while his hand is still intertwined with mine. He leans over and pulls me into a kiss, and I swear every time his lips touch mine, I get a shiver down my spine.

"Lizzie," he whispers against my lips.

"Hmmm?" I murmur before I open my eyes. He breaks away and cups my face. He runs his thumb over my cheek and across my bottom lip, then looks me in the eyes.

"I've never felt like this before. I knew you were different when I ran into you at the coffee shop, and then I realized it wasn't just luck that I met you again that very same night. I enjoy spending time with you. It feels so real when all I am ever surrounded by is fake." He pauses and lets out a long breath like he's nervous to say this, to open up to me. "Lizzie, it's everything about you. I know you're skeptical because of your past, and even I feel as though I should be nervous, but around you I feel calm. I feel like all is right in the world when you are close. Like all the pieces of my life have fallen into the right place." He leans in and gives me a chaste kiss to the lips, and then pulls back, dropping his hands. Without thinking, I grab his hand and squeeze it in mine while I stare into his eyes.

"It does feel real, and I can't seem to describe what it is about you that makes me feel like I can trust you. I don't trust easily, as I told you. But I still agree with what you said at the library. I will take a chance on this. On us. But that doesn't mean I'm not nervous. Not that you make me nervous," I correct quickly as he chuckles. "I just mean this 'at first sight' thing has thrown me for a loop. It's something that I would write about but not expect to happen in real life."

He takes both of my hands in his and kisses my knuckles as his eyes never leave mine. "I never thought this was possible either. When I was younger, my father told me about when he met my mother. He said he knew the instant he saw her that she was the one for him. He always told my brother and me that one day we would find the right woman and we would know right away. I guess I figured that he and my mother just got fortunate with love, but now I'm starting to believe what he was saying," he admits quietly.

"It's beautiful he believed that and passed it down to you and Sebastian. My parents definitely didn't have that sort of love, so I guess that's why I didn't believe in it. I suppose if I had been raised in a different environment I could see where you are coming from," I respond.

He takes a moment and gazes into my eyes. I feel as though he is reading all the things I haven't said to him. For some reason, I know he knows what I went through. Maybe not the full extent. But I think he can really see me for who I am, inside and out.

"We aren't our parents, Lizzie. We are our own people. We make our own way in this life with our own choices. That's what defines us, not our past," he says, as he rubs his thumb over my cheek and wipes a tear that's escaped my eye. How does he know exactly what to say?

"Will this be exclusive... between us, I mean?" I blurt out because I just have to know. I must know if there is someone else or if there will be. He looks at me like I have said something wrong, and I instantly regret asking the question. Of course, it's not exclusive. You have known him for two days. A small frown forms on his face, but before he can say anything, I pull my hands away and reach for the door. He leans further in to grasp my wrist firmly, but not to hurt me. He pulls me back toward him and says, "I would have never said the things I have said to you if I didn't want it to be just us. Yes, Lizzie, I want to be exclusive. I don't want any other woman. Now or ever. You are the most charming and real person I have ever experienced, inside and out, and I'm not going to let you go. And, no, I'm not sharing you." He cups my face again and says quietly, "I'm not like them, Lizzie. I'm not those other men you've dated. I will never cheat on you. They were fools. I need you to believe me. Please trust me." At his words, I melt into his hands and lean over, then give him a kiss. One that I hope shows him I believe him, or at least, that I want to believe him. He does seem different, and our situation is unique. He deepens the kiss; his tongue urges my mouth open, and I oblige. Our tongues explore the others, and we are lost in the kiss for what seems like forever. I pull back and smile. "I trust you, Miles."

With that statement, he's out of the car and opening my door for me. I take his hand as I step out, and he doesn't drop it as he walks me to my apartment. We arrive at the door, and I dig in my wristlet for my keys to unlock the door. As I open it, Miles pulls my body close to his and wraps his arms tightly around me. He's so tall and muscular, and I feel so safe and protected in his arms. Not just physically, but I feel like he will protect my heart, as well. He kisses the top of my head, and before we part, I take in his scent once again. It pervades my senses, and I don't think I will ever tire of it.

"Thank you, Lizzie, for allowing me the chance to take you out tonight. I have a packed schedule this week, but I will call you so we can arrange another date. I don't want much time to pass before I get to hold you again." He leans down and kisses my cheek.

I smile, looking up at him. "It was the perfect evening. Goodnight, Miles."

"Goodnight, Lizzie," he whispers in a low, seductive tone. He waits until I'm in my apartment, and then I hear him walking toward the stairs. I twist the lock, turn around as my back melts down the door, and I end up on the floor like a puddle with a huge smile on my face.

Sarah comes around the corner and sees my state, then starts to laugh. "You look like a smitten kitten!" she exclaims. I look up at her shocked.

"I am not. It was just an incredible night with an extraordinary man who may or may not be the man of my dreams." I laugh as I get to my feet. I take my heels off and toss them in by the couch, then slump down on it. Sarah plops down next to me staring. Obviously waiting to hear all the juicy details. We sit there for a while; I tell her about the library and the most romantic night of my life. I tell her about everything he said to me because I want her honest opinion. I need to know if Sarah believes what he said about me "being different" and wanted to "take a chance on us." She seems enthralled by the time I finish recalling the night. She leans over, puts her arms around me, and pulls me into a bear hug. When she pulls back, she has a huge, genuine smile on her face. "I think this could be the real thing, Lizzie. He sounds like he knows what he wants, and what he wants is you. I have never been on a date like that in my life, nor have I been told the things he said to you. I know you're hesitant, but not all men are the same as the ones that you were unfortunate enough to date before. I truly think you should give this a chance. You need to give yourself the opportunity to find love. You deserve that more than anyone I know. I love you, girl! Also, I like seeing this smile on your face. It suits you," Sarah states.

I think about what she just said, and in my mind, it makes sense. I do feel comfortable around him. Also, he wants to be exclusive. At least that puts my mind at ease a bit. I don't have to worry about him with other women when I'm not with him because, for some unknown reason, I really do trust him. And for reasons that I can't explain, I truly believe him saying he wouldn't hurt me. He is a genuine gentleman, and I would be foolish to let him slip through my fingers. Although, something tells me he wouldn't let me get away very easily. Miles is a man that gets what he wants. That much I can tell. Apparently, what he wants is me. It's still crazy to think about. I mean, this man could have anyone in the world. He is model material, and yet, I am the one that's caught his attention. I push out a deep sigh and remember the way his lips felt against mine. It was the best kiss I've ever had, completely obliterating all the ones that came before it.

Sarah and I say our goodnights and walk to our rooms. I quickly change into my pajamas and slide in the bed. I plug my phone in and set my alarm for work tomorrow. As I turn over in the bed, I hear my phone chime with a text coming through. I roll over and grab it to see who it's from. I smile when I see the quote appear.

Unknown: "You know you are in love when you can't fall asleep because reality is finally better than your dreams." - Dr. Seuss. Goodnight, beautiful.

Knowing this is Miles, I smile as I read the message over and over. He truly is sweet and charming. I adore that he loves books and authors as much as I do.

Lizzie: Goodnight, Miles. Xo

I put my phone back on my nightstand and turn over to go to sleep with a smile on my face and thoughts of that beautiful man running through my mind.

CHAPTER 9

Miles

It's Monday morning, and I am up and ready to go. I can't keep the smile off my face as I work out and dress for work. There is a definite pep in my step today. I keep going over the details of our date Saturday night, and it couldn't have been more perfect if I tried. She was absolutely stunning, and I feel so relaxed and genuinely happy with her. I feel like I have known Lizzie my whole life and everything just seems easy and natural with her. She is real and not pretentious. I feel like a horny teenager with my first crush, like I need to doodle her name on a notepad. I am eager to get to work so I can go over my schedule for the week with my assistant. I want to know the next time I can see her. I need to see her, desperately. I spoke to her a bit yesterday with some texts, but she was busy working, so I wasn't able to get the fill of her that I needed.

 I walk into Knight Publishing Company through the front doors. I smile and nod to the secretary behind the welcome desk. She smiles brightly and blushes. I hurry over to the elevators, while gesturing *hellos* to all my employees as they make a way for me to come through, like the parting of the seas. Some return the notion, and some look at me quizzically. Hmm, I know I don't have the best reputation for being approachable, especially at work. I suppose that's why I am getting these odd reactions to my apparent happiness. I make a mental note to do a better job of getting to know my employees, or at least be nicer. I guess I've been so stressed since my father's passing because I knew that they all depended on me to keep this ship afloat. I haven't been the best leader, as far as manners go. Once inside the elevator, I hit the button for the twentieth floor. We own the entire building, and every floor is a different department within the company. The twentieth floor is for the executive offices, mine and Sebastian's. With a deep breath, I lean against the elevator as I ride to the top. I take in the modern finishes that I incorporated after I became CEO. Marble flooring and gold sconces adorn the walls. Hanging on the back wall is a black and white abstract painting by a local artist.

I went to the opening of the art gallery and couldn't help but buy his whole collection. I'm not sure why, but they all seemed to speak to me. I smile when I think about them getting delivered. Sebastian looked at me like I had grown two heads. He said he could have made the same paintings with his eyes closed. I just scoffed and told my assistant to have our interior designer incorporate them throughout the building.

The door to the elevator opens, and I straighten up and walk out toward my office. I say a quick hello to Elaine, the floor receptionist. She smiles and gives me a seductive finger wave in return. I pass Elijah's desk, and he jumps up with his iPad in his hands to accompany me to my office. I hold up a hand to stop him. "Elijah, could you bring me a coffee, please? I didn't have a chance to get one," I say, and he simply nods, puts the iPad down, and runs across the floor to the coffee bar. I sigh and continue until I'm in the comfort of my office. I place my laptop case on the side of my desk and unbutton my suit jacket as I take a seat at my desk. My office is painted in a light gray that accentuates the white leather couch on the other side of the room. A plush rug is spread before it, above which is a glass cocktail table. My framed degrees hang behind my desk along with various awards the company has received over the years. To the right of my desk is a wet bar for when I pull late nights. It's stocked with my favorite Macallan whiskey.

I'm in my office for only a minute before I'm interrupted by Sebastian, who just swings the door open and drops onto the white leather chair in front of my desk. He's looking at me with a smug smile on his face, one that I want to punch off him. I haven't really spoken to him since I dropped him by his place after the club.

"Hey bro," he starts, "something going on that I need to know about?" he asks, as he studies my face. This makes me chuckle, which makes his eyebrows shoot up.

"I'm just in a good mood. It's a beautiful Monday, don't you think?" I reply with a grin.

"Okay, now you are really freaking me out. What is it? What happened?" he asks. I think I'm going to make him sweat it out a bit before I tell him about Elizabeth. His expression right now is priceless, and I am enjoying this.

"I don't know what you're talking about," I state, as I pull out my laptop from the case and place it on my desk, opening it and powering it up.

"I just came in behind you, and Betty from the welcome desk said you were greeting people in the lobby. She was concerned," he mentions, waiting on me to comment. I look up at him.

"Am I that much of a hard ass that I can't speak to my employees?" I ask feeling a bit guilty they think of me that way.

"Of course not. You just don't take bullshit, and maybe you've made more than one employee cry for something or other. It's not a big deal. I just want to know what has the mighty Miles Knight cracking a smile," he inquires with a chuckle. Before I can answer, Elijah knocks once and lets himself into my office. He places the steaming coffee on my desk as he opens his iPad.

"Thank you, Elijah. We need to go over my schedule

for this week to see if I can rearrange some things," I tell my assistant without looking at him or my brother. I can see them both looking at each other, silently wondering what the hell is going on with me, which just makes my smile bigger.

"Of course, sir. You have back-to-back meetings this morning with potential investors. I sent the information about them to your email, so you can review it before the meetings. After lunch you have a meeting with the board to go over the quarterly sales. I sent that spreadsheet to you, as well, and highlighted the most important divisions that need to be discussed. That's it for the day, as far as meetings are concerned, but there are several manuscripts that you need to either approve or deny. I have gone through your emails and flagged the important ones that needing to be addressed today." He finally pauses to catch a breath.

I lift my eyes from my laptop screen and reply, "Great, thank you for all that work. I am wondering if I have any meetings in the late afternoon or evening this week." He looks through my calendar, and then replies, "You have a meeting with Charles from HR tomorrow afternoon at 4 p.m. Then Wednesday, Thursday, and Friday, we'll will have the new interns here, and they will need to be settled and taken care of."

I think about this for a moment, then say, "Dennis can take care of the interns and get them settled. I will make a quick presentation about company expectations, and then he can get them squared away. Let him know and clear my afternoons on those days," I added, as I look back down at my computer and begin typing away. I can feel the eye lasers that are shooting at me right now, and I just smirk. I hardly ever reschedule meetings or make someone else cover them, so this behavior is very unusual for me, and they know it.

"Okay, that's enough," Sebastian declares. "I'm not leaving this office until you tell me what's going on." He sits back in his seat and crosses his legs. Elijah decides to join in and sits along with him in the other leather chair. I sigh and look at the two men in front of me. I contemplate what exactly I want to say. I tell my brother everything, and I know there will be more questions when Elijah leaves the office, so I keep it vague.

"I met someone, and I am trying to work my schedule so I can see her again, soon," I answer, matter-of-factly. Sebastian bursts into fits of laughter and slaps his hands on his thighs. Elijah just looks like I told him that Santa was real. I chuckle because they've have never seen me in a real relationship, just the casual fling, but I have never cared enough to clear my schedule.

"You're joking right? I mean you can't be serious. When would you have met someone?" Sebastian asks after he gets control of his laughter.

I smile as I say, "I'm not joking. I met her twice in one day, then took her on a date the next night."

"And so, you already want to rearrange your schedule for her?" he asks, incredulously. Sebastian will be the forever bachelor, at this rate. He never sees the same woman twice, which has caused many scandals in the past. He has at least begun to be more discreet about his afterwork affairs after Macie and our mother gave him quite the scolding. It was a pleasure to watch him turn as red as a lobster when our mother spoke to him about his "conquests".

"Elijah, will you excuse us?" He jumps up from his seat, nodding and makes his way out of my office, closing the door behind him.

I look at Sebastian with a humorless expression. "Her name is Elizabeth. We hit it off almost immediately. She didn't recognize me, which intrigued me even more. I ran into her again at the club opening, and we danced and talked for hours. Then, I arranged to have the library closed for us so we could tour and dine there. I know I sound crazy right now, and I feel crazy, believe me. I feel like I have been turned inside out and my world is upside down. She's everything that I ever thought I wanted and needed in a woman. She is intelligent, compassionate, stunning, and she was interested in me before she knew who I really am. And when I told her, she didn't act any differently. I can't get her out of my head, Seb. And I don't want to. She's gotten under my skin," I say honestly, trying to explain these feelings that are in my head. Sebastian looks taken aback and is silent for a minute.

"Wow, I was not expecting that. I don't know what I *was* expecting, but it definitely wasn't that. But damn, I'm happy for you, man! I never thought I would see the day that one woman caught your attention like that," he replies, then adds, "Just be careful. I don't want you to get taken advantage of. It's hard for us to know the good ones from the gold diggers," he winces as he says it. I know he means well, and he can't possibly understand that Lizzie isn't like that at all. But he will get a chance to get to know her because I don't plan to let her go anytime soon.

"Hey! Is she the black-haired woman from the club you introduced me to?" he asks quickly, as if it just registered to him that he may have already met her. I nod and smile.

"Yes, that was her." He lets out a whistle, and I glare at him from across the desk.

"Don't even think about it. She's *mine*." He holds his hands up in defense.

"Dude, I don't want your girl. I was just saying she is a looker!" I don't even want him to talk about her like that. I don't want any man to look at her like that. *Wow, when did I get so possessive?* It's such a weird feeling to have. But no one else is going to be looking at her the way I do. She's mine.

"Do you remember the stories about mom and dad and

their 'love at first sight' chemistry when they met in high school?" I ask. He nods and looks out of the large windows in my office. He sighs, and I can see the emotion in his eyes. He took our father's passing the hardest, I suppose, because he is the youngest.

Sebastian let's out a deep sigh, gets up to leave, and comes to pat me on the back, "Well, I guess that's enough of us wasting work time, brother. Better get back to it. See you in the board meeting later," he comments, as he strolls out of my office, closing the door.

I glance at the clock and see that Lizzie is probably at the bookstore now, so I decide to send her a text.

Miles: I am available several nights this week. Would you like to have dinner on Wednesday?

I wait and watch as the message goes from delivered to read, and then I see the three dots that means she's typing something. I smile as I wait.

Lizzie: Good morning to you, too! Wednesday works. I leave the bookstore around five. What did you have in mind?

I chuckle; she's a spit fire. I suppose I should have said something like "Good morning," but I was more focused on when I could see her again. I *need* to see her again. I need to hold her and kiss her perfect lips.

Miles: Forgive me. Good morning, beautiful. I was thinking that I could cook for you. Do you like Italian?

After I send the message, I wonder if it's too soon for her to come to my home. I mean, I'm not offering so I can sleep with her. But it would give us a more intimate time to get to know one another. As I am about to respond that we can do something else if she prefers, she responds.

Lizzie: Wow, you cook? I can hardly make boxed meals.

Lol! I love Italian, by the way. What time? Would you like me to bring anything?

Miles: I do cook, actually. My mother insisted I learn when I was younger. I see that it will be of use, after all. No need to bring anything but yourself. I will pick you up at six.

Lizzie: She sounds like a smart woman. I can't wait to see you put those skills to use.

Miles: Oh, you will see. Can I call you tonight?

Lizzie: I will be home around nine, from the restaurant. Maybe around ten? Unless you'll be passed out by then.

Miles: No, ten it is. Talk to you then, beautiful. xo

I reread our conversation, and now, I wish it was Wednesday already. But at least I will hear her voice tonight. For now, I've got to get to work. This company can't run itself. I dive back into my emails until it's time for my meetings. The day quickly passes with all the things I need to get done. By the time the last employee leaves, I check the clock and see that it's already seven p.m. I shut my computer down and send a text to Thomas that I am ready to leave. I lock my office up and head to the elevators. I have three hours to kill before I get to speak to her. *What to do, what to do?*

Man, I've got it bad.

CHAPTER 10

Elizabeth

This day is dragging by at snail speed. I keep glancing at my watch, and it only seems like a few minutes pass by every time I look down.

This morning at the bookstore wasn't bad, especially when I got a small break to text with Miles, when we made plans for our second date. I think I am equally excited and nervous at the idea of seeing his home. I've got all kinds of butterflies in my belly when I think of it. I immediately text Sarah and let her know about the second date, and she is all for it. If it wasn't for her encouragement, I don't think I could do this. She is always in my corner. Is it moving too fast for us to be alone at his place? My hands begin to sweat just thinking about it. I mean, I definitely want to go; but I'm also crazy nervous because he has this effect on me which makes me want to tell him my life story, then jump him. I rub my hand over my face. *I do not need to be thinking about that right now.*

Now I'm at the restaurant and it's a slow Monday. Most of the servers are standing around talking in the back. There aren't many patrons here tonight, and I'm hoping that maybe I will get out of here sooner. That way, I can get home and take a shower before Miles calls. I'm being silly about a phone call, but I'm nervous about that, too. What if there is awkward silence and neither one of us knows what to say? It will make me start rambling about random things, and that's the last thing I want to do. I don't want him to think I'm crazy. *Ugh, I feel the anxiety creeping into my mind.* I feel like a teenager with her first crush. *Calm down, Lizzie. You have been with him three times now, and there was never an awkward moment. Chill out and get a grip.* I take a deep breath and blow it out through my nose. I can do this.

As I'm sitting here thinking to myself, my boss comes over and says that he is cutting my section and one other because there aren't enough people in the restaurant. I jump up and begin cleaning my tables and closing out all the tabs. I roll some silverware, then head to the lockers to change back into the clothes I had on earlier today. When I'm dressed, I check my phone to see if I have any missed messages or calls and I don't, so I slide my phone back into my purse and head out the door. Once I'm on the street, the cool air rushes into my lungs. It's a chilly night, and I didn't bring a large coat with me today because the weather was nicer when I left the apartment this morning. But that's how the weather is in November. It could be snowing, or it could be sixty degrees. But right now, there is definitely a nip in the air. I only have a few blocks to walk, so I zip up the thin jacket that I have on and set off. Once I get to my apartment, I feel like a literal ice cube. I am so thankful that I was able to get off early so I can sink into a steamy hot bath instead of taking a shower. My body needs to thaw.

As I walk through the apartment, I see that Sarah must still be at work. That girl is a rockstar, but she is working herself to death. I slug out of my jacket, hang it up, and kick off my heels. *Ahhh*, so much better. I walk to the kitchen, pouring myself a glass of white wine, then take off to the bathroom to run a bath.

After the room is all steamy and the tub is full, I sink my cold body down into the water. It's marvelous. I have my phone playing some instrumental Christmas music because it's never too early for Christmas anything. Yes, I am one of those people that, as soon as Halloween is over, Christmas is on full fledge, except for the one day that is Thanksgiving. Then it's right back to the Christmas music and festivities. I rest my head against the tub and feel my body temperature finally thawing out from the brisk walk to my apartment.

When the water begins to cool off, I drain the tub and wrap my robe around me. I walk to my room and turn on the Christmas lights I have hanging over my bed, then I get dressed in some warn jammies. I get my wine glass from the bathroom along with my phone and see that it's almost nine, which gives me about an hour before Miles is supposed to call. I suppose I could text him and tell him that I got home earlier. Should I? I don't want to keep him waiting when I am free now. I'm suddenly really anxious. I down the rest of my wine, pour another, and sit on the bed with my legs crossed. I grab my phone and send him a quick text. He might not even see it until later. Who knows?

Lizzie: I got off earlier than I thought, so I am already home.

I put my phone down, reach for my laptop, and look over the manuscript I've been writing. I smile because I really like how this story is progressing. I was stuck for so long, and then almost instantly, my writer's block was gone. The words just began to pour out of me. I think it has something to do with Miles, which seems crazy because I barely know him. But he inspires me, and the hero in my story might possibly resemble him. I chuckle to myself thinking of writing about Miles when my phone begins to ring. I look down and see his name. My heart begins to feel like it's going to beat out of my chest. I answer the phone, "Hello."

"Hey there," he says.

Oh, his voice is so sexy, it just makes me want to melt. I can't help but have this huge, silly grin on my face. I'm so glad he can't see me right now. "How was your day?" I ask.

"It was good and busy. I had several meetings back-to-back today. How was your day, Lizzie?"

Man, oh man, the way he says my name. It just rolls perfectly off his tongue. "I can't complain. We did get some interesting books in at the bookstore, but none were first editions, which is what I look for almost immediately. And then my shift at the restaurant was slow. We weren't busy, and I was able to get off earlier than I thought. Then I froze on my walk home. Ha-ha"

"You walked home, alone?" He sounds upset.

"Yes, I do every day. I don't live far, so it isn't a big deal. I should have worn a thicker jacket today. I didn't realize it would be so cold tonight. I think I was a popsicle once I got through my apartment door. I definitely need to check the forecast tomorrow."

"Lizzie, it's not safe to walk alone at night, especially in New York. I will send Thomas to fetch you after work, so you don't walk home anymore."

"Wh-What? No. That's not necessary. Really. I do this all the time. It's not a big deal. Besides, I'm not taking advantage of your driver. He should be home with his family." I can't even believe he offered his driver. It's not like I'm a teenager. I've done this route so many times, I could do it with my eyes closed. I really don't know what he's getting so upset about. I'm certainly not going to use Thomas! Geez, that's the kind of thing the women he was talking about would do. I'm independent, and I have been for years."

"Lizzie," he growls, and his voice sounds like a warning. "I'm not letting you walk home alone at night. If you won't let Thomas drive you, then I will come pick you up. Plus, it will give me an extra reason to see you."

"You're not letting me?" I ask because, surely, I heard him wrong.

"Please be reasonable. You're with me now, and I don't like the thought of you walking. Please allow me to help. I didn't mean I'm not letting you; it wasn't the right wording. I would just rather know that you are safe and taken care of."

"This seems like the sort of thing the women you spoke of, that you attract, would expect from you. I'm not like them, and I don't want anyone to think that's why I'm with you. It's not. I have never had a problem before with walking. I don't mind it, really."

"I know that's not why you are with me." He seems to be getting upset with me, and I don't really know what to do. "I want you safe, Lizzie. I want to know if you are safe. It doesn't matter what other people think. They can talk to me if they have a problem, but I want to do this for you. Please, allow me to ensure your safety."

I really don't want to fight with him. Yes, I have heard stories about women being attacked at night, but not in this part of town. I do see where he is coming from. I just don't want to become dependent on him. I know he's worried; I can hear it in his voice. I don't want to be the cause of that. I guess if it's him picking me up, then it won't be as bad. Like he said, it would be another excuse to see him again. I sigh audibly and I know he can hear it.

"Miles, I don't want to take advantage of you. I know that you are a very busy man. But if it would make you feel better, then we can try out the ride and see how it goes. I do not want to be a burden by any means, and I could just as easily order an Ub-." Before I can finish, he responds.

"It's settled then. You can send me your schedule for the restaurant, and either I or Thomas will be there waiting to take you home. This is important to me, Lizzie. Thank you for allowing me to do this for you. And you could never be a burden. Anyways, enough talk of that. I want to know more about you. Tell me about your family."

Ugh, the dreaded "family" question. Obviously, it's unavoidable; but how much should I tell him? "Ah, my family. Where should I start? I was born and raised in Savannah, Georgia. I have one sibling, a brother named William. He is nine years older than me. I suppose I was sort of an 'oops' baby. He is married to his high school sweetheart, and they gave me two beautiful nieces, whom I don't see nearly enough. My parents, *ugh,* got divorced when I was twelve, and it was very unexpected and a difficult time. My father remarried almost immediately and wanted me to go to law school, so I could work in his firm one day. Since I didn't go that route, he refused to pay for my college tuition. Fortunately, I had a 4.0 GPA and got awarded several scholarships, but I still had to take out student loans. We had a huge fight because he paid for my brother's tuition but not mine. That created a larger chasm between us, which fostered an even more intense relationship. So, when I visit back home, I mostly avoid contact with him. My mother, on the other hand, has always been there for me; and I try and fly down to see her several times a year. What about you? Tell me about your family." I hope I didn't say too much. That just all came tumbling out of my mouth. It's more than I tell most people that have known me for a while, so it's strange that I just spilled everything like that.

"I'm sorry to hear about your parents. I can't imagine what that was like for you. I guess I also don't know what it's like to not have the approval of your father. I was groomed from an early age to take over the family company. I always knew where I would be going to college and what I would be studying. I haven't really thought about what I would have done if the choice was up to me. I do enjoy publishing. My parents were high school sweethearts, much like your brother and his wife. They were happily married right up until he had a heart attack last year. It was so sudden; no one got to tell him goodbye. I think that's what I regret the most. I was at a meeting, and I had my phone off; by the time I got to the hospital, it was too late." He takes a long breath, then continues, "And you know I have a brother, Sebastian. You met him at the club. He is three years younger than me, so we were always causing trouble when we were younger. My mother and I are remarkably close; she lives just out of the city. I try and visit as often as I can because I know that she is lonely."

"I can't imagine losing a parent that way. I'm sorry your family had to suffer through that. I'm sure he would be very proud of the work you are doing with the company," I remark. *I hope that he changes the subject because I would rather not go into details of my childhood.* I know I'll have to tell him at some point, but I'm not in the mood to go through that trauma in my mind.

"Thank you for saying that. Sometimes I wonder if I am filling his shoes. He was exceptionally successful, and I haven't scratched that surface yet. I really want to prove to the board that I should be there, as an asset, not just because it was my father's company." He pauses for a moment. "I've actually never told anyone about my concerns with the company. You make it so easy to talk to."

Wow, that's a remarkably high compliment. I could tell you the same thing. I feel like I have known you longer than I actually have. It's strange, yet comfortable. You know how I was telling you that I was drafting a book?" I ask.

"Yes, I remember you saying you were having trouble with it.

I smile that he remembers. No other man in my life has cared for this passion I have. "Exactly. I was at a point where I thought I might be better off giving up; but since I met you, the words have been pouring out of me like a waterfall. Maybe you are my muse." I chuckle. Then I feel heat creep up my cheeks. I shouldn't have said that. That was too much information, right? Now, he is probably going to freak out. *Lizzie, you must put a filter on that mouth!* Then I quickly add, "I guess maybe that wasn't the right thing to say. I'm just meaning, I think my writer's block has finally broken," I let out an exasperated breath.

I hear him smile as he says, "Why would my being your muse be a bad thing? I believe I would be a great muse. Even if I do say so myself…" He lets out a loud laugh, and I suddenly feel like he is making fun of me. However, he then adds, "Lizzie, it's a compliment. I'm happy that I've been able to help. Seriously, I haven't been able to get you out of my mind these past few days. I know how quickly this seems to be happening, but when you know, you know. I can just feel it and would love to read what you've been working on."

"Oh, I have actually never let anyone read anything I've written, except for assignments in college, and especially not you, being in publishing. I guess I don't take criticism very well. I'll be crushed if you think it's terrible. I also wouldn't want you to lie on my behalf and tell me it was good." I sigh. "I guess it's a tricky situation. While we are talking about my book, I just want you to know I'm not going to submit my manuscript to your company when it's completed. I know you would help it get to where it needs to be, but I want the writing to do that on its own. Do you understand? It has nothing to do with Knight Publishing, I mean, you are the best in the country. I just don't want any special treatment. I have something to prove to myself. I just… don't want anyone to think I'm getting special treatment from being in a relationship with you."

He's silent for a moment, and I regret even bringing up his company. What if he was waiting for me to bring up my book in relation to his company? What if he thinks I'm lying, and I'm just like every other woman that wants handouts? But on the other hand, I don't want to offend him by not submitting it. Ah, this is an exceedingly difficult situation. I run my hand through my hair and try to take a deep breath.

After a moment of silence, he finally speaks, "Lizzie, first and foremost, please believe me when I say that I know, in my soul, that you are not like the other women from my past. I know that's where part of that comment came from."

I can't believe he can see right through me, but it's the truth.

He then continues, "Secondly, I want to read your work, not because of my business, but because I am so captivated by you and want to see how you reveal yourself on those pages. I wouldn't criticize or placate you, but I understand if you aren't ready for that, yet. I know how intimate a book can be to its author. Can I also say I believe that your writing will speak for itself, no matter where you send it; so, there is nothing to be worried about. But finally, please don't exclude KPC because of our relationship. I want your book to be picked up by the best and wouldn't just publish it because of our relationship. The world needs to hear what you have to say, and I believe it will be incredible, even if I haven't read it."

A smile creeps over my face, and a blush makes its way up my neck. His sweet words make my eyes misty. He believes in me?

"Thank you, Miles, for everything you just said. You don't know how much everything you said means to me. But there's no reason to worry with publishers yet. It's not even completed. So," I say, trying to think of a topic change. "What will you be doing for the holidays?" I ask.

I hear him give a little chuckle and know it is because of my subject change. "Well, my brother and I went to my mother's estate for Thanksgiving. Our company hosts a

Christmas Gala that gives to a charity for mental illness and sickness in children around the city. I believe that's on December fifth. I haven't made plans for Christmas yet. My mother oftentimes travels to Italy to visit family during that time, so I'll most likely just be in the city. How about your plans?" he asks.

"The charity sounds incredible. It's great of you to get involved with those children, especially this time of the year. Plus, that's a very wonderful day to have a gala." I smile and laugh.

"December fifth? Is that day something special I need to be aware of?"

"Yes, particularly important. It's my birthday, sadly not the national holiday it should be, but such is life." I begin to laugh hard, then hear him laugh as well. "I'm just kidding you. I mean, yes, it is my birthday, but not a holiday by any means. Honestly, I try to forget the day all together. Although Sarah makes it exceedingly difficult, because no matter my objections, she always wants to celebrate. And once you get to know her, then you realize arguing with her is a losing battle."

"Well, now that I know your birthday, it will not go unnoticed. I may have to coordinate with Sarah." He laughs and the sound warms my heart.

"Oh, you don't need to do anything. That's only a week away! I'm sure you'll have your hands full with the gala. Please, don't go to any trouble for me," I say, even though I know I'm kidding myself. He doesn't want me to walk home alone at night; I'm fairly sure he will try and go all out for my birthday, which he doesn't need to do. My birthdays, since I was twelve, have been filled with disappointment, except for the ones that didn't include my parents. However, something seems to always go wrong. I would rather sleep through the day and wake up on the sixth.

He scoffs like I'm being ridiculous. "Lizzie, you are special to me. We are celebrating your birth. No arguments, because I know you're trying to brew up some excuse in that beautiful head of yours."

"Oh, so you think you know me, do you?" I say teasingly.

"Well, I'm working on it and looking forward to finding out more." Oh, my heart squeezes a bit at his words. This man is something else. He really is one of a kind, and I feel the walls around my heart slowly start to crumble.

"I look forward to that too, Miles," I say with a yawn.

"I heard that yawn. You need to get some sleep. We will talk tomorrow. I enjoyed our talk tonight, Lizzie. Goodnight, beautiful," he rasps in a soft, sexy tone that sends shivers up my body.

"I loved it too, Miles. Sleep well," I murmur as I disconnect the call.

I put the phone on my chest and fall onto my bed. I stare at my ceiling and recount the conversation we just had. I like him. I really like him. How did this happen so quickly? Is it fate? That's what he calls it and what Sarah says too; it just seems like a fairytale, which I've always believed to be exactly that, a tale. Not real. But even I can't deny there is this pull I feel toward him, and I don't want to resist it. I know what I told myself, but I would regret not giving him a chance. Miles Knight Jr. just might be my Mr. Darcy. That thought brings a smile to my face, and I drift off to sleep.

CHAPTER 11

Miles

It's Tuesday afternoon and I've been busy all day. I have only had a few moments to send off some texts to Lizzie letting her know I'm thinking about her. I'm going through some last-minute emails before I leave for the day when there's a knock on my door. In comes Elijah, my assistant.

With his iPad in hand, he sits in front of my desk and scrolls through some documents on the screen. "I have the guest list for the gala next week for you to approve," he remarks and hands me the iPad.

I scroll through it and see everyone that we invited to the gala. When I come to my name, I see there is a "plus one" beside it and I get an idea. The gala is on Lizzie's birthday, and I can invite her to this Christmas ball. I think she'll love it. I look up at Elijah. "This looks good. Add Elizabeth Brighton as my plus one."

"Are you sure, sir? You don't normally bring dates to these events." He looks at me skeptically. If he weren't the best assistant I've ever had, then I'd let him know it's none of his business. However, I just reply, "Yes, and I also need you to add her friend to the list, as well. Her name is Sarah McKenzie. Also, I want to order a special cake to be presented at the end of the night. It will be a birthday cake for Lizzie. I'd love for it to look like actual books, stacked on top of each other; the titles must be famous Jane Austen books, specifically *Pride and Prejudice*.

Find a bakery that can make that happen on such short notice. Price isn't an issue." He looks at me like I've lost my mind, but I shake it off.

"Yes, sir. Is there anything else I can take care of?" he offers. I think for a moment and shake my head. He rises and leaves my office. With that taken care of, I close my laptop, pull out my phone, and scroll through the contacts until I find the one I'm looking for.

"Mia, how are you? It's been a while, but I was hoping you could help me with something," I smile. Mia is my stylist, and she is a good friend of mine. I have no doubt that she'll be able to help me with what I have in mind. "I need an evening gown, shoes, and jewelry for a gala, but I want to be there to help with the decisions. This is for someone important to me. Are you available to meet this week, the sooner the better, as the gala is next week?" I ask. I must hold the phone away from my ear because she is squealing with excitement. I chuckle and we make plans to meet tomorrow at lunch. I thank her immensely, and then slip the phone into my pocket. I grab my laptop so I can get some work done at home, then leave my office.

As I walk into my apartment, I head straight to the bar to pour a whiskey, and then head to the balcony. I tun on the heaters and sit in an armchair overlooking the Hudson. I take a sip and place the glass down. I'm trying to think if there is anything else that I can do for Elizabeth to make her birthday even more special. I don't think we will have time to stop for a nice dinner beforehand, plus I know she will probably not want to rush with having to get ready. I wonder if Sarah already has plans for her birthday. I hope she'll be able to attend as well because I know it would make Lizzie more comfortable. I smile to myself because I already know what will make my girl more comfortable. *My girl.* That has such a nice ring to it. I get up and grab my laptop, bringing it back to the balcony. I didn't know Sarah's last name until I googled "Sarah PR New York" at the office. Fortunately, the first thing that pops up is the website for Club VIBE, and I know she did the PR work for them. I go through the website until I find her business details. I need her contact information to plan everything I have in mind. I find her telephone number listed, and without hesitation, I pick up my cell and call her.

She answers after a few rings, and I introduce myself. She sounds surprised to hear from me, but I explain what I have planned. She seems very excited. I ask if there is anything else I can do to make the day better, and she suggests a spa day. What an excellent idea! Fortunately, Lizzie doesn't have to work that day, so she'll have the whole day free. I invite Sarah to the gala, which she immediately accepts.

I am about to let her go when she says, "I just want you to know that I like you, Miles. I believe you are one of the good guys left, but believe me when I say, if you hurt her, then you will have me to deal with. She has been through so much in her life that she deserves all the happiness in the world." I begin to interrupt, but she continues, "I know you have only known each other for a short amount of time, but I see the way she looks when she speaks about you. The fact that you are going through all this to make her happy makes me happy. I just don't want you to lead her on if this is just a conquest you're looking for."

After she finishes, I'm speechless. I know Sarah is a good friend, who is very protective of Lizzie, but I want to protect her, too. I hate she hasn't had the best life, but I want to make her happy now that I'm in it. "I assure you, Sarah, I am very much invested in Lizzie. We have undeniable chemistry, and I'm not looking for a one-night tryst. I am all in and have told her that, as well. I want to prove myself to her. This has been a whirlwind of a relationship so far, but I believe I was meant to meet her that day; I'm not going to throw this away," I respond.

This seems to mollify Sarah, and I let her know that I'll send the spa and gala details to her as soon as I can, then we end the call.

I drain the rest of my whiskey and begin to think of Lizzie and her past. I only know the tip of the iceberg, but I want to know everything. I need to know what's happened to make her so untrusting with men. I won't ask Sarah because it's something I want Lizzie to be comfortable telling me herself. I know she isn't close with her father, but I just can't seem to understand that. I loved my father and, even though we didn't always agree on everything, I still can't imagine cutting him out of my life… before he passed away, that is. I look out at the river and suddenly have this urge to hear Lizzie's voice. I send her a text to see if she's still working.

Miles: When will you be off tonight?

Lizzie: I should be done around ten. Do you still want me to let you know when I'm finished, or should I walk home?

I let out a loud gruff at her text. She doesn't know how significant this is. She doesn't understand how serious I am about her. She's mine, and I'll be damned if I let anything happen to her now that I've finally found her.

Miles: You aren't walking anywhere, baby. I will be there at ten, waiting out front for you. I can't wait to see you.

Lizzie: Ok, Mr. Bossy. I'll see you then.

I chuckle at her response. Before I second guess anything, I send another text.

Miles: That's my good girl.

She doesn't respond, but I didn't expect her to either.

I have a couple of hours before I need to be there, so I begin looking up the best spas in the area. I can also ask Mia tomorrow when we meet for her to help me with Lizzie's wardrobe for the party. I have no doubt that she'll know the perfect place. I get up and turn the heater off, then head back inside. It's getting too cold to be out after the sun sets. I go to my kitchen and pull out a prepared meal from my housekeeper, throwing it in the oven. I sit at the counter with my laptop and finish some work I needed to get done before I left the office today. The oven timer dings, and I take my dinner out, grab a bottle of water, walk to the living room, and turn on the tv. I never realized how lonely this place seems. I'm sitting here alone, eating on the couch, and watching tv. This makes me miss Lizzie more, and I find myself keeping track of the clock. I won't be late picking her up. I really can't wait to see her beautiful face and feel her soft lips against mine. She has gotten under my skin in the most incredible way. I want to spend all my time with her. She's already constantly on my mind. As the time draws closer, I begin to get nervous just because I get to see her soon. I've never reacted this way to a woman. I feel like I have been put under her spell, but there is no other place that I'd rather be. *I have it bad!*

 I grab my keys and wallet, walking to the elevator. I hit the button for the garage, so I can bypass the lobby. I step out, and the chill in the air hits me in the face. Lizzie is not going to be walking home in this. She could get sick, or she could be hurt by some strangers on the street looking to cause trouble. I get in my car and blast the heat, pulling out into traffic, then heading in her direction. When I get there, I see that most of the patrons have already left. I pull into a space in the front and wait for Lizzie to come out. After a few moments, she emerges with a man following close behind her. I see her look back and say something over her shoulder, but she doesn't stop. Her face looks pale and unsettled, and seeing that, my stomach lurches. The man is stumbling around, and I see the look in his eyes, like he wants her. I feel my fists clench around the steering wheel. I hear the man yell something, but with my windows up, I can't make out what he says. Whatever it wis, Lizzie stops, immediately freezing in her tracks.

I instinctively get out of the car and walk toward Lizzie. She sees me coming and looks relieved. The man sees me but pays me no attention. He begins yelling at Lizzie, "It's your fault I cheated on you. All you cared about was that stupid book. You didn't have any time for me. You should have been a lawyer like your father wanted, you would be set. Instead, you have to make everything so diffic—" I cut him off before he can finish.

I walk up to him, facing him directly, eye to eye. "You have no right talking to her like that. I don't want to ever see you come near her again."

He looks at me, laughing in my face, and I can smell the liquor coming off him. "Lizzie, who is this? It can't be a boyfriend." He looks back at me and says, "Seriously man, don't waste your time on this one. She's not even easy. You could find anyone with your looks."

I look over at Lizzie and see the tears in her eyes. Obviously, this is the bitter ex that wanted Lizzie and a side piece, at the same time. All I see is red as I grasp his collar and lift him in the air with his feet dangling above the pavement. "You are never to see Lizzie again. Do you understand? I can make your life hell! Now get out of here!" I see the hesitation in his eyes, and he nods. I drop him to the ground, and he saunters off to a waiting cab and gets in. I immediately go to Lizzie and lift her up to my chest, so I can look her in the eyes. The sadness in them is overwhelming, and I just want to make everything right in the world for her.

"I'm so sorry," she finally says with a sniffle. "Jacob came in to get drunk and purposely sat in my section so he could harass me all night. He was begging me to get back together with him because he doesn't think it's a problem that he's still screwing his assistant. My manager insisted that I wait on him and wouldn't let me switch with one of the other servers. It's just been a crappy night. I'm sorry you had to see that. I haven't even heard from him since I found him with her six months ago." I place her back down and cup her cheeks.

I wipe my thumb over her cheeks to erase the tears and pull her chin up, so I can look her in the eyes. "You don't have to apologize about anything. No one should ever talk to you the way he did. He doesn't deserve you. And if I'm being honest, I'm glad he messed up, not because he hurt you but because it brought you to me." She looks up at me with a small smile, and I lean down to give her a deep kiss. I pull her waist against me, so she isn't cold since we are still standing outside. But right now, I just want to feel her pressed to me and to comfort her.

We break from the kiss, and she whispers, "Thank you for saving me. I don't believe he would have left me alone had you not been here. I suppose that doesn't help my case that I'm fine walking home alone at night." She chuckles. I just want to memorize that sound. I could never tire of hearing it. I kiss her forehead, walk her to the car, and open the door. She slides in, and I walk to my side to get in. I crank the car and turn the heat up because I can see her shivering. I pull out into traffic and toward her apartment. I move my hand to grasp hers, and we stay like that until I pull into her apartment. She looks over at me and quietly asks, "Would you like to come in for some tea or hot coffee?" I nod, then go around and open her door. We make our way up the stairs, still holding hands. She opens the doors, motioning for me to go in.

I help her out of her coat and shrug mine off, as well, and hang them next to the door. She begins to walk toward the kitchen, and I quickly grab her waist, pulling her flush against me. I brush stray hair out of her face and behind her ear. I lean down and give her a quick kiss, but I keep her held against me until I feel some of the tension in her body begin to melt away. I'm happy to be able to have that effect on her and that she feels safe enough with me that she can relax. The thought brings a smile to my face.

"So would you like coffee or tea?" she asks.

"Coffee, please. Decaf if you have it. I don't want to be awake all night." She agrees and heads to the kitchen. While she is busy in the kitchen, I take the time to look around her apartment. It's very neat and clean. There is a beautiful set of floor-to-ceiling windows that faces Central Park. I walk over to her bookshelf and peruse the books she has. As expected, many are British literature. Most of them look like she probably got them at the secondhand bookstore where she works. Maybe I can find some first editions for her. I know she would treasure them. I walk over to the opposite wall where I see some paintings. They look original.

"Who is the artist of these paintings?" I ask as I study them. I can feel the emotions pouring out of them. I enjoy books, but I also enjoy art. These paintings have me intrigued.

She walks up behind me with a cup of coffee. "I don't know how you take your coffee," she states.

I turn around and take the mug from her, then smile. "Black is fine."

She stands beside me as we look at the paintings. "These aren't anything special. I just hate bare walls and wanted something to fill the space, so Sarah insisted that we put them up," she explained.

I look down at her and ask, "So, you painted these?" I can't believe how creative and artistic she is. In all aspects of her life.

She looks embarrassed and replies, "Yes. I sometimes paint when I have a lot on my mind. It's more of an escapism. Some people journal: I paint. It's just to get the emotions out. They aren't intended to be seen, but Sarah loved them and wanted to hang them up," she continues.

"You are absolutely incredible! Do you know that? I have never met anyone like you before. You're the most unique woman. I'm captivated by everything I learn about you. I'm amazed by you, Lizzie; you are one of a kind."

She nudges me in the side with her elbow and says, "You are just being sweet. But thank you."

I take her hand and lead her to the couch, so we can sit down and talk. She breaks off and turns the lights on around her windows, then comes to sit next to me. She pulls her legs up to her chest and gets the throw blanket from the back of the couch to cover us. Silently, we stare out of the window and drink our coffee. We finish our drinks and place the mugs on the table in front of us. I grab her hand under the blanket and hold it in mine. I love feeling her warmth against me. Her presence is so comforting.

She looks up at me, and I know she probably wants to explain what happened in front of the restaurant. "The man tonight at work was my ex, Jacob. We broke up over six months ago when I walked in on him and his assistant in bed. It wasn't a pleasant sight. I haven't spoken to him since. He called a few times after I walked out on him, but I never answered. So, I couldn't believe he showed up at work tonight. I don't know what he was thinking. Although, he was always possessive when we were together," she says softly. I still at her mention of his being possessive. I don't want anyone to think of her as theirs; she is mine!

"I know exactly what he's thinking. He realizes what he threw away and wants you back. I could see it in his eyes," I say, looking into her eyes.

She lets out a laugh. "Yeah well, that's the last thing he'll get from me. He was the icing on the cake that made me conclude I would never find someone that would be faithful to me."

I squeeze her hand tighter and lean down. "I will never do that to you, Lizzie. I have never cheated in my life. It's not how I was raised. And I will never jeopardize what we have. Do you believe me?" I inquire.

She seems to think for a moment, then responds by kissing me. "Yes," she says against my lips. "I trust you completely. As crazy as that sounds. I feel safe with you. Is that too soon to say?"

I grip her waist and pull her into my lap, so I can be closer to her. I lean my forehead against hers as we look into each other's eyes. "No," I say. "I feel the same way. I like you, Lizzie. I like you very much." She closes her eyes and smiles. I take the opportunity to steal another kiss. This time it's deeper and more passionate. I can feel everything she's feeling and hope she can feel all the words I'm not ready to say yet. I pull her against me and wrap my arm around her, then she throws her arms around my neck to pull me down to her. Her fingers slide through my hair as my tongue explores her mouth. Once we pull away breathless, I lean down and kiss her forehead. She lets out a low moan and rests her head on my chest. She just fits perfectly in my arms. I wish we could stay like this forever. I close my eyes and take in this feeling. I'm very aware of her heat pressed up against my hardness. I want more than anything to flip her over and slide myself between her sweet thighs. I groan just thinking about it and try to think of something else before I make a move too quickly.

After a while, I feel her breathing slow and realize she is getting tired. "It's getting late," I whisper.

She responds with an, "I guess it is." She looks up at me and asks, "Would you like to stay the night? It's late for you to have to drive back to your place. It's not a big deal, if not—" She starts to get nervous and begins to ramble. I lean in and kiss her. "I'd love to stay." She smiles and rises to her feet.

She leads me to her bedroom. When I walk in, I realize it is decorated like the Regency era, 18th century. This only reiterates in my mind that Lizzie is one of a kind. I smile as I look around. She turns on her bedside lamp, and I instantly see the prized book she has in a glass case. I *am* going to try and find her another first edition. She grabs some clothes out of her dresser. "I'm going to change. Make yourself at home," she comments. I strip down to my shirt and boxers and get into bed. She comes back and is wearing yoga pants and a large University of Georgia shirt. She washed her makeup off and has never looked more beautiful.

She climbs into bed and turns to me. I wrap my arms around her and give her a kiss on her lips, cheek, and then on the top of her head. She sighs and puts her head on my chest while I rub her back. "Goodnight, Miles, and thank you for being there for me tonight."

I kiss her temple softly and whisper, "I will always be there for you. Goodnight, sweetheart." And just like that, we drift off to sleep like we've been together forever.

CHAPTER 12

Miles

I shift in the bed and feel her warmth beside me before I even open my eyes. I crack them open and see her beautiful, long black hair splayed across the pillow next to me. Her pouty lips, opened slightly as she sleeps soundly beside me, are so inviting. She has her hand on my chest, and its presence is the best feeling in the world. I sit there and stare at this stunning woman that has entranced me in such a short amount of time. I place my hand on top of hers, and she shifts a bit getting closer to me. She sighs and snuggles closer into my chest. This moment will forever be painted in my mind. I want to always go to sleep with her beside me and wake to see her beautiful face in the morning.

I wish I could tell my father that he was right. He said I would know when I found the right one. I wish he was here to meet Elizabeth. I know they would have gotten along spectacularly. She is so easy-going and considerate. How did I get this lucky? She is a beautiful blessing, and I will do everything in my power to show her how special she is to me.

As I lie in bed thinking, my mind strays to the gala. I get a large smile on my face thinking about the surprises that await Lizzie. I hope she wants to join me that night. It's a large, city-wide event; the news and paparazzi will be waiting outside to capture pictures of everyone entering. I don't mind the entire world knowing that she is with me; in fact, I want to scream it from the rooftops. However, I also know that can be a lot of pressure for someone that isn't used to being in the spotlight. But I'll be right there with her the entire time. Fortunately, Sarah will be there too, and she can possibly ease some of the tension out of the situation.

I push the negative thoughts away and focus on what I must do today. I need to get up and head back to my place to work out, shower, and get ready for work. Then I am meeting Mia about Lizzie's attire for the gala. I may need to make another call to Sarah to get her input on the type of dress and color Lizzie would prefer. Maybe she could even join us. I don't like keeping this from Lizzie, but at the same time, I want it to be a birthday surprise.

Bringing me out of my thoughts, my phone alarm goes off. I quickly grab it from the nightstand in hopes of not waking Lizzie up. She stirs a bit and looks up at me. I run my hand over her cheek and push some hair behind her ear. I kiss her forehead and whisper, "I've got to go, sweetheart. I need to get to my place to get ready for work." She pouts for a minute and nods. I can't help it, but I need to feel those lips. I lean down further and capture them in my mouth. It's slow at first, and then I put my hands around her waist and pull her on top of me. She gasps and looks down at me with her hair falling like a waterfall around us. I pull her face closer and seal my lips over hers once more. This time the kiss is more passionate, and I have to cut it short before I'm late for work. There is nothing more I would rather do than tear the clothes from between us and sink inside her sweet body. A groan leaves my lips as she wriggles on my crotch. I don't think she is doing it intentionally, but I have got to get out of this bed before I have her splayed out in front of me. A man can only be tempted so far.

I look into her gorgeous eyes and say, "Thank you for letting me stay the night. I wish I didn't have to leave so early."

She smiles. "The bed will get cold without you in it." *Is she trying to kill me?* It was already hard enough to think about leaving, without her saying that.

I kiss her forehead and tease, "I'm looking forward to our date tonight. I'll pick you up at 6." I slide out from under her, reluctantly, and begin putting my clothes on from yesterday. Maybe I should bring some suits to leave here. Just thinking that makes my heart squeeze. I have never wanted that with another woman. I turn back to look at Lizzie nestled in her covers and wish I was right back in there with her.

"I'll miss you today," she admits. I smile and sit on the edge of the bed, thinking she is finally letting her guard down for me, and it makes me the happiest man alive. I kiss her temple and tell her I must go. She sits up and pulls the covers down.

"I'll walk you out," she says. "I have to lock the door behind you anyways." I wish she didn't have to get out of the warm bed to let me out. If I had my own key, then I could do it for her; and she could just go back to sleep. I'll have to talk to her about that, but I don't want to scare her by moving too fast. As far as I'm concerned after last night, I don't want to spend another night apart. She could move in with me right now if she wants.

"I hate that you have to get up and get all chilly just to walk me to the door," I say.

"It's not a big deal. Besides, I wanted to. And don't doubt that I will run back and jump right into my warm bed," she says, flirting.

I hold my hand out to her, helping her out of bed. Her bedhead is the cutest thing I have ever seen. She is still breathtaking in every way possible, but seeing her pure and fresh in the morning has my mind wandering back to her sitting on me a few minutes ago.

We walk to the door with her hand still in mine and her head leaning on my arm. I take a moment to pull her to my front and cherish her warmth that I'm about to leave. I smell her vanilla perfume as I lean down and kiss the top of her head. She's nestled into my chest, and damnit, if it doesn't feel like our bodies were made for each other. I put my finger under her chin and pull it up so I can look at her. "I must go, sweetheart. I will call you when I get a chance today. I hope you have a good day." She slides up on her tip toes and puts her arms around my neck and kisses me. I kiss her back and hold her as close as I can. She is pressed firmly against me, and if I don't leave now, I will pick her up and take her back to bed, then have my way with her. I break the kiss and open the door. The freezing air hits me in the face and Lizzie starts to shiver.

"Make sure you lock the door, so I know you are safe," I order as I step out into the fresh morning air.

"I will. Have a good day, Miles. And thank you again for last night," she says as she leans on her door.

"I'll always be there for you. I told you that," I remind her, leaning in and kissing her one last time. I turn to leave and walk toward the stairs, pausing until I hear the door shut and the lock going into place. I smile because she does what I ask of her. I don't want to be worried about her; so far, she has indulged me, allowing me to help keep her safe. I get to my car, turn on the heat, and make my way back to my apartment. It's going to be a great day. I feel like a smile is my new dress code. I can't wipe it from my face. Lizzie makes me so happy and brings out the best in me. I want to make her just as happy as she makes me. I want, no I need to be, the best man for her. And I will be. I am in this for the long haul.

CHAPTER 13

Elizabeth

I close the door after Miles leaves and erupt into the biggest smile ever. Last night was incredible, well, except for the fiasco with Jacob, but Miles came to my rescue. He stuck up for me, and even told Jacob to never look my way again. He went all alpha male on him, and I've got to admit, that's sexy as hell. I never thought I would be into that kind of behavior, but damn that was hot. Miles is so confident, and his presence exudes dominance. His attractiveness just skyrocketed.

    I skip back to my room and get into bed where I can still smell where he was lying. *Mmm, he smells delicious.* I look at the clock and see that I can sleep for a few more hours before I have to get up for work. I set my alarm, roll over, and snuggle with the pillow Miles used. I can't wipe this stupid smile off my face. *Lizzie, you have it bad!* This is dangerous territory, but I agreed to jump right in with him; so, I must trust he'll catch me when I fall. And I'm doing just that, falling. I can only hope that this doesn't end in heartbreak. I try and push those negative thoughts away and concentrate on all the good that Miles and I have together, even during this short amount of time. I close my eyes and begin to doze off, and the next thing I know is my alarm's blaring for me to wake up. Geez, there is no way that was two hours! It feels like five minutes. I turn the alarm off and check my phone to see I have a message from Miles. I open it as quickly as I can.

Miles: Good morning, sweetheart. I enjoyed last night, and I can't wait to cook for you this evening. I'm already at the office and have a packed schedule today. I will call or text when I'm able. Have a wonderful day, beautiful. xo

Swoon. Could he be any more perfect? I mean, all girls want to wake up to messages like this. This man is something else. I reread the message, and again I have the largest smile on my face that it's starting to sting a bit.

Lizzie: Just waking back up and desperately needing my coffee fix! I may run to our little shop before work. I can't wait to see these cooking skills of yours. Just so you know, I can be picky, so I hope you bring your A game tonight! Have an enjoyable day! Also, thank you again for last night. Xo

I send the text and get out of my comfortable, warm bed that I don't want to leave, then stretch. I head to the bathroom and start a hot shower because it is quite chilly this morning. Once the steam fills the room, I step in the shower and just stand under the running water for a minute, feeling the warmth spread over my body. Once I'm warmed up, I bathe and wash my hair, then hop out of the shower. I put my watch back on and realize I'm on time today, which makes me happy. I hate to be in a rush. I towel dry my hair and put my robe and slippers on as I walk out to the living room. Sarah is still asleep, but she will be up soon. I start a pot of coffee in the kitchen and go back to the bathroom to blow dry and straighten my hair. It's a lengthy process, but it's worth it. I love when I have time to actually do my hair. Keeping it long is high maintenance, but I don't ever want to cut it. I finish with it, then put on a bit of makeup. I don't ever wear too much, just a bit of eyeshadow, eyeliner, mascara, and lipstick. My cheeks seem to also stay rosy, so there's no need for blush. I hate having foundation on my face because it makes it feel like my skin can't breathe. So, I just keep my makeup routine simple.

I go make myself a cup of coffee, then return to my

room, looking up the temperatures for today. I don't want to freeze to death by not having enough clothes on, but I also don't want to be hot either. The weather app says it will be a high of fifty degrees today and windy. I put the phone down and open my closet. This is the hardest part of my morning routine, finding something to wear. I have too many outfits, and it's hard to pick. I love clothes and shoes. I blame Sarah for being a fashionista and rubbing off on me. I chuckle to myself thinking of what she would say if I was to call her that. I pull out a pair of dark skinny jeans and some black knee-high boots. I run my hands through the sweaters I have and pull out an ivory one with a wide neck that hangs off one shoulder. I grab a teal scarf to give it some color. I pour the rest of my coffee into a to-go cup and top it off with some fresh creamer, then grab my phone and head back out to the living room where the full-length mirror is. I look and am pleased with my outfit choice. I won't have time to change, so this will be what I wear tonight to see Miles.

Sarah comes stumbling out of her room. "Need... coffee," she huffs.

I laugh as I say, "Just made a fresh pot. What's going on? Didn't get enough sleep last night?"

She grimaces and shakes her head. "I was up late working on a new project and fell asleep on top of all my notes. I even forgot to set my alarm; but thank goodness, I heard you out here moving around. I need a vacation!" She walks over to the kitchen and makes herself a cup of coffee, then sits at the counter with the mug warming her hands.

"I have some news," I announce, pausing for her reaction. "Miles picked me up from work last night because he is insistent I don't need to walk home alone. I'm so glad he did because guess who showed up at the restaurant last night?"

She looks at me and shrugs her shoulders. So, I go on

and exclaim, "Jacob!"

"No fucking way! I hope you told him to get lost. He's a piece of trash, Liz!" she hisses angrily.

"Oh, I know. He requested to be seated in my section, but my manager refused to let me trade the table with one of the other servers. So, I was forced to interact with him most of the night because he wouldn't leave. I think he was waiting for me to get off work to make his move." I let out a huff. "So, by the time I left work, he was so drunk he could barely walk. He was stumbling all about and followed me outside, shouting all these terrible things about me. Fortunately, Miles was there waiting in his car and saw the altercation. He jumped out of his car and got between Jacob and me. When Jacob kept running his mouth, Miles picked him up by his collar and told him to never speak to me again. Miles also, warned him that he would regret it if he did," I recount, as the words finish pouring out of my mouth, like the incident happened only moments ago.

Sarah's eyes widen, but she smiles at the same time. "Girl, you got yourself a good man. He's sweet and protective. You have to keep him around. He definitely has my stamp of approval," she quips.

"Well, that's good. I'm glad you approve. I have to get going. You know how Edith gets if I'm just five minutes early. I might as well be an hour late by her standards." I laugh because old Ms. Edith is a character, but I still enjoy working at the bookstore, even if it's run by a crotchety, old lady.

Sarah gets up from the counter, coming over and squeezing me tight. She steps back and places her hands on my shoulders, then says, "I'm happy that you're happy. I know you are because I can see the twinkle in your eyes when you talk about Miles. I understand you're apprehensive about this relationship and it's moving so quickly; but I have to tell you, when you know, you know. I think that's what you have right now. Don't fear this, Lizzie. He is a good man, and I believe he really cares for you. Don't run away. I know that's what you want to do, but I'm asking you to see this through. It might just change your life," she advises with a smile.

I grip her hands on my shoulders. "I love you, Sarah. You have always looked out for me, and I think you know me better than I know myself sometimes. Plus, you are right. I keep the thought in the back of my mind that I could just run away at any time, but that's not how I want to think in this relationship. If I do, then I won't ever fully give myself over to him."

I straighten my shoulders and hold my chin up. "Today is a new day, and I have a man that wants me. I'm not going to let the silly things in my head get in the way of that. I'm not going to run away this time, Sarah!"

She gives me another hug. I grab my coat from the closet, then my purse. "Miles is cooking for me tonight, so I will be home late. I'll text to let you know when. Love you," I say, as I step out into the cool New York morning.

I hear her yell back, "Does this guy have a brother?"

I laugh and holler back, "He sure does." Before the door closes behind me.

CHAPTER 14

Miles

I'm in the middle of a meeting with the board members of the company, and one of my employees is giving a presentation. I can't concentrate on what he's saying. All I hear is Lizzie's laugh, and I see her bright smile. I wish it was closing time, so I could see my girl. This day is crawling by, as I look down at my watch for what seems like the twentieth time since this meeting started.

The room falls silent, and all eyes are on me. I look up and see my staff waiting for me to speak. I'm thankful I'm quick on my feet and able to respond with something that satisfies the board, and they continue talking. I have to get my head on straight. I must prove myself to the board and the rest of this company, so this isn't the time to daydream. I push thoughts of Lizzie away and focus on the rest of the meeting.

Once I get back to my office, Sebastian comes in looking upset. "What happened to you in there? We need the board on our side, Miles. You were off in LaLa land instead of giving the pitch that we prepared. You're lucky I remembered it, or we would be in some deep shit. What's going on with you?" he nearly shouts.

I hate letting people down, but I have so much on my mind that I can barely concentrate at work. "I'm sorry, man. My head just wasn't in it today. Thank you for pulling us through," I reply, as I run my hands through my hair.

He looks at me for a moment, then asks, "Is this about Elizabeth? Are you really that serious about her? Have you even slept with her yet?"

That question rubs me the wrong way and I get defensive fast. "That's none of your business. Lizzie isn't some conquest that I'm after. She's the one. Just like dad said to us when we were younger, I know in my soul that she is it for me," I hiss as I look him straight in the eyes.

He pauses a beat and apologizes, "Dude, I'm so sorry. I didn't know all that. I mean I knew you liked her, but I didn't know it was already this serious. I'm happy for you, man. But you can't let her come between work. We have to keep this company running, and the board is breathing down our necks to publish something extraordinary. We can't drop the ball right now."

I nod because I know he's right. I am the CEO of this company, and everyone depends on me. I must figure out a way to balance my work and social life. That's not something I have ever had to do, but now that I have Lizzie, I've got to find a way to make this work.

Sebastian comes around to my side of the desk and slaps me on the back. "I truly am happy for you. When do I get to meet her, officially? The club meeting doesn't count."

"You will meet her soon. I'm cooking for her tonight, but we will plan something in the near future. Oh, I forgot to tell you that I'm bringing her and her friend to the gala next week. It's actually on her birthday, so I have a few surprises for her that day." I grin.

He just laughs and declares, "Man, you have it bad! You're smitten with this woman. I can't wait to meet her again. I'm heading out for lunch, want to join me?" he inquires.

"No, I have plans with Mia; it's part of the surprise for

Lizzie. I'll be back in the office later this afternoon. How about we do lunch this week sometime? I'll let you know when I'm free," I respond, hoping he's not upset that I don't have time for him. It's always been just us, especially when we started working here. I don't want our dynamic to change.

"Cool. No worries. Tell Mia hello from her favorite Knight," he jokes with a wink and walks out of my office. Geez, I don't even want to know what that meant. I shut down my laptop. Grabbing my suit jacket, keys, and phone, I head out of the office.

As I get to the boutique where we're scheduled to meet, I see that Mia is already here talking a mile a minute to the sales associate. Chuckling, I kiss her on the cheek. I've known Mia for years and she's dressed me for all kinds of occasions. She even organized my closet when I bought my new apartment. She certainly knows what she is doing. I pull out my phone and send a text off to Lizzie, while I wait on Mia to finish her conversation. I don't like her ex sniffing around her like he was last night. *What if I hadn't been there? What if I hadn't insisted that she allow me to pick her up?* My mind starts to swirl with all the possibilities that could have transpired last night, and I feel a tightening in my chest. I can't have anything happen to her. She is the one for me and the fuck if I'm going to lose her.

Miles: Just checking on you. I'm out running some errands, but I wanted to make sure you got to work safely.

I pocket my phone and glance at Mia to see if she finished her conversation. I was able to get back in touch with Sarah and she's available to meet today, as well. That gives me some comfort because she knows everything about Lizzie in order to pick out a dress she would love.

Mia spots me from across the store and runs over squealing. She jumps up and down when she reaches me and starts talking so fast, I can barely keep up. "I am so excited for this, Miles. I never thought you would be the type to go all out for a woman, but here we are. Ah, I can't wait to find something spectacular for her. What's her name?"

I smile and reply, "Her name is Elizabeth. I called her best friend, Sarah, and she is meeting us here as well." Speaking of Sarah, she walks in just as I say her name. She sees us right away and walks over.

"Hi, Sarah, thank you for meeting us. This is Mia. She's been my stylist for years and is eager to help us find something for Lizzie," I explain.

"It's nice to meet you, Mia. Thank you both for including me," Sarah says cordially.

"Girl, you do not have to thank me. I have been waiting for this day forever." She laughs.

The girls shake hands, complimenting one another's outfits. I can't help but chuckle. I guess they have made new friends in each other. Casually walking around the store, I look at all the different dresses. I honestly don't know what I'm looking for; that's why I insisted on help. I hear Mia clap her hands as she comes over to me.

"Okay. I have her size. Also, Sarah showed me a picture of Lizzie, so I could see what her coloring is, and O.M.G! I love, love, love her hair! It's gorgeous!" Mia exclaims.

They peruse the racks of beautiful dresses in the store, and Sarah selects various articles and shoes, then reserves them in the back. The theme of the gala is Winter Wonderland, which I believe Lizzie will love. Suddenly, Mia squeals with surprise as she pulls out a stunning silver, floor-length gown. Sarah quickly scurries over to her, and both girls ogle the dress. They both exclaim, almost in unison, "Perfect! Just perfect!"

Quite awestruck with the gown, Sarah exclaims, "This would fit her perfectly, and it would look fabulous with her hair! Plus, it so complements the theme of the gala. What do you think, Miles?"

I slide the material through my hands; the silk exudes luxury, so soft and cool to the touch. I can't help but imagine Lizzie in this dress. The gown, absolutely stunning and unique, is just like my Lizzie, Perfect! "It's perfect. Do you have shoes to match?" I grin and chuckle.

Mia runs over to the shoe department and selects some tall, strappy, silver heels that are the same color as the dress. "These will be perfect! She is going to be breathtaking!" she cries.

"Okay, I'll go purchase the dress and shoes. Is there anything else that she needs? I'm already going to Tiffany's after this, to get her something special to wear with this dress." I say.

"Wait," Mia shouts. "She needs a shawl. I'm sure it will be cold, and we don't want her freezing to death, even if she will look fabulous doing it!" She runs over to the other side of the store and chooses a classic, elegant shawl, styled with flecks of shimmering metallic, to add the finishing touch. "This is the one! Everything is going to go beautifully together!" The girls look at each other and both start clapping their hands. I laugh along with them.

"You are like the perfect man, Miles! Lizzie is one lucky woman," Mia coos.

"I assure you that I'm the lucky one," I tell her. "Mia, while I have you here, I need you to make two appointments for the 5th at the best spa and salon in town. It's for Lizzie and Sarah to enjoy before the gala. Send me the details as soon as you have them. Thank you both so much for your help today. I'm sure I will be needing you again soon." I half-way apologize. The sales associate comes over to take the items from me and wraps them up. I give her my card and turn back to Mia.

"By the way, Mia, Sebastian wants me to tell you 'hello'." She instantly blushes, and I definitely don't want to know what's going on there. Man, my brother is all over the place. He just can't help himself with a beautiful woman. She giggles, and we all say our goodbyes.

As I walk back out onto the streets of New York, Sarah comes up beside me, and says, "I really think this is such a kind gesture. Lizzie has never wanted to celebrate her birthday before, and I wrangle her into something every year by forcing her to celebrate. But I think this year will take the cake. I'm excited to see her face when she finds out everything. You're a good man, Miles."

I smile because I genuinely want to make her happy, but something that Sarah said doesn't sit well with me. "Can I ask you why she doesn't like to celebrate her birthday? Did something happen?" I ask.

Sarah looks at me for a beat, then says, "Her parents divorced when she was twelve, and after that, they would fight over who she spent her birthday with. She would have to have two separate parties because her parents couldn't be cordial toward each other for just a few hours, for her sake. I guess it got to where she would rather not even celebrate because it was too much for her. I was with her through all that time, and it hit her very hard." Sarah has sadness in her eyes after she finishes explaining. I can't even imagine what Lizzie had to go through. I grew up in a traditional house, so I never had to worry about separated parents. It sounds terrible, and I hate that she had to experience that, especially how much it has affected her adult life. I'm going to try and erase those bad memories by replacing them with happy and loving ones.

"It's terrible that she had to endure that. I suppose the divorce has something to do with her hesitance to trust men?" I say aloud, but mostly to myself, but Sarah hears me.

She turns to look me in the eyes, and I can see the truth there. "That's exactly where her trust issues come from. Miles, she's been through a lot. I talked to her this morning about it. I told her that you were worth the risk, to throw the doubts out of her mind, and let herself fall. I said that because I trust that you feel the same way about her that she does about you. Please don't hurt her," she mumbles softly. I put my hand on her shoulder, looking her in the eyes, so she can see the truth that I am about to say. "Sarah, I feel the same way. I'm falling for her. I know in my soul that she is the one. I won't do anything to lose her. I can't."

She gives me a smile. "That's all I wanted to hear. Now, send me the details for the spa and the gala, so I can start planning. And I guess I will see you soon."

"I'll send it all as soon as I get the details. Thank you again for coming out today and thank you for the talk. You are a good friend to her. I'm happy she has you." We hug and part ways.

Thomas picks me up, putting the items from the boutique in the trunk, and then drives me to Tiffany's. I really want to find something special. Something that makes me think of Elizabeth. She isn't ordinary, so the jewelry needs to be one of a kind. Once we arrive, Thomas comes around to open my door with a wide smile on his face. He's never brought me here, and so, he knows this woman is special. I have never bought a woman I've dated a piece of jewelry, so this is all new to me. As I get out of the car, I say, "Thank you, Thomas. I'm not sure how long I will be. Would you like to come in and help me look? You have a wife. This is all very new to me."

He chuckles and responds, "It would be an honor, sir."

CHAPTER 15

Elizabeth

As I'm walking down the busy streets of New York, my phone begins to ring in my purse. My mom's name appears on the screen, and I take a deep breath, then answer it. I haven't spoken to her in over a week, which is out of the norm for me. "Hey momma," I greet, answering the phone.

"Hey, baby, I haven't talked to you in a while. How are you doing?"

"I'm doing pretty well. I have just been really busy lately. What are you doing?" I ask before she can question me about what I have been busy with. I'm not ready to tell her about Miles. I don't know if I would have the answers to the inevitable questions she'll ask.

"I just sent out your package for your birthday. I hope it gets there in time. It should because I paid for express shipping. I haven't been able to get to the post office sooner. Sorry, baby. So, what have you been so busy with that you couldn't call your own mother?" I grimace because I knew she wouldn't let me get away without giving her some details.

"I actually have been doing quite a lot of writing when I've not been working. I got some much-needed motivation, and the book is finally taking shape in my mind as well as on my computer."

"That's great, Lizzie. I know you have been trying to get

that off the ground for a while now. How is the weather? Has it snowed yet? I always check your weather, but it's not always reliable."

I sigh in relief that she doesn't ask me about my new motivation. "It hasn't snowed yet, but it sure is cold. The other day it wasn't too chilly, but once I finished my shift at the restaurant, it was freezing. It goes back and forth. I'm sure the snow will come any day now, though."

"I can't see how you stand that cold weather. We like it down here in the south where there is hardly ever any snow. So, since you didn't come home for Thanksgiving, are you coming for Christmas?"

"I'm planning on it. I've already asked for a few days off, but it won't be a whole week like last year. I'll just come in and spend the holiday with you. Will William be in town?"

"Yes, he and his family will be here for Christmas Eve, and then at your father's home for Christmas."

I scoff. Yeah, I won't be going to see my father while I'm home; that's for sure. "Hmm, okay, well I need to get going. I will let you know what the dates are for sure when I know. Love you, mom."

"Hang on sweetie. William wants to know if you will go with him to see your father while you're in town. Apparently, he's been asking William to get a hold of you to invite you over. He hasn't been feeling well lately." A pit forms in my stomach at the thought of my father and his possibly being sick.

"Well, father has my number. But you can tell William that I will not be going with them. I'm just coming into town to see you."

"I really think you should go and see him, Lizzie. He misses you. You are still his daughter after all."

I am not liking the way this conversation is going. I don't understand why my mother, of all people, would be pushing me to see that man after everything he did to her and to us. I still can't believe William has a relationship with him. Am I the only one that can see him for what he really is? A liar, cheater, abandoner.

"We both know good and well that if your father did call you, that you wouldn't answer. That's not even a good excuse. But, anyways, we can talk about it later. I just want you to think about it, okay? Love you, honey. Have a good day," she chirps, as she disconnects the call. I pocket my phone and pull my coat tighter around myself, trying not to shiver.

Thankfully, the coffee shop is just around the corner. I can get out of this wind. As I approach the shop, I begin to walk a bit faster, so I can get inside. I open the doors and the aroma has my mouth watering. The shop's not busy, which I'm grateful for. Walking up to the counter, I order my usual under the name "Bronte." The barista smiles and winks at me, knowing that I always change up my name when I come here. As she prints the name on my cup, I stroll over to the sitting area and plop down in one of the overstuffed chairs. While I'm waiting, I pull out my phone, open the notes app, and type some things that have been on my mind for my novel. If I don't make notes somewhere, I will definitely forget my ideas when I get in front of my computer.

Once my name is called, I retrieve my drink and walk back to the chair to sit down. I have a little bit of time to sit and relax before I have to be at the bookstore. As I take the first sip, I close my eyes as the warmth slides down my throat and into my tummy. There is something about the first sip that isn't quite like the rest. I set my cup down and look around the shop. I haven't been here since last week when I ran into Miles. So much can change in the span of a week. Smiling to myself, I remember the way he looked down at me when we grabbed the coffee at the same time. The world around us ceased to exist, and we were the only two people in this tiny shop. My phone beeps in my hand, effectively taking me out of my daydream. My heart flutters in my chest when I see the message from him.

Miles: Just letting you know that I'm thinking of you. Xo

Lizzie: I came into "our" coffee shop to get out of the cold. I was just thinking about when we met last week.

Miles: Just knowing you are so close to me right now, makes me want to blow off my next meeting and come to you.

Lizzie: Well, I have to be at the bookstore soon anyway. But I wouldn't mind running into you again here soon.

Miles: We will have to arrange that, sweetheart. Heading into the meeting. I will call or text after. See you tonight.

Lizzie: Good luck in there. Talk to you later then. XOXO

Checking my watch, I pop out of the chair, grabbing my coffee and hurrying to the door. The few minutes I had to spare were used talking to Miles, and now I have to hustle to get work on time. I rush in just as I see Edith's car pulling up. Putting my hand to my chest, I take a minute to catch my breath as I put my coat and purse away. I busy myself with stocking the new inventory, and before I know it, my shift is over. I like Wednesdays because they are relaxed and mostly free from priorities. Except for the short shift at the bookstore, I have a free day. Grabbing my things from behind the counter, I call out to Edith before I leave, "I'll see you Friday, Edith." I hear her mumble something that probably wasn't for me to hear. Sighing, I walk out into the cold December air. I snuggle in my jacket tighter and start the short trek to my apartment.

Once I get home, I realize I have less than an hour until Miles will be here to pick me up. *Since he's cooking at his house, that means I can wear something casual, right?* So, I decide not to change from the outfit I have been in all day. I do, however, go into the bathroom to give my makeup a refresher. I run a comb through my hair from where the wind made it all tangly.

He called after his meeting, but I wasn't able to answer. He sent a message that his meeting went well. I'm happy about that. He's been stressing over the presentation, and now he will get the opportunity to relax tonight.

I check my watch, having five minutes to spare. In the short time that I have known Miles, I have found the is a man of punctuality. I run to the mirror in the living room to check out my outfit. It's the perfect amount of comfortable and cute. I left my hair flowing down my back because I think he really likes it that way. I hear a knock on the door and instantly get butterflies in my belly. I haven't even seen him, yet, but my stomach is doing summersaults.

I grab my purse and place my phone inside. I open the door and my breath catches in my throat. Wow, he is so handsome. He has a huge smile across his face when he sees me. Before I can get any words out, he has me wrapped up in a tight hug.

He leans down to where his mouth is beside my ear, and whispers out, "I missed you, today." Just feeling his breath on my neck send chills up my spine.

I pull back, so I can look up at his gorgeous blue eyes. "I missed you, too," I say softly. He gives me a small kiss.

"Let me grab my coat." I walk back into the apartment and pick my jacket up off the back of the couch. He takes it from me and holds it out for me to slide into. "Thank you," I say breathlessly because I can't get my breathing under control when he is this close.

"Always," he responds.

I can't deny that my heart skips a beat at his use of the word "always." But then, I come back down to earth and remind myself we have only been seeing each other for less than a week. 'Always' can change to 'never' in the blink of an eye. I smile up at him instead of replying to his comment.

"Are you ready for the best Italian you have ever eaten?" he questions.

I take this time to make the situation a bit lighter. "Oh, are we going out instead of you cooking?" I ask teasingly.

"Oh, very funny. Someone is being feisty tonight. I will be awaiting your apology after you taste my dinner." He looks at me with a wicked grin.

"Well, I'm starving, so I guess we better get you to your kitchen, then," I laugh out. He smiles and pulls me back into him as his lips crash over mine. It feels like he is starving for me, and I for him. He pulls his hands from my waist, cupping my cheeks, then breaks off the kiss gently. He gazes into my eyes for a moment, and then says, "Lizzie, you are breathtaking. You make me crazy for you." He kisses my forehead and drops his hand to grab mine.

"Ready?" He smiles at me like I'm the only person in the world he wants to look at or be with. Just with his looks, he is doing something to me. My heart begins to flutter again, and I can't help but blush that I know he probably sees.

"Of course," I reply. He leads me out of my apartment.

CHAPTER 16

Miles

Once we get into my car, I can't keep my eyes off her. She is stunning. But it's not just her looks that have me; it's her heart. She has captured my soul in this short week I've known her. I don't know if she realizes how bad I have it for her or how badly I want to tell her. But I don't want to scare her off by moving too quickly. Damnit, I want to spend every ounce of free time that I have with her. I grab her hand and hold it in mine as I drive down the road. I need the connection with her. She is too close for me to not reach out and touch her.

On the way to my penthouse, we talk about our day that we had today. Conversation flows easily and there is no awkward silence. Once we reach my place, I pull into the garage and park. I get out and go to her side to let her out. I grasp her hand in mine tightly and lead her toward the lobby. Once inside I nod to Colin behind the desk. I lead Lizzie to the private elevator that only goes to my apartment. When it opens up, her eyes widen even more than they did when she saw the lobby. The elevator has white marble flooring and gold sconces along the walls, then there's a large mirror hanging within an elaborate gold frame.

"Wow!" she exclaims. "This looks like a fancy hotel."

I chuckle as I look down at her. It does look like something you would find in a resort of some kind. I suppose that I have gotten used to it, so I don't notice anymore.

However, I do love seeing it through her eyes.

"I suppose it's a bit too fancy, but it was like this when I bought my place. I guess I don't really notice it." She looks at me with one brow raised, and it makes her look adorable. I can't help but smile. The elevator opens to my apartment, and I lead her out into my penthouse. She walks straight over to the floor-to-ceiling windows that look out over the Hudson. I walk up behind her and grab her hips.

"What do you think?" I ask, as I kiss the top of her head.

"It's beautiful. Breathtaking, really. Can I have a tour?" she asks, glancing over her shoulder at me.

We spend the next twenty minutes going through the rooms. Her favorites are the theater room and the kitchen.

"I still can't believe this kitchen. It's beautiful. My mother would have a fit if she saw this!" she exclaims.

I look at her a bit puzzled, "A fit?"

She laughs and says, "It's a southern expression. It means she would love it, basically. I forgot I was in the presence of a true New Yorker." She smiles.

"Ah, I guess I don't know the southern lingo. But I do know Spanish, French, and Mandarin. I suppose you will have to enlighten me with more southern sayings." I chuckle with a large grin my face.

"I speak French and Spanish, as well," she says. "It comes in handy when I'm working at the restaurant and tourists come in. I think my boss purposely puts them in my section, so they will be impressed with the establishment having someone that's multilingual." She shrugs.

As I begin to get the ingredients out to cook, I ask, "Do you like working there?" She takes a moment to consider my question, but I can see the answer written on her face. She doesn't like it. "It's not terrible. I'm sure others have it worse. And some, with no jobs at all. So, I can't complain."

That answers my question, but she won't admit it. She isn't taking her job for granted, and that makes me like her even more. She is so considerate of others and compassionate. I can't believe my luck that she collided into my life in that little coffee shop.

"Is there anything I can do to help? But before you answer, know that I am a terrible cook. I did not get that gene from my mother.," she laughs. The sound of her laugh makes me smile. I could record that sound and listen to it on repeat.

"I just want you to sit and relax. Would you like a glass of wine?" I ask.

She nods. "I would love white if you have it." I go to the wine cooler and pull out a bottle of white, then pour some into two glasses. I hand one to Lizzie. Before taking a sip, she smells the wine and a smile spreads across her face. Once she tastes it, she moans in delight. Oh, and do I want to hear her make that sound again, but me being the reason for it. My cock twitches in my pants as I watch her sip her wine. Her lips leave red marks on the side of the glass. She looks up at me like she knows what I'm thinking and begins to blush.

"This wine is delicious. Thank you. Are you sure there isn't anything I can help you with?" I walk over to the stool that she' sitting on. I take her glass of wine and place it on the counter. I cup her face and lean in for a kiss. The sweetness of the wine still lingering there and the taste that can only be described as Lizzie assaults my tongue. I could kiss this woman for the whole night and still not have enough. I pull back before this goes any further and we don't make it to dinner.

"I want you to sit right here and drink your wine. Plus, I don't want to have to call the fire department if something gets out of hand," I tease.

She gives me a playful shove. "You better watch out. I might not be great in the kitchen, but I am good at other things. Softball for one. I was too busy for cooking lessons because I was playing softball all the time when I was growing up." She points a finger at me, and I can't help but throw my head back and laugh.

"So, you think you can beat me at softball, say at the batting cages?" I ask while I get back to the kitchen and begin to prepare the dinner.

"Of course. Although it's been a while since I have practiced, I'm confident I will come out on top." She blushes at her double meaning. "Are there even batting cages anywhere around here?"

"Actually, there are. Sebastian and I have been to them several times over the years. I believe they are still open for business. I'll have to give them a call, so you can show me these skills you have. I must warn you; I won't go down without a fight," I reply, laughing as Lizzie does as well.

I get the dinner into the oven and walk around to the other side of the counter to lead Lizzie to the living room while we wait. "Oh, I love this space," she says. Once we are seated, she begins looking around. "Although, it definitely looks like a bachelor pad," she adds. I nod in agreement saying, "Well, I work long hours. I basically just use this place to crash after a long day. I haven't gotten around to decorating."

"You know, you don't have to go crazy, but maybe a few paintings on the walls might make it a bit cozier in here," she suggests.

I look around at the blank, white walls surrounding us and agree, "This place definitely needs something added to it."

"You wouldn't have any paintings you'd mind parting with, do you?" I turn to her and ask. She immediately begins to blush.

"I never should have told you that I paint. I'm not even that good! You will have to go to an art gallery and find something from a real artist," she replies, looking back at me.

I grab her waist and pull her closer to me, so our faces are inches apart. I cup her cheek and pull it up, so she is looking me in the eyes. I want her to believe me when I tell her this. "Lizzie, I love the paintings I saw at your apartment. I could feel your emotions pouring out of the canvas. Don't ever be ashamed of your work. I would love to have an Elizabeth Brighton original."

Our eyes stay locked for a moment longer, and then I pull her closer so my lips can hungrily press onto hers. I pull her into my lap, so I can have her closer to me. As she straddles me, she puts her arms on my shoulders and her hands begin pulling at my hair. I bite her bottom lip, and a small moan escapes her. I have a hand on her waist and one on the back of her head. I need to feel her closer to me. I want to feel her pressed up against me. I want to feel our bodies molding into one. As our kiss turns fierce, the oven timer goes off in the kitchen, alerting us that dinner is ready.

I sigh against her mouth because I don't want this to end, but I also don't want dinner to burn. I lean back and brush a few strands of hair behind her ear. "I've got to get dinner out," I whisper, not wanting to break this connection. She nods and moves to get up. I pull her back down quickly and place another scorching kiss to her lips. She gasps, and then moves off me, so I can go to the kitchen. As I walk that way, I have to adjust my arousal in my pants, willing myself to calm down.

Lizzie walks in behind me. "Something smells delicious. Maybe you can cook after all." She chuckles. I look over my shoulder and just to give her a wink. Once the pasta is out of the oven, I scoop some onto both of our plates along with some aromatic garlic bread.

"Would you like some more wine, babe?" I ask, as I take the plates to the dining room.

"Sure, I'll get it." She grabs our glasses and goes to the kitchen to refill them.

I take in the sight of her in my kitchen, making herself at home; it's the best damn sight I have seen. Seeing her here comfortable and in my home, it just feels right. *She* feels right. She is the missing puzzle piece that I've been without my entire life, and now that I have found her, I won't let her go.

She brings the glasses back, and I can't help but pull her in for a hug and a quick kiss. She looks up at me with adoration in her eyes and asks, "What was that for?"

I graze her cheek with my thumb and push a piece of hair behind her ear. "I just like seeing you in my kitchen. Here, take a seat so we can eat."

I pull the chair out for her and push her back in. Then I take my seat opposite her. She twirls some pasta around her fork and takes a bite, closing her eyes and letting out a little moan. "Miles, this is incredible. How did you learn to cook so well?"

"My grandmother is Italian, and I spent summers with her in Italy while I was in college. She taught me many recipes. It's a good thing you like Italian; it's my specialty. Other than that, my skills are a bit lacking" I confess.

She scoffs as she takes another bite, "I doubt that. Anyone that can make this, would be able to make something else, other than Italian. So how was Italy? I have always wanted to visit," she inquires.

I take a sip of wine and tell her about my trips. "I love Italy. The people and the atmosphere are beautiful. Venice is gorgeous. I will have to take you sometime. I believe you will love the sight." She looks at me with a huge smile on her face that lightens up the room, and a place in my heart constricts. I would do anything to keep that smile on her face. I want to be the one that makes her happy.

"I would love to go! It has always been a dream of mine. Ireland, as well. I guess I just want to travel in general. I feel like I haven't been anywhere," she says dreamily. I reach over and grab her hand in mine and look at her in her eyes, so she knows I'm being serious.

"I will take you anywhere you want to go. Just say the word and we will take off."

She laughs. "Well, thank you. But I'm fairly sure such a busy CEO can't just take off whenever he wants to. But thank you for saying that." I squeeze her hand tighter, so she looks back up at me.

"I mean it, Lizzie, we can travel wherever you want to go. I can work from anywhere if I need to." She nods, as a blush creeps up her cheeks.

"I guess I'm not used to this kind of treatment. You are so different than I thought you'd be. You've been most generous to me and kind. I guess what I am trying to say is that I'm glad I met you, Miles."

I get up and walk around to her chair, then pull her up against me. Holding her close, I whisper against her ear, "You are so incredible. How did I get this lucky?" A shiver runs through her at my touch. I love the way she responds to my simple touch. I want to always have this effect on her. I kiss her forehead, and she gazes up at me with unshed tears in her eyes.

"I'm the lucky one," I say, then cup her cheek and lean down so our eyes meet. "I know you have had it rough in the past with relationships, but I'm here now and I'm not going anywhere. This is it, Lizzie, you and me. You don't have to wait for the other shoe to drop because it won't. I'm going to treat you the way you deserve. The way those other idiots should have." A tear trickles down her cheek, and I wipe it away with the pad of my thumb. I kiss her moist cheek, and she sighs against my touch. She leans up on her tippy toes and kisses me. I pull her in closer and deepen the kiss, trying to show her exactly how I feel about her to give her reassurance about our relationship. I know that she has been put down in the past, but I am here to light her up. I want to be the man that she needs in her life, the man she deserves, the one she comes to when times are tough or when she needs someone to hold her up.

I love her.

Wait, I love her? I mean. I knew I had strong feelings for her, but I do love her. Damn, this woman has captured my heart and soul. I hold her tighter for a moment longer, then I grab her hand and lead her to the couch.

"Come sit with me, baby," I request.

CHAPTER 17

Elizabeth

Once we are seated on the couch, I look over at this devilishly handsome man that wants me. He wants *me,* of all people. I can't believe this is my life. For real, how did I get this lucky? It was just a chance meeting, and he happens to be the man of my dreams. I feel like I need to pinch myself and wake up from this fairytale. I know better than anyone that those don't exist, but he sure makes me want to believe in them. Maybe I am turning into a believer. I believe him when he says that it's us together. I feel the same connection to him. It's like there is a magnet pulling us together, and my resolve to fight it is getting lesser and lesser. I want to jump in headfirst and experience everything Miles has to offer. What's the worst that could happen? *You could end up with a broken heart again, Lizzie.* That's what scares me the most. Miles has the ability to consume my entire heart, more than anyone I have ever been with, and I don't know if I could come back from that if I were to lose him. But I can't turn away now. I am already in too deep. I don't want to turn away. Maybe I just had to kiss a bunch of frogs, aka my old boyfriends, in order to find my prince. Finally, I've found the right one. Miles is my Prince Charming. *My Mr. Darcy.* I smile as I cuddle up beside him.

"Dinner was perfect. Thank you for having me," I say, looking up into those beautiful blue eyes. He smiles down at me and kisses my temple which is such a tender place to be kissed. I feel adored when he does that.

"I loved being able to cook for you, Lizzie. And I love having you here in my apartment. I feel more at home having you here. I guess I didn't realize how lonely I was until I met you. So, thank you for giving me a chance," he tells me as he holds my hand and begins drawing circles with his thumb over my wrist.

I love when this man touches me. I feel the electricity shoot through my whole body, and I get goosebumps everywhere. "Thank you for stealing my coffee that day," I reply with a smirk.

He laughs aloud and it's a wonderful sound. I love seeing him this relaxed. Things between us flow so easy. It just seems right.

"Do you have any plans this weekend?" he questions. *Ugh, my birthday is this weekend.* I wonder if he remembers my mentioning that it is. It's the night of his gala that he was telling me about.

"I don't really. Although, I'm sure Sarah will drag me somewhere. Your charity gala is this weekend, isn't it?" I ask, even though I already know the answer. I, also, know Sarah will want to celebrate my birthday even if it's the very last thing that I want to do.

"Yes, the gala is Saturday evening. Would you like to spend Sunday with me? We can do whatever you want," he inquires.

"I would love to. I do have the weekend off. Did you have anything in mind?" I ask in return. He seems to ponder for a moment and a smile crosses his face.

"I have the perfect idea. Have you been on a cruise on the Hudson?" he queries with a twinkle in his eyes.

"No, I haven't. That sounds fantastic. I love being on the water. I grew up around it; we were always out on boats and such when I was younger. Can you arrange that with such short notice?" I ask.

"Oh, I have my way," he remarks with a sexy wink. As he pulls me into his lap, I wrap my arms around his neck and run my hands through the back of his hair. He closes his eyes as I slide my hands over his shoulders. Miles wraps his arms around my back and pulls me flush against his chest. His cologne rushes through my senses, and I don't think I will ever tire of it. He smells so good. How can he smell so wonderful?

"You fit perfectly in my arms, Lizzie," he whispers in my ear, resting his head on my shoulder. I 'hmmm' my agreement. It feels wonderful being in his arms. I feel safe and loved. I mean, not saying that he loves me, but it feels like he could. He pulls his head back up and looks at me.

"So, what kind of water activities did you do as a kid?" he asks.

"Well, as far back as I remember, we would go to the beach whenever we could. I was a beach baby for sure. I could stay there all day. My dad taught me how to ride waves on a boogie board, and when I got to be about eight or so, he taught me how to water ski. I practiced and practiced that whole summer and finally got the hang of it. I'd get to invite Sarah with us sometimes, and she learned as well. He would also pull us in a giant tube behind the boat. He'd go fast, taking turns sharply to try and throw us off. It was a lot a fun, but we also had to hang on for dear life." I laugh. "When I got a few years older, he taught me how to drop one ski, and I'd slide my foot behind the other and ski on one ski. That's called slaloming. Now, that took some practice for sure. It requires perfect balance. You can even start out on one ski, but I never mastered that. But yes, those are the water sports that we did. Those were good times," I say with a sad sigh. I didn't think Miles would hear it, but he did.

"Why does that make you sad to remember that? It sounds like it was a blast. I have never water skied, only snow skied."

I pause for a moment thinking of what to say. He takes my face in his hands and says, "Open up to me, Lizzie. Trust me." I let out a breath I didn't realize I was holding and begin telling him about my past history with my father.

"Okay," I say weakly. "I don't have a good relationship with my father now. He divorced my mom when I was twelve. I know that happens in a lot of families, but my parents didn't even fight, and if they did, they hid it very well. I was at a slumber party one night, and when I came home the next day, my father had moved out of our house. Like, that was it! He was gone. Just like that. He didn't leave town or anything, but he left me and my mother. My brother was in college and was living on campus, so it didn't affect him the same way. I guess I just felt abandoned. I was always a 'daddy's girl', and so I didn't understand why he left me there. After that, in an effort to gain my forgiveness, he began buying me all kinds of gifts: a cell phone, a car, and even a house." I take a breath and roll my eyes.

"He bought you a house?" Miles questions.

"Yes, well, it was supposed to be for both of us, so I could live with him until I finished high school. I think he may have stayed there a handful of times. The rest of the time he was with his girlfriend, living at her house. So, I basically lived by myself while I went to high school. Obviously, that probably sounds like a dream come true, but it wasn't. I'd never felt so alone in my life, even though I had tons of friends. I tried to do as many extracurricular activities as I could, so I was always busy, However, when I would get home, I was always alone. I even had to make myself something to eat by myself, and I don't even cook. I guess that would have been a good time to learn," I say with a sarcastic chuckle." Anyways, it sucked. He basically left me twice." Tears begin to stream down my cheeks, and Miles brushes them away with his hands.

"I'm sorry you had to go through that, and at such a young, impressionable age. I can't imagine. Yet you have grown into an amazingly strong woman," he assures, as he kisses my forehead.

"I had to grow up fast. And I realized that anytime I was upset with him, he would buy me something to make up for it," I sputtered. "It took me a while to figure out that presents were not what I wanted; I needed him, my dad. Because he wasn't ever there much, it drove a wedge between us. I started declining the gifts and refusing to see him as much. Once I went off to college, I had to cut ties with him because it wasn't healthy for my mental state. He married the woman he was dating, and she has children my age and a little older. He took to them as if they were his own, and I felt like I was the ugly stepchild, looking in on his new family. I couldn't compete with that, and I didn't want to. It hurt too much!" I rest my head against Miles' chest, and I take in a deep breath. He wraps his arms around me, hugging me tightly. I don't know how long we sit there like that, but he gives me exactly what I need. His strength pours out of him and into me.

He pulls back so I can look at him and says, "I see why it's difficult for you to trust people. I think I would be the same if I had been in that situation."

I just nod in agreement. "Sarah is the only one that knows this story, and that's because she was there when I went through it all. I've never told anyone else," I admit, looking into his eyes. He rubs his hands up and down my back in a comforting motion.

"Are you scared that I'll leave you, like he did?" he asks quietly. I stare at him for a moment. How can he know that? How can he already read me so well?

"Yes," I confess. Since all that happened, it's always

been my fear that the people closest to me will leave me. His betraying and abandoning me like that instilled this fear in me, and it's hard to shake it off. I guess that whole experience with him, and then my own terrible romantic failures, just make me feel like it's inevitable.

"Listen to me," Miles says sternly. "I'm right here. I'm not going anywhere. I have never met anyone like you, Lizzie. I've never wanted someone so badly in my life. You are everything I have been waiting for, and I'll be damned if I let you slip through my fingers." He pauses and says more calmly, "I will never cheat on you. When I'm not with you, you are what fills my mind. You are my endgame, Lizzie. Please trust me with your heart. I'll keep it safe."

I smile and put my hand to his chest. "I trust you, Miles."

He smiles and lightly kisses me. It's tender at first, and then it becomes passionate. We only pull back when we need to catch our breath. "Good girl. Now let's go to bed," he says, standing up with me still in his arms.

I manage to squeak out a shaky, "Okay." Hearing the words 'good girl' really does something to me. I like it. I want to be his good girl. I want to make him happy.

He holds me close as he walks us toward his bedroom.

CHAPTER 18

Miles

The next morning when my alarm goes off, I shift my arm to turn it off before it wakes Lizzie. Turning back toward her, I pull her body closer, loving the warmth and feel of her body pressed against mine. My hands rove over her hips and down her legs. She has the softest, creamy skin. I groan as my hands slide over her smooth belly. I pull her hip back further, so she can feel what she does to me. She brushes her sweet ass against me, and I try to think of anything other than pinning her to the bed and marking her as mine. Moving a few strands of hair, I kiss her neck and see goosebumps erupt over her skin, even when she isn't fully awake. Her vanilla perfume fills my senses, and I have to force myself to put a pause on this. I told her that she's my endgame, and I meant it. I've got to break down the walls around her heart before we can become intimate. I don't want her to regret anything, especially not me. It's going to be hard as hell but will be more than worth the wait. She is worth everything, and I want to give her everything that she deserves.

Last night, she opened up a lot, which has given me more insight into what's going on in that beautiful head of hers. I now know, to an extent, how she has been hurt in the past. My mind immediately goes to her ex who was following her the other night. I need to know his story. I must keep my girl safe, and she isn't going to be with him lurking around. I could see the crazy in his eyes. Maybe he was on drugs and not just crazy, but I don't want him anywhere near her. That thought makes me see red and has my fist clenching at my side.

Looking back down at my sleeping goddess, I notice her black hair splayed across the pillows. I can't help but stare at this beautiful woman in my bed. She has very quickly become everything to me. I want to wake up every day with her in my bed or our bed. After telling me about her father last night, I felt our relationship shift into a deeper connection. She has never told anyone about that, and it makes my heart swell with pride. She trusts me enough with those memories. I have fallen so hard for Lizzie. I wish I could stay cuddled up with her all day, but I have to get up and get the day started. I look out of the windows of my room and see the sun hasn't come up yet. I give Lizzie a kiss on the cheek and slide out of bed. I don't want to wake her this early, so I leave her to get more rest.

I pull on my workout clothes and head to my gym. After I put in my ear pods, I jump on the treadmill. I don't even hear the music; my thoughts are back on my girl sleeping in my apartment. I wish this was our apartment. I don't ever want to be away from her. I want her here when I go to work and when I get home. Her presence is what I have been missing, and I don't want to know what it feels like when she leaves today. I wish I could talk to my father right now. I wish he could give me advice. I know Lizzie is the one for me. The amount of love coursing through my bones tells me she is my soulmate. However, I don't want to move at a pace that isn't comfortable for her. If it were up to me, I would have movers at her apartment today. I want to protect and care for her for the rest of our lives. Thinking of protection for Lizzie, I kick my machine up a notch to work off the extra anxiety. I don't want him anywhere near her. I don't even want her to work at the restaurant. She doesn't need to, especially if she comes and lives with me. I could give her everything she ever needs. Knowing she is used to being on her own and values her independence, I doubt she'll allow me to care for her financially. That's why I wish I could talk to my father; he could advise me as to what do. I just need to bring it up to her. I told her I would be honest with her from day one, so that means with what I'm thinking, as well.

My thoughts wander back to Lizzie moving in with me and my heartbeat accelerates. That's such a huge step, but ironically, it doesn't faze me at all. I feel completely comfortable with Lizzie. I can be myself around her, not my CEO persona that I have to display most of the time. I can relax and just be me. I need that balance in my life, and I finally found it in the form of a beautiful, curvy, and brilliant, brown-eyed girl. Or rather woman. A smile crosses my lips when I think of that song, I'm going to add that to my workout playlist. *Brown Eyed Girl* by Van Morrison is a catchy tune, even if it's about a guy reminiscing about his lost love. Although that's not our situation, I can appreciate the love he has for her and yearn for the adventures he sings about.

Glancing down at my watch, I see I've reached my cardio workout goal. I slow the pace to a cool down and wipe my face with a towel. Once off the machine, I transition to weightlifting. Grunting through the various sets, I finally place the bar on the bench press rack. I sit up, wiping my face and neck, then chug from my water jug. I sit for a moment longer as my heart rate adjusts to its normal pace.

I finish in the gym, grab a fresh towel on the way out, and walk up the stairs toward my bedroom. When I walk in, I see the bed is empty, and my heart starts pounding in my chest until I hear the shower going. I take a deep breath and smile that she's comfortable enough to shower here. I can hear her singing some pop song along with the music on her phone. Walking over, I knock at the door. I crack it a little and say, "Good morning, beautiful. I hope I didn't wake you."

"You didn't. I needed to get up and run some errands before going to the bookstore," she replies.

"Do you need anything in there? There are extra towels in the cabinet and a robe if you need it."

"Thank you, that would be great. I'll be out in a minute."

I shut the door and head to the kitchen to make my morning shake. My back is to her when she walks into the room a few minutes later. I turn around and look at this stunning angel in front of me. Her raven hair is damp, running down her back. Her face is void of all makeup, but she's still beautiful. Wearing the navy robe that I keep in the bathroom, I notice it's too large for her, which makes me chuckle. I'll have to get a smaller one for her. I make a mental note to tell my assistant today.

"You have never looked more beautiful," I tell her. I hear a little scoff come from her lips, and it only makes me want to prove my point even more. "I would hug you, but I'm all sweaty; you would need another shower," I say, wagging my eyebrows at her so she knows what I mean. She laughs and gives me a small shove.

"I'll just kiss you then," she replies as she leans up on her toes to reach my lips. Hers are so soft and plump that I want to kiss and nibble on them all day. She pulls away and rests back on her feet.

"So, is there coffee?" she asks expectantly. I grimace because I haven't become accustomed to her need for coffee first thing in the morning. She isn't quite a morning person, the way I am.

"I can get Thomas to go get you some. It will only take a few minutes. I suppose I need to get a coffee machine. I normally get it on the way to work or while I'm there." She looks at me with horror in her eyes.

"How can you not have a coffee machine? You literally have every other appliance in this place! It's like the most important fixture in the kitchen. I could argue it's more important than a stove!" she exclaims.

I tilt my head back and belly laugh. This woman is something else. I love her silly, whimsical side. However, I think she's pretty serious right now, though, if her facial expression indicates anything. In fact, I'd say I pissed her off. I definitely need to add that to today's shopping list. I hold my hands up in defense.

"Sorry, baby, I know coffee is your lifeline in the morning. I should have known better," I say, still chuckling a bit, but I scoot out of punching range.

"You should have. I don't know anyone that doesn't have a coffee machine. That's simply crazy. I guess I'll pick up a cup or three while I'm out." She smiles, adding, "You're going to need to fix this situation." As she walks away, she mumbles, "I can't believe my boyfriend doesn't have a coffee maker!" If I wasn't already smiling, I would be now. That's the first time she's called me her boyfriend, and I would be lying if I said I didn't love it.

I run up behind her as she's walking back to the bedroom. I scoop her up, spinning her around, until she starts squealing and laughing. I put her down and smash my mouth down on hers. I need her lips on me like I need another breath. I can't get enough. Once we pull away, she's panting and looking at me with awe in her eyes.

"What was that for?" she asks breathlessly, smiling while a blush breaks out over her cheeks.

"I just couldn't help myself. I wanted to get you riled up. I needed to taste you again, anyway," I croon, as I tuck her hair behind her ear. "Plus, I heard what you called me under your breath, and I had to get you in my arms," I whisper into her ear, as I suck her lobe into my mouth.

She gives me a radiant smile and declares, "Go shower, Miles! You're soaked, and honestly, don't smell that great." She giggles.

I gasp and hold a hand to my chest in mock horror. Smiling, I suggest, "You sure you don't want to join me?"

Arousal flickers in her eyes for a moment, before she straightens up and replies, "You're going to be late for work, and I've got to get dressed and head out." I smirk, giving her a wink and walk into the bathroom to shower.

"Suit yourself," I return, before closing the door behind me. I hear her groan, which makes my cock jump at the sound. I need her badly. *Soon. Very soon.*

CHAPTER 19

Elizabeth

I text Sarah as soon as I leave Miles' apartment and ask her to meet me for coffee. She quickly responds back that she's on her way. I sigh in relief because I need some girl talk ASAP. Like *serious* girl talk. Maybe I'm freaking out over nothing, but I feel like things with Miles are going too fast. I guess the whole interaction this morning seemed so domesticated. It felt like we've been together for months, not just a mere week; and it scares the shit out of me. Knowing Sarah will be able to talk me through this gives me comfort. If anyone can talk me off the ledge, it will be her.

Putting my phone away, I amble to the coffee shop where we plan to meet. I glance around but don't see her yet, so I head to the counter and order our drinks. As I grab the last available table, I sling my bag on the empty seat, so no one will come grab it. The nerves coursing through my body right now could energize me enough to run a marathon. Coffee probably isn't the best thing to drink. I already feel like I could have a heart attack, with how fast my heart is racing. I'm not even sure where this anxiety came from. Everything was great this morning, waking up in Miles' bed. I could still smell where he had been lying when I woke up to his empty bed. His cologne sent shivers up my spine as I rolled over onto his pillow, before getting up and taking a shower.

How could I have let myself fall for someone so quickly?

Am I out of my mind?

I just swore off men two weeks ago and now, here I am spilling my most inner insecurities to a man I've known such a short time. I can feel myself begin to spiral when I hear the barista call "Jane." I look around to see if anyone else is going up to the counter. When no one moves, I know it's my order. *Yes, I know that I'm crazy to use different names.* Maybe I'm all around crazy since I seem to be dishing my heart out to an almost stranger. No, he's not a stranger. Ironically, he's never seemed like a stranger. My thoughts have completely overtaken me by the time Sarah plops down in front of me.

"What's wrong?" she asks, as she studies my face and my foot bouncing at an unnatural pace. "First, before you even start talking, slow down and take a deep breath. That's the only way we are going to get through this. Did you get decaf? I don't think you need anything else," she remarks, gesturing to my body language.

I can't help but smile; I love this woman. I shake my head no because, obviously, I didn't think about decaf until after the fact. I take some deep breaths to calm my racing thoughts and put some sort of order to them. They don't need to come out as a jumbled mess when I decide to speak. I concentrate on the air going in then out through my mouth. Over and over. Sarah takes a sip of her coffee, pulls off her jacket, and lays it on the back of her chair.

"Okay," I begin, with a bit of a tremble in my voice that I know she hears. "I told Miles about my dad last night. Like, I told him everything. Everything that no one knows except you. It just spilled out of my mouth like vomit," I blurt because I really don't know any other way to say what I did. I keep that part of me locked away in a box, guarded with metal locks. My mother doesn't even know the extent of my pain. Only Sarah. She was there for me when I needed her, and she didn't leave me like my father did. She stayed and helped me put my life back together.

"Okay, so you opened up to him. Did he not take it well or something? You are going to have to walk me through this. I know you don't trust anyone with that part of yourself, but I can see how you feel about him. It's natural to share your pasts with each other," she expounds, then reaches over, putting her hand on mine. I didn't realize I was drumming it against the table. I instantly feel her calmness wash over me.

Unshed tears prick at my eyes as I look at my best friend. "No, he took it extremely well. He comforted me and asked if that's why I don't trust easily. It's like he was looking into my soul. All I could do is nod, and he pulled me in close to his chest. It was actually the most amazing reaction I think I could have gotten," I say breathlessly. "He leaned back and pulled my chin up, so I could look at him, and he said that he will never hurt or cheat on me. Miles mentioned that he truly believes I am meant for him. That I'm his endgame, and he isn't going to let me get away," I reveal, summing up everything.

Sarah squeezes my hand, and I look up to see a huge smile on her face. "I knew I liked that man. He's good for you, Lizzie. Listen to me. We've both had our share of terrible boyfriends, but I honestly think he's the one for you. I know it's so soon, and that's why you are scared, honey; but I think you will regret it if you walk away from this," she says gently. I know she's right about regretting it, but I'm also terrified he'll hurt me more than anyone ever has in my life.

"And this morning, we were acting all couple-y, like we have been living together. He got up to work out, leaving me to sleep. Then I woke up, took a shower, and put on *his* robe!" I exclaim, but all Sarah does is smile wider. *She isn't understanding the problem.* "Sarah, it's only been a little over a week. I can't be in this deep already. I'm scared to death that he is going to smash my heart, worse than it ever has been. I won't recover; I know I won't. I need help. I am freaking out! Please tell me what to do," I plead.

Sarah takes a deep breath, sits up in her chair, and squares her shoulders, like she is going into battle. This slightly frightens me since I don't know where she is going to take this conversation.

"Lizzie, you had a shit of a childhood after your father left. You can't keep living in the past. I know it haunts you. I wish I could have kicked your father's ass." She chuckles, but continues, "Just because you were dealt a bad hand, does not determine the outcome of the rest of your life. Lizzie, you are a beautiful soul. You love others. You're compassionate and giving. You are insanely creative. You're hilarious and fun to be around. It's time for someone else to see what I see. Not all men are like your father, in fact, most aren't. And most men aren't like the dirtbags you have dated. Those were all unfortunate relationships. Even though the relationships crashed and burned, you learned from them. You know what qualities are most important to you in a partner now. I haven't met my soulmate, but that doesn't mean I don't believe he's out there. I will meet him when the time is right. Now is your time, Lizzie. You read all those smutty romance novels. You escape into them. It's time you believe that kind of love is real." Sarah squeezes my hand again, and I'm left speechless. I didn't think she believed in soulmates. I didn't believe in them.

I take a napkin and wipe my tear-stained cheeks. "Thank you for saying all of that. I didn't know you believed in everything you just said. I guess I'm just scared. Well, I know I am. My own father left me. My own blood left me, and that betrayal is always in the back of my mind. I feel like if my father didn't love me enough, then how can anyone else. I know I have these deep-rooted issues; I've just got to get passed them," I murmur quietly.

She looks at me for a second and says, "You know, I will always be here for you. *Always.* You are my person, Lizzie.

We are soul sisters. *Forever.* Don't forget that." She pauses and steadily looks at me, but with a different expression than one I've ever seen before. "I want you to think about what I'm about to say without freaking out on me, okay?" she asks, quirking her eyebrow.

I nod even though I feel a bit uneasy about what she might say. "I think when you go home for Christmas, you should stop by and see your dad." She holds up her hands to stop me from interrupting her, "This isn't for your dad, honey; it's' for you. You should take this opportunity to get your life back from him. You are giving him too much power over your life. The fears he has instilled in you are running the show. He lives halfway across the country, yet he is still occupying your mind. His abuse is living rent free. You need to face him. I think even telling him your side of the story or how you felt through it all, would begin to heal you. Hell, write him a letter. You are best at putting your soul down on pages. Write him, Lizzie, tell him what he did to you. Take away his power over you. I promise you'll feel lighter without carrying around this shit on your shoulders every day. I'm not saying to forgive him. That's up to you. But you deserve to be happy, and I think this is the first step in that direction. Otherwise, how will you be able to ever fully give yourself to Miles and believe the things he tells you?"

I sit in stunned silence. I don't know whether I should be mad that she thinks I need to talk to that man or feel hopeful that she's right. The table is quiet for a few moments, as I muster the strength to respond.

"I'll think about it, Sarah. I know that was hard for you to tell me, but I'm thankful that I have a friend that will give it to me straight, the way you do. I don't want to be weighed down any longer, but I just don't know how to go about this. I have been running for years. That's why we are in New York. I'm a runner. I always have been, but you're right. Nothing can happen with Miles if I don't get my head on straight." We both stand up and hug each other. Sarah has my back. That's all I need to remember. I'm not alone in this.

She pulls back, wiggling her eyebrows at me. I can't help but laugh because I know what's coming. "So, now that that's out of the way, I'm going to need some details on Mr. Tall, Dark, and Sexy," she announces with a huge grin. We pull our jackets on, grab our coffees, and walk toward the door. Once we get outside, I take a deep breath, feeling like everything will be okay. I look over at her and see she's waiting on all the details. As we walk down the street, I tell her all about my dream man, Miles Knight.

"Oh, before I forget to bring it up again, is Miles taking you out for your birthday this weekend?" she questions as we come to a stop before crossing the street.

"No, he has some charity gala that night. I also told him that I don't celebrate it unless you make me." I let out a laugh, making me feel lighter than I have all morning.

"Yeah, I'm not listening to that crap this year. We are celebrating. I'll come up with something perfect for you!" she exclaims as she grabs my hand and leads me across the street.

"Sarah! I'm staying home! You can't convince me otherwise. Just because you have in the past does not mean it will happen this year. In fact, I'm beginning to become immune to your begging. So, that's that!" I declare, matter-of-factly, even though I don't believe a word I'm saying. She doesn't either. I know she'll drag me somewhere, and I'll end up having a fun time. That's how great of a best friend she is. She knows just what I need, even when I don't.

"Whatever, babe. You keep telling yourself that while we go in here and find something fun to buy," she replies, pulling me into one of our favorite thrift shops in the city.

CHAPTER 20

Elizabeth

Sarah convinces me to call out of work so we can spend the entire day together—something I think we both need. We shop and run errands all day, and it's just what the doctor ordered. We find some fun 1950s cocktail dresses in a thrift shop close to our apartment, and I just had to get them. I love dressing up in clothing from different eras. Plus, I got things accomplished that have been on my to-do list forever! When we finally get into the apartment, I drop the bags in my room and come out, falling on the couch. Wow, I'm exhausted. After all the emotional talking, and then walking. Man, it was a workout. Sarah can shop 'til she drops. I think we'd still be out there if the weather had permitted, but thankfully, I was saved by the snow. We cut the shopping trip short. It's the first snow of the season, and it is beautiful as I watch it silently falling beyond our floor-to-ceiling windows.

I've gotten to talk to Miles a few times today. He texted a couple of times to see how my day was going and to let me know he's thinking about me, which made me smile like a Cheshire cat. Sarah looked at me and laughed. She knew exactly who I was talking to, which made me blush, something that seems to be happening a lot lately when it comes to him. He called back later while we were in another store, but it was too loud with the overhead music and all the other customers.

Sarah comes from the kitchen with two glasses of wine

in her hands. I take one of the glasses. "Thanks girl, you read my mind."

She just laughs. "After the day we've had, wine is definitely in order. So, should we order something for dinner?" she asks, while she ruffles through our collected stack of take-out menus.

"Yes! I'm starving. You shopped me to death, and now food is imperative, unless you want drunk, hangry Lizzie to come out," I warn, pointing my finger at her.

"Oh, anything but that!" she exclaims, holding her hands up. We both burst out laughing. I don't even think we're laughing at my silly joke anymore. We are just deliriously tired and hungry. Tears stream down my cheeks we laugh so hard.

"Italian?" she queries.

"No, that's what I had last night. Miles cooked for me, by the way. On top of everything, the man can cook," I shake my head in disbelief. Is there anything he doesn't do perfectly?

"Wow, okay. At least you didn't have to and chance the possibility of poisoning the poor man," she quipped, lifting her eyebrow at me to argue with her. I don't do so, but I do throw a pillow at her head, and we start the laughing fit all over again.

After what seems like an eternity, our Chinese food finally gets delivered, and it takes us no time to devour it. Watching some sitcom on TV, drinking wine, and laughing, we both enjoy our much-needed girls' night.

Before I realize it, it's eleven, and I forgot to call Miles. I look for my phone, which somehow is squished between the couch cushions. When I try to turn it on, I see that it's dead. Dread fills my mind. I don't know how long it's been dead. I get up quickly, run to my room, plug it in, and plop down on my bed. It takes a few minutes to charge enough to turn on, and when it does, notification after notification chimes out. I pick up my phone and see all the missed calls and messages. Not all of them are from Miles, which relieves me a bit, until I open the ones from him.

Miles: Hey, beautiful. Are you still out shopping in this storm? Call me.

Miles: Lizzie, I tried calling you, and it went straight to voicemail. I'm just leaving the office; it's 9:30. Please give me a call and let me know that you're okay.

Miles: Lizzie, I'm getting a little worried. If I don't hear from you soon, I'm going to check on you at your apartment.

The last message was sent thirty minutes ago. I quickly pull up his contact information and hit call. It takes a few minutes for it to ring. I pull the phone closer to my ear so I can hear better. It's faintly ringing. Just then a loud knock comes from the front door. Startled, I jump at the sound, but then I hear Miles' voice calling my name, "Lizzie, are you in there?" His voice sounds strained and angry. I run to the door, pulling it open quickly. My heart is beating out of my chest. This situation escalated fast, but I suppose I'm the one to blame since I didn't let him know I was home.

When the door opens, I suck in a deep breath as I see the man in front of me. He's in his suit still, but he's shrugged off his jacket at some point and rolled up his sleeves. His hair is disheveled like he's been running his hands through it or running from the parking lot. Soaking wet from the snow and rain, he looks at me in bewilderment.

"Miles, I—," Without letting me finish, he wraps his arms around me as tightly as I can stand. We are still in the doorway; he is holding me like he'd lost me, and I was finally found.

"Miles, I'm so sorry," I whisper. "I was hanging out with Sarah, and I didn't realize my phone had died. I lost track of time. I didn't mean to make you worry," I apologize, as I pull back to look at his face. He still hasn't spoken a word to me, and my heart is still drumming in my chest. He lets go of me, closes the door behind him, and then turns back to face me.

"What the hell?" Sarah exclaims, when she slides into view and sees Miles. Obviously sensing we need to talk, she just says, "Nice to see you again, Miles. Sorry, we lost track of time. We were having a much-needed girl's night. I'll see you all later." Then she quickly walks to her room, shutting the door quietly.

I look back at Miles, willing him to say something. *Anything.*

"Miles? Please say something," I plead, pulling him toward me. He looks down at me for a moment before he speaks. I can see the turbulence, in his normally beautiful blue eyes. He rests his forehead against mine and lets out a deep breath.

"Lizzie, you have no idea how worried I've been about you. I kept trying to reach you but couldn't. I didn't know if you were still out, or if something happened to you. I've never felt so helpless in all my life. Please don't do that to me again. I thought you could have been hurt, or maybe had run into that stupid ex of yours. There were just so many things running through my head" he expresses, with a solemn voice. I'm momentarily speechless. I didn't think he would react like this. Seeing the desperation in his eyes, I can truly feel the affection he has for me. The love is bleeding out for me to see. In that moment, I believe everything he's said about us belonging to each other, and that we're meant to be together.

A few tears slide down my cheeks because I have put this man through so much tonight. Even done unknowingly, I feel terrible. I've never had someone worry like this about me, other than my parents and Sarah.

"I'm sorry," I murmur, again. I don't know what to say or do that can make this right. He's soaking wet and freezing cold. So am I, from where he's been holding me. I pull back from his embrace and take his hand, leading him through the apartment to my room.

"Let me get us some towels." I leave him, going to the bathroom to fetch several towels. When I return, he's standing in the same spot. Leaning up on my toes, I bring my lips to his.

Hanging on to the front of his shirt, pulling him closer to me, and kissing him with the affection my words haven't spoken. Miles grabs ahold of my hips and pulls me flush against his chest. I can feel his magnificent body through his drenched shirt. Suddenly, I am desperate to get him out of his shirt.

Pulling away, I begin unbuttoning his shirt. One at a time, while I look him in the eyes. When I get to the bottom, I lift the shirt from his pants. As I run my hands up his torso to his chest, he shivers and digs into my waist harder. He helps me yank the shirt from his shoulders, and I drop it to the floor. Grabbing the towel from the bed, I dry off his body the best I can while distracted by his touch. His once turbulent eyes have darkened with desire. I can't help but bite my bottom lip, as the sexual tension builds inside me. He groans when he sees my mouth, and I see his restraint snap. He pulls the towel from my hands, dropping it to the floor. The next second, I am up pressed against the wall. Miles holds me up while my legs wrap around him. I can feel the bulge in his pants, and I can't help myself. Rubbing against him, I wrap my arms around his neck to tug him closer. He brings his mouth down on mine and the kiss is deep and aggressive. He grasps my waist tighter, and I think he might leave marks. I'm too consumed with passion to care. I *want* him to mark me. I *need* him to. His tongue desperately tangles with mine, as I moan out his name. A growl releases from his throat, as he pulls back from me. Pushing some hair behind my ear, he speaks softly, "Lizzie," in my ear. "You make me so wild. I can't stop thinking of you when you aren't near." A shiver runs through me. He kisses down my neck, as goosebumps explode over my whole body.

I have never been this affected by a man in my whole life. The way he kisses and touches me, sets my body on fire. My body ignites being near him. The way he looks at me, like I'm the only one in the world he sees. I now know that this pull isn't a normal feeling. Sarah is right, saying she believes Miles is the one for me. I believe it, too. Knowing this doesn't make me less terrified, but at least I know where my feelings lie. They are buried deep in the man holding me so tightly.

Miles continues kissing and licking down my shoulder. Pulling my tank top strap down, he kisses and nibbles on my collarbone. The feeling has me throwing my head back, opening myself up for him. He continues across my chest and up the other side of my neck. He pulls back, cups my cheek, kisses my forehead, temple, nose, cheeks, and then my lips. It's a softer kiss than before, but just as passionate. He expresses his feelings, which his words don't at the moment. Breaking the kiss, he gazes deep into my eyes and searches mine as if trying to read my thoughts.

"Lizzie," he rasps, as he strokes his thumb over my cheek. "Do you feel this connection between us? Do you feel like I do?" he queries, imploringly. Resting my hand on his chest, I can feel his racing heart awaiting my answer.

I look up at him and nod. "Yes, Miles. I feel it all. I've never felt this before in my life," I admit. The smile that spreads across his face, makes my breath catch. The sight of this beautiful man in front of me is hypnotizing. I lean into him, bringing his lips back down to mine. I wrap my arms tightly around him, hoping that I never have to let go.

My body begins to shiver, and I realize I've become just as wet as he is. Having been pressed up against his damp clothes, my pajamas cling to my skin. My back is up against a cold glass door, which leads to a little porch attached to my room, giving it direct contact with the elements outside.

"Are you cold, baby?" Miles asks as he lowers me to my feet. I nod, as my legs wobble a bit before finding my balance. His hands never leave my sides, holding me up until he's sure I'm stable. He leans down and kisses my forehead.

"I can't wait any longer, baby. I *need* you. I need to be inside you. Please tell me you're ready. I don't want to rush you into anything," he assures as he ghosts kisses over my jaw and down my throat. He looks me in the eyes, asking for permission.

"Yes," I croon. "I need you, too." He grabs my tank top, slowly pulling it over my head. As his fingers skim across my flushed skin, he drops the shirt to the floor. His eyes travel down my exposed skin, then his hands run over my black lacy bra, thumbing my already hard nipples. A whimper escapes my lips at his touch. He grips my waist pulling me closer and sucking my nipples through my bra. The sensation of the lace and his hot mouth against me is driving me wild. I clench my thighs together, trying to quench the ache that's building. He kisses his way back up my chest, until his lips are on mine once more.

"Are you wet for me, baby? If I slide my hand between those gorgeous thighs, will you be soaked through your leggings?" he inquires softly as he licks a path back down my neck.

A whimper falls from my lips because I'm so turned on. I haven't had sex in months, and I know sex with Miles is going to be epic. His dirty mouth makes my eyes roll back in my head, at the sheer sexiness of it. "Yes," I manage to reply. "Yes, you make me so wet, Miles." After a loud groan, he lifts me in his arms and throws me onto my bed. I squeal and laugh as I bounce up from the bed. The laughter is soon quelled when I see the look in Miles' eyes. The unadulterated lust and passion I see in his addictive blue eyes is beyond anything I have ever seen. He leans over me, kissing my stomach lightly as he hooks his fingers into my leggings and panties. Ever so slowly, he slides them down my legs, perusing my body as he goes. I lean up, unclasping my bra and letting it fall to the bed. Naked and exposed before him has me feeling self-conscious, until I see the look in his eyes.

"You are perfection, Lizzie. The sexiest woman I have ever seen. Damnit, you're fucking stunning," he declares.

A smile crosses my lips as I feel my body blush under his gaze. and the need to see him naked is strong. Sitting up, I crawl to the edge of the bed. Dragging my fingers down his perfectly sculpted chest, I make my way further down until I reach his belt. I glance up to see his bright blue eyes have darkened to almost black. I grasp his cock, feeling the huge evidence of his arousal and suddenly, I can't get his pants off fast enough. I pull the belt from the loops in one swift motion, dropping it to the floor. Miles is already unbuttoning his pants and pulling them down. His erection springs free, slapping his abdominal muscles as it dances between us. Shucking off his shoes, he steps out of his pants. I take a moment to let my gaze roam over this magnificent specimen in front of me. Seriously, this man should be a model. I hmm my approval, while biting my bottom lip. I hear a curse fall from his mouth as I scoot back on the bed and look up at his face.

"Lizzie, if you keep looking at me like that, this is going to be over a lot sooner than I want it to be. Lay back, baby. Let me see that wet pussy. Let me see what I do to you. You can already see what you do to me," he says, stroking his cock, while putting a knee on the bed. I lay back breathlessly, watching in rapture as he caresses himself.

"Fuck, you are so wet," he growls as he grabs hold of my

knees, spreading them wider. There is a hunger in his eyes, as he rubs his fingers through my wet lips. My back arches off the bed from the way he is working his fingers between my thighs. My body begins to shake, as he continues working my clit back and forth. His fingers alternate between rubbing my clit and thrusting inside me. I feel the pleasure building as more wetness gushes out. Miles groans at the sight and lowers himself on the bed, with his face between my legs. "I'm going to taste this pussy. I want these juices all over my face, baby," he rumbles as he locks eyes with me. His tongue darts out of his mouth and through my folds. I cry out on contact and buck my hips closer to his face. He presses down on my hips, keeping me in place. Miles takes teasing to a new level as he sucks my clit, until I'm squirming under the pressure. Just when I feel the heat pooling in my lower belly, he backs off and presses kisses up my inner thigh. When he mirrors the ministrations on the other leg, I start to beg, "Miles, please, I need mor—" But he cuts me off by thrusting two fingers deep inside of me. He flicks his tongue back and forth along my slit, and then alternates to sucking. As if he knows exactly what my body needs; he licks, sucks, flicks, and fingers my pussy in the most tantalizing rhythm that my whole-body flushes as the pressure builds up rapidly. I open my eyes and see his gaze searing into mine. An orgasm ricochets through my body, unlike any I have ever experienced. Every nerve in my body is ignited. I grip his hair as I gush all over his face. "Miles! Miles! Fuck, yes!" I gasp as the air leaves my lungs. I collapse limply back onto the bed. Miles continues lazily licking and sucking, until I'm a quivering mess.

"Lizzie, you are my new favorite meal. I won't ever get enough of that. Fuck, you are so sweet," he swears as he sits up licking his lips. I can see my arousal smeared all over his lips and chin, and the sight makes me want him even more. His admission makes me whimper in response. I have never in my life been talked to like this, and it's hotter than I could have imagined. I never knew dirty talk could be so sexy, but hot damn, Miles takes it to a new level.

He slowly crawls up my body, nipping and kissing a path along the way. Finally, he brings his mouth to mine in a scorching kiss. As my own taste invades my mouth, I moan, trying to pull his body closer to mine. Leaning against one arm, he trails his hand over my body in slow, seductive strokes, like he is trying to memorize every part of me. His cologne drifts through my senses, making me drunk on lust. He pulls his lips from mine as he stares deep into my eyes. He pushes the hair from my face and tucks it behind my ear. "I need to be inside you, sweetheart." He trails kisses up and down the column of my neck and behind my ear. A sob slips past my lips, as I nod in response.

"Yes, please. I need you, Miles." He moves off me and grabs his pants. He pulls out a condom and tosses it on the bed beside me. In that moment, I know that I don't want anything between us. He climbs back on the bed, and I grab his face in my hands because I need to see the look in his eyes when I say this. "I-I'm clean, Miles and I'm on birth control." He groans and puts his head on my shoulder. I think I've said the wrong thing until he looks back up at me.

Running his thumb over my cheek, he asks, "Are you sure, Lizzie? I would love to be inside you with nothing between us. I'm clean as well. I've never gone bare before, baby. You are the only one I have ever desired to do this with."

"I never have either, I want you," I admit.

"Fuck, Lizzie, you are going to be the death of me." Miles places another kiss to my lips as he reaches down and places himself at my entrance. He pushes in gently and I can feel my walls stretching to accommodate him. I'm not a virgin but fuck, this feels like my first time. He is pushing in and out, slowly inching his way in. I frown at the slight pain.

"Am I hurting you? You're so damn tight, baby," he moans.

"You're just so big. I'm okay." He pushes my knees up to my chest, opening me up wider for him. He uses this position to thrust himself completely in one plunge. The sudden force takes my breath away, making me gasp. He holds still, letting my body adjust to him. He leans down and kisses me, then looks back up at me.

"Are you okay? Please tell me I can move." I nod, unable to form the words. He starts to thrust in and out. Slowly at first, then harder and faster, each shove quicker than the last. I can feel every inch of him, and I have never felt so full in my life. With each stride, my pleasure begins to build higher and higher, tempting me with falling over the edge at any moment. He cups my breasts and thumbs over my nipples, bringing my body right to the brink of another orgasm. "Open your eyes. I want to see you as you come. Come for me, baby." He tweaks my nipples, and the pain drives me headfirst into another orgasm. The pleasure is so intense, it is almost too much to handle.

"Miles, yes, I'm coming! Miles!" I scream. He seals his lips over mine to silence me with his tongue. Wave after wave of pleasure washes over me, as he continues hitting all the right spots inside my core.

"Good girl. You are so responsive to me." He grins. "Fuck, your tight little pussy is milking me. I'm going to come. I'm going to fill you up," he murmurs in my ear. The words make me clench tighter around him. "You like hearing that don't you? You like being my good girl? I can feel how much you like it." He groans as I feel hot ropes of his come coating my walls. Jet after jet fill me up, until I can feel our combined juices spilling down my ass. It's the most erotic sensation I've ever had. As his motions slow, he leans his elbows on either side of my head. He takes his time kissing along my jaw, from one side to the other, then kisses up my cheeks to my forehead. Then he presses his forehead to mine and stares into my eyes. "You're mine, Lizzie. *Mine*."

"Yes, I'm yours." I nod, overcome with emotions. I've never felt like this before. He's more than anything I could have ever imagined.

"That means more to me than you know because I am all yours." A tear escapes my eye, as his words sink into my mind. *He's mine*. He's everything I have ever wanted, and he's all mine. Miles uses his thumb to swipe the tear away and kisses the wet spot on my cheek. "All yours, Lizzie. All yours," he whispers against my ear.

As he pulls out, he leans up to see his come dripping out of me. "Fuck, that's hot. Seeing my seed deep inside of you, claiming you," he groans, then gets off the bed and wraps one of the towels I got earlier around his waist. He opens my door, walking out but before I can ask what he's doing, he is back with a wet washcloth. Leaning on the bed and opening my legs, he cleans up our mess. I'm momentarily speechless because I have never been cared for like this. My cheeks flush with the warmth I feel in my chest for this man.

Once he's satisfied, he throws the towel and cloth into my hamper, then crawls back into bed. He pulls the covers down and helps me get under them as well. Miles pulls my body flush against his and brings the blankets up to cover our bodies. I am laying on my side with my head in the nook of his shoulder, my arm draped over his chest. He lays his hand on top of mine while his other is rubbing my back. I let out a sigh of contentment, and a yawn escapes my lips. Miles chuckles. "Will you stay with me tonight?" I question.

He cups my cheek and whispers, "There is no place I would rather be." Then he leans down and pulls another sweet kiss from my lips.

"Go to sleep, sweetheart. It's late."

"Goodnight," I say, wrapping my arm around him tighter, afraid he might vanish into the night. Closing my eyes, I smile to myself knowing Miles will be here in the morning. That's the last thing I think of as I drift off to sleep.

CHAPTER 21

Miles

I awaken to the sound of knocking on Lizzie's apartment door. I run my hand over my face and glance at my watch. *Shit.* That'll be Thomas at the door. I sent him a message last night, letting him know the situation and that I would be needing a clean suit today. He has the code to my penthouse and said it wasn't a problem. I figured I'd be awake by now. Normally, I am, that's for sure, but when Lizzie is asleep next to me, I sleep better than ever before. She comforts me in ways almost impossible to comprehend. I take a moment to look down at the sleeping angel in my arms, and my heart wants to burst from my chest. God, I am a lucky bastard to have her. I hear my phone vibrating and know it is Thomas telling me to get my ass up. I chuckle softly to myself to keep from waking Lizzie. Sliding out of the bed, I pull the blanket up around her neck and look around for last night's clothes. When I pick them up, I remember how drenched they got from the snow and rain. Fuck, I can't answer the door naked. Thomas has obviously seen some things in his time with me, but he doesn't need to see that, and neither does Lizzie's roommate, Sarah. I glance around and see a robe hanging on the back of the door. Rushing over, I pull it on the best I can and tie the straps. It doesn't take a mirror to know this thing barely covers my ass. One wrong move in any direction and something is going to be showing. I scrub my hand over my face knowing I have no other options. A sigh slips from me as I pull open Lizzie's bedroom door. The cool morning air comes rushing in and bites my sensitive areas. I am taken back as I jump a bit at the sudden temperature change.

Shuffling to the door, I try to hold the front and the back of the robe in place. I look through the peep hole to make sure it is, in fact, Thomas; I don't want to give anyone else a show. As I unlock the door and open it, I see Thomas' expression change to horror as he eyes me up and down.

"Well, this is definitely a different look for you, sir. Purple looks good on you." He chuckles as he hands me my suit.

"Laugh all you want. There wasn't anything else. That's why you are here. Thank you for this, by the way. You're a life saver," I state, gesturing to the clothes. I hang them beside the door and turn back to him.

"Of course, sir. Here are your coffees. Will you need a ride to work this morning, or will you be taking your car?

"I'll take my car today, so I can spend a bit of time with Lizzie before I head into the office. Thank you for grabbing these coffees, as well. She will be thrilled."

"Not a problem, sir. It's good to see you like this, if I may say so."

"Like what, Thomas?"

"Happy. Genuinely happy. She must be pretty special."

"She's the one," I confess.

"Well then, don't let her get away. I've never seen you like this, and I've known you most of your life."

"I have no intention of letting her go anywhere. Thank you, Thomas, for all that you do for me." He pats me on the back before turning on his heels and heading toward the stairs. I close the door and lock it. I grab my suit and the coffees, then make my way back to Lizzie's room.

Hanging the suit behind her door, I place her coffee on the nightstand. I take a large gulp of mine and sit on the edge of the bed. As I stare at this perfect creature bundled in covers, she shifts a bit before her eyes flutter open. My breath catches in my throat at the sight of her striking brown eyes. A lazy smile ghosts her lips as she looks up at me. "Miles," she whispers. Putting my coffee down next to hers, I lean over and kiss her soft, pouty lips. I wrap my hand in the back of her hair and clench to pull her closer to me. She moans and the sound sends a jolt straight to my cock. All I can think about is sinking back in between her legs. I pull back and place a small kiss on her forehead. She closes her eyes and smiles.

"Thomas brought you a coffee, sleepyhead," I remark, as I brush the hair out of her face. Her eyes pop open immediately with a shocked expression.

"Wait, what? Also, are you wearing my robe?" She covers her mouth to muffle the laugh.

"Well, I couldn't very well walk out there naked. What if Sarah came out of her room? Also, Thomas would not have been pleased either. Although, he did mention that purple is a good color on me. Maybe I should keep this robe. What do you think?" Standing up, I do a little twirl. She lets her hand fall and gives me a full belly laugh at my shenanigans. Her laugh sends a ping to my heart, and I find that I want to keep making her laugh. I want to always be the reason for her laughter.

"Miles, I can't believe you answered the door like that!" She covers her eyes. "Poor Thomas. He is probably scarred for life." She's laughing with tears in her eyes now. She sighs and looks over to her nightstand where she sees the cup from Raven's Brew. Lizzie bolts upright, causing the blanket to fall. Which exposes her breasts to me, making my mouth water to take one in. She quickly covers herself as her cheeks redden.

"Sorry, I forgot I wasn't wearing anything." Looking down, her fingers fidget with the bedspread.

I grasp her hands to still them. "Lizzie, look at me." It takes a moment for her eyes to find mine. I see the uncertainty there and can't stand it. It concerns me that she could be embarrassed in front of me, especially after last night. "Lizzie, you never have to apologize to me. There isn't anything to be sorry for. I love your body. I thought I made that perfectly clear last night, but if not, let me tell you this. You are the most stunning and captivating woman I have ever seen in my life. Whether you are naked or have twenty layers. Do you understand me? Never hide from me." Pulling her chin up, I express sincerity in my eyes. She averts hers for a moment, then she looks at me and nods. I kiss the tip of her nose and hand her the cup of coffee. She takes a sip and closes her eyes, as the flavor floods her mouth. I knew my girl would enjoy having her special coffee in bed today.

"Thomas brought me a suit for work and I had him stop to get coffees as well." She moans as she takes another sip.

"Thank you so much. You spoil me."

"Always," I say kissing her forehead. "I need a quick shower. You stay in bed and drink your coffee. I'll be right out." Getting up, I grab my suit and head to the bathroom. Before leaving the room, I hear her laughing again. I cover my ass with my hand as her laugh grows louder.

After showering, I put on my dress pants and undershirt. I head back to the bedroom with the rest of my clothes and enter to see Lizzie making the bed. She is wearing some sexy black yoga pants that hug her curves perfectly. Her long hair sways over her t-shirt that hangs off one shoulder. Across the front reads, "Books are cheaper than therapy." The sight brings a smile to my face. I love that we share the same passion for books. She walks over from the bed with a smile on her face, and my heart squeezes at the beautiful sight. She is absolutely stunning. Unquestionably gorgeous and totally mine. I kiss the top of her head as she wraps her arms around me.

"Have a good shower? Sorry it's so small, compared to yours at least."

"What did I tell you about apologizing to me? Sounds like someone needs a reminder." I pick her up quickly and toss her onto her bed. She squeals and tries to get away, but gripping her legs, I hold her still. I lay down on top of her and bring my mouth to hers, taking in a deep kiss. I taste the sweet coffee and something else that is entirely Lizzie. I growl as she hooks her legs behind my back and begins to rock into me.

I lean back and she's biting her lip, smiling. Damnit, this woman is going to be the death of me.

"I have to finish getting ready. I have a meeting to get to, and Sebastian will kill me if I'm late." She huffs and pulls her legs away. I instantly miss the feeling of her wrapped around me. I sit up and pull her into my lap.

She tilts her chin so she can look up at me. Her eyes enrapture me. She strokes her hand over my chest, and I can feel her heat wash over me. She looks like she is contemplating something. I don't want that; I want her to be able to talk to me about everything. Cupping her face in my hand, I smooth my thumb over her cheek. "What's going on in that beautiful head of yours?" I ask.

She looks stunned for a moment. "How did you know I was thinking of something?" she queries, still rubbing my chest.

"I just know by looking at you. What is it? You can talk to me about anything, Lizzie. I keep telling you that."

She takes a deep breath and stills her hand as she

speaks. "I was just thinking that if you didn't have plans for Christmas, you could come with me to Savannah. I know it's several weeks away, but I'm sure you have plans with your brother or friends. I remember your saying that your mom oftentimes travels to Italy. Anyways, it's your call if you want to come. I mean, it's Savannah, Georgia and definitely nothing like New York. I don't want you to be alone. It was just something that I thought of today. You can totally say no." She pauses for a moment and takes another breath. I smile at how cute she gets when she is nervous. I just want to kiss every inch of her. A kiss might be necessary to stop her from rambling on. She had me hooked the moment she asked me to come. She continues, "I mean, I guess it is presumptuous of me to think we will still be together by then, right? I mean a lot can happ—" I don't let her finish.

    I place both hands on either side of her face and capture her lips with mine. I pull back from her lips and trail my mouth down her neck, biting her earlobe. She lets out a soft gasp. I smile because I know that's one of her sweet spots. She moans, running her fingers through my damp hair. "Miles," she whines, breathlessly. With the slightest touch, I graze her side and move the hair out of her face as she bites the bottom of her lip. A groan comes from my chest at the sight of it. Kissing her forehead, I comment, "I had to do something to get you to stop rambling on. Of course, I want to go with you to Savannah. I'm not spending Christmas without you." Giving her another kiss, I lift her from my lap, so I can stand. I grab my button-down shirt from the hanger and put it on. She stands up and begins to button up my shirt.

"I wasn't rambling. I was just giving you a chance to say no and not feel bad." She pouts. I put my finger up to her mouth before she keeps going. She gives me a sassy look that makes me chuckle. This woman is something else. I can't get enough of her.

"As far as us not being together by then, we will be. You don't ever have to doubt us, Lizzie. Remember what I told you last night? I am yours." She nods with a smile, so I let my finger drop and pull her back against me. I love this woman. I want to scream it from the rooftops, although I want it to be special when I tell her. I kiss her temple and rub her back.

"I'm yours too, Miles." She reaches up on her tip toes and gives me a quick kiss before finishing my buttons. Handing me my tie, she steps back raking her eyes over me. "You are so sexy in a suit," she hums in approval. I give her a wink as she rolls her eyes and grabs her coffee before sitting back on her bed.

***

"Thank you for meeting with us today. We have picked up this new manuscript, and we need to go over marketing and distribution. I have a few mockups for the design and layout that you will see in a moment on the screen," Olivia says, as she switches on her presentation to the screen in front of us.

As usual, I'm sitting at the head of the conference table. Sebastian is on my left, leaning back in his chair and looking smug. He has been the one pushing this book. I, personally, don't think it's as great as everyone else, but I was out voted. I am still holding out on that one book that grips me and won't let go. I know it must be out there. I zone out while the presentation continues just thinking about finding the perfect author. I already work so late, going through the manuscripts, that my assistant drops on my desk. He filters through them, and then hands over the ones that he thinks will be marketable.

I glance back to Olivia, head of marketing, and she is pointing excitedly at the different slides she has created. The rest of the table is paying attention, while I'm just sitting here letting my mind wander. I really need to focus. I have to continue to build this company up. It's our family legacy, and I've got to keep up the momentum my father created before he passed away. I push the thoughts away and focus back on the meeting.

"Once we decide on the cover, I'll send it straight to our printing company. We need to get the pictures out along with the synopsis so we can present it as an upcoming novel. The author says she has an open schedule to work signings and readings that we'll set up with our PR team. Any questions?" she inquires once her presentation is complete. A few people around the table ask some questions, but most everything was covered already in the meeting. I know this will be a good selling book but it's not anything special. It's a story we have all heard before, just written differently. Most books are. It takes a special talent to get the characters to jump off the pages. An author has to breathe life into their novel; it's the beauty of books. The characters come to life and captivate the reader, so they are as much a part of the novel as any of the characters. That's what makes a best-seller.

After all the questions have been answered, I stand and button my suit. "Thank you, Olivia. That presentation was highly informative. Get me the final cover mockup so I can sign off on it. Alright, great meeting." I'm the first one out the door.

Once I get back to my office, I lean back in my chair, rubbing my hands down my face. My thoughts instantly go to Lizzie. *My Lizzie.* I didn't want to leave her this morning. I never want to leave her. She is my comfort. She is my breath of fresh air. She's brilliant. A slight smile adorns my face, thinking about her love of literature. It's a passion we both share. I sit up quickly as my heart begins to drum in my chest. Lizzie is the answer! I haven't even read her work, but I know she's the one. Her novel will be the best seller this company needs to push forward. I know it is. I begin to think about how happy she will be to have her work published. I know she worries about our relationship causing favoritism, but she's going to have to understand that we met for a reason. Not only is she the one for my soul but also for this company. I need to read what she's written. It's like a thirst that won't be quenched until I get my hands on it.

We will be spending the whole weekend together, even though she only knows about Sunday. She doesn't know the plans that I have for her tomorrow, celebrating her birthday. She will get a delivery in the morning with instructions for the day. She and Sarah will be pampered at the spa and salon that I was told is the best in the city. Once they get home, I'll have her dress delivered. I don't want her to see it until it's time for her to put it on. I can't wait to see her in it, and I can't wait to see the look on her face when I pick her up. She is going to be devastatingly beautiful. Perfect, as always. I know every man and woman will be looking at the beauty on my arm tomorrow. I'm excited to show her off to the world, however, there is a part of me that's anxious that the attention will be too much for her. At least Sarah will be there to soften the experience.

I need to finalize all the details and surprises for tomorrow, so everything goes to plan. I want it to go off without a hitch because I love this woman. I want to give her everything in the world. She enchants me and brings a light into my life that I didn't know was missing. I want to show her what she means to me. Father always taught us that, "Actions speak louder than words." I intend to show her the love I have for her for the rest of time. Always.

CHAPTER 22

Elizabeth

I've had a smile on my face since I woke up this morning. People I've passed on the street have looked at me funny, but I don't care. I feel like I'm floating on a cloud. After getting everything off my chest yesterday with Sarah, spending the night with Miles was just what I needed. I'm happy. I feel lighter today. I've been thinking about what Sarah said about my father, and I'm going to write him a letter. I think that will be the best way to get everything I have ever felt off my chest. I don't think I could say it to his face, and I might get anxious, not getting it all out. That's what made me decide the letter is the best way to go. After all, just like Sarah said, this is for me, not for him. It's me that needs to move on, and I will.

I'm sitting at the café down the street from where I work. I don't have to be there for several hours, but I wanted to get out of the apartment and get some fresh air. I'm sitting at a little table outside, and it's cold while also a bit overcast; however, I don't mind. When it's overcast and cloudy or even raining, it doesn't make me sad; in fact, it puts my mind at ease. There's supposed to be some more snow coming in later tonight. I lean back in my chair and stare up at the sky. The clouds slowly move across the sky, changing and creating new shapes. I close my eyes, and my mind takes me back to when I was a child. I was lying on the ground, looking up at the sky with my dad. We were sharing what each cloud looked like to us. We would make up stories to go along with them. I smile, thinking back to that special moment where there were no problems, no divorce—just us and the clouds. I open my eyes as a tear falls down my cheek. I pull out my notebook and pen, knowing what I need to do.

Dad,

I am writing to you because there are some things I need to get off my chest. I feel like this is the only way to fully express what I need to say. This letter does not come from a place of malice but of one where I need to heal in order to live.

When you left mom and I was twelve, I came home to your abandonment. Even though you were divorcing mother, you left me that day, as well. You didn't sit me down and talk to me, but instead, you left without a word. I felt lost, betrayed, lonely, and heartbroken. In my mind, we were the best of friends, close as a father and daughter could be. I was only twelve; I didn't know what I did wrong to make you leave me. Even though you were still in the same city, you were oceans away in my mind.

One thing that always made our family situation worse, after the divorce, was my birthdays. A should be celebration would turn into a nightmare over who would 'have me' on the actual day. You and mom couldn't be in the same room with each other, so I had to choose, or it was chosen for me. I absolutely hated my birthdays. I didn't understand why you couldn't be civil for a couple of hours for me. Why couldn't you? It was my special day, and it's one that, since then, I still hate. It brings about the memories I want to stay buried deep inside. My sadness eventually turned to anger; that's why I quit playing softball. I couldn't stand the sight of the fields where you had been coaching me since I was five. You knew I was angry with you; so, to appease me, you bought me gifts. Gifts never healed the terrible chasm I had in my heart. Buying me broke my heart even more. Gifts were easy for you, but I didn't need that. What I needed was my father.

I lean back in my chair and look over what I have

written. Tears escape my eyes once more. I wipe them away with the sleeve of my sweater. *Am I doing the right thing by writing this? I'm bringing up all these old feelings that I don't want to relive.* Unfortunately, though, I think Sarah was right. I have to get through this, so I can move forward. I don't want to drown in this misery any longer. I continue to write and write, getting out all the poison from my system. I let him know how angry I was that he moved on so quickly, how I've always felt like he had to have been cheating on my mother for him to go from her to another within the blink of an eye.

Once I got to high school, you even bought that small house, in hopes I would come live with you and eventually forgive you for breaking up our family. I even moved there trying to mend our relationship. However, that didn't work either because you left me again, a second time. This time you left me to go live with her. My own father, my best friend, left me again. So, I was alone, again. Any other teenager would probably have loved getting her own house to herself. I didn't. I saw it as another abandonment. And this time, it was just me that you left. It was hard to believe I was even a lovable, worthy person when my own father left me twice. What had I done to deserve this? What was wrong with me? Was I disgusting or something? I tried my hardest at everything I did to try and get some sort of acknowledgement or approval from you. It was exhausting, trying to be the best at everything. The sad part was I never felt good enough to receive your love again. I always doubted you.

I have carried this pain with me every day since all that happened. I fear to get too close to others because, inevitability, they will just leave me like you did. I loved you like no other and thought you loved me the same way. You broke my heart. I never wanted to go through that again! I dove into books because my reality was so terrible that I needed to escape. I suppose I can thank you for my love of books; however, I still use them as an escape from reality. I understand that some marriages don't last, but when you grew up in a happy home with parents that don't fight (or make it known that they aren't happy) and then the one I love the most in the world drops the divorce bomb. It shattered everything I knew. I didn't know who to trust because you hid your true feelings from me.

Having these early experiences in my life has, unfortunately, shaped my decisions, as an adult. After many failed relationships, I believed that was all I was destined for. Sarah has been the only constant in my life. But I can't live like that anymore. I needed to get these feelings, fears, and insecurities out of my mind, so I can be whole again. I need it. I hope this explains my absence from your life these many years. I wish we would have had better communication. Obviously, I was too young to know how much of a necessity communication really is. But now I know. Thank you for taking this pain from me as you read this letter, even if you never read it. Thank you for no longer having power over my mind and my soul. You are still my father, and I truly hope that one day we will get through this mess of a relationship. I know it can never be the same, but I want you to know I miss those good days. I've learned never to take anything for granted. Although you didn't die, I feel as though a part of you did, the part that was tethered to me. Maybe we can mend that connection. I hope so.

Love,

Lizzie

I put the pen down and take a deep breath. That brought up old feelings that I had buried deep down, and they all just poured out onto the page before me. I feel like I just unloaded a ton of baggage I'd been carrying for years. I feel... lighter. I feel hopeful. I look back up at the clouds and smile. I'm proud of myself. I've been running from this for so long, and I can finally stop, turn around, and face it head on. I'm not saying I'll heal overnight, but this was definitely a step in the right direction. I check my watch, and I can't believe I have been writing for two hours. The waitress came by a few times to refill my water, but I didn't realize I've been here that long. I put up the letter and my pen. I leave some cash on the table for her tip, get up, and sling my bag over my shoulder.

    My smile returns as I think of Miles. I will get to see him tonight when he picks me up from work. The thought of seeing him again sends butterflies to my belly. He has gotten under my skin in the best way possible. I love him. *Do I love him?* Yes, I do. I can't deny it any longer. I know it's crazy and fast and scary, but I think that's why they call it, "Falling in love," because you jump into the unknown with your eyes closed and hope they'll be there to catch you. And I know he will be. Miles will be there to catch me. Well, he already has.

***

The shift tonight has been a disaster since the minute I walked in the door. We have been so busy, on top of having two new servers training tonight. They would accidentally bump into everything. Food and drink trays were knocked over. I got covered in alcohol. Trinity, a waitress that's been here as long as me, got a tray of salads knocked onto her. She didn't hold her tongue, and I think the whole restaurant heard her curse at one of the new girls. Our manager was rushing around putting out figurative fires all night long. Everything has been so hectic, and I haven't had a chance to check my phone all night. Normally, I can sneak away and text Miles or at least read a message that he's sent me. I forgot to tell him what time I get off, so I'll probably just end up walking home tonight even though my feet are killing me. I don't want to have to wait for him to get here when I can walk faster. My last table finally leaves, and I cash out my tickets and begin cleaning up my station. The bar stays open a while longer than the rest of the restaurant, so there are still customers there, but none that I've got to deal with. I take my tickets and payments to my manager to sign me off for the night, so I can go change out of these nasty work clothes. I grab a trash bag on my way to the back because I need to wash my uniforms, especially the ones from tonight. I just want to shower this night off me. I open my locker, take out my phone, and see I have a message from Miles. Instantly smiling by just seeing his name on my screen, I open the message.

Miles: Hey beautiful, sorry I won't be able to pick you up tonight. Sebastian and I have to go to dinner with a new investor that we have been trying to sign with us. I sent Thomas to you, so he'll be waiting outside when you are finished. Hope you have a good night. I will call you later. xo

I smile at his text but can't help but be a little disappointed that Miles won't be here to pick me up. I was hoping I could wake up with him on my birthday tomorrow. I know he's busy and is working hard to make sure that Knight Publishing Company stays at number one nationwide. I can't imagine the stress he is under in that position. Even being groomed to take over doesn't take away from the stress of having to step into his position because of the passing of his father.

I send a text to Sarah telling her I will be home soon. I'm not sure if she has plans tonight or not. She has been secretive the past few days when I mention my birthday. I know she's got something planned and was hoping to find out what, so I can psych myself up for it.

Lizzie: Heading home soon. Thomas is dropping me off, so no Miles tonight. Are you home?

I put my phone down and change clothes. I grab my jacket and bag, then shut my locker. Grabbing my phone and the dirty uniforms, I walk through the restaurant and out the front door. Just as Miles said, Thomas is waiting right out front. Once he sees me, he's out of the car in a flash and has the back door open for me with a huge smile on his face.

"Good evening, Miss Brighton."

"Good to see you, Thomas. Please call me, Lizzie." I slide into the warm car and wait while Thomas walks around to get in the front. "Thank you for picking me up. I could have walked easier than you having to wait out here for me."

"No, ma'am. I don't mind waiting at all. This time of night isn't a suitable time for a young lady to be walking the streets. It isn't safe."

I nod because I know I won't be able to argue with him. He works for Miles, after all, and it's on his insistence that I do not walk home. It doesn't take long to get there. By the time we park, snow has begun to drift slowly down. He walks me up the stairs to my door, even though I insist I'm fine.

"Thank you again, Thomas. And thank you for the coffee this morning. It was wonderful."

"You are very welcome, Miss Lizzie."

"Have a safe drive home," I call out to him as he descends the stairs back to his car.

When I open the door to the apartment, I don't hear Sarah. She never wrote me back, so she must be out. I kick off my boots inside my room, and then I start a load of laundry. Once I get that going, I grab a wine glass from the kitchen cabinet, open a bottle of Moscato, and pour myself a large glass. Taking a quick shower, I wash the ick and grime of work off me. Washing between my legs, I feel the soreness from last night and smile as the memories flood into my senses. That was the best sex I have ever had in my life. Not that I am an expert, but damn it was good. I rinse off, wrap myself in a towel, and go to my room to put on something warm and comfortable. With my wine in hand, I take out my phone to message Miles.

Lizzie: Just getting home and out of the shower. Are you still out?

As I am waiting for him to respond, I see that Sarah sent me a message while I was in the shower.

Sarah: I am out with some coworkers. I will be home soon. Not trying to stay out all night tonight. Love ya.

As soon as I read her message, I see a text pop up from Miles, but then my phone shuts off. I sigh, reaching to my side table to get my charging cable. This phone does not stay charged very long anymore. To be fair, it is several years old, and I am surprised it has lasted this long. I need to make plans to get a new one whenever I have free time. This one is definitely unreliable. As I wait for the power to come back on, I get my laptop and open it to the last page I wrote on my manuscript. I reread the last paragraph, so I know where I left off. I begin typing away. A few pages later, my phone rings. Looking at the ID, I see it's Miles. I answer right away.

"Hey! I've been waiting to hear from you."

"Lizzie, I got your message and have been trying to get in touch with you since." I wince at his tone. Damn phone.

"Ugh. It's this stupid phone. I saw you messaged me right back, but then my phone turned off. It has been acting up lately. I plugged it in and was waiting for it to charge and turn back on."

"I'll get you a new phone. You can't have one that's undependable. I must be able to get in touch with you. Or, what if something happened and you needed to get in touch with me?"

"Calm down. I'm already planning to get a new one. I just have to figure out when I have some free time. I guess I could go tomorrow."

"No. I'll get you one. Plus, tomorrow is your birthday, baby. You don't want to stand in line for hours on your special day."

"Miles, you are not getting me a new phone. It's my responsibility, I ju—."

"Lizzie, will you stop being so difficult and let me help you? I could have it delivered right to you. You wouldn't have to wait in line. I can just make a phone call, and it would be ready."

Sometimes I forget about the billionaire status that is tied to Miles' name. I forget that he can get whatever he wants with a snap of his fingers. "Miles," I sigh. I don't want this to turn into an argument. He is used to getting his way, but I don't want him to spend all his money on me. Well, not saying he could even spend all of it in a lifetime. I guess I don't want to be a burden or seem like I'm after him for his money.

"I'll take that as a yes then. I'll get you the newest one, so there won't be any issues with my being able to get in touch with you. Now, how was work?"

"We were very busy. There were new servers in training, and it did not go well. I had a platter of alcoholic drinks spilled all over me because one girl wasn't looking where she was going and ran right into me. It was awful."

"That's unacceptable. Are you all right?"

"Yes, of course. That isn't the first time something has been spilled on me, and I guarantee it won't be the last. It's just part of the job, unfortunately."

"I wish you didn't work there. It sounds like it's more trouble than it's worth."

"Well, we can't all own our own companies, Miles. Besides, this is temporary until I finish my novel. I was working on it when you called."

"Oh, really? How is it coming along?"

"Really well, actually. I think I will be done with it soon."

"Wow, I didn't know you were that far along. When will I get the chance to read this Lizzie Brighton original?"

"Well, I don't know. You read manuscripts all the time. Those, I'm sure, are the best of the best. I don't want you to look at me differently if mine totally sucks."

"Lizzie, how could you ever think something like that would color my opinion of you? Besides, I know it will be brilliant because you are. I believe anything you touch turns to gold. So, I have no doubt that you have a best seller on your hands."

"Thank you for saying that. You're being very kind."

"Look at the clock. Happy birthday, baby. I wish I was there with you right now."

"I do, too." A yawn escapes my lips.

"You sound tired, Lizzie. Get some rest, and I will talk to you later today, birthday girl."

"I am exhausted. Are you home?"

"I am. I got home right before I called you this last time. Seb is here because I recorded the Princeton basketball game. We knew we wouldn't be able to watch it live."

"Oh, that's good that you're getting some brother time in. Just wanted to make sure you were home safe. How did the meeting go? We've only been talking about me. I'm so sorry!"

"Lizzie, I will always want to talk about you. But it went very well. Seb and I were able to sway them to invest in our company. So, it was a very good dinner."

"That's such great news! I'm proud of you."

"Thank you, sweetheart. Now, get some rest. I need to as well. Someone kept me up late last night. However, my brother is waiting for me. He ordered pizzas and everything, even though we just ate. I need to go make sure he isn't trashing my apartment."

My cheeks begin to flame when I think about last night. I smile, though, thinking about Miles getting on to Sebastian for being messy.

"I could argue the same thing, that someone kept me awake last night. Go have fun with your brother. Goodnight, Miles." *Oh, how I wish you were here with me right now.*

"I will. Goodnight, my sweet Lizzie."

I hang up and pull my laptop back over to me. I have a few more pages I think I can write before I fall asleep tonight.

CHAPTER 23

Miles

After the dinner with the new investors, Sebastian and I had plans to come back to my place to watch a basketball game I recorded. Since the dinner ran later than I had thought, I figured we would reschedule our get-together, but Seb wanted to come anyway. We drove separately to the restaurant because there were some last-minute details I needed to get done before tomorrow.

    I get to my apartment and see Sebastian's car is already here. I'm sure he let himself inside and is already making a mess. I love my brother, but he can somehow make the worst mess in just a few short minutes. I'm almost thinking it's a special ability. I feel sorry for his future wife because she will have her work cut out for her. The thought makes me chuckle aloud as I park my car. Thinking of wives makes me think of Lizzie. I am going to marry that woman. I love her. I would ask her right now if I didn't think she would probably freak out. Oddly, it doesn't make me want to freak out. Dad was right. She's the one. I knew it the moment our hands touched, and I looked down at her at the coffee shop.

    I walk through the lobby and wave hello to the door attendant. I reach the private elevator, put in my code, and get inside. My thoughts are on Lizzie and the type of ring I want to have made for her. She is unique in every way, so she needs something equally as special. I will have to make a few phone calls to some jewelers next week, so I can get the ball rolling on that. It will take a while to make anyway. I walk in my penthouse and am slammed with the smell of pizza and beer.

When I enter the living room, pizza boxes are sprawled on the table and a few empty beer bottles. "Make yourself at home, did you?" I ask, tossing him the empty bottle on the couch. I walk over to the bar and pour myself a whiskey.

"Of course. Got here a while ago. Where have you been?" he queries.

"I had to make a phone call for Thomas to pick Lizzie up tonight. Then I got stuck in traffic. You left just in time to miss it."

"Why does she need to be picked up? She can't get an Uber?"

"She doesn't live far from her work, and she usually walks home alone at night. I put a stop to that," I grunt as I slump down on the couch next to Seb.

He looks at me incredulously. "You really are in it deep with this girl, aren't you?"

A growl comes out almost involuntarily. "She isn't just some girl. She's the one, Sebastian. Her name is Lizzie. Remember it," I say with some grit to my tone.

He holds his hands up in defense. "I didn't mean anything by it, bro. I guess I didn't know it was so serious. You haven't known her very long."

I take a sip of my whiskey and look over at him. "Remember what father told us about when he met mother? How he knew that instant?" I inquire, but know he remembers.

"Of course. He told us that story all the time growing up. I didn't think you believed in that."

"I didn't. Not until I met her, and then I understood. I knew that everything father said was true; you just know when you meet that person. I knew that instant. I thought I was going to be a bachelor forever or at least for a lot longer, and I certainly didn't think I would find this kind of connection with anyone."

"You sound like a chick, dude. But seriously, I'm happy for you," he says as he chuckles. "When are you going to properly introduce us?"

"Tomorrow. She will be at the gala. It's her birthday, and I have a few surprises planned," I reply with a smile.

"Oh hell," he groans as he rolls his eyes at me, and I can't help but chuckle.

"Yeah, keep talking like that. Wait until it happens to you," I quip, turning on the tv.

"Don't wish that on me. I'm happy being single. I don't need one woman when I can have many. Bachelorhood suits me," he swears, taking a sip of his beer.

"Whatever you say, bro. I'll make sure I'm there to tell you 'I told you so.' Just give it time. I'll be right back. Let me go change and call her to make sure she got home okay." Seb rolls his eyes as I get up and jog to my room.

I change out of my suit and into a pair of sweats along with a Princeton t-shirt. I talk to Lizzie for a little while until I hear her yawn. I know she needs to get some sleep because tomorrow is going to be busy for her. I'm excited thinking of everything I have planned for her. I just hope I haven't gone overboard. After we hang up, I return to the living room and see Sebastian, reclining and scrolling through his phone.

"Wow, I thought you might have fallen asleep back there. Now, can we please watch the game before I see any updates pop up on my phone?" he questions as I sit down on the couch.

"Yes, princess," I say, as I push play.

We sit back and watch the game, eating pizza, drinking, and just having some good brother time. We may have just had a work dinner, but we always have room for pizza. Princeton is winning, which is who we are pulling for. We both went to college there and still follow the team, especially since we both played the sport back in the day. I enjoy watching, but I miss the action of being right there on the court. Sometimes, Sebastian and I play a bit, but we have been so busy lately that we haven't been able to. Once the game is over, Princeton having won, I get up and start cleaning up this mess we made. Seb helps a bit by putting the extra pizza in the fridge, but that's about it.

When he gets ready to leave, he comes and claps me on the shoulder. Even though he is younger, he is about an inch taller than me. "I'm happy for you, man," he states with a lazy smile.

"Thanks. I am too. You good to drive, or do you want the guest room?"

He looks at me for a moment, and then says, "Actually, I think I'll go crash in the guest room. I think I had too many beers." I laugh and am relieved he doesn't want to drive. I probably would have insisted that he get an Uber. He heads up the stairs, and I shake my head smiling. I finish straightening up and head to my room. I happen to look at the time and realize it's three in the morning. I'm glad I was talking to Lizzie earlier when the clock turned twelve. I got to be the first person to wish her happy birthday. I wonder if she is still awake. I told her I would call her but didn't realize what time it was. I send her a quick message to see if she responds.

Miles: Hey, birthday girl. I'm sure you are asleep, but Seb and I just finished the game.

I sit on the edge of my bed and wait to see to see that she's read the message. After a few minutes without a reply, I put my phone down and go take a shower. Once I'm out, I dry off and slide under the covers. I reach down and grab my phone before I turn the light off. I click the screen and my heart speeds up. A new message from Lizzie pops up.

Lizzie: I think I was half asleep. I was writing but guess I dozed off with my laptop on me. How was the game?

I smile at the message. She's so cute when she sleeps. I wish I was lying beside her right now with her wrapped in my arms. Although, sleeping isn't what's on my mind.

Miles: We won. Seb and I had a fun time hanging out. We have been so busy with work, so it was good to take a beat and hang out.

Lizzie: See? I told you that you needed to relax. And I'm glad your team won. I think I need to see you play sometime, so I have proof that you really can.

Miles: Is that so? You aren't going to take my word for it?

Lizzie: Nope. I'm going to need to see it, in person, of course. Maybe... shirtless?

Miles: Do you want me to play basketball, shirtless? What is the benefit of that?

Lizzie: Oh, that benefit would be all mine. Although, there is a possibility that it could distract me from your 'skills.'

I laugh when I read the last message. This woman. I can't get enough of her fun personality. The way she makes me laugh. She is so comforting.

Miles: Well, I want both, to distract and not. It's a bit of a dilemma. So, does this work both ways? You will show me your softball skills, shirtless?

I can see her smirk in my mind when she reads my message.

Lizzie: Of course not! You can't play softball naked! Are you crazy?

Miles: For you, I am.

I take a deep breath waiting for her reply.

Lizzie: Are you?

I blow out a breath and think of what to reply. I type a few responses and delete them. I delete the message I was working on and call her instead.

"Hey," she answers softly.

"I wanted to hear your voice. And as an answer to your question, you know I am crazy about you. I told you last night that you are mine and I am yours. You are truly an extraordinary woman, Lizzie."

She lets out a small gasp that makes me smile. I know she heard me tell her last night; but I want to keep telling her, so she doesn't have any reason to doubt us.

"I feel the same way, Miles. I can't believe it. It's been such a short amount of time since we met. But I feel so comfortable with you."

My smile gets so large my cheeks begin to tremble. "I'm glad, baby. I want you to be comfortable with me, and for you to trust me with all of you. Your heart, body, and soul. Lizzie, I want the honor to protect them. I'm not going anywhere."

"I know you aren't. I believe you." I hear a muffled yawn on her end, and I know she's exhausted. I'm being selfish keeping her awake.

"I just wanted to hear your voice, sweetheart. Get some sleep."

She chuckles, "Okay, goodnight for real this time."

"Goodnight, baby."

I end the call and put my cell on the nightstand. I'll call Elijah tomorrow to get Lizzie a new phone. That is a must have. I turn the light off and roll onto to the pillow that smells like her from two nights ago. I take a deep inhale of her scent and smile into the pillow, as I snuggle up to it.

CHAPTER 24

Elizabeth

"HAPPY BIRTHDAYYY, LIZZIE!!!!" Sarah comes rushing into my room, squealing as she jumps on my bed. I groan and put a pillow over my head.

"Sarah, what time is it? Have you lost your damn mind?" I inquire because, surely, she doesn't think this is the best way to wake me up, especially this morning.

"It's 8 am and high time to get your sleepy ass out of this bed, so we can start the birthday celebration!" she yells, as she snatches the pillow from my face.

"Can you just go celebrate without me, then come back and tell me how it went? With coffee, preferably," I say, whining as I sit up in the bed. Miles and I stayed up late talking on the phone, and I didn't expect to be awaken so early today. It's my day off for, Pete's sake!"

Sarah jumps off the bed and scoffs just as I hear a loud knock on the door that startles me. I look at Sarah, and she doesn't seem surprised at all. In fact, she seems happy. What is she up to?

"Well, get up birthday girl. That's for you!" she exclaims as she yanks the whole comforter off the bed. I pop up and put on my robe in a rush, so I don't freeze to death, while she is standing in my doorway with her arms crossed and wearing the largest grin I've ever seen.

"What are you up to Sarah? Why can't you go get the door?" I say exasperated. She pulls my arm and drags me through the living room to the door of our apartment. Just as I am about to peek through the hole, the loud banging returns, and I almost fall over from being startled and half asleep. I can't take this much stimulation before coffee! Sarah pulls the handle open for me without looking to see who it is. I almost protest when I look up and see Thomas, Miles' driver. I open my mouth to say something, but there are no words. I just stare at him for a moment, and he begins to chuckle.

"Happy birthday, Miss Lizzie. These are for you," he advises with a wide smile on his face. I didn't even notice he's holding a large bouquet of the most stunning flowers, and a package. As he hands them over to me, I can't help but smile as a giddy feeling flutters in my stomach. What did Miles do this time? Sarah takes the flowers and heads to the kitchen, leaving Thomas and me in the doorway.

"Thank you, Thomas. You didn't have to go through the trouble to bring all of this to me. Would you like to come in for a cup of coffee?" I ask, feeling a bit awkward at what the protocol for this is. I don't want him to have to have come all this way on a Saturday just for me. The thought makes me a bit uneasy. Just as if out of thin air, he pulls out a cup of coffee that I instantly recognize as my favorite coffee shop logo appears. He must see the awe on my face because his smile broadens even more than I thought possible. He hands the cup over to me, but before I take a sip, I see the name on the side, "Austen." A chuckle escapes me. Miles thinks of everything. He pays so much attention to the intricate details. My cheeks burn from the smile that has permanently attached itself to my face since I first saw Thomas at the door.

"I must decline the offer, Miss. You have plans to get to. I will be down in the car when you and Miss McKenzie are ready," Thomas replies, and before I can ask further questions, he takes a bow and heads to the elevator.

"Thank you!" I call out to him as I shut the door. Before I can wrap my head around the fact that he said he will be waiting for us, Sarah tugs me into the kitchen where she has put the flowers in a beautiful glass vase. They are sitting on the kitchen counter next to the package Thomas left.

"Open it! Open it!" Sarah exclaims.

I skip over to the counter, set my coffee down, and inspect the box.

"Do you know what this is all about? You didn't seem surprised to see Thomas at the door."

She shrugs her shoulders with a coy smile and slides the package closer to me.

The package is a thin white box with a black satin ribbon wrapped around it. I pull at the edge of the bow, and the ribbon falls away. As I open the box, my heart begins to race. I have never been treated like this in my life. I feel like a princess, getting all these gifts and surprise deliveries. When I lift the lid off, I see a cream envelope with my name written on it, which I instantly recognize as Miles' handwriting. With trembling hands, I open the envelope carefully and pull out the handwritten card.

My dearest Lizzie,

Happy birthday, my love. Today is a celebration of your life; without it I wouldn't have you in mine. I will be forever thankful. I want you to enjoy this special day beginning with a bit of relaxation. Enclosed are your and Sarah's passes for Eden Spa and Salon. I am told it's the best of the best. Enjoy your time. Thomas will take care of anything else you need. When you arrive home, expect another package.

"There are as many forms of love as there are moments in

time." – Jane Austen

Yours,

Miles

A gasp escapes my lips as I reread the note. I press a hand over my mouth as I continue to stare at this beautiful note. *Or love letter.* That's what it seems like, and my heart is bursting at the thought. I can't believe he is going through so much trouble to celebrate my birthday. He even included Sarah, and I cannot be happier about that. He knows how much she means to me, and the fact that she gets to be a part of this makes me ecstatic. I start to jump up and down as I pass the note over to her so she can read it. She does so quickly, but I suspect she already knows what Miles has planned today because her smile only grows wider. However, she doesn't seem surprised. The thought of them working together for me has me feeling all kinds of emotions. But mostly *loved*!

"Wait, Lizzie, you only opened the card. There is something else in this box," Sarah points out. I look over my shoulder at the package; I didn't realize there's something other than the card inside. However, if it was just a card, it could have been sent in an envelope. I mentally face palm my head. I need to finish my coffee, so my brain can catch up with all this craziness that is going on this morning.

I run back to the kitchen and take a big gulp of my coffee. I seriously could get used to this. My favorite coffee delivered two days in a row. Lucky me. I put the cup down and stare at the package. The gold tissue paper is neatly folded and a circular sticker with the initials BMK in a script font is the holding it together. Benjamin Miles Knight Jr. Of course, he has his own stationary, which would include these beautifully intricately designed stickers.

I peel off the sticker and place it on the back of the card because I want to keep it as a memento. I'm careful not to rip the paper; it looks too fancy to mess up. Pulling back the tissue, I choke on my own intake of air when I see what Miles has gotten me. I pick up the brand-new iPhone in disbelief. How did he already get this? We literally just talked about this less than twelve hours ago. Looking up at Sarah, I show her the new phone with my mouth still open wide in disbelief.

"Lizzie, you do need a new phone so bad! That is so sweet of him."

"Yeah, but I literally just told him last night that my phone has been acting up. Like hours ago, and here I am, holding a new phone. I did also tell him I would get it myself when I have the free time," I explain, exasperated.

"Well, he has personal assistants, so I'm sure it isn't a big deal to get that for you in such a short amount of time."

"I know that. It's just..." I trail off, thinking about how getting gifts like this makes me think of my father.

"Don't say it. I already know what you're thinking. Miles really cares for you. He wants to spoil you. Technically, it's a safe gift to give because your phone is so awful that it barely works. It isn't dependable. He is not like your dad," she says, reassuringly.

I look down at the box in my hand and realize she's probably right. I am putting too much thought into this. "I guess you are right." I open the box and take out the phone. It's so much bigger than the one I have. This must be the newest one there is." I power it on, and instead of the usual beginning start screen, I see a text.

Miles: Happy birthday, baby. I know you said you could get this yourself, but I wanted to do this for you. This way you can take some great pictures of your special day, and I will have peace of mind knowing that you have a way to get in touch with me any time you need to.

I smile again, thinking about this sweet man. Even though I feel exasperated with him for getting me this present. I know he means well, and it comes from a place of caring.

"Well, I guess we need to take a selfie with my new phone to document this day."

"Yes, ma'am!" she squeals as she comes up beside me, and we pose for the photo. I snap the picture and smile at how great it turns out. I guess it really was time for an upgrade. So… maybe I love this new phone, just a little. Okay, maybe a lot. It is pretty impressive, and I haven't even had time to play with it yet.

Sarah turns on our Dance Party playlist on the Bluetooth speakers, and I begin to spin and frolic about the apartment. Sarah starts laughing at me but joins in on the fun too.

"I can't remember the last time I saw this bright face on your birthday! Let's get this party started!" she says, then takes my hands and dances around with me. After our short impromptu dance party, we dress quickly and make our way down to Thomas to take us to the spa. I have never been to a spa, so I have no idea what to expect. I wonder what all Miles has arranged for us to do while we are there.

"I'm nervous," I whisper to Sarah as we drive down the road. She grabs my hand and gives it a small squeeze.

"This is going to be so great! All I want you to do is relax. Miles put this together to pamper you. It's your birthday, girl!" she emphasizes. I can see the excitement written all over her face. I take a deep breath and know she's right. This *is* going to be awesome!

The Eden Spa and Salon is known for entertaining the rich and famous, according to a quick search on google, so I certainly feel out of my element when we pull up in front of the building. The outside is sleek and modern with glass double doors that open to what can only be described as an oasis of luxury.

Thomas comes around to our side of the car, opening the door for us and letting us know that the spa employees will tell him when we are ready to be picked up. *Seriously, is this real life?* I pinch my arm and let out a whimper. Yes, definitely not a dream. Sarah locks her arm through mine as we walk up to the entrance. An employee is there to open the door for us with an unnaturally happy smile on her face. It makes me chuckle internally. This is totally not me, but it's sweet of Miles to arrange this for my best friend and me. Most guys won't think to include their girl's bestie, or even go through this much trouble for a birthday. It's literally just another day of the week to me, but apparently not to Miles.

We walk up to the counter. Before I can utter any words, the receptionist says, "Welcome to The Eden Spa and Salon, where all your worries dissolve away. You must be Miss Brighton and Miss McKenzie. We already have your rooms ready per Mr. Knight's request. Please, follow me."

Before I can even confirm our identities, she whisks us away. Sarah is squealing as we walk along and see all the things the spa offers. I look at her with a vexed expression. I feel like I'm walking through a dream. This place is insanely opulent and lavish. I can't help but feel a little uncomfortable being out of my element. I mean, my hair is in a messy bun, and I'm wearing leggings and a sweater, for fuck's sake. I'm sure they are wondering how I managed to get access to this spa, and I'm sure they all know it was the famous Miles Knight that arranged it. I cringe on the inside. What I must look like. *Ugh.*

They take us inside a room that can only be described as something you would see in a queen's mansion. Gold decadence surrounds the room with lightly colored, opulent upholstery. It looks like nothing should be touched, let alone lie naked on to get a massage. We are instructed to remove our clothes and put on the lavish, warmed white robes they offer to us. *WARM! The robes are warm. I can't even, right?* I can't decide if this is comical or outright crazy. People live like this? For real? Did Miles really think this would be something that I would enjoy, or that I am this type of person? I have never done anything this ridiculous in my life. I am not saying that I'm not up for a massage, because I have heard they are amazing, but I'm sure I can find a hole-in-the-wall place that can get the job done.

While I'm having my inner crisis in my head, I look over at Sarah. She seems super comfortable and relaxed. How is that possible? I need alcohol, like an hour ago. Just when I am about to say just that, servers knock at the door and bring in mimosas on a silver platter with assorted brunch, finger-foods. The whole setup is insane, but I don't shy away from the mimosa. I down the first and ask for another. I will need it to get through this adventure. When I get the second glass, I swallow a not so lady-like gulp and can feel my jitters start to melt away. Maybe this isn't as bad as I think it will be. Sure, it's something I will never arrange for myself. Just because it's new and somewhat scary doesn't mean I can't enjoy the hell out of it. *Cheers to getting my spa on!*

A few hours later, they usher Sarah and I to the limo where Thomas is waiting for us. I'm a bit tipsy and my body feels like Jell-O from all the massaging that's taken place. It may also be from the number of mimosas I drank. Either way, I'm feeling great. I'm not complaining as much as I did when we got there. That is one of the best experiences of my life. I wish I could take one of the masseurs home with me, so I can get a rub down every day. I giggle to myself when that thought crosses my mind.

We get in the car; Thomas takes us back to our apartment. When we reach our door, there is a large box waiting. I look at Sarah quizzically, and she just smiles, then unlocks the door. I grab the box and head inside. This birthday is getting crazier by the second. I know Miles said there was going to be another package when we got home, but I figured it would be smaller or maybe, I don't know, himself. That would be the best gift, but I know he has big plans tonight with the charity gala.

As I place the present down on the coffee table, I stare at it for a moment. I'm not sure why. I'm not expecting anything to pop out of it; it's just I didn't expect anything today. Today isn't a day that I care to remember. I still haven't gotten a phone call from anyone in my family wishing me a happy birthday. Although, that's putting too high of a hope on that situation. I guess I am just overwhelmed with everything that he's already given me, so I'm not sure if I'm ready for something else.

Sarah comes and flops down on the couch, which makes me flop up a bit, and we start laughing. "Well, open it already. I can't stand it. I need to know what else that beau of yours has up his sleeve," Sarah gushes, as she slides the box closer to me. I roll my eyes, but I'm secretly wondering as well. I pull the same beautiful black lace ribbon off and take the card off, then open it up.

Lizzie,

I can't wait to see you in this tonight when I pick you up at eight p.m. A few friends of mine will be stopping by to help with anything you need. Happy birthday, darling!

Yours,

Miles

What on Earth is he talking about? He has the charity ball tonight. *Oh my... no! Surely, it's not what I'm thinking.* "No way!" I exclaim, as I open the box, unfolding the tissue paper. I gulp when I see a gorgeous silver gown, encrusted with small diamonds that make the shapes of delicate snowflakes woven all over the dress. On the bodice there are small snowflakes that are arranged on glittery, silver lace. The lace extends out to the arms of the dress, making it appear to be long-sleeved, even though it's sheer. Shocked, I hold the dress up to my chest, and then look at Sarah, who is gazing at me with so much excitement in her eyes.

"Did you know about this?"

"I sure did. Miles called me about the gala and asked me to come help pick out a gown for you. I met with him and his personal shopper, then we found this gem. Miles' eyes were glowing when we showed it to him, and he said he couldn't wait to see it on you."

I'm speechless. My mind is completely blown away! Never in my wildest dreams did I think I would be going to a ball, or a gala rather, but still. Holy shit, this just got intense. There will be so many people. Everyone will see us together and know I'm just a plain Jane, whereas Miles is like prince charming around here. Everyone knows who he is. Ironically, I didn't know it was him when we met, but I don't keep up with things like that.

"Sarah, I can't do this." I shake my head and look down at the beautiful dress in my hands.

She hops up from the couch and clasps my shoulders with her hands. "Listen to me, Lizzie Brighton! You are brilliant and gorgeous and outgoing! You deserve this! Yes, there will be tons of people there, but guess what?"

"What?" I ask, quietly.

"I'm going with you! Miles didn't want you to feel uncomfortable, and he knew with me there that I would have your back. And I do. He has thought of everything and has gone above and beyond to show you how much you mean to him. It's pretty incredible, if you ask me."

"You're coming too!" I squeal.

"You bet I am. I have my own dress that will be here any minute, along with our very own makeup and hair stylists. We are going to be the talk of the gala!"

"Wow. I think I might be in shock right now. Sarah, Miles really did all this for me?"

"He did. Lizzie, that man has it bad for you! And I know you feel the same. Take this chance. I know it's scary, but a good scary, right? I mean, this is fairytale, once-in-a-lifetime shit." We both start laughing. This is absolutely crazy, and yet, I am so excited I feel like I could jump out of my skin. I can't wait to get all dressed up. I mean, secretly, what girl doesn't want this magical experience?

I lay the dress over the sofa, and then grab Sarah in the tightest hug, expressing to her everything I need to say with just our embrace. And she understands. When we pull apart, there is a knock on the door. We glance at it, then back at each other. Unable to contain our excitement, we jump and dance, making our way to the door. Let the fun begin.

CHAPTER 25

Miles

Thomas calls to let me know that Lizzie and Sarah made it back to their apartment safely and that the last package and personal stylists have just arrived. I know Lizzie is probably overwhelmed with everything going on right now. However, I am hoping that she is excited about tonight. I can't wait to see her. I know I went a bit overboard with everything that I planned for her today, but I am hoping that it shows her how much she means to me. I just want to spoil her like she deserves to be.

I have been itching to call her all day. I want to know how everything is going, but I wanted to give her the day to spend with Sarah and not have me interfere. With everything taken care of ahead of time, I have had a lot of spare time on my hands today. I went down to my gym to work off some nervous energy I had built up over the events of tonight. I just want everything to be perfect for my Lizzie. *My Lizzie. She truly is mine, and I will never let her go.*

Sebastian has been here all day since he spent the night last night. His tuxedo was already sent here because he knew he would be getting dressed here. It's a bit of a tradition that he comes to my place before a large event like this. We usually sit down together and enjoy a whiskey before we are swept away to endure a night of entertaining guests and being the center of attention. We enjoy setting these charities up but attending them is a different story. When my father was alive, at least most of the attention was on him and my mother. But since his passing, unfortunately, the press has shifted their attention to Sebastian and me.

I'm in my living room, looking out the windows, imagining what Lizzie is doing right this moment. Is she enjoying being pampered? I take a sip of my whiskey and swirl it around in my glass, as I look out across the Hudson. Sebastian sneaks up behind me and claps me on the back.

"Starting the pregame without me, bro?" he asks with one eyebrow raised.

"I didn't know when your lazy ass would get down here and join me. Besides, I just poured this. You aren't that far behind."

"I'm sorry I don't wake up at the ass crack of dawn on the weekends. I don't know how you do it, man. We even went to bed after three last night. How are you even functioning right now?" he questions as he pours himself two fingers of whiskey from my mini bar beside the windows.

"Well, for one, I went back to sleep this morning for a bit after I took care of some things. And then when I got back up, I went down to the gym for several hours, working off some extra tension that I had. That gave me an extra boost. Maybe you should get back to the gym; you're looking a bit soft," I say chuckling as I take another sip of my drink.

"Oh, is that right, old man?" he fires back.

"I am only two years older than you, and you're just jealous I'm in better shape than you. It's probably all that junk you eat." I love getting a rise out of him. I know he works out just as hard as I do. However, he does have a penchant for junk food and beer.

He laughs and bumps me with his shoulder, then walks past and plops down on my couch. "So, what has you so engrossed that you take to gazing out at the scenery?" he gives me a quizzical look.

"Just thinking about Lizzie and wondering how her day is going. I arranged for her and her friend to go to an exclusive spa this morning and sent Mia and Liam over to her apartment to help them get ready for the gala," I inform him, not even sparing a glance his way. I know the incredulous facial expression I would see. I smile to myself. I can't wait to see him go through this love shit. It's intense. Not that I would trade it for anything, but it's unlike anything I have ever experienced. I feel like I am constantly questioning my actions because I don't want to fuck up and lose her, whereas I am a man that has always been sure of my actions inside and out of business. I have always been confident, but Lizzie has me all tied up from the inside out, and I don't know which way is up. I am just hoping that I'm enough.

"Fuck, man. I can't wait to meet my future sister-in-law. Does mom know about her?" he asks, genuinely curious.

"I spoke to her a few days ago and mentioned Lizzie. She is excited to meet her tonight. What do you mean, your 'future sister-in-law'?" I know he can see right through me. I just want to know what he sees. Does he see the lovesick fool I feel I've become?

"You know exactly what I mean. I'm surprised you don't already have a ring. I mean you don't, do you? That's the kind of thing you must tell me first man. We have to shop for a ring together or some shit, right?" I burst out laughing, turning away from the window and joining him on the couch.

I don't have a ring, yet. And I think I will make you come with me. You'll need the practice," I smile, draining the last bit out of my glass.

"First of all, stop jinxing me with that shit. It isn't going to happen. I enjoy my playboy status. By the way, did you mention that Lizzie has a friend coming with her tonight? Is she hot?" I glare at him, standing to refill my glass.

"Stay away from Sarah. She's Lizzie's best friend, and I don't want to have to beat your ass for breaking her heart," I growl as he holds his hands up in defense.

"Dude, chill. I was just giving you shit. I was only about ten percent serious about if she is hot or not. Besides, I'll meet her tonight." He smirks, then gives me his trademark wink as he jumps out of the way before the pillow I throw has a chance to hit him in the face.

"All right, that's enough. Go get dressed. We have to leave soon."

"Yes, sir," he responds, giving me a salute of his hand. I roll my eyes as he walks off to his room. If I didn't care about being late tonight, I'd go beat his ass right now. I pour two more fingers of whiskey and head to my room to get dressed as well.

Looking into the mirror as I straighten my bow tie, I hear Sebastian calling from the living room that it's time to go. The buzz in my pocket also alerts me that Thomas is downstairs waiting. Satisfied with my appearance, I walk out of the bathroom and over to my dresser that has Lizzie's present from Tiffany's I picked up. I stash the classic blue velvet box into a tuxedo pocket. A flutter of nerves shoots through my body at the upcoming monumental night. By tomorrow, all news outlets will have pictures of Lizzie and me gracing their covers. I love the thought of claiming her to the world, but I worry what her reaction will be. No matter what, I'll help her through it. It's not an option for me to walk away now, and I won't allow her to either. She is it for me. I've already claimed her body, and I will claim her heart. The way she looks into my eyes tells me I'm already close. I check my watch and see we are running behind schedule, which is something I never do. I look around quickly, making sure I have everything and jog out of my room.

"Took you long enough. Hoping to impress a certain someone tonight?" Seb quirks his mouth with a devious smile. I could punch it right off him.

"Cut the shit. You know how important this night is for our company, and for me," I scold him, slapping his back harder than necessary. "Now, are you done whining so we can go?"

He chuckles to himself, muttering something about being whipped, and walks toward the door. Locking my door with the pin pad, I follow behind.

As we pull up to Lizzie's apartment, I let out a breath I didn't know I was holding. Parking at the entrance, Thomas hops out of the car to collect the girls. Sensing my nerves, Sebastian speaks up, "It's going to be great. She obviously likes you, for some reason," he adds a bit quieter, and I smile at his attempt to lighten the mood. "Tonight, is about helping those children; it's a bonus that Lizzie will be by your side. You've got this, bro." Looking over at him, I see the sincerity in his eyes.

"Thanks, man," I let out another sharp breath. Emerging from the limo, I see Thomas, and my heart stops when I see the most stunning Lizzie walking beside him with her arm linked in his. She is speaking to him, so she hasn't seen me yet, which gives me the opportunity to drink her in from head to toe. The silver jeweled gown hugs her every perfect curve and shimmers with every step. The light, reflecting off the diamonds, making her look ethereal. Her dark hair, softly curled, falls loosely down her back. Just as I glance at her face, her gaze locks with mine and another Jane Austen quote comes to the forefront of my mind. *"Their eyes instantly met, and the cheeks of both were overspread with the deepest love." - Jane Austen*

As she gets closer, I stand up straighter, smoothing my

hands over my tuxedo and trying to dispel some last-minute nervous energy. I stroll over to meet her, taking her hand in mine. A charged current passes between us, and I can see it in her eyes that she feels it as well.

"Darling Lizzie, words can't describe how absolutely stunning you look tonight," I praise, bringing her hand to my lips and pressing a small but lasting kiss, while keeping my eyes locked on hers. A shiver runs up her arm, and I smile at the affect I have on her. The reassurance that this attraction isn't one-sided makes my heart leap with joy. Placing her hand back at her side, I glance over at Sarah. "You look beautiful, as well, Sarah. May I steal your friend for a moment?" She nods and continues toward the limousine. Turning back to Lizzie, I grasp her hands in mine and bring her body closer to my own. I shift some hair off her shoulder to whisper in her ear, "Happy birthday, baby."

Goosebumps erupt over her uncovered skin around her chest. "Miles," she moans, and the sound instantly sends a jolt to my already stiffening cock.

"You clean up nicely," she compliments, as her eyes twinkle up at me.

After kissing her neck, I step back and look down at the magnificent woman before me. Even in heels, she's still a bit shorter than me. I reach into my tuxedo and pull out the blue box I placed in there earlier. Lizzie gasps, putting her hand to her mouth. "Miles you have done enough already!" she exclaims, looking from the box back up to me.

I could never do enough, sweetheart. I saw this and immediately knew that this was meant to be yours." I lean forward and gently press a kiss to the side of her neck; I am instantly struck with the scent that is entirely Lizzie, vanilla mixed with a hint of something feminine, yet understated, a combination that renders me momentarily incapacitated.

Pulling myself from her body proves difficult, but I want to see her open her gift.

"Open it, baby."

"Miles, this is all too much! This entire day has been incredible! And oh," she gasps, as her hand covers her mouth, "I didn't even get to say thank you for everything that you've done for me today. The flowers, the coffee, oh, and the phone, Miles, I told you I would get that! The spa was incredible and simply everything you did for me was so much more than I even deser..." I stop her mid-sentence by holding my finger over her sensuous mouth before she finishes what I know she'll say next. She was going to say she didn't deserve anything, and I won't have my woman believing any of that. She deserves the world, and I will do all I can to give it to her.

"Open it, Lizzie!" I say more forcefully than I should, but knowing it's what she needs to hear. She opens her mouth to protest but closes it back just as quickly. Looking down at the box in her hands, I can see she is trembling slightly, possibly from the cool night air or the anticipation of what's to come; but it makes me nervous all the same. Cautiously, she slips off the ribbon and I grab it so she can have her hands free to open the box. As I hear the box open, my eyes immediately find hers, so I can see the first true reaction she has to this gift. She sucks in a deep breath and her mouth forms an 'o' shape, but it's her eyes I can't look away from. They show all her emotions, and in an instant, a lone tear makes a trek down her beautiful cheek. I catch it with my thumb before it falls any further. At that slightest touch, her eyes turn to mine, and I see exactly what I was hoping to see. Love. I see the love in her eyes. Even if we haven't uttered those words to one another, the feelings are there all the same, and I can see it glowing from the deep pools of her eyes.

"Miles, it's the most beautiful necklace I have ever seen. It's so unique. I've never seen anything like it before!" She beams up at me.

"It's unique like you are, Lizzie. When I saw this piece, I knew the only place it belonged was around your neck. Please, let me do the honors." She nods, handing the necklace over to me so I can fasten it. I skim my fingers over the column of her neck and more goosebumps appear over her skin. Lizzie sweeps her hair up into her hands, so I can clasp the necklace in place. Once she lets her hair back down, she takes the pendant in her hand and studies the piece closer. I knew she would love this. The platinum Victorian key pendant on the necklace is adorned with an intricate pattern of diamonds. This necklace holds more meaning than I think she knows. It's the key to my very soul that I have entrusted to her.

"I love it!" she whispers, looking back up at me. I almost tell her right then that I am in love with her and that I think I have been since the day she marched into that coffee shop, stealing my coffee. I smile when I think back on that day. It could have been like any other day, but it was the day I met her, and my life changed.

A whistle sounds behind me, and without looking, I know it's my jackass of a brother trying to get us to hurry up. I just want to stay in this bubble a little while longer, but the gala awaits.

I hold my arm out and Lizzie wraps her hand around my forearm, as I lead her to the limo. As I help her into the seat, I steal a quick kiss to her cheek. She looks up at me with a sparkling twinkle in her eyes, and I thank my lucky stars I have this woman in my life.

CHAPTER 26

Elizabeth

The feeling of this silky dress caressing my body sends chills up my spine, but nothing compares to the feeling of Miles' warmth pressing against me as we make our way to the charity event. His large hand rests on my lap, making me wish we could time lapse this event and go back to my apartment, or more specifically my bed. *I haven't been able to get it off my mind, the way he thrust inside of me over and over, while pressing his glorious weight on top of me. Fuck I'm getting wet just thinking about it.* I look up at him and admire his sculpted jaw line and cheek bones. He's beautiful in a Greek statue sort of way. He looks regal and seeing him in a tuxedo amplifies this effect on me.

"Are you staring at me, sweetheart?" he asks, squeezing my thigh a bit tighter and making a gasp escape my lips. He just smirks at me because he knows his effect on me. *Ass.* Two can play this game.

"Actually, I was about to tell you that you missed a spot shaving," I comment with a devilish smile on my face. His smile falters for a moment before I burst out laughing, which earns me a pinch on my side.

"Hey!" I squeak, getting the attention of Sarah and Sebastian, both looking at me at the same time.

"Looks like someone is feeling feisty tonight," Miles leans in and whispers in my ear. The warmth of his breath caressing my neck sends sparks through my body.

"Well, it is my birthday, after all, and Sarah insisted we start the celebration early with a bit of bubbly." I'm pretty sure she could sense my nerves throughout the whole apartment and wanted to give me a bit of liquid courage, especially since the Knight men are so important here in New York. I will be on the arm of one, making me a target for attention tonight. Just thinking about it makes me start to fidget with the clutch in my lap. Miles notices and rests his hand over mine. He takes his other hand and slides it up to cup my cheek, then turns my face to look at him.

"Take a deep breath, baby. I know this is very new for you, but I want to show you off to the world. I'll be right by your side. You have nothing to worry about." He gives me a quick kiss and turns his attention to Sebastian, asking him a question I didn't hear because I was in my own little world. I notice that Sarah looks stunning in her white gown. I told her she could use it as a wedding gown one day when she meets someone, and she gave me this look, as if to say I was crazy. I just laughed and went back to getting myself dressed.

The car begins to slow, and I realize we have already reached our destination. We are in line to be dropped off at the red carpet. There are so many people everywhere with cameras snapping and spotlights that can be seen from outer space. My anxiety begins to rise because I hate being in large crowds. Usually, if I have to be in them, I act like a wallflower and stick to the outskirts to avoid conversing with people that I don't know. Miles doesn't understand how uncomfortable I am with this. He grew up in the limelight, and I'm sure he is used to all the attention that comes at these types of engagements. I, on the other hand, am out of my element. I look from the window to Sarah, and she is already looking at me. She can see the panic written across my face. She leans over and places her hand on my shoulder.

"Look at me, Lizzie. Take a deep breath. You look stunning, and you are here with Miles. Just relax and try to have a pleasurable time. I'm sure there are many women who would trade places with you in a heartbeat, so be proud that he chose you," she whispers and gives my shoulder a squeeze, as the car comes to a stop in front of the main entrance.

Thomas comes around to our door and opens it, letting Miles climb out, buttoning his tuxedo jacket as he stands. Then he leans over and offers me his hand with a megawatt smile on his face. *Damn, this man is hot!* I slide my hand in his, and his firm grasp on me gives me the strength to step out of the limousine. *Deep breaths, Lizzie.* As I stand, I can hear people shouting Miles' name from all directions with their cameras and phones out to capture our every move.

Miles puts his arm out for me to take and leads us toward the entrance. Blinding flashes continue as we make our way up the red carpet. We are asked to pause several times for pictures, and Miles obliges, while wrapping his hand tightly around my waist and pulling me close to him. I can't help but look up at him and smile. He looks down at me as well, giving me a wink. Then he places a kiss to my forehead in front of everyone. I can't believe he really is claiming me in public.

"Miles, who is your date?" one camera man shouts.

"Mr. Knight is she your girlfriend?" another yells, with a microphone pointing at us.

My heart starts drumming in my chest. So many people are shouting at once and no one is getting answers; it's making them seem desperate. I feel like one of them might be crazy enough to jump over the rails, separating us, to get the inside scoop. Miles just moves along, holding my hand and waving to people as we pass.

Finally, we are through most of the chaos and climbing the stairs to the entrance of the ballroom. Lifting my gown, I try not to fall on my ass as I hold my clutch in the same hand, which is proving to be a bit complicated. I am clearly not used to this sort of fancy lifestyle, but I hope it doesn't show. The last thing I ever want to do is embarrass Miles in front of all these people.

Stepping inside the Cipriano Wall Street ballroom takes my breath away. The beautiful architecture along with the Winter Wonderland theme makes the space stunning. There are several extravagantly flocked Christmas trees all around the room, decorated in only white and silver. The whole interior is decorated much the same, and it gives the space a very Christmassy but glamorous feel. There are high top tables scattered around the walls and circular dining tables in the middle of the room with white, linen tablecloths, adorned with magnificent, magical-looking center pieces, close to a stage where a band has begun playing music.

Pulling me away from my perusal of the ballroom, a server comes up to us offering champagne in beautiful crystal flutes. Miles hands one to me, and then takes one for himself. I quickly down the contents in one gulp and place the flute back on the tray, grabbing another in its place. Miles looks down at me with concern in his eyes, and I feel like I've already done something wrong. I guess I shouldn't have done that, but I needed something to drown the nerves that are bubbling up in my belly. The server walks off to greet more people, and Miles pulls me off to the side of the room where no one has gathered.

"Lizzie, talk to me. What's going on in that beautiful head of yours?" he inquires, while stroking my hand with his thumb.

"I'm sorry. I just…" closing my eyes, I try to think of the best way to explain. Looking back up at him, I continue, "I'm just nervous. This has all been so much. I know how much this event means to you, and I am trying to fit in because I don't want to embarrass you. But it's so nerve wracking with all the attention being on you and indirectly on me because I am here with you. It's just a lot to take in. I'm sorry, Miles." I close my eyes again, willing my tears not to fall.

"Lizzie, first of all, I told you never to apologize to me. I meant that. You especially don't ever need to feel sorry for telling me what you are thinking." He pulls me closer and rubs his hand down my back in small, comforting strokes. He lifts my chin up to look at him as he continues, "Second, I didn't really give you an option of coming. I'm an asshole, Lizzie. I was so worked up, wanting you to have the perfect birthday that I didn't stop to think that maybe you wouldn't feel comfortable with all the attention. I am truly sorry." He lets out a deep breath and pulls me right up against his body, muscles tense beneath his jacket.

"This isn't your fault, Miles. You didn't know, and you've made my birthday feel like a fairytale. I even got to dress up for a ball at the end of the day," I say with a little chuckle, hoping it will relax him a bit.

"Please forgive me, Lizzie. We can leave just as soon as I make my speech. I never want you to be uncomfortable." He runs the back of his hand up and down my cheek.

"No! I want to do this with you. I was just shocked is all. I wasn't prepared for being bombarded on our way in here. That was intense!"

"That's understandable. I should have warned you, and that's on me. You are incredible, you know that?" he whispers the last part in my ear, kisses the side of my neck, and calmly soothes the fear from my body. Miles instills comfort and safety in me. I'm not sure what it is about him, but it calls to me, and I can't help but be entranced by it.

"You're not so bad, yourself," I thankfully respond. He

can tell he's helped me over my panic. He cups my face in his hands and places a soft kiss on my mouth. He groans at the contact, and I can't help but agree. He feels so good pressed against me.

"Come on," he suggests, grabbing my hand and kissing it quickly. "Let's find our table. It should be right up front."

I feel relieved we were able to talk about what was going on in my head. I'm thankful he can already tell when something isn't right with me, and I don't feel like I have to bottle things up with him. I can be an open book, and he will still accept me. It's such a strange but welcome feeling.

We arrive at the table where Sarah and Sebastian are already sitting. Miles pulls out a chair for me, and then seats himself. He scoots my chair closer to him, which makes a small screeching sound, but he just shrugs his shoulders and puts his hand on my thigh. He kisses my forehead, taking a sip of his champagne. I look over at Sarah, and notice she has a huge smile on her face, watching the interaction between Miles and me. I can't help but blush.

"I was wondering where you both ran off to," she ponders aloud. Before I can say anything, Miles answers for me.

"I wanted a moment alone with *my* girl before everything begins," he enunciates as if it's the most casual thing in the world to call me 'his girl.' *Swoon.*

Sebastian clears his throat and places his champagne flute down on the table before speaking. "I have been getting to know Sarah, but I don't know much about you. Tell me about yourself, Lizzie." Before I get a chance to respond, Miles and Sebastian are out of their seats, buttoning their tuxedos, and smiling at an elegant older woman approaching the table. Without an introduction, I know this is their mother. Anyone can see the resemblance a mile away. Another round of butterflies erupts in my stomach. I didn't know I would be meeting their mother tonight, although I should have known. I didn't even think about it. The men take turns leaning down and giving their mother a sweet peck on the cheek. Miles leads her toward me as I stand.

"Mother, I would like to introduce you to Elizabeth Brighton. Lizzie, this is my mother, Amelia Knight." I reach my hand out to shake hers, but she surprises me by pulling me into a tight hug. A smile dusts my face as this woman embraces me. When she releases me, I speak up.

"It's so nice to meet you, Mrs. Knight," I say with more confidence than I feel.

"Please, dear, call me Amelia. You are even more stunning than my son let on." I give her a small smile and look at Miles, who has a huge smile on his face. He gives me a wink that makes my knees feel weak. I glance back at his mother and see her smiling with her hands laced together. I get the feeling they've had a deep conversation about me, which makes me both excited and nervous. Miles takes his mother's hand and leads her to her seat on the other side of the table.

"Mother, this is Sarah McKenzie. Sarah is my Lizzie's best friend," he advises, gesturing to her. A small gasp escapes my lips at his admission of my being his, to his mother no less.

"It's a pleasure to meet you, Mrs. Knight," Sarah acknowledges her gracefully.

"Oh, you girls are so polite. Please, call me, Amelia," his mother says graciously. Sarah gives her a nod and a warm smile.

Miles comes back to his chair, leaning over, giving my cheek a chaste kiss, and telling me he is going to the bar to get a drink for his mother.

"Would you like anything, darling?" I gaze up at this

gorgeous man that treats his mother well, and I can't help but to be in awe that he chose me to be his, I still can't wrap my head around it, but I've never been so happy to have bumped into this total stranger in my entire life.

"No, but thank you," I answer.

"I'll join you. I need one, as well," Sebastian states, walking toward Miles.

Miles leans over and whispers in my ear, "Will you be okay while I'm gone?" I nod and smile at his thoughtfulness.

Both men head toward the bar, and I can't help the deep affection I feel when I look at Miles. I turn my attention back to our table, and Amelia has her focus on me. I can't help but feel a bit nervous. *What if she doesn't think I'm good enough for her son? What if she thinks I'm after his money?* A sick feeling settles in the pit of my stomach. I raise my champagne flute to my lips, take a large sip, and concentrate on the bubbles that glide over my tongue.

"Elizabeth, it seems you're just as smitten with my son as he is with you. I know that look all too well. It was one my late husband and I shared."

A pang of sadness hits me at her words. How terrible it is to lose the love of your life. I can't imagine. "I'm so very sorry for your loss, Amelia."

"Thank you. I miss him every day, but I wouldn't trade what we had for anything." I nod my head in understanding. As I am about to respond, Miles and Sebastian return to the table. Miles gives his mother her drink, and then takes his place by my side. He slides his arm around my shoulder to bring my body closer to his, and I'm engulfed in his cologne and the scent that is all his own. I slowly let out a deep breath and inhale this man beside me. He drops a kiss to my forehead before he takes a sip of the whiskey he got from the bar.

"I'm going to be giving a speech soon. Being the CEO, I'm expected to start this charity event off. Then we can walk around and look at the items in the silent auction," Miles murmurs in my ear.

"That sounds fun," I reply, nuzzling closer to him. He hums his approval at my movement. The sound sends chills through my body.

CHAPTER 27

Miles

Standing at our table, I button my tuxedo and lean over to give Lizzie a quick kiss to her forehead before I walk to the stage. A little flurry of nerves shoots through me, which catches me off guard. I am used to talking in front of crowds. I've been doing it for most of my life and never given it a second thought. However, tonight I know Lizzie will be watching me. This will be the first time she sees the CEO me. Climbing the steps to the stage, I walk over to the podium just as the band finishes playing their set. The chatter in the room begins to quiet as guests start noticing me. Taking a solid, deep breath, I begin my speech. "Good evening, ladies and gentlemen. As most of you know, I am Miles Knight with Knight Publishing Company." I pause as cheers erupt through the ballroom, and I glance at Lizzie, who has a wide smile on her face. It makes my heart flutter at the sight. "Thank you all for taking the time to be here tonight for this special charity event. The Knight Foundation contributes to many charities throughout the year, but this one has always held a special place in my heart. The Children's Fund for Mental Illness helps those who suffer from various conditions, so they get the therapy, medication, and support they need to grow to become thriving individuals in our community. Many children with mental illness go undiagnosed in our country and/or are unable to get the help they need. The Knight Foundation strives to help pediatricians and early childhood educators by funding the extra tools needed to assist in screenings and proper medical services for all children under their care."

"The reason this charity is dear to me is because I have seen, firsthand, the difference in a child without help, and then with her getting the aid she needed. It was a small miracle for that family, and if we can help more kids like her, then we can build a stronger foundation and support system for other children, as well, to prosper and grow up to be important members of our society. Thank you all for supporting our cause by helping these wonderful children. Lastly, again, thank you for attending tonight's event. There is a silent auction that will begin soon. The prizes have been donated from many businesses and families throughout the city. If we all come together, we can help these children. Enjoy your evening." I wave to the crowd who have now gotten to their feet to applaud. I shake hands with our foundation treasurer, who then goes on to explain how the silent auction will work.

As I walk off the stage, trying to get back to my girl, I am stopped several times by associates and clients wanting to thank me for the charity auction. Some want to talk business, and I have to excuse myself politely. Many people come to these charities to network, which is something I am not interested in doing tonight. As I round the corner to our table, I see Lizzie laughing and talking with Sarah and my mother, which makes my heart happy that they are all getting along. I knew my mother would love Lizzie, but seeing it with my own eyes confirms, in my heart, that Lizzie is the one for me.

"Miles, you were amazing up there. I had no idea how huge this charity was. I am so proud of you," Lizzie gushes as she stands, pulling me into a hug as I get to the table. I squeeze her body close to mine and drop a kiss on the top of her head, her vanilla and coconut scent floods my senses. I take a moment to breathe her in before I let her go.

"Thank you, sweetheart." I give her temple another

small kiss.

"Miles, you always give such wonderful speeches, dear. Your father would be so proud of you," my mother states as she dabs her eye with a cloth to catch an unshed tear. I walk over and give her kiss on the cheek.

"Thank you, mother. He taught us well," I reply, winking at Sebastian. "Lizzie, I'm going to the bar. Would you like to join me?" I ask. She nods, placing her clutch on the table, then walking toward me. I take her hand and place it on my forearm as we make our way through the crowd. We get stopped several times by more business associates, and I get the chance to introduce my beautiful girl on my arm. Seeing her face light up as I introduce her as my girlfriend gives me great satisfaction, but I can't help but want to introduce her as my fiancé or wife. Everyone she meets seems to be totally besotted with her. I can't help but get a little jealous that I'm having to share her with others.

Once we make it to the bar, we only have to wait a moment before we're served. "What would you like?" I lean down, asking Lizzie in her ear. I love seeing the goosebumps covering her skin when I whisper so close to her. She looks up at me with a knowing smile, like she knows that I know the effect I have on her.

"I think I would like a glass of Moscato, please," she says to the bartender. He takes a moment to look her up and down with an appreciative smile, then looks to me silently asking for my order. I take that moment to pull Lizzie closer to me, keeping my hand on her waist. The bartender pales when he sees the glare, I'm giving him.

"Macallan for you, sir?" I nod as he gets our order. I reach out grabbing Lizzie's chin to bring her eyes to mine. "Have I told you how stunning you are?" Her cheeks blush at my compliment, which makes me smile wider. She doesn't know how beautiful she is, but I will spend the rest of my life telling her, until she finally believes it.

"Yes, I believe you have. It's all thanks to you and this gorgeous dress."

"No," I state, adamantly. "It's all you, baby. That dress would look like rags on anyone else. It was made with you in mind. You're breathtaking!"

"Here are your drinks, sir." The bartender places them in front of us. I pick up the glass of wine and hand it to Lizzie, then take my glass.

"Would you like to look at the lots in the silent auction?" I ask Lizzie, as we walk toward that section of the ballroom.

"Sure. I've never been to one," she answers. Leading her in that direction, I place my hand on her lower back, loving the feel of her against me.

Everyone needs to experience it at least once. I am curious to see what all we have available this year. Let me know if you see something you like." She looks at me incredulously.

"I am not letting you bid on something for me with everything that you have already done today, Miles," she insists.

"Well, technically, it would benefit the charity." I smirk down at her when she looks up at me. She just sighs as we walk around, looking through the auction. There are antique cars, boats, destination vacations, all-inclusive spa packages, tickets to sporting events and concerts, but just about everything else you can imagine also.

Lizzie stops in front of a trip to Ireland and reads the details. Up until that point, she's just been looking at the different exhibits. However, something about this one catches her attention. I stand back and watch her as she looks at everything that the trip includes. I don't want to break the moment for her, so I continue past her to look at other items while keeping my eyes on her. I wonder if she has ever been to Ireland. It's such a beautiful country. I would love to take her there. I think she would love it, especially with her literature background. Many well-known authors in the eighteenth and nineteenth century were Irish born, although often considered English authors. It wasn't until the twentieth century, when Ireland petitioned for independence that scholars reclaimed those authors and their works to be known as Anglo-Irish literature.

I look down at the auction item in front of me and it grabs my attention. A gun metal gray 1967 Shelby GT500 Mustang would look amazing in my collection. As I am reading about the car, I hear Lizzie's laugh, and it pulls my attention away from the car. When I look up, I see Timothy Alexander, standing far too close to my girl. He is grinning like he won the lottery. He's a known playboy in this crowd; it shouldn't surprise me that he zeroed in on the most beautiful woman in the room to try his luck. Unfortunately for him, she's already taken. It pisses me off more that he already saw us together, and he is taking this time when I'm not beside her to make his approach. My fists clench at my side as I walk over to where they are talking. Coming up beside Lizzie, I grab her waist and pull her close to me, making Timothy have to take a few steps back. "There you are, baby." I say, looking down at her.

"Timothy, I haven't seen you in quite a while. Hope you're doing well." I hold my hand out for him to shake. He nods, shaking my hand.

"Very well. I was just looking at this trip in the auction, and I met Elizabeth. Seems we have a mutual interest in Ireland."

"I see," I reply to Timothy. Looking down at Lizzie I say, "The auction is almost over, do you want to head back to the table? I'm sure Sebastian and Sarah are wondering where we went off to."

"Oh, you're right. I didn't tell her I wasn't coming right back. It was nice meeting you, Timothy," Lizzie tells him politely as I lead her away from this fuck face, trying to move in on my woman. Once we get back to the table, it's empty. I pull out Lizzie's chair for her and take my place beside her. The band has started up again, and there are many couples on the dance floor. When I see Sebastian dancing with Sarah, I can't help but chuckle. She must have asked him to dance. He never does unless he's forced, and the idea that Sarah must have done that makes me smile.

"Seb and Sarah seem to be getting along." I point to where they are dancing, and I hear a gasp coming from Lizzie.

"Wow, I definitely didn't see that coming. He is not her type at all. Maybe they were just bored sitting here," she ponders. I take her hand in mine, kissing her knuckles. She looks back at me and smiles.

"You just can't keep your hands to yourself, can you?" she queries laughingly.

"Not where you are concerned," I admit as I pull her in for a kiss. When we pull away, I see mother approaching the table which gives me the perfect opportunity to go bid on the trip to Ireland as a surprise for Lizzie. I wasn't going to leave her at the table alone. I stand and pull the chair out for mother and tell them I will be right back.

Walking quickly toward the silent auction tables, I find the Ireland trip I'm looking for and put my name down. I see Timothy bid as well, and the need to outbid him overwhelms me. I place an outrageous bid that pretty much guarantees my winning. I put the pen down and head back to our table, just in time to see Sebastian leading Sarah back as well. He looks... happy? Interesting.

I slip into my seat, while my mother and Lizzie are talking. I glance at Seb, and he just winks at me. I warned him about messing with Sarah. I may have to give him a little reminder although, I am pleased that she seems to be comfortable with him. Maybe she is a one-night kind of girl. Not judging at all, I just don't want it to blow up in our faces.

The band continues to play, so I rise from my chair and hold out my hand for Lizzie. "May I have this dance?"

"Of course." She smiles shyly and places her hand in mine as I help her from her seat. I guide her toward the dance floor just as another song starts playing. I recognize it instantly as, "Say You Won't Let Go" by James Arthur. I love that this will be the first song we dance to. Once we get onto the dance floor, I pull her close to my chest. Taking her hand in mine and placing the other on her waist, I begin to dance us around the floor with the lyrics weaving their way through us. I look down at her, and again, I can't help but feel so incredibly fortunate to have met her. I lean over and sing some of the lyrics in her ear as we sway to the music. I feel her body melt into mine, and it's the perfect fit.

"Everyone is looking at you, Miles," she whispers, as she looks around the room.

"Lizzie, you are the most exquisite creature I have ever had the pleasure of meeting. Trust me when I say, it is you they are looking at. They're all jealous that I'm the one that has you in my arms." She looks up at me with a mix of wonder and love.

"Baby, I wish I could frame the way you're looking at me with those gorgeous brown eyes. I feel like I can see everything you are feeling. You take my breath away," I murmur, nuzzling my nose along the column of her neck and feeling her shuttering breath.

"No one has ever said anything like that to me before," she breathes out. Leaning down, I bring my lips to hers. I lift my hands to cup her face. People around us continue to dance, but I stop and look in her eyes, seeing everything I'm feeling reflected back at me. I must tell her I love her, and I know she feels it as well.

"Lizzie, I..." I'm cut off from what I was about to say by a drunk Timothy. He grabs ahold of her arm, trying to pull her away from me. For a moment, I am stunned that we were interrupted, but it soon turns to anger when I realize he means to take her from me.

"You don't mind if I cut in, do you, Miles? Surely, you can share this beautiful woman," he slurs a bit as he continues to pull on Lizzie's arm. When she winces from the pain, I see red. I take his hand from her arm and squeeze until he draws back, then I step between them. Lizzie moves behind me as people begin to stare.

"You will never lay another finger on her again. Do you understand?" I seethe as his steps falter a bit. Instead of agreeing, he steps closer with a sleazy grin on his face.

"And what if she wants me to touch her? Huh? I bet she's easy if she is here with you. She has those fuck me eyes, and I think I..." Before he can finish his disgusting little speech, my fist connects with his face, and he falls flat on his back in the middle of the dance floor. Combined gasps come from all around us, but the only thing I'm concerned about is getting Lizzie out of here. I turn around and see all the color has drained from her face. I step closer and pull her body against mine. I can feel her trembling beneath my touch, and it only ignites my rage further that someone would dare lay a finger on her like that. I pull back and raise her chin up, so I can look into her eyes.

"Are you okay, baby?" She silently nods, but I can see that she is far from all right. Sebastian comes up to us with Sarah trailing behind him.

"What the hell just happened, man?" Seb asks, looking from me to Timothy lying on the floor.

"He put his filthy hands on her and was trying to fucking say she wanted him to. He didn't back down with my first warning, so I took him out with the second." Sebastian nods in understanding. He looks at Lizzie, and then at me.

"Get her out of here. I'll handle this. Sarah can stay here with me, and I will get her home safely." He claps me on the shoulder, and I give him a nod in thanks.

I turn back to see Sarah trying to console Lizzie, but that's my job now. I take her hand in mine and lead her away from the crowd that's gathered around us. Pulling out my phone, I message Thomas to meet us at the back entrance as soon as possible.

"Miles, slow down. You're scaring me." I instantly come to a stop, turning to look at her.

"Baby, look at me. I will never hurt you. I was trying to get you out of there before reporters start swarming in. Timothy went too far. I don't like people touching what's mine. You're mine, Lizzie." I trail the back of my hand over her cheek and kiss her forehead. After a moment, she takes a deep breath and looks up at me.

"Thank you for getting me away from him and the rest of the crowd, for that matter. I'm sorry. I didn't mean to be the cause of a scene, especially here at your charity event." She drops her gaze to the floor and sighs.

Cupping her face with both hands, I force her to look at me in the eyes, so she knows what I'm about to say is the truth.

"You did nothing wrong. Timothy was drunk, and he was so far out of line. He had an opportunity to walk away, but he didn't take it. I'm not sorry I knocked his ass out. He was asking for it. I'm not going to apologize for making a scene either. I know it made you uncomfortable, but I won't have people being disrespectful to you. It doesn't matter where we are. I will always be on your side. Do you understand me, Lizzie? It's you and me baby. Always. Now, come on. Thomas is waiting for us." I slide my hand into hers and lead her to the back entrance of the Cipriano ballroom.

Thomas is waiting for us as we step through the doors. I usher her into the car and climb in after. Thomas takes off down the road, and I pull her onto my lap. She instantly snuggles up to me and rests her head on my chest. I feel a weight lift from me knowing she is safe in my arms. I rub my hand up and down her back and give her a kiss on the top of her head. She relaxes into my body, and I squeeze my arms around her to pull her in closer. I never want to let her go. Now, I don't want to let her out of my sight. I know that's irrational thinking, but I can't stand the thought of something happening to her and my not being there to help. We arrive at my penthouse twenty minutes later. I open the door before Thomas gets to us, and I help Lizzie out.

"Thank you, Thomas, for getting us out of there. Has Lizzie's bag already been brought up?" I ask.

"Yes, sir, I dropped it off earlier," Thomas replies.

"Sebastian and Miss McKenzie are still in need of your service tonight. But then, I want you to take tomorrow off and spend it with your wife. I can drive us anywhere we need to go. Thank you again." I insist as I lead Lizzie to my private elevator.

The only thing on my mind now is getting this dress off her. I need to be inside her... *now*. I need to hear her screaming *my name*. She is the only thing that can ease this anger and adrenaline currently coursing through my body. I wanted tonight to be special, but it's going to be rough.

CHAPTER 28

Elizabeth

Miles pulls me into his elevator as the doors close. He turns to look at me with pure lust in his eyes, then growls, "Fuck, I can't wait any longer to taste you." He grabs my waist and slams his lips on mine in a possessive and ravenous kiss. He pulls me tight to his body, and I am overheating from just his touch. Burning from the inside out, it feels like electricity is shooting all through my body. He groans as our tongues tangle together making the kiss sloppy but erotic. Pushing me up against the wall, he cinches my gown up to my waist, and I take the opportunity to jump into his arms, locking my legs around his back. He squeezes my ass in his hands and a soft cry escapes my lips. Feeling his hard cock pressing against my core, I can't help but rock up and down against him. I'm so hot and oblivious to our surroundings by the time the doors open to his penthouse. I didn't realize he started walking us toward his bedroom, until I notice the light from the elevator sliding closed.

The penthouse is dark. The only light being the illumination from the streetlights below and the full moon streaming through the large bank of windows to the right of us. The murmurs of traffic from a distance are the only noise, other than our mouths on each other. Holding me closer, Miles kicks open his door that was left ajar. His lips leave mine just for them to shift down my neck. He knows my sweet spot and is going right for it. While nibbling my ear, he strokes my wet, needy pussy.

"Miles, I need you so bad. Please," I whine into his ear. As he moves his mouth down my neck, he begins biting, then soothing the sting with his tongue. The pain from the bites melt to pleasure, and I am overtaken with the desire to feel his naked body against mine. I undo his bowtie and throw it to the floor as we get closer to the California king-sized bed. He sets me down on my heels, holding onto me while my legs steady themselves. My dress falls back down into place, with noticeable creases, where he was holding it so tightly in his hands. His beautiful eyes bore into mine, and I can see hints of their blue hue from the moonlight.

"I need you out of this dress. Now!" He turns me around quickly, with one hand remaining on my waist for support. I hear him curse under his breath when he realizes the dress has about a million buttons to undo. I smile to myself, when I remember Sarah cursing about getting me into the damn dress in the first place.

"Why the hell did I buy a dress with this many buttons? *Fuck that*." I gasp as I feel his hands shredding the dress, until it's a pool of silk and lace on the floor. I'm left in a silver silk thong and matching strapless bra. I feel him drop to his knees behind me, and he begins caressing my ass in his hands, then licks and kisses down my spine.

"Miles!" I exclaim. "I literally had that dress for less than a day," I cry out. Not particularly caring about the discarded clothing but needing to say something to keep myself in this moment. Instead, I begin floating away on a cloud of pleasure.

"I'll buy you ten more," he vows between kisses. "I don't give a fuck. I needed you out of it. That was my solution," he utters, with a husky growl in his voice. He drags his hand down the strip of material between my ass cheeks, finding my wet slit. His fingers press against the sticky fabric between my legs, and I gasp. As he pushes it aside and slides a finger inside me, I press back against him, wanting him deeper.

"Damn, baby, you are so wet. Did I do this to you?" I nod my head, unable to form the words I need to answer.

"Answer me, Lizzie. Who makes this pussy so wet?" he grinds out, then sliding another finger through my folds. He presses his thumb on my clit and the sensations of it all make my legs weak, but he wraps his other arm around my waist. He holds my body against him, while he sucks and bites my ass cheeks. He begins to remove his fingers because I haven't answered him.

"You, Miles. Only you" I yell as he slams three fingers into my tight pussy. The burn of the stretch has me in a daze and feeling my climax building. He bends me over the bed, shoving my ass in the air. I cling to the thick white comforter, as he presses in a fourth finger. Tears threaten to spill from the intense pleasure. I know my makeup is smearing all over his bed, but I'm beyond being able to care.

"Good girl," he praises, making me clench down on his fingers. The fucking praise I get from this man makes me want to do anything he tells me. He continues pushing his fingers into me rhythmically, as his thumb circles my clit with more pressure. Heat is coursing through my blood from his ministrations, and I come undone when his tongue slides between my cheeks. It runs up to my virgin rosebud, thrusting inside. I scream out his name as my orgasm ricochets through my body, hitting every nerve ending in its wake. He continues working me through my climax, until I feel like a quivering mess.

"Lizzie, you are the sexiest woman I have ever seen. When you come undone on my hand, it's a beautiful sight. Fuck, how did I get so lucky? I want to tie you to my bed, so you can never leave." I shiver, as he slides his fingers out of my pussy, and I instantly miss the feel of him inside me. "Mmm, baby, you taste so sweet. Like a ripe piece of fruit," he rasps, as he sucks his fingers clean. The erotic sound of the slurping makes me gush even more. I feel it drip down my thigh. He must see it because he chuckles. "You like me talking dirty to you. Don't you?" He slaps my ass hard, and the pain sparks something deep inside me. "You like that, don't you, Lizzie? You like being my little slut?" He slaps the other cheek, then soothes it with his tongue.

"Yes. It's so good. I want to be your good girl," I assure him.

"I know you do, baby. You want me to be in control? You trust me to give you what you need?" he questions, kissing my burning ass, where he spanked me two more times.

"I trust you, Miles," I whimper. He keeps me bent over the bed, as he lifts one ankle and takes my high heel off, then throws it somewhere behind us. He does the same with the other shoe and wraps his arms around my middle, pulling me up from the bed then turning me around to face him. I find him on his knees in front of me, seeing him like this ready to worship my body, makes my heart beat wildly in my chest.

Sliding his hands over my waist, he leans in to kiss both of my hip bones. "This needs to go." He gestures to my thong. Grabbing it, he shreds it from my body, adding it to the ruined pile of silk. "Miles!" I gasp.

"What? I thought you trusted me. I needed it off." He smirks, like he didn't just shred thousands of dollars from my body. I roll my eyes at him, which I realize is a mistake the moment I do it. "Did you just roll your eyes at me? I guess your ass isn't sore enough then." He's off the floor in an instant and turning me around. He spanks both cheeks in rapid succession, with more force than last time. A sob escapes my lips, as a few tears run down my face. The sting is both painful and pleasurable. I never knew I was into that, but I guess I am. He knows more about me than I do, apparently. "Now, how is this perfect ass feeling?"

"It stings, but it also feels good," I shriek, not sure if I can take any more. He quickly flips me back over and crashes his lips down on mine. The taste of myself on his tongue is erotic. Tingles spread through my body as he runs his hands up the side of my ribs until he reaches my bra. With the flick of his wrist, it unclasps and falls from my body. Miles breaks the kiss as my breasts spring free before his eyes. In the next breath he's lavishing my nipple with his tongue, while tweaking the other with his fingers. I close my eyes and moan at the pleasure building up within me again.

"Look at me baby. I need to see your eyes on me." I open, tilting my head down to see his hooded gaze connecting with mine. As he sucks my nipple in his mouth, I grab his wrists to undo his cuff links. Then I grab his jacket, sliding it off his shoulders and he quickly shakes his arms loose. His hands are right back on me like magnets. He moves his mouth to the other breast, keeping his eyes locked on me. He rotates between biting, licking, and sucking, and I know he's marking me. The incident from the gala must still be at the forefront of his mind and he wants everyone to know who I belong to. I feel like I should be offended but find that I don't give a damn because the truth is, I do belong to him. He has my heart, soul, and body. I don't think there is anything I wouldn't agree to if he asked me. That's how far gone I am for the man before me.

He lifts me by my ass and throws me onto the center of the bed. The motion makes my curves jiggle a bit, so I go to cover myself. "Don't you dare. Don't hide from me. I want to see all of you. I *need* to see all of you." I lie there, chest heaving as he starts unbuttoning his shirt.

"That necklace is stunning on your naked body. That's how it was meant to be worn, but only around me." He smirks down at me, as I brush the pendant with my fingers, loving the cool metal against my heated skin.

"So, you can rip up my gown, but I have to wait here for you to undo all those buttons?" I say teasingly, with a grin on my flushed face. I find that I like getting him riled up.

"That bratty mouth is going to get you in trouble one day," he promises. In the next moment, buttons are flying across the room, hitting different surfaces, making it sound like rain on a tin roof. He rips the shirt from his body, adding it to the pile on the floor. I sit up and crawl toward him. My beautiful necklace thumping against my chest with every move. His gaze, still locked on me, becomes raw and intense as I inch closer toward him. Leaning up, I run my hands over his abdominal muscles up to his sculpted chest. The heat radiating off him, mixed with his salacious stare makes me grow desperate for him to be inside me. I run my nails down his body, and a groan vibrates from his chest. Locking eyes with his as I unbuckle his belt, ripping it from its loops. Seeing his hard dick through his pants, I squeeze and rub it as I unbutton his pants. In one swift movement, he tears his pants down his body and stands before me completely naked.

My mouth waters at the sight of precum dripping from his shaft. I lean forward, licking the slit as the erotic saltiness flavor that is Miles explodes on my tongue. Cupping his balls in one hand, I place the other on his ass. I lick him from tip to base and back. I swirl my tongue in a circular motion around the tip, before sucking it inside my mouth.

"Fuck, Lizzie, your mouth is perfect around my cock. Can you take me all the way, baby?" I hum, with him still in my mouth and move forward, trying to take his hard length further into my hot, wet mouth. He grabs a handful of my hair and begins pumping himself in and out, going further each time. "Keep those eyes on me, gorgeous." I do as I'm told as he pounds himself into my mouth. Holding still until I gag, then slowly sliding it back out. I start to pull away because I don't have much experience with this, and I don't want to disappoint him. As if reading my mind, he brushes the hair from my face and wipes the tears away.

"You are taking me perfectly. Let me show you what I like." I nod to him, as he angles my chin higher to give him better access to the back of my throat.

"Hollow your cheeks out and relax around me. Let me in, baby." I do what he tells me, and his grip on my hair tightens. The pain sends shivers down my spine and straight to my pussy. He thrusts in hard and stays for a moment before sliding out and doing it again, all while giving me the praise I desire. I want to be his good girl. I get wetter every time he praises me.

"The only place I am coming tonight is inside that tight pussy of yours." He pulls me back by the hair, and his cock slips from my lips with a pop. He leans over me, cupping my cheeks as he gives me a bruising kiss. He slips one hand from my face, bringing it to my chest to gently push me back on the bed.

"Scoot up the bed, baby." I grip the sheets and slide backward, and as I move, he prowls closer to me on the bed. Miles slides his muscular body up mine, dragging his hard cock between us until it's positioned right at my core. He rests his body on one elbow, while his other snakes around my head, holding me in place. He brings his lips down on mine and it instantly becomes intense. *Deep. Dominating. Possessive.* It feels like his lips are giving me all the unspoken emotions coursing through himself.

I move my hand between us and line his cock up with my entrance. The moment it's there, he doesn't waste a second before thrusting completely inside me. He swallows my scream, and continues driving inside of me without giving me the time to adjust to his huge size. Digging my nails into his arms as the pain turns to pleasure. My back arches off the bed, pulling him in closer. Miles starts licking and sucking down the column of my neck until he gets to the place behind my ear, which makes my toes curl. I can't stop my hips from rising to meet his every thrust.

"That's my good girl. Come for me, baby," he croons in my ear. I cry out as he hits that perfect spot over and over, until I am falling headfirst over that edge of pleasure that's been building. My body shudders violently as my orgasm rocks through me, sending waves of rapture through my soul.

Miles slips out of me, and before I can protest, he flips me onto my stomach, bringing my ass up in the air. Before I can catch my breath, he's behind me again, pounding away. His thrusts are deeper than I knew was possible.

"My cock fits in here perfectly." He spanks my sore ass and continues to drive deep into me. "Who owns this pussy?" he demands between grunts.

I move my head to the side, so I can look back at him when I reply. "Yours." It's all I can get out of my mouth. He's taking my breath away with every pump. I never knew sex could be like this. *This electric. On fire. Magnetic. Passionate.*

***

Miles

"Hell yeah, it is." *Thrust.* "You." *Thrust.* "Are." *Thrust.* "Mine." I squeeze the globes of her ass in my hands, as I pound into her, no doubt leaving more marks. Marks that further prove Lizzie is mine. *Today. Tomorrow. Forever.*

"Yes!" she cries out into the sheets. I reach around her waist and begin circling her clit in rhythm with my plunges. I want her to come again when I do and I'm close. "I'm yours, Miles!" Hearing those words uttered from her lips, has me coming in her tight little pussy. Rope after rope of come fill her ripe body, and for a minute, I wish she wasn't on birth control. I want to see my seed take root in her womb and watch as her belly swells with my child. That thought has my orgasm going off again, filling her so much that it's dripping down my balls and her legs, collecting on the sheets below. Slowing my motions, I lay my body over hers. Careful not to crush her, but I want to have skin-on-skin contact. I bury my head in the crook of her neck, kissing any spot I can reach. I want to worship every inch of Lizzie's body. I can't get enough of her, and I know I never will.

As our breathing slows, I finally pull out, rolling on my back and bringing her body with me. She snuggles into my side as I hold her close to my side. Lizzie wraps her arm around my chest and holds her head up to brush a kiss against my neck. Goosebumps explode over my skin at the sensation of her lips on me. After the mind-blowing sex we just had, my whole body feels tingly. Almost electric. Like there was a live wire in our bodies, sending out sparks.

"Stay here." I kiss the top of her head and roll out of the bed. Walking into the ensuite, I start a bath. I know I was rough with her, but I couldn't help it. Timothy pushed me to my limit, and I had this possessive drive in me to fuck her hard. I needed to fill her up, so every damn person would know who she belongs to. Just thinking about that fucker makes me clench my fists. I let out a deep breath and shake him from my mind. I need to take care of Lizzie now.

Walking back to my room, I see her sprawled out on the bed with the sheet covering half of her body. Her messy, but gorgeous black hair covering the pillows surrounding her. Her eyes are drooping like she could fall asleep at any minute. Walking over, I lift her from the bed. The sudden movement jars her awake and she tenses until she realizes I have her in my arms.

"I drew you a bath, sweetheart. I want you to soak and relax." I lean over the tub and place her feet in, allowing her to lower herself into the water. She winces when her ass touches down, but her face quickly morphs into bliss. I put a few drops of lavender essential oil and some bath salts, so it should soothe her aching ass and pussy. I bought the oils and salts with her in mind. She mentioned loving taking baths, and I wanted her to feel at home here.

"Mmm, this is amazing Miles. I love baths, but I don't have the time to take them often." She closes her eyes and rests her head against the towel I put at the end of the tub, so her head would be comfortable. "Aren't, you going to join me?" she inquires, opening her eyes to look up at me. The sight of her in my tub, my bed, my home makes my heart skip a beat. I suddenly don't want her to leave, ever. I want her to live here with me. I know I want to share my life with her.

"I will. I have to take care of something first." I dim the lights and turn on some soft music through Bluetooth in the bathroom. Leaving her in the tub, I walk back to the bed and strip the sheets. I don't want her to sleep on dirty linens, even though I like the idea of sleeping on our mixture of pleasure. I get a clean set and make the bed quickly, so I can join Lizzie before the water becomes tepid.

Coming back into the bathroom, I'm rendered speechless at the goddess in my tub. Her wet hair looks like silk cascading down her creamy body. She has her eyes closed, but her toes are tapping to the rhythm of the music playing. She hasn't noticed me yet, so I take this opportunity to really look at how exquisite Lizzie is. Not just on the outside, which is absolutely phenomenal, but on the inside as well. She is kind and passionate. She's had a rough go of it, but stayed strong no matter what she thinks. She allowed herself to open up to me, when I didn't know if that was something she would be able to do. But she has overcome so much, and she is the most precious thing in the world to me. If I had to sell my soul to keep her, I wouldn't hesitate.

"I can feel you staring, Miles." She smiles, before opening one eye and looking at me.

"I couldn't help it. Just enjoying the view. I have never seen anything more magnificent in my life. You, here with me, in my tub." I groan, just thinking about it. "It just does something to me. Scoot forward, so I can get in behind you, baby." She leans forward, as I slide in behind. I wrap her in my arms and pull her back against my chest. She lets out a contented sigh, resting her head on my chest. I grab the sponge and squirt body wash on it, then begin lathering up her arms and legs. Going slowly, I wash around her breasts, and she lets out a small sigh. Then I move further south, until I am cleaning her pussy. She jerks a bit at the first contact, so I pull away.

"Did I hurt you, baby?" I ask, concerned, knowing I was

too rough on her. Guilt slams into me hard.

"I'm okay. Just a bit sore. The bath is helping," she replies, bringing her hand up to rub the back of my neck.

"I'm sorry, baby. I'll make it better." I kiss the side of her head and reach my hand between her legs to start massaging her clit in slow, sensual circles. It doesn't take long before she is writhing in my lap, and my cock has taken notice of her ass rubbing so close to it. I close my eyes and try to suppress the urge to take her again. When I am around her, I feel insatiable. I want to constantly be inside her.

She slowly turns around to face me, straddling my lap and trapping my hard cock between our bodies. "Don't be sorry. I loved every second of it. I would have told you to stop if it was too much. I promise," she replies. I move a strand of hair, which has fallen into her face, and cup her cheek. Pulling her to me, so I can kiss her pouty, swollen lips. I lick the seam and she opens for me, allowing my tongue to lazily glide into her mouth. She sighs into the kiss, bringing her hands around the back of my head and threading her fingers through my hair.

Chill bumps break out over her skin, and I pull back a little. "Are you cold, baby?" She just slowly nods her head and gives me another quick kiss. I lift her off me, grabbing a towel from the heated rack and wrapping it around her. I snag one as well and quickly dry off, then tie it around my waist. I lift her up onto the countertop, grabbing another towel to wrap her hair in, so it dries faster. Opening one of my drawers, I pull out a toothbrush that hasn't been opened yet and hand it to her.

"Wow, you're prepared," she remarks as she takes the toothbrush from me. I give her a wink. She hops off the counter, grabs the toothpaste, and brushes her teeth. Fortunately, this bathroom was built with a Jack and Jill vanity, so there are two sinks and plenty of counter space. After we brush our teeth, she puts her toothbrush next to mine, and I smile at the sight. Tugging her from the bathroom, she sees I remade the bed, and the look of shock on her face sends a jolt of pleasure through me.

"I can't believe you changed the sheets. Or that you even knew how." She laughs and nudges me in the stomach.

"Oh yeah? Is that how it is? You don't think I can do everyday things?" I raise my eyebrow, giving her a smirk, and she takes off across the room to get away from me. She isn't fast enough, and I grab her, throwing her onto the bed. We are both laughing as I tickle her ribs through the towel. I love the sound of her laughter and I want to keep making her do it. The sound is so comforting. I lean down and kiss her forehead, cheek, eyes, nose, and then her mouth.

"Let's get some sleep, sweetheart." She nods and I pull her up, taking her towel and tossing it in the hamper along with mine. I pull the covers back and pat the bed. I slide in behind her, wrapping my arm around her waist and pulling her flush against me. I let out a deep sigh of contentment.

"Miles, I'm happy. You make me happy," she murmurs a few minutes later. I smile into her hair and kiss her head.

"Me too, baby. Me too." I close my eyes and drift off to the most peaceful sleep I have ever had.

CHAPTER 29

Elizabeth

Darkness.

It surrounds me, threatening to pull me into its shadowy depths. I've been here before, but I don't know which way to go. I need to run. I need to escape this blackness, before it drags me under. My throat clogs in fear as I see a dark, hooded figure closing its large hands around me. It's done. Over. It got me. I thrash around trying to escape it, but no one is around. Just me and my demon. He's here to take me like before. It's just like before, except I've never been caught. Wait, I hear my name. Where is it coming from? He can hear it, too, because his grip on me loosens. I hear it again. Miles.

"Lizzie! Wake up, baby. I'm right here." I jolt awake with fear still coursing through my body. Opening my eyes, I see Miles leaning above my body. Cradling me in his arms; the look of worry is written across his face. I close my eyes to try and remember the nightmare, and this time I can actually remember pieces of it.

"Good morning, beautiful. I was worried about you." Miles kisses my forehead, down the side of my face, and a quick kiss on my lips.

"I'm okay. It was just a nightmare. I'm sorry. I have those sometimes." I try to think back to the last time I had one, and I think it has been a couple of years. I don't even remember what happened later that day, but I'm sure something terrible happened. That's the way these dreams always work, ever since I was a child. It's like they are a forewarning of something malicious to come. I try to scoot away from him, so I can go to the bathroom and get a cold, wet washcloth to put on my head.

"You aren't okay. You were yelling out in your sleep and were flailing about on the bed. What were you dreaming of baby?" he questions as he pulls me further into his arms.

"Um, can you get me a wet washcloth for my face?" He rests me against the pillows, then jumps up, runs to the bathroom, and returns a moment later holding the cloth. He climbs back into bed and takes the washcloth, running it along my face. I close my eyes and soak in the coolness against my overheated flesh. He continues to rub the cloth over my face and neck, until he can see that I have calmed down.

"Can you talk to me now, sweetheart?"

"It's just this night terror I get sometimes. I don't really know what brings it on," I say with a quiver in my voice. Miles threads one hand through my hair, and the other skims over my skin, leaving goosebumps in its wake.

"You've had this same dream before?" Miles looks at me with concern in his eyes. I hesitate for a moment. How do I tell him that when I have this dream, it means something bad is going to happen? He would probably think I'm crazy or something. Maybe I am just getting sick this time because it can mean that, too.

"Just... Ugh, yes, I've had this same dream before. I had it the night before my parents decided to get a divorce and have had it a few times since then. Every single time I have it, there seems to be something bad that happens that day. I promise I'm not crazy. Maybe I just have this bad dream and coincidently, something happens the next day. But the dream is so dark and scary. I never know where I am, and there is no one around. The only thing I know is that I need to run, to get away from the darkness. It's like instinct; I know that I have to run. In today's dream, I actually saw a dark, hooded figure which grabbed me. That's never been a part of the night terror before. Normally, it's always the same." I take a few deep breaths, because I don't want to have to relive the dream over again.

"Just take some deep breaths; I'm right here. I'm not going anywhere. I'm not going to let anything happen to you. It was just a dream. It doesn't mean something bad is going to happen, okay? I'll always protect you. Do you trust me?" Miles queries.

"Of course, I trust you, Miles. You have already proven that you'll take care of me. Maybe the dream stemmed from what happened at the gala last night," I say, looking up at him. His jaw tenses like it did last night when that man had his hands on me.

"You don't have anything to worry about," he murmurs as he gives me a sweet kiss on the lips. I cover my mouth quickly. "No! I've got morning breath!" I try to get off the bed, but I'm hauled back against him with a thump.

"Do you really think that's going to give me pause?" I turn my head into one of his luscious pillows and giggle as he tickles my ribs.

"Miles! Mercy! Mercy! You can't tickle me five seconds after waking me up! That's a criminal offense." I shove back against his hard chest, but there is no escaping him. His arm tightens around my waist, and he presses my back against the mattress. He lowers himself on top of me. And just like that, the dream drifts further and further from my memory, until I'm not scared that something sinister awaits me today.

"How come you got to brush your teeth? I can smell your minty freshness," I pout. He pulls my bottom lip into his mouth and nibbles before letting it go.

"That's because I've been up for hours. I got in a workout and a shower, all while you were being a lazy bum in this bed." I see the huge smile on his face, before he lowers his head and begins kissing my neck.

"You could have awakened me, you know." I declare, only half serious. I'm not an early riser unless it's necessary. Working out doesn't seem too important at that time of day.

"Yeah and endure your wrath?" He chuckles as his eyes come back to meet mine. He's in a playful mood this morning, and I like seeing this side of him. It's a vast difference from last night. Ah, last night was a whole new side of Miles I hadn't seen before.

"I suppose there's no hiding that I'm not the best morning person in the world. However, if it involves you, I think you would have that on your side. Being with you makes me happy, so I suppose that means even if it is crack thirty in the morning." He chuckles and leans his forehead against mine, bringing a hand up to cup my face. His thumb strokes my cheek, and the look in his eyes is no longer playful, more thoughtful.

"Lizzie, do you know how much you mean to me?" he inquires. I'm not sure if he's actually asking, or if it's rhetorical. So, I bring my hand up and cover his that's on my face.

"I think I can imagine," I whisper.

"I don't want you to imagine, baby. I want you to know." He takes a deep breath, closing his eyes. My heart begins beating wildly out of my chest, not knowing where he is going with this. His eyes open and find mine again. "I'm in love with you, Lizzie. You are everything I never knew I needed, and everything I know I can't live without. You are the piece of my heart that's been missing all my life. It's like a beautifully but uniquely shaped puzzle piece that fits perfectly in a puzzle. I love you baby." He leans in, giving me the softest of kisses as he trails his lips over my jaw and to my ear. "You are my world, Lizzie," he rasps. Feeling his warm breath against me sends shivers running through my body.

"Miles." I pull his face up to look at me. I open my mouth, but nothing comes out. I know I am in love with this man, but can I tell him? It's only been a couple of weeks, but I know what I feel. I think it's real. Obviously, we don't know everything about each other, but I feel like we know the important things. I do feel like I know his heart. While my mind rambles on, he places a finger over my mouth.

"I don't want you to say anything if you aren't ready. I just want you to know what's in my heart. I need you to understand my actions from last night. Never in my life have I felt so territorial or possessive over someone. I wish you didn't even have to leave this apartment, so then I would know you were always safe. Obviously, I know that's ridiculous. I just want everyone to know you are mine. And you *are* mine, Lizzie. You may need time to come to terms with that, but we were meant to be together. We were meant to get our coffee orders mixed up in that little shop. I never thought I believed in destiny, but I can't deny it any longer." He pulls his finger back from my lips and replaces it with his. Our chaste kiss soon turns into a passionate tangle of hands, roaming all over the place. Miles grabs me around the waist and rolls us, so he is lying on his back with me straddling his body. I gasp, as the sudden movement places his hard cock against my wet core. I can't help but rub back and forth, wishing his gym shorts weren't between us. Just as I lean over his body to kiss up his chest and up the side of his neck, an alarm goes off on his nightstand. A loud groan escapes my throat, and Miles chuckles at my reaction. He pulls his phone from the table and silences the alarm.

"Time to get up and get the day started, sweetheart.

Although, maybe this should be continued in the shower." He gives me a wink, and in a flash, has us out of bed and heading toward his bathroom. Setting me up on the cool granite countertop, Miles turns and starts the shower. I hop down quickly, grabbing my toothbrush and brushing the gross morning breath away. Once the steam starts billowing out of the shower, Miles scoops me up again and opens the shower door and sets me down under the stream.

"You do know I can walk, right?" I tease as I splash some water down his perfectly sculpted body. I don't think I'll ever get used to seeing that kind of immaculateness. *I don't care if that's a word or not. That's exactly what I'm staring at.*

"Maybe I like keeping you close and taking care of you. Ever thought of that?" he counters, giving me a cheeky smirk.

"Well, that's sweet and all, but I don't want you to hurt your back. I'm not small, Miles," I argue.

"Lizzie, turn around and let me wash your hair. We aren't wasting time talking about things of no consequence. You are the perfect size for me, and I will carry you around if I want to. If I couldn't do it, then I wouldn't. That's the last time we will discuss that, princess," he asserts, then leans over, kissing my cheek and reaching for his shampoo bottle. Instead of responding, I close my eyes and soak in the wonderful sensations of Miles massaging the shampoo in my hair. I love the fact that I'll smell like him today. His shampoo's scent is so masculine, and I revel in the fact that I spent the best night with this beautiful man. Now he continues to care for me.

"Miles, thank you for such a wonderful birthday. I don't think I ever properly thanked you for everything, but it was the most special day." I peek back at him as he lathers the ends of my hair." The sight of him doing that sends butterflies to my stomach.

"I wanted to make your day special. Birthdays *are*

special, Lizzie, and it broke my heart to know that you try not to celebrate them anymore. I wanted to do everything I could to make it memorable. Not to change the subject but we are going to go through tons of shampoo bottles with your hair being this thick and long." I burst out laughing; he is such a guy.

"Just wait until you see how much conditioner and other products I use, and then how long it takes to dry. Maybe I should cut it off," I imply, not seriously. I like having long hair, even with the upkeep being insane.

"Don't you dare! I love your hair. I was just simply stating a fact. Maybe we should buy stock in hair product." He chuckles as he takes the shower head down and begins rinsing my hair.

"We?" I ask skeptically. I mean I guess I'll be spending some nights over here, but he seems like he is talking long term. I'm sure it was just a slip of the tongue. I shouldn't have mentioned it. Inwardly, I cringe that the question slipped through my lips.

"Yes, *we*. For when you live here, and before you say anything, I am aware that I'm moving fast; but now that I have you, I'm not letting you go. If I had it my way, you would be moving in here today," he declares.

I am stunned into silence. I feel tears pooling at the sides of my eyes, and I'm glad that I'm facing away from him. I don't want to give him the wrong impression, that I wouldn't love to live with him. I'm just terrified that this is all going to fall apart right in front of my eyes. I mean, we are basically from different worlds. My parents went to school together and knew each other for a long time, but their marriage still turned to shit. I have only known Miles a little over two weeks, but somehow, I feel comfortable with him. Like maybe, this really was meant to be. Miles puts the shower head back in place and turns me around. He sees my face, and I quickly turn to look at something else. I don't want to look him in the eyes. He cups my cheeks and pulls my face to look up at him.

"We are not your parents or anyone else you've had a relationship with. I know that's what you're thinking," he announces as his thumbs rub away the tears that fell to my cheeks.

"How did you..."

"Because I know you, Lizzie. I know how you think, and I knew how throwing that major surprising bomb out there would affect you. I don't want you to be upset. I'm just telling you how I feel. I love you, baby, and that's not going to change. Here." He takes my hand and places it over his heart. "Do you feel that? My heart beats for you. Only you. You are it for me. I couldn't be surer about anything in my life, and I *will* do whatever it takes to prove that to you, over and over again. Do you understand me?" he asks.

"Yes." I lean my head against his hand and close my eyes as I feel his heartbeat strumming under my hand. Opening my eyes, I look up at his piercing blue orbs, looking down at me with love and devotion. "Miles, I love you." A look of shock crosses his face before he hauls me up his body. I lock my legs around his waist to keep from sliding down his slick body. He ravishes my mouth, and then leans his forehead against mine. We stand there, gazing into each other's eyes for a moment with the steam from the shower surrounding us.

"Lizzie, you've made me the happiest man in the world. I love you, baby." Tears are now streaming down my cheeks in a steady flow, but they are happy tears, and he knows that. I can feel his erection pressing against my pussy, so I wiggle back and forth to see his reaction.

"Fuck. You don't know what you do to me, baby." He slams his lips over mine and presses me up against the shower wall. In one swift motion, he's inside of me, stretching me as he thrusts up into my core, repeatedly.

"Yes! Harder, Miles! Right there!" I chant, as he plunges into me. He reaches between us and strums my clit. It doesn't take either one of us long to reach our peaks and fall over the edge. Breathing hard, he slips out of me and places me down on the floor of the shower. Kissing along his chest, I laugh and declare, "I think that makes showering counterproductive, if we just end up getting dirtier." I smirk up at him.

"Don't you know that's the best type of shower. Here let me wash you up." He takes his time, washing me softly, paying close attention to my breasts and pussy. I think he is trying to get me riled up again, but I try to think of other things until it's my turn to wash him. Then I get payback by making sure I take special care in washing his cock. By the time we are done, he is cursing under his breath about needing a cold shower. I can only laugh as we dry off.

Sitting on the bed in a new, fluffy white robe Miles says he got for me, I pull the book out of his nightstand and take a look at it. Turning it over, I smile seeing that it's *Sense and Sensibility*, another classic by Jane Austen. I open the book to where he has a feather bookmark placed. I see the passage he has highlighted, and it takes my breath away.

> **"It is not time or opportunity that is to determine intimacy; it is disposition alone. Seven years would be insufficient to make some people acquainted with each other, and seven days are more than enough for others." - Jane Austen**

"I see you found my book." I look up at Miles. He's coming toward me with perfectly fitted jeans and a black shirt, showing off his glorious body. I am momentarily rendered speechless until I remember what he said.

"Yes. I didn't know you genuinely like Jane Austen. I thought you had memorized a few lines to impress me," I admit, which earns me a brilliant smile from him.

"Lizzie, you wound me. I am in publishing. Of course, I know all the great books. I wouldn't be particularly good at my job if I didn't. I came across this passage a few days ago and wanted to show it to you. Even Austen knew that people could fall in love in a few days. We're the ones she's talking about. We don't need years, Fuck, I knew when I met you at the coffee shop. It was confirmed even more when I saw you again that night." He takes the book from my hand, placing the bookmark back in its spot and setting it back on the table. He pulls me up off the bed and hugs me tightly, placing a kiss on my forehead.

"Now you need to get dressed for the boat trip. While you do, I'll make you some coffee. I may have purchased a coffee maker that has more buttons and gadgets than I know what to do with, but I am confident I can make something drinkable." I can't help but laugh at the image my mind conjures up of Miles making coffee with a fancy machine.

"You bought a coffee machine?" I ask incredulously. I know he didn't have one the last time I was here, and it's sweet that he went to the trouble of getting one.

"Of course, I had to. Apparently, it wasn't acceptable to live in this fancy apartment without one. Someone may have mentioned that the last time they stayed the night, so I knew I had to remedy the issue for the next time they stayed over. I didn't want it to be a deal breaker for not having one," he teases me.

"What am I going to do with you?" I implore.

"Hmm, I'm just throwing this out there, but how about keeping me?" he suggests, sounding insistent.

"I just might have to. I guess it depends on how good

the coffee is." I chuckle, as I push him away, so I can get dressed. After changing into casual clothes, drying my hair, and applying a small bit of makeup, I come out of the bathroom and run right into Miles' hard body.

"I was bringing you your phone. It has been going off for about ten minutes now. I wanted to make sure everything was okay." He hands me the phone, and I see I have several missed calls from my manager at the restaurant. Ugh, I know she is going to want me to come into work. Several people must have called out for her to have called me this many times.

"It's my manager at The Ziti Dish. She must need me to come in to work," I mumble with a wince, looking up at Miles.

"But it's one of your days off. Isn't there anyone else she can call?" he questions with a stony expression on his face. I know he made plans for us to go on a cruise on the Hudson River today, but the truth is, I could use the money. Plus, my manager knows that I'm reliable; that's probably why she has called me so many times.

"Let me just give her a call back to see what she says." Miles shrugs and walks away. I know he's aggravated, but he doesn't understand having to work two jobs.

After calling Rachael at The Ziti Dish, my suspicions are confirmed. There are several parties scheduled tonight, and a few of the servers called out. I couldn't tell her no because I know she's freaking out. She has always had my back when I needed extra shifts or if I got sick and needed time off, so I feel like I owe it to her to come in and work tonight. I walk into the kitchen where I see Miles reading the manual to the most futuristic coffee maker I have ever seen. I smile to myself, leaning against the counter, watching this wonderful man of mine try to figure out how to make me a cup of coffee. After buying this ridiculously expensive coffee maker, we could run our own coffee shop out of his apartment. Well, if he figures out how to work it.

"I heard you walk in; you know. So, I know you are checking out my ass." He does a little shake of his hips and turns his head over his shoulder to wink.

"Well, if you must know, I was looking at this fine piece of machinery that makes the best coffee in the world apparently." A deep laugh bubbles up from Miles, as he doubles over the machine and sets the manual down.

"Well, I guess I need to up my game," he comments, turning around toward me with his muscular arms crossed over his chest. I stand and admire his bulging arms before walking over to him. When I get close enough, he wraps them around me. His cologne fills the air between us; I inhale the masculine scent. I breathe him in deeply, wanting to bathe in his scent. He smells like home. Miles *is* my home. I smile when I think that. I love this man.

"How about we stop and get a coffee on the way to your apartment?" he leans in and murmurs in my ear.

"You heard me on the phone? I'm so sorry, Miles. I know we had plans today, but my manager is desperate. She has always helped me when I needed it. I feel like I owe it to her, ya know? Besides, she said she would get me out of there early, so it won't be a late night. I'll make it up to you." I insist.

"Lizzie, there is nothing to be sorry about. But you really don't have to work there anymore. I was serious earlier. You can move in here and spend your time finishing your book. Then you can start writing the next one," he proffers in all seriousness.

"I'm not moving in here and quitting my jobs, Miles. How would I make a living? What if my book is a flop? Then I would have to go out and find new jobs. I'm not just going to let you pay for everything. That's not fair to you." Miles kisses me, stopping my argument. Something he's very good at doing.

"We'll talk about it later. Now come on. Thomas is downstairs." I relent by grabbing my bag and following Miles out of the door to his elevator.

CHAPTER 30

Elizabeth

After spending a fairytale birthday with Miles, walking into work shocks me back to reality. I let out a deep sigh, trudging up to the bar. Rachael is talking to some of the wait staff.

"Lizzie, I'm glad you could make it. Thank you so much for coming in on such short notice. There are three different parties scheduled tonight, with more than fifteen people in each one. Since you are the best at large groups, I want you to work on those. Everyone will help you with whatever you need." Rachael stresses these words, looking back at the other staff to let them know she means it. I can't help but smirk. Rachael has R.B.F., resting bitch face, so to others, she can seem a bit scary. However, she has always been kind to me.

"Thanks Rach, I'm going to go get changed and make sure everything is stocked for tonight." She nods, as she continues to lecture some of the new hires who were here the last time I worked. Hopefully, they won't cause any problems tonight. I just want to work these parties and get out of here. I wonder what Miles is up to. He mentioned he was going to call Sebastian and see what he was doing today. I wish I was with him right now, on the Hudson River, like we had planned. Unfortunately, duty calls. Miles was disappointed. I know he was, even if he didn't say anything. Hell, I'm disappointed, but people were depending on me. I need to figure out some way to make this up to him.

Opening my locker, I put away my coat and purse, then sit down with my phone. Scrolling through my notifications, I see I missed a call from my mother and my brother. Panic courses through my body until I begin listening to the voicemail from my mother.

"Hi sweetie, I was calling to tell you happy birthday. Did you get your package? I hope you and Sarah had a wonderful day yesterday. Call me back and let me know what y'all did to celebrate. Also, before I forget, I need to know what days you will be home for Christmas. I can't wait to see you! Call me back. Love you."

I miss my momma. I can't wait to see her for Christmas. That reminds me, I need to speak to Rachael about getting some days off. I need to talk to Miles, as well, and see when will work for him. Since he runs an entire company, I'll work my days off around his. I love that he said he would come with me. That makes my heart skip a beat. I'm nervous and excited for him to meet my family. I smile as I open our messages and type out one about Christmas.

Lizzie: Hey babe, my mom called earlier and wants to know when I'm coming home for Christmas. Let me know what days work for you, and I will work around those, since your work definitely takes precedence over mine. Also, I miss you. Just want you to know. After hitting Send, I listen to my brother's message.

"Little sis, where are you? You never answer your phone. Anyways, happy birthday. I'll give you your gift when you are in town. Call me back. I need to talk to you. Love ya."

I know exactly what he wants to talk to me about. He has been pressuring me to go and see my father when I'm in town. I don't think I am ready for that; I'm not sure I ever will be. That reminds me of the letter I wrote him. I haven't decided if I'll send it to him or not. It felt good to get the words out on paper, so I don't know if I really need to send it and open up all those old wounds. I've wasted enough time not getting dressed for work, so I put my phone down and change into my uniform. Making sure everything is in order, I leave the locker room and clock in.

True to Rachael's word, the wait staff help me with any needs I have during my shift, and it ends up running smoothly. The parties come and go with smiles on their faces and on mine, too, after all the tips I made tonight. After closing out all my tickets and printing my end of the shift receipt, I clean up my section.

As I go to take off my apron, I hear a familiar voice behind me, making the hairs on the back of my neck stand on end. "Hey there, beautiful." That eerie, smoke induced, raspy voice sends shivers over my body, gearing up my fight or flight reflex. I turn around and come face to face with Jacob Mathis. I take a few steps back, but he just takes the same number of steps forward.

"W-what are you doing here, Jacob?" I stammer nervously. He comes closer, and I realize I can't back up any further because I'm against the wall.

"Oh, Lizzie. Aren't you happy to see me? I came here for you, little lamb. I want you to come home with me. We need to talk about us," he proclaims, then puts his palms on the wall beside my head. I try to duck down and move away, but he leans over and blocks my path.

"There is no us, Jacob. Now, will you excuse me, so I can get my work done?" I insist with a bite to my tone. Looking around, I try to see if there is anyone that can see us or come to help me if things escalate. Unfortunately, we are in a corner that's already cleaned for the night. It's unlikely that anyone will come over here. My palms begin to sweat because he was very possessive when we were together, and he's acting even more so now that we aren't. I can smell the alcohol rolling off his breath as he leans down to whisper in my ear.

"I'm not going anywhere, little lamb. Not until you agree to come with me. You belong to me, Lizzie. You need to get it through that head of yours. I don't know why you thought Miles Knight would stop me from getting you. Besides, he and his brother never have a girl more than once. I'm sure you know that by now," he snarls with a twisted smile crossing his lips. Those words hit my heart with a thud, and I feel like I'm going to be sick. He grabs ahold of my arms firmly, when I try to maneuver around him. Suddenly, my nightmare is glaring at me. This is exactly what I saw in my dream. The monster from the night terror is staring down at me, but in the flesh. I'm a lamb being led to slaughter.

I try again to escape his hold on me, but his grip only tightens. I emit a gasp from the pain. Abruptly, my breath leaves my lungs like I've been struck with force; but the only thing that hit me is the knowledge that this isn't going to end well. *I can't breathe. I need air.* I must get away from Jacob. He's drunk and stumbling, but he's still much larger than I am; I've never seen him act this crazy before. Tears begin to form in my eyes, but I look away so he can't see my fear. Swallowing the lump in my throat, I barely manage to get out words.

"Jacob, I'm not leaving with you. We are over. You made sure of that when you slept with your assistant. That was more than six months ago. Why are you suddenly coming around again?" I grill him. He squeezes me harder, and I can feel the bruises he's going to leave on my arms.

"I can have whoever I want, whenever I want. But you look better on my arm, and if I'm going to make partner at the firm, then I need you there to look pretty and get me the promotion. I need to be riding on your father's reputation too. Plus, I saw you and Miles Knight looking extra comfortable together on a red-carpet last night for some gala, and I couldn't let some other shit swoop in and take you." He tries to rub his thumb down my cheek, but I flinch on contact.

"Now, am I going to have to drag you out of here, or are you going to be a good girl and walk out with me? You know, I still have the key to your apartment. I could come get you tonight while you are sleeping. Or I could send someone over there now to check on Sarah. She's home, isn't she? I think I watched her walk up the sidewalk to your apartment not too long ago," he growls dangerously, and I feel a cold shiver run over my body. *What would he do? Would he hurt her? How the hell did I ever end up dating this man? Was I blind to his psychotic behavior, or did he just make me see what I wanted? He sure hid it well.*

Tears blur my vision, as I look up at his manipulative, calculating eyes. I can't let anything happen to Sarah. I try to think of a plan, but my mind is eerily blank. I wish I had been able to tell Miles when I was going to be off tonight, because he would already be here waiting. *Think Lizzie, think.* If I could just get to my phone and call the police or to the bar where I'm sure a manager is.

"Okay, I have to go change before I can leave," I tell him. "Go have a drink at the bar. Tell Henry I said it's on the house. I'm sure he remembers you. I'll meet you over there in a minute," I state with confidence I don't feel. Holding a shaky smile, I'm hoping he believes me.

"Oh, sweet little Lizzie, do you think I'm that fucking stupid? You aren't getting away from me. We are leaving *now*! And don't think about yelling. I have a friend waiting to hear from me. He's parked right outside your apartment. I'm sure I don't need to tell you what that means for your friend." He yanks my arm, forcing me to walk toward the front door beside him. I'm about to have a full-blown panic attack now. I don't have a phone, and he's not going to let me go. I don't know what he'll do to me or Sarah if I make a scene here. Shit, I have to go with him. As we start to walk, I look all around, trying to catch anyone's awareness, but no one is paying us any attention. I can feel my legs about to give way from fear, and I stumble a bit. His grip tightens so hard, I let out a whimper. Afraid, I look at him. The way he gazes at me is something I will not soon forget. Such venom and hatred! I don't even know this man in front of me anymore. He's turned into something evil. As we approach the doors, tears fall freely down my face because I know this is it.

As he goes to push the doors, they suddenly open with a hard swing. Miles stands fiercely in the doorway, his eyes piercing us. Jacob grips me even tighter, and more tears flood down my face. Miles clenches his fists and roars, "I thought I told you to never talk to her again. I'll fucking kill you for touching her!" Miles shouts, stomping inside and slamming the door behind him.

Jacob holds up his free hand and thunders back, "Look, Knight, Lizzie is mine! You tried to scare me off last time, but I'm here to take what's mine! Don't be stupid and get in the way."

Before he can say anything else, Jacob is on the floor with blood spilling out of his nose. Miles pushes me to the side and swiftly lunges toward Jacob, beating him beyond recognition. "I warned you not to come around her! Fucking piece of shit is what you are!" Miles continues pounding into him repeatedly. Jacob seems to have lost consciousness, but that doesn't stop Miles.

"Miles! Stop! You're going to kill him! He isn't worth it," I scream. A crowd begins to form, and I hear someone yell to call 911. At least the police will be here soon. I try to reach out and grab Miles' hand before it flies back down to hit Jacob, but I get caught in the crossfire. His elbow connects with my eye. I stumble backward, hitting a table before falling to the ground.

"Fuck!" I hear Miles's shout. Gasps sound all around, and before I can open my eyes, I'm being lifted from the ground. The sudden change in elevation makes me dizzy. I look up to see that I'm in Miles' arms. He has a hard expression on his face. I want to reach out and stroke that expression away, but the shock of everything has me frozen in place. I take a deep breath as he sets me on the nearest table. His bloodied hands are shaking as he cups my face. His thumb caresses my eye where I got hit. I whimper at his touch, and his face quickly turns pain stricken.

"Lizzie, please forgive me! When I saw his hands on you and the tears in your eyes, I couldn't stand it. I had to get him off you. The things he was saying made the anger rise up in me, until I snapped. Forgive me, please, baby! I didn't know you were behind me, and now I've hurt you." He pauses for a moment. Unshed tears start falling from his beautiful blue eyes.

I grasp his wrists, since his hands are still holding my face. "Shh," I whisper as I rub his forearms up and down, trying to get him to calm down. "It was an accident. You saved me from him. He said I couldn't get away from him; if I did, then he had someone waiting at my apartment to do something to Sarah. Shit, I have to get to her!" I go to stand up and almost fall over from lightheadedness. Miles's strong arms wrap around me tightly, keeping me close to his body.

"Calm down, Lizzie, he is unconscious. I'm sure Sarah is fine."

I look up at him with anger radiating through my body. He doesn't know she's okay. He doesn't know if Jacob had some sort of agreement with his friend, that if he didn't call by a certain time, or something, he was to go into our apartment. I saw a whole new side to Jacob tonight, and I am terrified. I go to push Miles' body away from me because I need to get to my phone. I hear the sirens in the distance and know the police are going to be asking a million questions. All I care about right now is Sarah. I have to know if she's okay. I push harder and back away from his embrace.

"You don't know that she's okay! Don't try and placate me. I must get to her!" Once I'm free, I run to the back of the restaurant to the lockers, but I feel Miles right behind me. I open my locker with shaking hands and pull out my phone. My stomach drops when I see all the messages and calls from Sarah. Panic taking over, I fall to the floor and dial her number. Tears streaming down my face, I let out a huge breath when she answers the phone and sounds okay. That's all it takes for me to turn into a mess on the floor.

"Lizzie, where are you? You should have been home by now. I was getting worried!" she exclaims. Her voice sounds anxious, but she doesn't sound hurt. I'm such a mess I'm unable to tell her what happened. I think everything from the nightmare this morning, to the shit show tonight, has come crashing down on me. I'm inconsolable by the time Miles joins me in the back room. He leans down and pulls me into his lap. He takes the phone from my hands and calmly recounts tonight's events to Sarah. Before I realize it, he's off the phone and holding me tightly against his warm body. He kisses my forehead and rubs his hand up and down my back to calm my nerves. After a few moments, I look up at him, resting on his chest.

"Lizzie, I'll always do anything to protect you. You are mine. Mine to adore, mine to hold, mine to love," he murmurs softly into my ear. He brushes his nose against my temple, and I melt even more into him. I don't have words to respond to him, but I don't think he meant for me to. He continues to caress my body, and I can feel the tension and anxiety begin to fade away.

A few minutes pass in silence, before the door opens. In walks my manager and a police officer. My heart begins to hammer out of my chest again, because I'm not looking forward to having to recount everything. I especially don't want Miles to get in trouble over this. He picks me up from his lap, helping me stand, then he does as well. Before I can speak, Miles pulls me to his side and addresses the officer, "I want a restraining order in place. Jacob Mathis is to come nowhere near Elizabeth, or he will look worse than he already does." I'm stunned, and just look up at him. He seems taller and more masculine than I've ever seen. Not that he ever lacked that, in any way, but he's standing his ground, protecting me. It feels good having someone in my corner. It makes me feel like he might really be able to keep me safe. After tonight, I feel like I'll need it. The officer nods and looks at me.

"I need a statement of what happened, Miss. Also, from talking with the other patrons at the bar, it seems he assaulted you first. Would you like to press charges?" he questions, while taking out his notebook and pen.

"If I press charges, does that mean I'll have to see him again in court?" I fret because I never want to see him again. And then a thought comes to mind. Jacob, himself, is a lawyer; he's going to get out of this somehow. He's a dirty lawyer, just like the partners in his company. Panic begins to bubble up inside me.

"Yes, you would see him in court," the officer replies and slides his notebook across the table toward me. I sit down in front of it. My hand is slightly shaking as I take the pen. I look at Miles and he gives me a reassuring squeeze on my shoulder.

"I'm afraid to press charges. I don't ever want to see him..."

Before I can finish, Miles interrupts me saying, "We will be pressing charges. You can let Mr. Mathis know we will be seeing him again." He speaks directly to the officer, not looking at me. My mouth is gaping wide. *Did he not hear what I just said? What is he thinking?* I clear my throat and look at Miles.

"Maybe we should discuss this in private," I urge, trying to be stern. But I'm still quite shaken by how horrible tonight has gone. He gives me a firm gaze that tells me this isn't up for discussion. I didn't know he could be so domineering. I mean, I knew he was protective, but this is something on a whole new level. It almost scares me at what he would do to someone. This is the second day in a row that he has hit someone on my account. A thought creeps into my mind. *Miles is going to see that I bring more trouble than I'm worth, and he will leave me.* I take a deep, staggering breath. Writing my witness statement with fresh tears trailing down my cheeks, the salty tears begin to burn the eye that got hit. I can feel the pressure of it, and I know it's already swelling. It'll probably continue to do so until I can get some ice on it. I can barely see out of it as I try my best to recount all the events of this whole fiasco, hoping I don't leave out anything.

CHAPTER 31

Miles

I glance down at my strong girl as she fills out her statement. I didn't know what time to come pick her up because she didn't know when she would be finished. Depending on what time the parties left, determined when Lizzie would be off the clock. Grief fills me as I realize I could have gotten here too late to save her from that maniac. The thought makes me tense, causing my stomach to churn. *What if I had sent Thomas here instead of me? What if Jacob had managed to take her?* My mind begins spiraling, but I manage to keep control for Lizzie's sake. She needs me right now, more than ever. I need to be her rock through this. I need to show her how strong she was through this whole ordeal. She hasn't said much, but I know there will be a meltdown soon. Once she truly realizes what she went through tonight, Lizzie will be vulnerable. And I will be there to hold her hand.

A thought comes to mind, and I grab my phone from my pocket. Scrolling through the contacts, I find the one I'm looking for—Travis James, owner of the largest security company in New York. I shoot off a quick message for him to call me as soon as he can in the morning. I need to get Lizzie and Sarah's apartment safe, and he is the only person I trust with the job.

I met Travis when we were freshmen at Princeton. We were roommates and both of us were there to play basketball. We became as close as brothers over the years. I have no doubt that he'll be able to supply the security Lizzie and Sarah need now. She may fight me on this, but it isn't up for discussion. With this psycho ex of hers, she can never be too cautious. Hopefully, Jacob will spend some time behind bars, but I'm not naive enough to believe he will remain there. I'm sure he'll be out tomorrow on bail, and I bet he'll go for her again. He doesn't seem like the type to take a loss. Before I pocket my phone, I shoot a text to Marcie, our PR manager. I need to let her know what happened and to be on the lookout for videos and images that I know were taken tonight. I don't want this incident to get to the media. They'll have a field day with it, and it could negatively impact my company. She is already dealing with a bit of fallout from the gala incident. Thankfully, the press was mostly gone when I hit Timothy.

Putting my phone away, I look back down at Lizzie, seeming to still be in shock. She is no longer crying but looks deep in thought. After finishing her report, I quickly jot down what I saw and everything that happened once I got involved. We hand both of our testimonies to the officer, who has been talking in hushed tones with the manager the whole time.

"Thank you for coming out tonight and for seeing to that restraining order," I point out, handing him my card. "Please call me if there is anything else that needs to be done to get this fucker off the streets and behind bars." Nodding, the officer takes the reports and packs up his things. Pulling Lizzie to her feet, I lean down to steady her so we can get out of here. I need to get her home, and I know Sarah is anxious to see her, as well. Before we can leave the locker room, Rachael clears her throat, making us both turn around to look at her.

"Hey, you doing, okay?" Rachel asks Lizzie. She gives her a shoulder shrug and fresh tears begin to stream down Lizzie's face. "I hate to do this, but I had to call Sergio and let him know what happened here tonight. It's my responsibility to report these types of situations to him." She pauses and takes a deep breath. Whatever she has to say, it doesn't seem like it will be good news. Whatever it is, it's making Rachael fidget with her hands. I don't know how much more Lizzie can handle tonight. "Unfortunately, he views this place as family friendly, and he doesn't want this type of drama to drive away business in the future. Obviously, he knows it wasn't your fault, Lizzie, but he wanted me to let you know that tonight would be your last shift. He said he would pay for your shifts next week, but that tonight was the last time you would be on the floor. He also mentioned that he hated to lose you because he knows how much of an asset you are. Unfortunately, it's company policy. Oh, I'm so sorry, Lizzie. I hate that you are going through this." She pulls Lizzie from me and hugs her tightly, rubbing her back as Lizzie slumps into her embrace. Small tears form in both of their eyes, as they let each other go. "I will keep in touch. Take care of her," she says directly to me. I nod my head, and Rachael all but sprints from the room.

"What am I going to do?" Lizzie whispers, looking up through the left eye that isn't completely swollen shut like the other. Fuck me. I can't stand the sight of her like this. She looks so broken and fragile. I know she'll get through this because she's strong, but it's going to be a rough road ahead.

"For starters, we're going to get your eye checked out and make sure you don't have a concussion. Then we are going to your apartment. You and Sarah are going to pack a bag to come stay with me tonight. I'm not letting you out of my sight, and I will feel better knowing Sarah is safe as well. I have a friend that will be going to your apartment to install a state-of-the-art security system, but in the meantime, you both will be staying with me. I met Travis in college, and he's the best of the best with security. He will make sure your apartment is safer than Fort Knox." She just bobs her head up and down. I know this is too much for her to process right now, so the best thing I can do for her is make the decisions. She doesn't need to think about anything more than she has to.

As we walk out to the main restaurant, I see that most of the patrons have cleared and only a few employees, some officers, and the emergency medics remain. One of the EMTs comes up to us and asks Lizzie if she needs to be checked out.

"Yes, she does. She was hit pretty hard in the eye, and then stumbled back, hitting her head on a table as she fell. I think she needs to be checked for a concussion," I interject, before Lizzie has a chance to reject the checkup. Instead, she remains quiet and follows the medic.

"Very well. Come with me, and we'll get you checked out," the female medic replies, then leads us through the front doors to an open ambulance. Lizzie climbs up onto the seat, and the medic begins doing various tests. While I sit there and watch, I pray there is nothing terribly wrong with her. Her eye has swollen completely shut by the time we get out here, so the EMT is having to pry it open to track her pupil dilation. I feel terrible that I'm the cause of the pain she is in right now, but I keep reminding myself it could have been so much worse if Jacob had taken her.

After the evaluation is complete, Lizzie is released with the instructions to take it easy for the next week. She's got to ice her eye several times a day and take anti-inflammatories every eight hours for the pain and swelling. She did end up having a mild concussion, but the medic said it shouldn't cause any problems, that rest is the best thing for her. I will call my doctor in the morning to come and take a look to confirm everything is okay. With Lizzie, I can't take a chance.

Once we get to her apartment, Lizzie steps through the door, and Sarah jumps up to embrace her before anything is said. "I was so worried about you. Miles told me about Jacob! I can't believe that piece of shit would do that. He better be locked away for a long time. Gah, I can't even imagine what you went through. Who on earth would have thought something like this would happen, especially the day after your birthday. And you weren't even supposed to be there today. I thought you were going to be home tonight since I wasn't here when you came by to get your uniform. Shit, come sit down. I'm sorry. Thank you, Miles, for taking care of her and that asshat." She leads Lizzie to the couch while I close the door and lock it. As I sit down beside Lizzie, I pull her against me and rub circles along her back.

"Can you get her some ice and some ibuprofen?" I request. Sarah hops up and quickly returns with the items. "Sarah, I would feel better if you and Lizzie stay at my place tonight. Since Jacob had people here watching you, I think it's safer if you come home with me." She nods her agreement. Thank God, because I don't have the energy to have an argument over their safety. "Can you pack a bag for Lizzie, as well. Make it for several days. I'm going to take some time off this week, so I can watch over her. She does have a mild concussion." Lizzie turns her head to me with a sad-looking expression.

"Miles, you don't need to do that. I'll be fine. I mean, I'll stay with you, but you don't have to take time off from work.

I'll be fine once I wake up in the morning."

"Shh, it's happening, baby. I already sent a message to Seb, and I will call my assistant in the morning to work on clearing my schedule. It isn't a problem at all, so there is no need to worry about it. I just want you to concentrate on healing." Lizzie sighs, resting her head back on my chest. She takes the medicine and puts the ice pack on her eye, flinching as she does. Sarah gets to work packing their bags, and we are out of their apartment thirty minutes later.

I give Sarah a quick tour and show her to one of the guest bedrooms. "We are up the hall if you need anything. I'm going to get Lizzie settled in."

"Miles, I just truly want to thank you for saving her. She is everything to me, and I don't know what I would have done if you hadn't been there. I just can't even think about it, or it will give me nightmares." Sarah sniffles. Hearing the word "nightmare" brings me back to this morning when I woke Lizzie up from one. She mentioned she gets them before something bad happens to her. *Shit.* I take off down the hall to our room. I must get to her and make sure she's okay.

***

Elizabeth

Miles comes barreling into the bedroom startling me. He's wearing an odd expression as he approaches me on the bed.

"Baby, Sarah just mentioned the word 'nightmare,' and it made me think about the one you had this morning. You said it always means something bad is going to happen. Is this the kind of thing that happens?" he wonders aloud, after getting on the bed and pulling me to his side.

"Nothing ever happened that was this violent. Usually, I just have shitty day from something happening out of my control. Apart from my parents' divorce, this is the worst thing to happen. I don't really want to talk about it anymore, though, Miles."

"Me neither. It's finished. I will take care of Jacob and anything else that has to do with him. Everything is going to be okay, Lizzie."

"Thank you, Miles, for everything."

"No need to thank me. Now let me go run you a bath, so you can relax a bit before bed." He kisses my forehead, shifts me to the side, and gets off the bed. I watch him walk away and am amazed at how much I love this man. He takes care of my mind, body, and soul. I hope to never be parted from him.

"It's ready, baby," he calls from the bathroom, pulling me out of my daydreams about him. I roll over to the side of the bed, and he's there to lift me up. I can't help but laugh at him.

"You know, I distinctly remember telling you that I can walk myself." He chuckles and kisses my neck, sending shivers down my body.

"And I think I told you that I want to carry you around," he retorts with a grin. He sits me down on the cool counter next to the sinks and begins taking my clothes off. He slowly unbuttons my shirt, while his eyes never leave mine. He pushes the shirt over my shoulders and down my arms, leaning over to kiss me on the lips. I close my good eye and let myself go to the sensations of having his hands on my body. He gently kisses my cheek and down my neck to my collar bone. Goosebumps erupt over my skin, and I can feel him smile against my skin. He loves knowing he has this effect on me. Leaning back up, he grabs my waist and sets me down on the tile floor. Bending down and resting on his knees, he reaches up to unbutton my pants and gently pulls them down my hips and over my ass to my legs. I step out of them and am left in only my panties and bra. Miles wastes no time ripping my panties from my body and unclasping my bra in one swift movement.

"You are so perfect, baby. Everything about you. I love you," he vows as he stands to his full height where I have to crane my neck to look up at him.

"I love you too, Miles." I step into the tub while he holds my hand to make sure I stay steady, and I lower myself into the wonderful steaming water. Closing my eyes, I slink back until my head is propped on the side of the tub. I can feel the tension melting away.

"I'm going to go get some things ready for you for

tonight. I'll be back to check on you in a little bit," Miles announces before he leaves the bathroom.

"Okay," I murmur, but I'm not sure he heard me.

Sitting here in the quiet, I can reflect on what went down tonight. I really can't believe how the events unfolded. I reach up to touch my swollen eye and wince at the pain. I may not believe it, but I can feel the proof. All the possible outcomes run through my mind until I have to force my mind to quiet down. Nothing good will come from dwelling on it tonight, but I admit it has gotten me spooked. *Shit*. I don't have a job at the restaurant because of that bastard. He just continues to screw me over. I'll have to start looking for something new tomorrow. Or at least online. I'm sure people will turn me away if they see the state of my face right now. I saw it briefly in the mirror, and it sickened me. I don't see how Miles can stand to look at me. Taking a deep breath, I submerge myself into the water. When I come back up for air, I feel like any residual anger and mental pain from tonight has been washed away.

"You ready to get out, sweetheart?" Miles asks in a low, husky voice that has my pussy quivering at the sound. I peek open my good eye, and see my handsome man changed into a pair of sweats and has a bare chest. My mouth waters at the sight.

"I'm ready." I reach out to grab his hand, and he helps me out of the tub, wrapping me up in a warm, fluffy towel. After wringing my hair out over the tub, Miles pulls the plug and guides me into the bedroom where he has my pajamas laid out on the bed. He puts my clothes on and hands me my brush.

"I don't think you want me to brush out your tangles. I can't imagine I would be good at that, and I don't want to hurt you anymore than I already have," he grimaces, turning away to throw the towel into the hamper.

I take Miles' hand and pull him to the bed. "You can't feel bad about my eye. I don't. I'm so thankful that you were there. Please know that. You saved me, Miles. *You*. You were the only one there for me, and you will never know how much that means to me. Okay?" I squeeze his hand and look up into his beautiful eyes, moving a piece of hair out of the way, which has fallen across his forehead.

"Okay. I just hate to see you in pain. Brush your hair. I have some medicine for you and an ice pack for your eye."

After all that, we finally get into bed, and I sink right in, almost falling fast asleep. Until I remember something I thought earlier, and I have to get off my chest or I will continue to worry about it.

"Miles?"

"Yeah, baby?"

"I was just thinking about something and wanted to get it off my chest." He pulls me closer and pulls my chin up, so he can look me in the face.

"What is it, Lizzie?" he asks.

"I was just thinking about everything that's happened in the past two days, first with Timothy at the gala, and then with Jacob tonight, I was wondering if you thought that maybe I'm going to be too much trouble for you. I don't want to cause any trou—" Before I can finish, he shushes me.

"Lizzie, listen to me loud and clear. First, you will never be too much trouble for me. Those incidents weren't even something you caused. It was just unfortunate circumstances where you happened to be in the middle. Okay?" he says sternly as he strokes my face with the back of his hand. "Second, I want you to know that I knew right away you were it for me. I never had any reservations or second thoughts. I saw you in that coffee shop, and I knew in my bones that my soul already knew yours. I felt mine calling out to yours. I love you so much, Lizzie. I can't be without you."

My left eye begins to water at Miles' beautiful words.

"Thank you. I really needed to hear that. I felt an instant connection to you too. One I couldn't explain logically. I just knew you were going to be a big part of my life. It scared me at first, but now I know I'm exactly where I am meant to be."

Miles leans down, pressing his lips to mine and giving me all the love, he feels for me.

"Get some sleep, my love."

CHAPTER 32

Elizabeth

The next several days go by in a blur. Staying in bed and resting, per Miles' insistence, has been both nice and aggravating. I don't think I've rested this much since I had the flu in college. Miles doesn't let me lift a finger. He has taken the responsibility of caring for me to a whole new level. I can finally open my right eye without any pain, but there is still some nasty bruising around it. I had to call Edith at the bookstore to tell her what was going on and that I wasn't going to be at work for the week. She seemed sympathetic in her own way, but she was a little upset by the end of the phone call. However, she wished me well. Miles' friend came to our apartment a few days ago to set up the security system, so Sarah is staying there now.

I called my mother the day after the incident and told her everything about Jacob, and I also told her about Miles. She asked a million questions and was overly excited to learn he would be coming home with me for Christmas. I was finally able to open the birthday present she sent; it was a beautiful, monogrammed leather journal. It has been perfect to make notes about the book I'm writing, since I am holed up in bed.

My phone rings, and I see that it's William. I'm sure mom told him about what happened last weekend, and he is calling to check in.

"Hey, bro."

"Lizzie, fuck don't scare us like that."

"Geez, Will, I wasn't trying to get kidnapped."

"That's not what I'm saying." He drags in a deep sigh,

then continues, "We've just had a lot going on lately, and I can't lose my little sister."

"What's going on? Is it the girls? Is it Whitney?" I question in a rush. Now, I feel terrible for not calling him back sooner. He obviously is going through something.

"No, no, they're all fine. It's dad, Lizzie. He's sick."

"What's wrong with him, Will?"

"I was hoping we could have this conversation in person when you're home for Christmas, but its gotten worse. Dad was diagnosed with early onset dementia about six months ago. He's been getting progressively worse, faster than the doctors predicted. In fact, he had to be put in a senior living facility." I gasp, even though I somehow knew, deep down, that something was wrong with him. Tears well up in my eyes as I listen to William tell me everything that's been going on in the past months. I feel terrible for putting this all on Will and for not coming home more often.

"I feel like I don't know what to say. I have a lot of questions, but none I can verbalize right now."

"I know, Lizzie. Just take some time to process this. I think it would be a promising idea to see him when you come home for Christmas. There are still some days that he'll recognizes me, and I want you to have that. I know y'all have had your problems. I just want you to think about it okay?" I take a deep breath and nod my head, even though I know that he can't see me.

"Okay. I will. I'm so sorry."

"It is what it is. It's a terrible situation for everyone involved. I'm not upset with you if that's what you're thinking. I love you, sis, always."

"I love you too, Will. I'll call and let you know when I will be getting home." We say our goodbyes and hang up. I just sit there, staring at my phone until I hear Miles clear his throat. The bed dips with his weight as he comes to sit next to me. When I look up at him, I see concern written all over his face. I had the call on speaker phone, so I'm sure he heard everything, which really suits me, because I don't think I can recap anything right now.

"I'm so sorry, baby. I heard the news." Miles lies down on the bed and brings my body over to his, so my head is resting on his chest. A few tears escape my eyes and pool on the shirt he's wearing.

"I don't really know what to say," I admit to him.

"You don't have to say anything. Just know I'm right here when you need me, if you want to talk." He leans down and kisses the top of my head, and a new wave of tears erupts from my eyes.

You never know how much time someone has left. I felt like I had forever to make things right with my father, and now there's a possibility he won't even know me if I go see him. Stupid early onset dementia. Why did he have to play football all those years? William said the doctors mentioned that repetitive brain injuries from years of playing contact sports could have led to this diagnosis. Also, his elevated level of alcohol consumption. His doctors have been telling him for years that he needed to stop drinking. Did he listen to them? No, he didn't, and now we've got to deal with this shit.

Well fuck him.

He did this to himself.

Literally, he did this to himself.

Fuck.

Why did he have to do it?

I still can't believe it. What am I supposed to do with this information. I'm still trying to process everything that happened last weekend, and now I get hit with this information. I'm suddenly so exhausted, so I close my eyes and fall into a fitful sleep.

***

Miles

I lie here watching her sleep, but she isn't doing so peacefully. She keeps jerking and jumping, and there seem to be a million different emotions showing on her face as her lashes flutter. I grab my phone from my pocket while trying not to disturb

Lizzie, so I can order us some dinner. I think it's time for her to get out of this bed. I know just the place to call and have it delivered. Once the order is placed, I pull her small body closer to mine, squeezing her tightly and hoping it will comfort her fretful sleep.

Rolling out of bed, I leave Lizzie to rest and walk to the front door to grab our dinner delivery.

"Thanks, man, keep the change." I slip the kid a large tip for getting the food here so quickly. I paid online, but I still want to help those that earn tips for a living, like Lizzie did.

"Thanks, sir," the boy responds with wide eyes once he realizes how much his tip is. I just smile and take the bags from him.

I place the bags in the kitchen, and then go to the balcony to turn on the heaters, so we can sit outside but not freeze our asses off. Lizzie loves being outside, and she loves the view from the balcony. Even though there is a little layer of snow, I think it will be romantic to snuggle up and eat out there.

Looking through all the drawers, I try to find a lighter or some matches for the candles, but I can't find anything. I think back to the last time I even lit anything. I remember that there are some matches in the bathroom I used to light candles for Lizzie during one of her baths this week. I admit, I have gone overboard this week with keeping her in bed and resting. She does not make the best patient. I chuckle, thinking about how she was ready to get out of bed by the second day. I had to threaten to tie her to the bedposts to keep her there. Her eyes blazed fire when I said it, but I don't think it was all anger, and it's something I want to explore later. Fuck, that makes my cock twitch in my pants just thinking about it. Calm down, boy. It's been days of sleeping next to Lizzie but not being able to make love to her. It's taking a toll on my body as well. My resolve for letting her rest is wearing thin.

Running up to the bathroom but keeping quiet, I rummage through the drawers until I find the matches. Sprinting back down the stairs, I grab the blankets and candles, then head out to the balcony to set everything up.

Once I'm pleased with how it turns out, I walk back up to our bedroom to wake Lizzie.

"Wake up, sleepyhead. I ordered dinner," I whisper in her ear, rubbing her back in circles, trying to wake her up softly. The covers start to rustle, and I see her lustrous brown eyes flutter open. I get a shot to my heart at the sight. I lean down and bring my lips to hers. She arches her lush curves against me; if I don't pull back soon, we won't get to the special dinner I planned. With a groan, I kiss her forehead and pull away. "None of that... yet. I have a surprise for you."

"What is it?" she queries, sitting up.

"Well, it won't be a surprise if I tell you, right? Come on, baby. I'm carrying you, so you better keep your eyes closed until I tell you. Got it?" I smirk at her irritated expression.

"Yes, sir." I shouldn't like hearing her say that as much as I do, but damn, does it do something to me. Picking her up with an arm on her back and one under her knees, I cradle her body to mine.

"Good girl. Now close your eyes," I rasp in her ear, then notice the goosebumps that cover her neck and I'm sure down her arms. I've discovered my girl has a praise kink, and I love it. I use it whenever I can, and I see the heat behind her eyes.

When I open the balcony doors, Lizzie goes rigid in my hold.

"Are you kidding me? It's freezing outside, Miles," she squeals and digs her head further into my chest. I walk over to the heated section and set her down on the sectional that's covered by an overhang to protect it from the elements. The heaters are doing their job, and it's nice and toasty over here.

"Keep them closed a second longer, baby." I pull a blanket over her lap and lean down in front of her.

"Okay, open," I softly command.

Her eyes open the instant the words leave my mouth, and I can't help but smile. She loves surprises. She looks me in the eyes, and then past me when she notices all the candles around us. She brings her hand up to cover her mouth as a tear slides down her soft cheek.

"You did all this? For me?" she asks in awe. She's still looking around, catching sight of the candles with a backdrop of the frozen city below us. I can see the flames dance in her eyes when she looks back at me. I lean up and give her a quick kiss.

"Of course, this is for you, baby. I wanted to do something to get you up and out of bed, also have a little romantic dinner," I explain.

Lizzie jumps off the couch and into my arms in an instant. "I love it so much. Thank you. This is so beautiful." She sits back down on the sectional, brings her legs up under the blanket and crosses them, placing her hands in her lap. "So, what's for dinner then? I'm starved!" she exclaims.

"I got Mexican from that little place over by your apartment. Sarah mentioned it was your favorite."

"Yes! It's so, so good! Thank you, babe!" she gushes. "Just wait until you try it!"

"All right, well, let me go get it." I rise to my feet, kiss her forehead—which I know she loves—and I get our dinner. My stomach growls when I smell the food in the kitchen. I guess I didn't realize how hungry I was either.

When I get back to Lizzie, I stand there transfixed by the scene before me. It's the same one I just left, but for some reason, it's hitting me in a different way from this angle. This is what I want. I want Lizzie here, in this apartment. I want her to live here, so I can surprise her and do these small gestures for her whenever I want to. The thought of her moving in overpowers me, and I know I will be insisting she move in with me by the end of the night. She looks over at me, and my heart skips a beat. The sheer beauty of this woman, inside and out. Lizzie is the epitome of a goddess.

"Here it is," I declare, placing the bags down on the table. I take out each dish and arrange them in front of us. I grab two bottles of water and pass one to her, then tell her," Dig in!"

"Mmm, this is delicious. I definitely needed this. Do you like it?" she questions.

"Of course, I like it. It's food." I laugh. "But seriously, it's incredibly good. I'm glad I know about this little place now."

Once we get our fill, I lean back and rest my head on the back of the couch, looking up at the sky. It's a beautiful open sky. Unfortunately, the city lights obstruct the viewing of many stars; however, a few brighter ones can be seen. Lizzie leans back against my chest. The smell of her shampoo never ceases to make me happy. Everything about her makes me happy. She is my forever. I bring my arm down and rest it on her lower back as we sit in silence and look off into the distance.

"This is nice. Being out here with the snow but staying warm and being able to look at the city. I love it out here."

I take this as an opportunity to bring up her moving in with me. With a gentle touch of my hand, I pull Lizzie's chin up, so our gazes are locked.

"What if it was your balcony, too?" I ask, heart pounding.

"What do you mean?" she queries as she gazes into my eyes.

"I mean, what if you moved in here with me and this was your balcony, too? Would you like that?" I rub her cheek with my thumb soothingly.

"Really? You want me to move in with you?"

"Yes. I don't want you to leave when you get better. This week has been one of the best of my life and I want to have you with me forever. I want to go to work and know you will be here waiting for me when I get home. I want this to be your home too. Please say yes. Please say you will move in with me, baby."

It takes her all of three seconds to jump in my lap and yell, "Yes!" Loud enough I'm sure the neighbors can hear, but I don't give a damn. My girl isn't going anywhere. Fuck, just letting that sink in makes me ecstatic. With a wide smile on my face, I lift her up into my arms and spin her around and around. She starts laughing, then throws her arms and legs around my body. I can feel the love she has for me radiating through the depths of her soul. I lean down and catch her lips with mine. The kiss is slow and sensual at first, and then it becomes hungry and feral. A groan escapes my mouth as I clutch her tighter in my arms. I pull back for a moment to look at my stunning woman. I still can't believe this is real life. This woman right here wants me. She wants me as much as I want her, and we're going to be living together.

Leaning over with her still in my arms, I grab the remote for the heaters and turn them off along with the twinkling lights I put up. I look around and most of the candles have already blown out from the breeze, but I blow the rest out and slip us inside through the sliding glass doors. Moving quickly through the apartment, I walk us toward our bedroom. I'm going to spend the night worshipping her body and telling her all the ways I love her.

CHAPTER 33

Miles

Being back at work after having a week off is exhausting. I was working some from home, but the number of meetings that got rescheduled is ridiculous. Now poor Elijah is trying to call and schedule them for this week. It's difficult because the holidays are right around the corner, and most everyone already has their schedules locked down. However, he is trying nonetheless to get these meetings scheduled. Some may have to wait until after the New Year.

When I got back from my leave, I told Elijah I'd only be here for a week, and then I would be gone to Savannah, Georgia. He looked like he had seen a ghost. No doubt he was wondering what was going on with me lately. I never take days off, much less weeks at a time. I just told him to get done what he could this week, and then he'd have a long vacation while I was away. In fact, I told him to write a company memo that the office will be closed from December 24th through January 1st. Joy replaced the shock as he jumped into his work for the day.

Sebastian strolls into my office and closes the door. I have been waiting for him to come in since the memo went out thirty minutes ago, and I didn't discuss this with him prior. I'm sure he's pissed, not at the time off, but at my making the decision without his input.

"So, a companywide holiday, huh? What's brought this on?" he inquires as he settles into the leather chair in front of my desk.

"I'll be going with Lizzie to Savannah, Georgia, to spend Christmas with her family," I casually reply, scrolling through the emails Elijah sent to me.

"How's she doing after everything? Mom has been worried about her," Sebastian adds.

"She is better as far as the Jacob situation goes. Since he is in jail and was denied bail, Lizzie at least feels safe leaving the apartment. Her father is a whole different situation. She doesn't know what to do about that. I want her to take the opportunity to see and talk to him when we are down there because I know she will regret it if she doesn't. Her brother said he is already forgetting him, so she needs to talk to him while he still knows who she is."

"And she doesn't want to talk to him?"

"It's complicated. She does but she doesn't. I'm going to try talking her into it by telling her I wish I could speak to our father once more. Hopefully, she'll listen to me."

"I'm sure she will. She knows she needs to. I'm sure she's simply scared. From what you've told me, she's been carrying this baggage around with her since her teens. I'm sure she needs that closure." He takes a breath and continues, "Do you think this company break is a good idea? I get you want to spend that time away, but you just got back from a break, even if it was warranted. I just don't want the board breathing down our necks because they think we're being reckless."

"I'm going to call for an emergency board meeting by the end of the week. There are some things I need to discuss with them, and they have to do with father, his ideals, and his work ethics with this company. He wouldn't want us working ourselves to death." I rise from my chair and go to my mini bar to pour myself a whiskey. I need something strong for what I'm about to talk about. "Would you like one?" I gesture to an empty glass. He shakes his head no, and I return to my desk chair. "Seb, I never told you this, because I didn't want to admit it to myself, I think. The day before father died, he and I had an argument." I sigh, taking a large gulp of my drink, loving the burn as it cascades down my throat. "He was spending more time at home with mom, and I argued with him that we needed him at the office. Or rather, I needed him here. I wanted to learn everything possible before he retired, and he just told me that I would get it eventually. He said I had a good head on my shoulders. That he'd built this company and taught us well; we would be ready when they time came." I close my eyes, remembering the day like it was yesterday. "He told me work wasn't everything, and that I'd do good to remember that. Maybe he knew his time was running out, and he wanted to spend as much time with mom as possible. I'm not sure. What I do know is I continued to berate him until he hung up on me. I didn't call him back. I let my pride get in the way. The next day he died, and I think, as a way of punishing myself, I have been working myself like a dog because I didn't think I deserved to be happy after that phone call." I down the rest of my whiskey as a tear falls down my cheek.

"Damnit, Miles, why didn't you tell me? I'm your brother. We are in this together, man. I would have told you what an asshat you were being. Our parents wanted us to have lives outside of Knight Publishing. Don't you remember dad coming to all our basketball games when we were younger? He wouldn't have done that if he was obsessed with work. We grew up with significant role models. Dad didn't spend every waking hour here, and in return we had a present father to raise us. You were simply scared you wouldn't be able to fill his shoes once he was gone, but that's no reason to punish both of us since he died. This company is doing great. Better than great actually. Our numbers are up higher than they've ever been. We got this, bro. Now that I know the reason behind closing the office down, I'm all for it. I need a vacation from dealing with your punk ass." Sebastian gets up and comes over to slap me on the back. "I love you, Miles. I'm sorry you've had that on your chest for the past year but thank you for finally telling me. Thanks to Lizzie, you finally realize that working isn't everything. I think I should call her myself and thank her myself for getting your head out of your ass." We both laugh, and he goes to walk out.

"Thank you, Sebastian. What are you going to do for Christmas. I'm sure you are welcome to come with us."

"I actually have a cute little blonde I want to spend some extra time with. And before you say anything, don't. I do not want to hear it," he orders with a smile. I chuckle as he walks out, closing the door behind him. The love bug is going to bite him, sooner rather than later, and I can't wait to have a front row seat.

Thinking about love, I need to hire packers and movers for Lizzie's apartment. I press the intercom button for Elijah's desk. "Yes, sir?" he answers immediately.

"I need you to get with Lizzie and hire a moving company to pack up her things in her apartment and move them to mine. This needs to be completed as soon as possible. Thanks, E," I respond, before hanging up the call. Getting that out of the way, I text Lizzie to let her know.

Miles: Hey, baby. Elijah is going to call you with movers' info. What are you up to?

Lizzie: Hey! That was fast. We can wait until after the holidays. I'm sure everyone is booked.

Lizzie: I'm working on my book today. I am almost done. I sent it to Sarah to read and asked her to let me know what she thinks. I can't believe it has finally come to fruition.

Miles: I'm so proud of you! You know you can send it to me, and I can take a look at it.

Lizzie: I know. Let me see what Sarah says about it. Oh, Elijah is calling. I love you.

Miles: I love you, baby. I won't be home late.

Smiling, I put my phone down and get to work on the piles of work that accumulated while I was out.

CHAPTER 34

Elizabeth

"Hey momma. Miles and I will be there this weekend on the 21st," I inform her over the phone.

"That's great, sweetie. I was wondering if I was going to have to come up there and drag y'all down here myself. What is your flight information, so I can be there to pick y'all up?"

"Actually, we are taking Miles' private jet, and I think he rented a car, so I can show him around but not have to use your car, in case you need it."

"He has his own jet? Goodness, Lizzie, I can't wait to meet this man. I feel like I'll be meeting a celebrity or something."

"Mom, please don't overdo it. He isn't a celebrity. At least down there he won't be. I just want to have a relaxing week, okay? I've got to go."

"Okay, sweetie. I can't wait to see y'all. Love you."

"Love you too, momma."

Putting my phone down, I get back to editing my novel. I can't believe I am almost done with it. I started it so long ago, then my life got derailed by Jacob and his needs until mine didn't exist anymore. I just stopped writing. Then, after meeting Miles, it's like I got my second wind, so to speak, and I've been writing during any free time I've gotten since. Now I am staring at a finished word document with over 120,000 words on it. It's surreal that this moment is finally here. The only problem I'm having now is producing a pen name. I want it to be one that means something to me, and not just random. I was thinking E.M. Austen, since that would take the first letter of mine and Miles' names and the last name would be the name we confused each other over at the coffee shop. I wanted to pick something that represented both of us since this is our love story. He doesn't know it yet, and I didn't really know it when I started writing again, but that's what it has become. Life imitates art and it's exactly what our love story has become, art.

My phone rings, and I look down to see that it's Thomas. He must be downstairs.

"Hi, Thomas."

"Hey there, Miss Lizzie. I'm downstairs whenever you're ready."

"Okay, I'll be right down."

I hang up the phone and slip it into my pocket. I grab my keys, slide on my boots, and grab my jacket as I head out the door. On the elevator ride down, I contemplate everything that's happened this month. It's been a whirlwind of romance and suspense, almost like I'm in my very own romance novel. But seriously, I met Miles and everything has been at high speed ever since. I'm excited about going home and relaxing for a few days. I know he's looking forward to it, as well, because of how hard he's been working. Stepping out of the elevator, I pull my jacket on and walk out of the lobby toward Thomas where he's waiting for me with the car. He is taking me back to my apartment, so that I can pack some things to take to Miles', and I also want to spend some time with Sarah. I feel like I haven't seen her since my birthday, even though she has been over to the penthouse to check on me several times. Everything has just been so crazy since then. Jacob is in jail, at least, and I hope he stays there. They found a large amount of cocaine on his person and in his system, which galvanized his attempt at kidnapping. Our lawyers said he could be in there for five to ten years; so, fingers crossed.

"Good afternoon, Miss Lizzie."

"Good afternoon, Thomas. Thank you for taking me to my apartment. I could've gotten a cab, but Miles insisted."

"Of course, he did. A young woman like you doesn't

need to be riding in taxis around the city, not when I can take you wherever you need to go."

"Well, thank you again."

I slide into the back of the car, and Thomas shuts the door behind me. On the way, I pull out my phone and text Miles.

Lizzie: Thomas just picked me up. Heading to my apartment to pack a few things. Then I'll be with Sarah for a while.

I immediately see text bubbles appear where he's writing me back.

Miles: Sounds good. Elijah sent out the company memo for the holiday, and everyone is going nuts around here. Glad you are getting some time with Sarah.

Lizzie: I'm sure everyone is thinking something is wrong with the Big Bad Miles Knight! Lol! I'm happy for them.

Miles: Yes, well, apparently, that's what love does to you. My brother thought something was wrong too. He will learn soon enough. Evidently, he is 'seeing' someone. I didn't get any more details than that.

Lizzie: Hmm, I wonder if it's serious?! Anyways, I'm at my apartment. Love you.

Miles: I doubt it. He might be an eternal bachelor. Love you, babe. Have fun, and I'll see you tonight.

Walking up to my apartment is bittersweet. I'm happy for this new chapter with Miles, but it feels like the end of an era since I won't be living with Sarah any longer. Unlocking the door, I call out for Sarah; but I hear the shower going, so I walk through the living room to my bedroom and sit down on my bed. Looking around at everything that needs to be packed causes panic to start rising in my stomach. The thought of Miles and my relationship not working out scares me, and then what would I do? Would I move back here? Will Sarah have a new roommate by then? Would I have to go back to Savannah? Probably, if my book doesn't sell, because I wouldn't have enough money to rent a place on my own.

I am in a full-blown panic attack when I hear the

shower turn off. The bathroom door opens, and I hear Sarah coming in my direction.

"I thought I heard you in here. Oh no. What's wrong? What is it, Lizzie?" Sarah grills me; One towel is wrapped snuggly around her body and her hair is wrapped up in another.

"I was ju-just thinking," I hiccup with tears and snot running down my face.

"Hey, hey, hey! Take a deep breath. In and out. In and out," Sarah instructs.

"What will happen if Miles and I don't work out? What if-if we break up? Do you think we're moving too fast?"

"Lizzie, look at me. You and Miles are in love. If you don't work out, then you will get your ass back here. I don't plan on getting another roommate. I got a big raise at work, and I like this apartment, so I'm not planning on moving. So, if something unfortunate were to happen, which I really don't think will, you'll have a place to fall back on. Everything could fall apart tomorrow, but what if everything falls together, and you get everything that you have ever wanted?" she poses and hands me a towel that was on top of my hamper, so I can wipe all the crap off my face.

I just nod because that puts me at ease a bit. Then I remember something else she mentioned. "Wait! When did you get a raise? And congratulations! I am so proud of you!" I squeeze her in a tight hug.

"It was this past week. With everything that's been going on with you, I didn't mention it."

"Oh. Sarah, you can tell me anything, anytime ever. I promise. Nothing could keep me from being so proud of you!"

"I know, girl! I just wanted you to get better. Here, let me get dressed, so we can go grab a coffee. Sound good?"

"Of course. Now you're speaking my language!" I chuckle and wipe away the last remaining tears. Sarah gets up to get dressed, and I go to the bathroom and try and fix the mess I'm sure my face has become.

"I'm going to borrow some makeup," I call out. I'm

going to miss this. I won't be able to borrow her stuff all the time anymore. That's another sobering thought. I look at myself in the mirror and see a brightness in my eyes that hasn't been there in a long time. I know the reason for it is Miles. He breathed life back into my battered soul, bringing me out of my comfort zone and into a universe filled with love and happiness.

A few hours and a couple of coffees later, I'm on the way back to Miles' penthouse, or rather our penthouse. That is definitely going to take a while to get used to saying. I gave my official manuscript to Sarah, since she's going to be my PR person if this novel takes off. She assured me she would send it to all the best publishing companies in the country, so now I just have to wait. Since no one at Knight Publishing Company will know who the author is, I told her she could send it to them. I just didn't want any preferential treatment, but since I am using a pen name, that no longer concerns me.

Thomas helps me into the elevator with the bags I packed. "Do you need me to come up with you to get these in their proper places?"

"No. Thank you, Thomas. You have done plenty. I can get these. Thank you for all your help today."

"It was a pleasure, Miss Lizzie. Have a good evening."

"You as well, Thomas."

Once I waddle into the apartment holding all my bags, I drop them at the entrance and take a deep breath. I realize I don't feel the fear I felt a few hours ago. That's why Sarah is my person. She's helped me through almost everything in my life and continues to help me every day. She is truly an amazing person.

"Lizzie, is that you?" I hear Miles call from the kitchen.

"Yeah, just getting in," I yell back.

He comes out of the kitchen, and my heart skips a beat at the sight in front of me. Miles has his tie off and the top few buttons of his shirt are undone. He's rolled up his sleeves to the elbows, showing off his sinewy muscles. My mouth waters at the sight. He crosses the room in quick strides and lifts me in one fluid motion, then presses me up against the wall, my legs automatically going around his waist.

"I love that I'll be able to do this any time I want to," he murmurs in my ear, sending shivers down my body. "Mmm, you smell so good. Anytime I smell vanilla, I instantly look around to see if you're nearby. You have ruined me for baked goods, my love." A deep chuckle rumbles from my chest.

"I think you can manage."

Miles' lips rapidly cover my lips, and his whiskey-tinged tongue collides with mine. His hands, tangling in my long hair, provokes intense emotions that permeate my body. I pull back just a moment and stare up at my piercing, blue-eyed knight. He may not be in armor, but he is no less the hero to my story.

CHAPTER 35

Miles

Today we're flying out of New York City and heading to Savannah to spend Christmas with Lizzie's family. Thomas came upstairs to help get the bags down to the car while Lizzie is running around the penthouse making sure we have everything we need. While she's preoccupied, I walk into our large closet and open a small, hidden drawer that no one would know about unless they were told. I take out the little blue box, flipping it open and looking at the ring I had custom made for Lizzie a few weeks ago. Not long after we met, I knew she was the one; and I didn't want to wait forever to pop the question. This little trip seems like the perfect time. I pocket the box and walk out of the closet, just in time to see Lizzie coming up the stairs toward me.

"I forgot my laptop. I need to take it in case I hear back from any publishing companies while we are gone," she insists, as she flies past me to grab her laptop bag. I wish she would've sent her manuscript to our company, but she's big on getting her book published based on its own merit, which I can understand. She also said that Sarah is the one that sent her manuscript out because she's going to be Lizzie's PR rep.

Once we get down to the car, Thomas closes our door, and we head toward the airport. Since we are taking my personal jet, we don't have to go through the busy terminals. We can just pull right up beside the plane, which is exactly how I like it. I don't fly commercial unless I absolutely must.

"Are you excited to be going home, sweetheart?"

"I am. It seems like it's been forever since I was there. I couldn't make it for Christmas last year, so it's been a while.

I know my mom will be happy to see me and meet you," she replies.

"Have you thought about going to see your father while we're there?"

She wrings her hands in her lap at my question. I'm sure she assumed I would bring it up eventually, but I want to have a serious talk about this with her.

"I haven't had much time to think about it honestly. With the incident at the restaurant and then finishing up my manuscript, I guess I have been avoiding thinking about it," Lizzie answers.

Thomas rolls down the privacy window to let us know we made it to the tarmac. We unbuckle, and I help Lizzie out of the car. Thomas goes to meet with another member of the staff to help bring our bags on board.

"Thank you, Thomas. I hope you have a Merry Christmas. Tell your wife hello from us and to relax this season. Please, call me if you need anything while we're away." I clap him on the shoulder and lead Lizzie up the stairs of the plane. When we reach the top, we' escorted on by two impeccably dressed flight attendants. Right off the bat, I can tell they are trying to impress me and get my attention, and I see Lizzie tense up at the sight.

"Ladies, I appreciate your joining us on this flight, but please refrain from making any more forward gestures toward me. I only have eyes for my fiancée." Both women's eyes are as large as saucers when I finish speaking, and they quickly avert their eyes from us, but not before I see them check Lizzie's hand. That pisses me off. For all intents and purposes, she is my fiancée, or my wife, for that matter. I don't need a crowd to pledge my love to her. I would be happy to take her to a courthouse as soon as possible, but I'm sure she wants a dream wedding, and I'll give her anything she wants. I lead Lizzie over to a set of seats that face the window. She seems nervous, and that's the best seat in the house. I raise my hand to gesture over an attendant.

"Lizzie, sweetheart, what would you like to drink?" I ask her as she gets settled into her seat. She looks up at me, then the attendant, and veers her sight back to me. "Vodka with cranberry, please," she requests sweetly.

"Whiskey for me. Thank you." I grab Lizzie's hand and bring it up to my lips, kissing her knuckles. I can see her shoulders relax at the contact, and my heart soars knowing I have that effect on her. "Tell me what's going through your mind."

"You told those women I' your fiancée," she states not asks.

"I did. Does that bother you?"

"No. No, that's not it. It's just that I'm not your fiancée unless moving in with you means more than I thought it did."

"I think of you as my fiancée, Lizzie. I don't want anyone else. Just you. But if it bothers you, then I won't mention it again. I never want to make you feel uncomfortable."

"Miles, that's not what I'm saying. I like the sound of it," she blushes as she says it. I subconsciously feel the ring box in my pocket that is itching to be taken out and given to her. I'll have to plan something soon.

After a few moments, the flight attendant returns with our beverages, and then I excuse her for the rest of the trip, unless we need them again. I don't want to be disturbed. Lizzie takes a big gulp of her drink, then rests it in the holder as the plane begins to ascend further down the runway. Soon we are up in the air and the grip of her hand on mine is like a vice. However, I know something that will take her mind off the flight. Leaning over to whisper in her ear, I ask, "Are you a member of the Mile High Club, baby?"

She gasps as she looks me in the eyes. "N-no. I'm not," she stutters but gives me a small smile.

I place my glass down after drinking the contents in one swallow, then put my hand out for Lizzie to take. She hesitates for a moment, looking around to see if anyone is watching us. "I sent them away, baby. They won't bother us."

"Okay." She grasps my hand, and I lead her to the back of the jet where there is a king-sized bed waiting for us. I made sure to have it ready in case we decided to use it. Looks like we will after all. Closing the door behind us, I click the lock into place and turn to see Lizzie sitting innocently on the edge of the bed.

As I step toward her and place both hands on the sides of her face, I gently murmur, "You are stunning, Lizzie. So perfect." My lips descend onto hers, and she moans into my mouth, allowing my tongue in to taste her tangy cranberry flavor. While I kiss her, I start taking her clothes off as fast as I can. She does the same in return, grabbing my pants and pulling the belt free, then throwing it to the floor. I pull my mouth away from hers, so I can get her shirt up over her head. My mouth instantly finds her pert nipples through her lacy bra, that barely contain her breasts.

"Mmm, yes, Miles. That feels so good." I switch nipples and use my fingers to tweak the other. I feel her unbuttoning, and then unzipping my pants, yanking them down my legs, along with my boxer briefs. A moment later, her hand is caressing me in the most tantalizing and agonizing way. I need more. I push her back against the bed and throw my shirt off over my head. I lean down and pull her leggings down, leaving her in her panties. I can see how wet she is through her matching lacy thong.

"Who makes you this wet, Lizzie? Whose pussy is this?" I question, as I slide my hands slowly up her smooth, milky thighs, reaching her panties and tearing them off in one swift movement.

"Yours, Miles. Only yours." Lizzie begins to pant at my slow perusal of her wet pussy.

"Good girl." Hearing those words makes her wetter as I fall to my stomach with my mouth right at her center. Fuck, her smell is something that makes my mouth water. I could eat and suck on her for the rest of my life, and never get my fill. Sticking my tongue out, I run it up her center, to her clit, and flick it a few times. Then I suck hard, making her arch off the bed. I'm sure the staff can hear her, but I don't give a fuck. This is my plane, my employees, and they all sign NDAs before they set foot in this jet.

I bring my fingers up to her nipples, twisting and pulling as she screams out my name. Her orgasm crashes through her, as she comes all over my face. I lick up every last drop and climb up her body. Pressing mine against hers, so she can feel my hard cock urging into her. She can make me rock hard by just looking at me, but when she screams my name, I am hard as steel.

"I love tasting you and making you come on my tongue. It's so hot, baby."

"Please, Miles, I need you inside of me," she begs.

"Yes, baby, beg for it. Beg for my cock to fill you up."

"P-please fill me up with your cock. I need it so badly, Miles. I need you. *Only you*," she emphasizes.

"Fuck yes." I thrust into her in one punishing motion. I kiss her swollen lips, so she can taste herself on my tongue. Her eyes roll back with every deep plunge of my cock. I slow my motions because I want this to last longer. If I kept that pace, it wouldn't. I want to feel her, all of her. My hands roam all over her body, memorizing every surface as I go along. Kissing along her jaw and down her throat, nipping and licking along the way.

I pull out of her for a moment so I can reposition us. I roll us on to our sides, turning her to where her back is to my chest, so I can feel her ass pressed up against me. Sex on my side has never felt so intimate. Thrusting back inside as I nibble on her ear, Lizzie screams out as another orgasm flows through her body. The feeling of her clamping down on me, milking me, is like no other in the world. It takes me right over the edge with her.

Having her smell, taste, and feel so close to me, skin to skin, makes time and space have no meaning anymore. There is only Lizzie. She is everything all at once. *My everything*.

***

Elizabeth

Once cleaned up, we go back to our seats at the front of the jet. The ice in my drink is completely melted, and you can see the different layers of liquid in the glass. Miles sees me eyeing my glass and asks the attendant to get us fresh drinks. Somehow, he always knows what I need. He knew I was nervous about flying, so he took me to bed and had his way with me. Two orgasms later, I have no qualms about flying. Honestly, I've never felt so exhilarated in my life. He brings me out of my comfort zone, but then replaces it with solace.

"Lizzie, there is something I've wanted to tell you about my father before he died. I have been holding it close to my heart because I was too proud to admit I did something wrong, but I'm ready to talk about it with you." Miles takes my hand in his and squeezes.

"The day before my father passed away, I called him while he was home with my mother. He had taken a half day off from work, and I was aggravated because there were things that needed to be done at the office. He argued that the work would still be there tomorrow. But I continued to berate him for being needed. I wanted him to keep teaching me everything he knew, for when he retired. I thought I had to be prepared for any and everything. My father argued that work was not what life was all about." He takes a deep breath and continues, "I yelled at him for spending time with my mother because he would get to go home to her that night, seeing her then. He got so upset with me that he ended the call, and I never called him back. It resulted in me staying at the office until midnight that night, trying but failing, to get everything done." He sighs, taking a sip of his whiskey. "Those awful words were the last things I ever said to my father. He passed away the next day from a massive heart attack. And I've been punishing myself ever since, by almost working myself to death."

"The thing is, when I remember my childhood, my father never worked crazy hours. He was always at all my brother and my basketball games. He was there for all the holidays and birthdays. He wasn't just there physically; he was there with us in those moments mentally. I don't know where I got so lost along the way, that I felt the need to be the best. I worked hard and for long hours to make that happen. I want to be like my father with you, Lizzie. I don't want to get so enveloped in my work that I neglect you or the family we create one day." He sighs, looking out the plane window.

"I am telling you this for two reasons. The first being

I want you to hold me accountable for my work. If I get to where I am overworking myself, I want you to be there to pull me back. I know that you will be the only one to do it because you're already having that effect on me. I didn't think twice about staying home for a week to care for you, and I didn't bat an eye when I gave the whole office a week off. I want them to be happy as well. The only way my employees can work their best is to not work them to the bone. The second reason I wanted to tell you this is because I don't want you to regret the last moments you had with your father. I want you to be able to try and reconcile. Even if it doesn't happen, you tried and that's all anyone can hope for."

Tears streak down my face from everything Miles just confided in me. I can't imagine holding all that in for so long. It must have been eating away at him. I wish he would have been able to have spoken to his father one last time. I realize I don't want that for me. I need to see him when I get home.

"I had already been thinking about going to see my father. I wrote a letter to him a few weeks ago; it listed everything I felt from my point of view. I want him to know how I feel. I never sent it, and I didn't know why. Now I know it's because I need to do this in person. Not only for me, but for him as well. Will you come with me? I don't know if I'll have the strength to do it without you."

"Lizzie, you never have to do anything alone again. I will be with you, always. But I want you to know that you are stronger than you think. You have been through so much and yet, you're the most caring and compassionate person I know. You are utterly amazing. But it would be an honor to accompany you."

"I love you, Miles," I profess.

"I love you so much, baby," Miles croons.

***

"Mom, you didn't have to go through so much trouble for us." I try to persuade a frantic Sandra as she runs around cooking all kinds of dishes for Miles and me. I tried to help, but she knows the extent of my culinary skills, so she shooed me out of the kitchen.

"I just wanted Christmas morning to be perfect," she responds.

"Why? We normally have lazy Christmas mornings," I retort.

"It's just special having you and your brother here and y'all's significant others, all under one roof. Go take this eggnog around and see if anyone wants some. Breakfast will be served soon enough." She hands me the fancy glasses and the glass jar full of eggnog. I take this as a defeat and retreat to the living room to serve everyone.

CHAPTER 36

Miles

I climb the stairs two at a time to retrieve the ring box I stashed away the moment we got here. We just finished a huge Christmas breakfast and Sandra is keeping Lizzie occupied, until I can get everything set up for the proposal. I asked Sandra for Lizzie's hand in marriage the night we got here, and to say she was happy would be an understatement. She and I hit it off instantly, and I have no doubt that she and my mother will get along very well.

Once I get down to the back porch, I see that Lizzie and her mother are enjoying a cup of coffee. They are watching William's darling little girls play in the backyard. Opening the sliding glass door, I step out and Lizzie turns her attention to me with a smile that stops me in my tracks. Her raven black hair is glistening in the Savannah winter sun and her magnetic brown eyes pull me right to her. I lean down capturing her lips with mine for a moment before pulling away.

"I seem to have forgotten a gift for you upstairs, sweetheart." I grab her hand and pull her up to me, placing her coffee on the table behind her. As I pull the book from behind my back and present it to her, she gasps and puts her hand over her mouth.

"How did you find this?" she whispers, taking the book from me.

"I made several calls and went to many different secondhand bookstores. It was finally Edith that called. A copy had come in while you were home resting from the accident. I immediately went out to get it, then stopped and got lunch on the way home. You didn't suspect a thing." I chuckle when I see the shocked expression on her face.

"Edith was in on this?" she asks, adorably shaken.

"She was. She seems to have taken a liking to me. But anyways, when I finally found this book, I knew it was meant to be," I reply.

"I've been looking for the first edition of Jane Austen's "Pride and Prejudice" for several years. This one is in perfect condition too." She opens the book and closes her eyes. She breathes in the old book smell she loves so much. I wish I could bottle that smell for her. I guess I'll just have to build her a library so she can smell it anytime she wants. As she opens her eyes, I see the glistening of tears. She's about to say something, but changes course when she realizes the bookmark that I placed in there.

"Miles, your bookmark is in here. The one from your copy of "Sense and Sensibility" by Jane Austen. I would recognize it anywhere. I love ravens and I have never seen a real feather from one before. It would make a perfect quill." As she starts to ramble, I stop her before this begins going in the wrong direction.

"I put that there because I knew how much you loved it. It's always reminded me of Poe, whom I know you love as well. Anyways, read the second paragraph on that page that's marked for me, baby." She looks at me suspiciously for a moment, and then obliges.

"Okay," she replies and takes a deep breath.

"It is truth universally acknowledged, that a single man in possession of a good fortune, must be in want of a wife." She finishes the Jane Austen passage and looks down at me. I dropped to one knee while she was reading, and she was none the wiser. Lizzie chokes on a bit of air when she sees me down on a knee before her. Taking the book from her hands, I place it down beside us. I take her trembling hands into my own.

"Lizzie, from the moment I saw you in that coffee shop, my world has been turned upside down in the most perfect way possible. It was fate that brought us together that day, twice actually." I chuckle when I think back to seeing her at the club the same day. "You see, I go after what I want and what

I want is you. You have bewitched me, body, heart, and soul. I am completely and utterly in love with you. Lizzie, please allow me to take care of all your needs and wants. Let me make you as happy as you make me every single day. I want to be the reason that your beautiful brown eyes sparkle. I need you like I need the air I breathe. You are the crazy little puzzle piece that fits my proud and arrogant one. You have made me a better man by seeing the best in myself. Please, Elizabeth Brighton, will you be my wife?" I finish with a single tear sliding down my cheek. Lizzie nods her head several times before she says anything. By now, everyone in the house is on the porch watching us, but I only have eyes for Lizzie.

"Of course, I will marry you, Miles. You are everything I never knew I needed. You make me the happiest I have ever been, and I want to spend forever and a day with you. I love you so much," she says as she wraps her arms around my neck. I kiss her quickly and pull her back to bring the little blue box from my pocket. As I flip it open, I see how wide her eyes become. The ring has a four-carat oval diamond with three brown diamond baguettes on either side that remind me of the color of her eyes. I had this specially made, and it came out perfect.

I take the ring out and slide it on her finger. It's a perfect fit, just like us.

"It's beautiful, Miles. I have never seen anything like it."

"That's because there isn't. There isn't anything like you, so your ring had to be the same. Unique. It's custom made, with your deep striking brown eyes as inspiration. I love you, Lizzie."

"Oh Miles, I love you so much! Thank you for making me so happy."

"No, thank you, Lizzie. You are my soulmate, and I am just too thankful to have found you."

Cheers erupt around us as I stand up and pull Lizzie into my arms. I could never describe the love I have for this woman. She is truly the full moon to my midnight sky. Unique.

Elizabeth

As I open my emails, I see that I have one from Knight Publishing Company. There are several others from multiple publishing companies, as well. This one sticks out the most because the subject reads: "We want to publish you!" I squeal in excitement, as I jump up and down. Miles comes running into the room, with a look of worry written across his face.

"What is it, Lizzie?" he questions, trying to read my expression. I don't have the words, so I turn my laptop for him to see. He falls to his knees with the largest smile on his face. He grabs my hips, pulls me close and rests his head on my stomach.

"You have got to be kidding me! You sent your manuscript to us, and I didn't even know it. I haven't heard your name. Sebastian called me earlier and told me about a new author that sounded extraordinary. The name was something Austen." Then, I see the recognition in his eyes. His mouth gapes open, seemingly speechless.

"I made a pen name. I wanted it to be unique and special like us. I used the first letters of our names and the last name Austen because that was the first name associated with us. So, E.M. Austen is me, Miles." He jumps up moving the laptop to the side and picks me up. Twirling around the room, both of us are laughing and crying at the same time. Happy tears, of course.

"I am so proud of you, baby. I knew you could do it. We have to celebrate," he shouts as he continues swinging me about.

"I think we already did." I say gesturing to my engagement ring I haven't been able to take my eyes off of.

"You are truly incredible, Lizzie," he murmurs in my ear, then kisses my forehead. I love this man so much. He is my everything too.

CHAPTER 37

Elizabeth

The black Audi rental car comes to a stop in front of the Palmetto Senior Living facility. The building is bright white stucco, with large, black plantation shutters. Palm trees are scattered throughout the beautiful landscaping. There are benches for sitting areas scattered throughout the property. Some are facing the ocean, and I know those would be the ones my father would choose. I know why my family chose to put my father in this place. He's always loved the sea. It was something we always had in common.

The clouds overhead are swirling about, as the wind strengthens. There is a storm coming. It's quite fitting, actually. There is a storm inside me that is raging, about to spill over. There is nothing I can do to stop it. I came here for a reason and as much as I would rather run away, I know this must be done. I let out a deep breath as I look out the window at the ominous weather. Miles cuts the engine and reaches over to grab my shaking hand. He gives it a firm squeeze, letting me know he's right here with me. I'm not going into this alone, and I'm thankful for that. I glance over at Miles, and I see the concern in his eyes. I didn't want to be alone today, and he was happy to accompany me. I attempt a small smile, but I know it's weak.

"Are you ready?" he queries. I don't think I'll ever be ready, but I nod. He pulls my hand up to his lips and gives it a quick kiss. Getting out of the car, he comes to my side to help me out. I take his hand like it's the only lifeline I have. I'm sure he can feel the tension rolling off me in waves, as we walk into the center. He opens the large door and ushers me inside, then places his hand on the small of my back. A simple act, yet so comforting. As I approach the main desk, I look around at the hustle of nurses, staff, and patients. The air is sterile and clinical, which only makes this situation more real.

"How may I help you?" The receptionist interrupts me from my thoughts as I glance back at her.

"S-sorry, I am here to see Alan Brighton," I reply with more confidence than I feel. She types at her computer, and then asks, "What is your relationship to the patient?" My mouth goes dry because I haven't acknowledged he was my father for many years now. I clear my throat and Miles pulls me closer to his side. The instant warmth from his body soothes my racing heart.

"Daughter. I'm his daughter, Elizabeth Brighton," I inform her. She studies me for a moment, then looks back down at her computer.

"Oh yes, I see your name under visitors. If you don't mind, can I see your I.D. just to confirm. It's policy procedure," she explains. I pull out my license and hand it over to her, as she surveys the card. She quickly hands it back and gives us directions to his wing of the center. Miles laces his finger through mine, as we walk down the corridor. I feel like my feet are growing heavier the closer we come to his room. I glance at the room numbers on the doors and feel sweat begin to coat the back of my neck. Within minutes, we are in front of room 143. The door is cracked, but I'm not able to see in. I stare at his nameplate and different instructions for care, which hang to the right of the door. Before I can push it open, a nurse comes along.

"Can I help y'all?" she inquires, looking between Miles and I, and then back at Miles for a beat too long. A spike of anger unfurls in my stomach, but Miles pulls me closer to him. He obviously felt her wandering eyes as well.

"We are here to see Alan Brighton. This is his daughter, Elizabeth," Miles replies while keeping me close. She looks shocked by his admission. Probably because she didn't know he had a daughter. Why would she? I'm sure I've never been mentioned, and this is my first visit.

"Well, I'm glad you could visit. I'm sure your father will

be pleased to see you. He's been quite lucid this morning, so you have a good chance of having a real talk with him." I just nod as Miles replies with a "thank you." I gather any remaining mental strength and walk into his room.

His back is to us as we enter, looking out of his window. He's sitting in a leather recliner that I'm sure he insisted needed to be in his room. It's always been his favorite chair. You can see the ocean from his room, and I imagine he sits in that chair a lot. I can see the amount he's aged since the last time I saw him. His hair is completely gray and balding in the center. I take a few deep breaths and walk around the side of his chair, so he can see me. He looks up at me and for a moment I feel like he doesn't recognize me. But then I see a flicker in his eyes as he says, "Elizabeth." A small tear escapes my eye as I nod, and I quickly wipe it away. He looks behind me, and I move to the side to introduce Miles.

"This is Miles," I inform, looking at my father. "Miles, this is my father, Alan Brighton." Miles approaches, reaching out to shake his hand. My father hesitates briefly, before accepting his hand.

"It's a pleasure to meet you, sir," Miles remarks. Knowing he can feel the tension in the room, Miles looks to me and asks, "Would you like me to go grab us a couple coffees? I think we passed by the cafeteria." He looks at me with questions in his eyes. Asking if I want him to leave and if I am okay. I just nod. I need to do this part alone.

"Coffee sounds great, babe."

"Can I get you something, Mr. Brighton?" he asks. My father just shakes his head and continues looking out the window. Miles leans down and kisses my forehead, then gives me a squeeze before leaving the room. I stare at the door for a moment before I work up the courage needed to talk with my dad. I take a deep breath and look back at my father. It's a miracle he even knows who I am. With the reports from mom and William, I knew he would most likely not know who I am.

I take a seat under the window and look my father in the eyes. It's been so long since I've been this close to him that my anxiety spikes in my stomach, making me feel uneasy.

I can tell the years haven't been kind to him. He looks much older than his actual age. There are more wrinkles than I remember, and his skin doesn't have the usual glow from being in the sun. My heart aches, and I know I need to get this over with before I chicken out.

"Dad, I wanted to talk to you. I know we haven't talked much over the years, but I wanted to come see you," I admit softly, feeling more and more insecure about this conversation.

"I know why you're here, Elizabeth," he responds as he glances at me, and then back to the window. I take a deep breath, unsure of what he'll say next. I wipe my sweaty palms over my jeans and look up at him. He's looking at me now. Not saying a word, just studying me.

"I know that I'm sick, and my mind comes and goes. It seems like it's in a fight every day to see if I'll be able to make an appearance or not. You caught me on a good day it seems. I'm surprised you cared enough to come." A blast of anger shoots through me at his harsh words, but I hold my tongue.

"I came because there are things that I have wanted to get off my chest for years now, and I never told you. I guess I have been holding onto them like a grudge, and I never knew the impact it was having on my life until recently," I confess, while fidgeting with my hands, unable to look him in the eyes.

"So, you are here to tell me all the ways I have messed up and things I've done wrong over the years then, huh?" he grits out, no longer looking at me. He's looking at the storm that's about to wreak havoc over us, both figuratively and literally. I can feel the sting of tears in my eyes, but I don't dare let them drop. They are a weakness to him, and I will never get through this if they fall now. I feel a knot in my throat, only seeming to intensify with every passing moment. I know I need to respond, but I'm lost for words. For once the words aren't flowing through me. They are firmly lodged in my head and refusing to be set free. I let out a long breath and pull my gaze up to him. *I can do this. I CAN do this.* This isn't just for me and my baggage I carry, it's for him and my forgiveness that he needs to know he has.

"Dad, please look at me. Please give me the time to get

out the things I need to say before you say anything. Please give me this opportunity to share with you the emotions and feelings I've kept buried for far too long now. This is something I think we both need." As I stare into his eyes, waiting for him to respond, he doesn't say anything, but he gives me a slight nod. So, this is it. This is my chance to get everything out in the open. I pull my chair closer to his and take a deep breath to steady my nerves.

"When you and mom got divorced, I was devastated. I thought we had the perfect family. Even my friends thought that. I never even saw y'all fight. So, not only was it a shock to me, but I felt like the breath in my lungs had been knocked out of me." I take another deep breath and look to him as he continues looking out at the storm.

"I was so angry at you for ruining everything. Obviously, I didn't know the details, and they were spared to me because I was only twelve. There was no reason in my mind that I could manifest to justify that kind of behavior. I understand that it was juvenile thinking, but that's what I was. A child. So, I became angry, and I directed that at you. We had been so close for as long as I could remember. You always said you were the big finger, and I was the little finger," I recite as I hold up my hand and gesture to the pointer finger and the middle finger that came together to touch. He sighs and looks at my hand I'm holding up in front of him. His lips turn down slightly for a moment, and then his attention is back outside. I take another deep breath and continue.

"When I got to high school, you began buying me gift after gift. I think it was how you wanted to show me that you still cared, but all I wanted was you. The cell phone and the convertible were great for a while, but the shine wore off, and I was still left completely alone. Then you bought the house that you said we would live in together and I was ecstatic. I thought everything was going to be okay after that. So, I left my childhood home and my mom to move in with you. I can count on one hand the days you actually stayed there with me. Before I knew it, I was alone again and you were off with Evelyn, living at her house. The only commonality with all these scenarios is that you left me at the end. I wondered why she was so special, and why she had to take all your attention.

So, I began to think your love for me was conditional. I felt I had to perform at high standards, or you wouldn't look my way. I studied my ass off in high school and was almost the valedictorian, but I was beat out. I got so many awards, honors, and scholarships. I was so proud of what I had accomplished, especially with all the extracurricular activities. You were proud too for a while, until I told you what I wanted to study in college." I pause letting the silence swirl around us. The only sounds were the thunder crashing from the storm and the patients and staff chattering beyond his door. He doesn't say anything because he knows I'm not done and I'm thankful for that. I don't want to fight. I want to free this poison from my system and finally clear the air with him.

"Through college, I would call you with good news or good grades just to get some semblance of reassurance from you. I was left always wanting more. I would get off the phone and scold myself for still needing your approval in my life when you clearly weren't even a part of it anymore. I struggled with this for so long until I couldn't take the rejection any longer. I don't even know if you thought of it as rejection. This is all based on my point of view. I've never known your side of the story. Once I was older and suspected you got a divorce to be with Evelyn, I didn't even want to look at you. You had been my hero for my entire childhood and then seeing you in this new light made me sick. The thought of you cheating on mom, and me for that matter, was more than I could bare. So, I distanced myself from you. I didn't even want to look at you." I see his jaw clench. He is grinding his teeth so hard that they might crack. I take another slow breath and continue.

"For several years, I looked for others to give me the love that I wasn't getting from you. I went through heartbreak after heartbreak, overlooking red flags that could be seen a mile away. I just wanted that relationship, that connection with someone. Eventually, I began not trusting anyone or their motives. The only constant in my life had been Sarah. She stayed by my side through the good and the bad. The truest form of friendship that I have ever been gifted with. I felt that I always had to be this perfect version of myself, or I wasn't lovable. Until recently, I felt as though all men couldn't be trusted. Just like how I trusted you and you still left me.

So did all my boyfriends, and with other women as well. I found myself in a very dark place and I couldn't see the light no matter how much I clawed at the surface. I finally hit rock bottom. I knew something had to change and that something was me. I had to be enough. Not for others, but for myself. I had to learn to love me at my best and worst so that I could allow others to love me. It was a long hard road and it's one I still stumble on along the way." I pause as the words I have been holding in for so long are now out in the world. I feel like I have been ripped open for all to see but this is the next stage in my healing. I am exposed and vulnerable. This was something that had to be done before I was left without a chance to tell him how I felt. He glances over to me, and I know he can see all the emotions shooting through me in this moment. Pain. Relief. Anxiety. Hopefully, he sees my love for him. I reach over to grip his hand in my own.

"Dad, I'm only telling you how I have felt all these years. I need you to know the damage that stemmed from the divorce. This is my perspective, not yours. Mine. I'm not trying to change the past. The die has been cast. We can only move forward, and I'm stronger now. I guess it really is true that what doesn't kill you will only make you stronger." I chuckle half-heartedly. With what I have said, I feel like a weight has been lighted off my shoulders. One that until now, I didn't realize was so heavy. I can breathe. I close my eyes briefly as tears trickle down my cheeks. I think of the anxiety of coming here and the fear of confronting him. The relief that it is out in the open now has me unable to hold the emotion in any longer. I feel my father place his other hand over mine and more tears begin falling at the gesture. I open my eyes and look up at him. He takes a moment and then speaks.

"Elizabeth," he pauses as he closes his eyes for a moment, "I am truly sorry for all that you have been through because of my actions. There are things that I should have done differently. I always thought you were so strong. I never saw this struggle within you. I hate that as your father, I couldn't see the obvious turmoil that was going on inside you, and at such a young age." He takes his hand off mine and scrubs it down his face where I see a lone tear fall. My stomach sinks for him because I didn't want to upset him. I wanted to mend our broken relationship. Before that could happen, he had to know what he had either knowingly or unknowingly done to me throughout the years. He looks back out at the storm that has just turned to rain.

"You know, the ocean has always reminded me of you," he proclaims. "Not just because we always visited here when you were younger. Most people don't know how powerful an ocean is. You are like the ocean, Elizabeth. You are both wild and calm, dangerous and beautiful. You are so strong and always have been, even if you think of your past as a weakness. You prevailed and came out on the other side. You may draw back, but you push forth just as much as the tides do." He looks over at me and wipes the tears from the side of my cheek. I try to memorize this moment so it will be with me forever.

"Please, forgive me for not being what you needed. I'm here now." He leans over and kisses my forehead as another tear escapes his eye. As I get up, I hug him as tight as I can without hurting him.

"Of course, I forgive you, daddy. It's all water under the bridge," I whisper into his ear with a smile on my face and fresh tears in my eyes. I sit back down, and he pats my knee a few times, then looks back out to the ocean.

"You know, I asked to be facing the ocean, so I could see you every day, Elizabeth. I see you in the waves, always. Your reflection shines through, and I know that you're okay because of how strong you are. You'll be okay when I'm gone. I love you, slugger," he states, looking back at me. I am caught off guard by his confession, but more so from the softball endearment. He always called me that when I was younger. As he holds his hand up, he shows the two fingers close together, the gesture that I had reminded him of earlier. I hold my hand up to his and mirror the same expression. He gives me a small smile and looks back to the ocean.

"I love you too, daddy," I utter softly. The words feel both foreign and familiar on my tongue. His gaze never leaves the window, but his body stiffens. I put my hand back on his, and his eyes snap to mine with confusion in them. The sudden change captures the breath from my lungs. Sadness falls over me like a fog at the different man sitting beside me.

"Dad? Are you okay?" I ask quietly. He pulls his hand from mine with confusion still written on his face.

"Who are you? I'm not your father. I don't have any children. Where am I?" he asks me suspiciously. I stand up quickly to move back, so he doesn't get more uncomfortable of how near I was sitting to him.

"Dad, it's me, Elizabeth. We've been sitting here talking for the past hour. Do you remember?" I question even though I know the answer. My heart feels like it is breaking into pieces. He scoffs and tries to stand from his chair, but he's unsteady on his feet. I reach out to help him, but he swats my hand away. As he begins to mumble, I struggle to make out what he is saying. I grab the nurse pager and push the button. I am completely and utterly at a loss of what to do in this moment. I just stand there with my hand over my heart, trying to ease the pain. I watch as my father backs further away from me because he doesn't recognize me anymore. I know at that very moment that I've lost him. It's as though God knew exactly how much time I needed with him, and he gave it to me, but not a moment longer.

As the nurse rushes in, she sees the state my father is in and gives me a sympathetic glance. She gets him to the edge of the bed, and he sits as she gives him a dose of medicine. I assume it's something that will calm him down. I'm rooted to the spot, unable to move. I feel like I'm watching that sad scene from "The Notebook" when Ally and Noah have one moment together where she remembers him, and then it quickly fades away. I can't help the fresh tears beginning to stream down both sides of my face. I wipe them away, but they're quickly replaced with new ones. Suddenly, I can't breathe again. I must get out of here. As I quickly snatch my purse from the table and make it to the door, I glance back at the man I've known all my life. He no longer knows me, and I know I have to get out of here. The rawness of our conversation, followed by this episode, has my mind reeling as I run past the nurses' station and down the hallway from which we came. I hear someone shouting behind me, but I can't make out the words. The only thing I can focus on is getting out of here.

I burst out of the double doors in the front of the building, and I'm greeted with the beautiful rain I saw from the window. I don't stop running. I take off toward the ocean, getting soaked in the process. I run until my lungs are burning in my chest, and I no longer feel like I'm suffocating. I make it to the sand and drop my purse to the ground. I hold out my arms and take in the rain, facing the sky with my eyes closed. The rain is cleansing me of this afternoon, of the emotions that just keep pouring out of me. It's washing it all away, more than anything ever could. I have always loved the rain. The clouds pour their hearts out to me, and I soak up every bit of it. I don't know how much time passes, but I'm suddenly wrapped in large, warm arms. I open my eyes and look up at Miles. He has rain dripping from his eyelashes as he looks down at me with concern, but ultimately, love in his eyes. I let my eyelids flutter shut and push my face into his chest. He kisses the top of my wet hair and rubs a hand over my back. He doesn't tell me we need to go, because he knows I need this and is here for me. He continues comforting me until I have no more tears left in my body. I feel numb from the emotions and the cold rain. He picks up my purse and scoops me up into his arms as he walks us back to the car.

"I love you, Miles," I mumble softly. He leans down and kisses me on the forehead.

"I love you, more," he replies as he tucks me into the car. I take one last look at the treatment facility, then close my eyes and rest my head against the seat. I did it. It was hard, but I was able to get everything off my chest. I'm sad my father didn't recognize me toward the end, but I am so thankful that at least, I did what I came here to do. Miles reaches over and takes my hand in his. He rubs his thumb in soothing motions across my wrist and I melt into the seat.

EPILOGUE

Elizabeth

Brightness.

  It surrounds me. I take a deep breath. The smells are fresh and airy. Opening my eyes, I am lying on the ground looking up at the different clouds forming in the sky. I smile and look to my right, seeing my dad lying next to me with a huge smile on his face as well. He's pointing up at the sky and speaking, but I can't hear him. I only see the pure joy on his face to be lying here in the grass with me. Then he grabs my hand and links them together. I feel his hand. I feel the wrinkles and callouses showing his age. This isn't a memory. It's something else. Are we really here? The wind blows, and I close my eyes, loving the feel of the breeze on my face. I have an overpowering feeling of happiness surrounding me. I open my eyes and he is gone, but I'm not sad or scared. I feel at peace and most of all, love.

  I wake to the sound of people bristling about. Was that a dream about my father? It felt so real, like I was right there with him. Maybe I really was there.

  A knock sounds from behind my bedroom door. I'm in my childhood bedroom because today is my wedding day. Miles and I decided we wanted to get married in Savannah, where I grew up. So, after a year of planning, here we are, the day of our wedding.

  "Come in," I yell to the mystery person behind my door. William steps into my bedroom and sits down at the end of my bed. I sit up, pulling my covers up to my chest. I love my brother, but he doesn't need to see what I sleep in every night. I giggle at the reaction he would have just seeing me in a tank top without a bra on.

  "So, it's the big day, huh? It looks like mom might have

invited the whole city with the state of things downstairs." I laugh, because I can only imagine what everything looks like. We decided to get married in her backyard, overlooking a small lake. The service will be relatively small with family and close friends. However, the reception will be in downtown Savannah, at a huge historical building that hosts weddings from time to time. There will be tons of people at the reception. I allowed my mom and Miles' mom, Amelia, to arrange everything. I've been busy with my novel becoming a number one bestseller. I've been booked on talk shows and done countless readings and signings in the past year. It only made sense to let them do the work, since they were more than enthusiastic about it. Miles was right, our mothers love each other. I think they speak to each other more than they do their own children. It's great that they've gained each other in their lives. They have many things in common.

"Yep. It's the big day," I respond.

"Are you nervous? You know we can use the secret hand gesture and I'll get you out of here before anyone can blink." He chuckles.

"I can't believe you remember our old sign we'd use!" I exclaim, hitting his shoulder and laughing. "But, no, I won't be needing it. I'm not nervous at all. I'm just excited. I am ready to begin this new chapter of my life with Miles."

"Well, good. Just remember what you have to do if you need anything. But in all seriousness, I didn't come here to give you an out for your wedding. Father gave me this letter to give you on your wedding day. I've been holding onto it for you." He hands me an envelope with my dad's handwriting on it. It reads: For your wedding day. I let out a shaky breath, looking back up at Will. He has the same unshed tears in his eyes as my own.

"Thank you," I tell him quietly, not sure what else to say. He goes to stand up, then stops and turns his head to gaze at me.

"Don't take too long. Mom has makeup people here that are ready for you. I told her to give you a few, okay? I love you, sis. I can't believe you're old enough for me to walk you down the aisle," he jokes. He walks toward the door to leave but stops when he hears me speak.

"I love you, Will. I'll see you out there."

Once Will leaves, shutting my door behind him, I look at the envelope in my hands. With trembling fingers, I open the letter to read it.

Dear Elizabeth,

This letter is supposed to be opened on your wedding day. I hope that, however I am with you today, whether it be physically, mentally, or spiritually, I hope you can feel my presence. I have always been with you, baby girl. I'm sorry I let us get disconnected over the years. I take full responsibility for that. You have grown up to be an extraordinary woman, baby girl. I am so proud of you for pursuing your dreams and not letting your old man get in the way. I want you to have everything out of life, Lizzie. I want you to be happy. I want you to build a home with family and fill it with all the love and devotion you didn't receive from me as a child. I want you to always remember that I love you. I'm not telling you that everything is going to be all right but find the things you are passionate about and don't forget to fight for them. Fight for the ones you love, always.

I met your husband-to-be today when he came and asked me for your hand in marriage. I had just spoken to you, then I had a short episode where dementia took over. By the time you left the room, I had come back, and he was there. Miles is good for you, Lizzie. I could never part with you for someone less. He's a good man, and I know he will make you happy. You'll be able to lean on him when I'm gone. I know you will cry, and I just want to tell you it's okay. I' always be a part of you. You are the best part of me, and I want you to know that. Keep this letter for when you need me, baby girl.

I think it's time for me to leave, but I'll never leave you. You can always find me when you look up at the sky. I will be there among the clouds we used to watch go by. Life isn't always a fairytale, but there also isn't light without darkness.

I love you so much, Slugger,

Dad

With tears streaming down my face, I reread the letter and am so thankful that he'll be here with me on my big day. I think that's what my dream was about this morning. I believe he's in heaven and looking down on me on my special day. I smile at the thought. Brushing the wet hair and tears from my face, I get up and walk downstairs to get ready to marry the love of my life. I'm finally getting my happy ending.

ABOUT THE AUTHOR

L. B. Martin

L.B. Martin lives in South Carolina with her husband and two children. She spends her free time reading, writing, and drinking all the coffee. L.B. majored in English literature in college with a minor in British Lit. She loves all things book related. Her husband is a gaming streamer, so when he is playing, she is reading away.

L.B. Martin began writing as a form of therapy.

"My words spill from my mind to the pages in effort to rid myself of the demons tucked away inside. My hope is that readers will be immersed into my world and come out feeling hopeful and full of purpose." -L.B. Martin

PRAISE FOR AUTHOR

"'The Write Knight' is a sensational, wonderful, emotional debut. L.B. Martin has done an exceptional job of making you fall in love with her characters and balances the great and not so great moments.

Miles and Elizabeth believe the opposite about fate and being able to find 'The One.' When she swears off all men, Fate intervenes and throws them together, and their connection can be felt from the first meeting.

The world building was really great, just like the characters. You'll fall in love with them from the start. I'm itching to get my hands on Sebastian's story. I absolutely love that the characters were relatable.

Having said this, L.B. Martin's debut is one of the best I've read, and I can't wait to see where her writing journey takes her."

- CHASITY MAHALA, EDITOR

BOOKS IN THIS SERIES

Knight Publishing Company

Knight Publishing Company, the largest publishing company in the U.S., is not only known for its best-selling books but also for the men who own the company. Miles and Sebastian Knight are two of the most eligible bachelors in New York. These two brothers are known for their playboy life styles but no one seems to be able to tame them until fate blows their way. Will these two ever meet their match? And is there a third Knight that no one knows about? Pick up this series and find out!

The Write Knight

Life isn't always a fairytale...

Lizzie hasn't had the easiest life. With old wounds from childhood trauma and boyfriends past weighing her down, she has sworn off all men, even if she does meet one that checks all her boxes. He will just break her heart, right? They all do in the end. Maybe Miles Knight is just what Lizzie needs to conquer her inner demons.

Miles is used to being in the spotlight but when a chance encounter with a mysterious Lizzie, who doesn't know who he is, takes place, he knows without doubt that he has to see her again. Will he be able to find her? And when he does, will he be enough to override the trauma that she has experienced.

The Starry Knight

Life isn't always a work of art...

Sebastian and Stormy's story coming 11/17/2023

The Last Knight

Life isn't always a battle...

Samuel's story coming early 2024

Made in the USA
Columbia, SC
23 August 2023

9aaa085f-fa51-42ae-9362-f2d48013d777R01